THIS IS WHERE I AM

KAREN CAMPBELL is a graduate of Glasgow University's renowned Creative Writing Masters, and author of *The Twilight Time*, *After the Fire*, *Shadowplay* and *Proof of Life*. A former police officer, and council PR, Karen Campbell won the Best New Scottish Writer Award in 2009. She lives in Galloway.

www.karencampbell.co.uk

THIS IS WHERE I AM

KAREN CAMPBELL

BLOOMSBURY

LONDON · NEW DELHI · NEW YORK · SYDNEY

First published in Great Britain 2013
This paperback edition published 2014

Bloomsbury Publishing Plc
50 Bedford Square, London WC1B 3DP

Bloomsbury Publishing, London, New Delhi, New York and Sydney

A CIP catalogue record for this book is available from the British Library

ISBN 978 1 4088 3273 8
10 9 8 7 6 5 4 3 2 1

Typeset by Hewer Text UK Ltd, Edinburgh
Printed and bound in Great Britain by CPI Group (UK) Ltd, Croydon CR0 4YY

For Abdul and Farida

PART ONE

AWAY

I. JANUARY

SCOTTISH REFUGEE COUNCIL

Scotland has a fine tradition of welcoming and assimilating incomers; indeed the very name 'Scotland' is believed to derive from the Scoti, an Irish tribe who themselves may have originated in Egypt. And, for generations, waves of immigrants have continued to enrich and strengthen the nation. The Scottish Refugee Council is an independent charity dedicated to providing support and information to people seeking refuge in Scotland today.

Staffed by a team of employees and volunteers, the charity moved to its current Glasgow offices in 1999, when Glasgow City Council became the first UK local authority to sign up to the Home Office Dispersal Scheme. This saw a massive and immediate increase in the SRC's client base, with around 150 requests for help each day.

Working hard to raise awareness of refugee issues and to influence policy in both Scotland and the UK, the SRC offers a one-stop advice centre to refugees and people seeking asylum, carries out research, training and community-based programmes, and campaigns for fair treatment. Since its inception, the charity has provided support to refugees from countries such as Uganda, Vietnam, Chile, Bosnia, Kosovo, Iraq and Rwanda, amongst many, many others.

Entry to the SRC offices is free.

★

SO. HOW DO these things start? I'm sitting in the waiting room, thighs damp, with my tights sticking to me, wiping my palms on my unfamiliar skirt. It's been years since I've had to dress so smartly, and it feels strange, constricting after a decade of soft jersey leggings and loose tops where the stains don't show. *Come on, come on* is hissing in my head, willing them to come and get me, or me to get up and leave. I don't think the room's particularly hot; it's me. Me and my unpredictable plumbing and my panic flaring.

Would you look at that sweaty woman? Someone should tell her: the health centre is next door.

I'm too young for hot flushes. I am. But youth is relative; I'm double the age of the other two with me, and I know they're both thinking add-on-ten again. The odd time I've had to give my age, you see people do a double-take. Even the doctor. *You're . . . forty-four?* Said doubtfully, before writing me another prescription for pills I doubt I'll take. I've got plenty.

What am I doing here? This isn't me; I live flat and bland. And I must have decided this would be fine, that I would remain that way. It was safer. It was tea after shock, the calm after the storm, the exhausted, whimpery quiver after tears. Damp circles are spreading

4

in my armpits, seeping into silk. Surreptitiously, I check for stains; am confronted with the flush of my sad wee chest. My sister's jacket-collar falls in embroidered points, hiding the worst of it. I should have taken the thing off as soon as I came in. Now, I'm stuck wearing it for the duration. What if they offer to take my coat? Have I brought any perfume? A dull ache tells me I'm grinding my teeth again. I relax my jaw, creaking it from side to side to loosen gristle hinges. The girl opposite looks slightly alarmed. I pretend to cough instead.

That's what truly started it, I think; the beginning. Or the end. My teeth. Made me get out of bed and go in search of Panadol and be so unbearably ... awake. I promise it was Panadol. I still have a cupboard full of the heavy-duty stuff: Co-dydramol, Tramadol — I think there's even a little liquid morphine left. But I keep them just in case. In case one day I really need them all, at once, down in one, laid out in my best nightie with my head reaching out to ...

Well.

A bee swirls into the waiting room. The girl across from me draws her arms and legs inwards, but her eyes dart frantically as the bee tours the room. As she's also been sipping from a bottle of organic lemonade ... well, of course it makes a bee-line for her. Ha! Now who's making funny faces?

Compared to the open-plan chaos outside, we three are in a quiet enclave. Occasionally, you hear a raised voice or a baby crying, but, tucked in this little anteroom, we are insulated. Apart. We do not need, and are not yet useful.

I'm aware of the young guy over to the left of me swaying his neck. It is a cobra-dance, he means to make eye contact. Make me speak.

'Worse than a job interview, this.' His chin comes up in a collusive, backward nod, inviting me to agree.

'Mmhm.'

'I mean, if they knock you back . . . no that they will, but if they *do* . . . It's a bit like a blind date, this.'

Bee-girl tuts, which makes me go immediately on his side.

'I know what you mean.'

'I've no really done much volunteering before. You?'

'Not really.'

He nods again, I smile. Resume my mental wanderings.

'I mean, I help with my wee brother's football team and that.'

'That's good.'

'Yeah. There's quite a few wee asylum kiddies at the school. Ach, you feel heart sorry for them, don't you? Plus . . . I know I shouldny say. But I thought it might help me get work. Paid work, you know?'

Bee-girl snorts. Small noises, some slurping and a mobile face have been her only contributions, but already I dislike her. I imagine her living in an earnest bedsit, eating only wholemeal bread and mung beans.

'So, what got you into this?' He directs this, pointedly, at me.

Och, just the usual. Drugs. That and cruising for young boys.

Imagine if I actually said that? If I told him how I'd passed this lad, he must have still been in his teens, with a sign that said *Hungry and Homles*. It was written on the inside of a KFC carton, and that intrigued me. I don't know how it is with other people, but

6

sometimes I walk past these folk; sometimes I give them money. It's a terrible thing to admit, but I activate my internal judge. You know, do they have a sad-eyed dog, do they look like a drug addict, do they shake their wee cup with menaces? Do they smile, are their eyes downcast, their clothes clean, tattered? Do they sit respectfully at the side of the pavement or sprawl grubbily in some poor soul's doorway? If they are one of those gypsy-looking women from Eastern Europe then I think: *No.* You didn't flee oppression. You're just here on the make. But if they're a thin, haunted African boy who cannot spell and can offer only a shame-filled glance, well, you stop, don't you? Only this time, I spoke too. Actually asked him his name. Why? To make the exchange less clinical, perhaps? To make up for all the times I do walk past? Because the sky was a clear pale blue and the days were shifting oh, I don't know, I just did, I just said it.

He had raised his hand a little higher.

'I'm Deborah,' I persisted. 'What's your name?'

He'd nudged the KFC box with his foot. It was clever, because the writing was on the inside of the lid and the box itself was where he would receive his money. But it was unclever too, because then, when you notice that, you immediately think, *oh so he can afford KFC, can he? Well, he canny be that destitute.*

I put my hands on my knees and scrunched down low, so our eyes were virtually level. He refused to meet my gaze. Gently – I promise, it was incredibly gently – I shifted one hand to rest on his shoulder and my God, it was as if I'd stabbed him, or he thought my hand was made of fire. He juddered and cowered; one fluid movement with several parts which resulted in the upper half of his

7

body shutting like a penknife, keeling over away from me. As if I was the dirty one. I let his shoulder alone. 'There's no need to be like that.' Then I straightened up. 'I was only trying to be friendly. You know? I didn't have to stop.'

His neck drooped to the ground. Dark, like planed oak like a dark-shaped tree branch angled on the road like wood only wood like we didn't have to stop.

Oh. The bee is pirouetting. I focus on it twirling like a November leaf. In the background, in our waiting room, the guy on my left is waiting for his reply.

'You just want to help, don't you?' I say vaguely.

This satisfies him, I think. How long did I leave him hanging? Time has taken a very amorphous quality – and language, and sense actually. I have difficulty concentrating now. I digress. A lot. It's as if my thoughts are a dandelion clock. I see one, and I chase after it, and then another one birls by and they're so tiny and meandering they can't really amount to a whole. So I try not to assimilate them. I just follow them, whichever one catches my eye.

And I *did* want to help that boy with the KFC box. But I continued haranguing him; it had become a point of honour. 'I mean, we're both human beings, aren't we? What's so wrong in asking for your name?'

I'd taken my purse from my handbag. 'I was going to give you money anyway, it's not a test. I just thought it would be nice to –'

He must have registered some kind of irritation in my tone – I don't think there was – I felt more embarrassed than anything to be honest – but he, too, straightened up. With his eyes held firmly down, he placed one palm flat on the pavement and – whoosh – up he came. I got a bit of a fright, the quickness of him when he had been so hunched and slothful. I backed away, conscious I was look-ing behind me and to either side. The street was terribly empty, which is just as well, because, the next second, he took my hand. His mournful face turned in the direction of the alley that ran between the two tenements behind us. And then it wasn't 'just as well' at all. *He's going to drag me in there.* There was no one I could call out to, there was only the man in the paper shop the next block along. Would he hear me if I screamed but I couldn't. I couldn't make any noise, couldn't move. And the boy stood too, suddenly docile again. Head down, still holding my hand. His other hand, the thumb of his other hand was hooked inside the waistband of his dirty jeans and in one vile and clarifying moment I knew what he thought I wanted.

It was daylight in a broad, suburban street. *I was old enough to be his mother.*

Disgusted, I pulled free. Emptied the contents of my purse, everything: the twenty-pound note and the pound coins, the bits of fluff and the coppery snash, all of it tumbling in like a tawdry waterfall. All that evening, my hands smelled of coins and fish. I didn't sleep. Spent hours before the light returned staring across our street. Wondering what would drive someone to do that, and feeling righteous rage and feeling . . . ugly.

Months before, I had taken to devouring the obituary column, my own columns of workings scrawled alongside, showing how I had added and subtracted to extract each age of death. *Older, older.* And then, the occasional triumphant: *Younger.* I stopped playing that game when I found myself fleetingly superior to *Clarke: Alan and Connie*. Who had lost their baby son.

What will I say if they ask me at the interview?

My new pal is called out of the waiting room. 'Fraser Blair. Could you come on through, please?'

'Right. Cheers.' The lad jumps up. Brushes down his trousers with clenched fists. Upright, he is surprisingly small, his hands and head (especially his ears) all out of proportion to his condensed frame. The girl looks up and frowns.

'Good luck,' I say.

'Right. Cheers.'

The girl swigs her lemonade.

I didn't go out for three days after the boy and his box. Sometimes, I wish Callum didn't have a pension, that the mortgage was not paid, because it would force me to go outside more. I would have found a job by now, engaged with the world. But then, look what happens when I do. Left unable to open a window for fear the ghosts will come in. I couldn't sleep at all. Nothing unusual in that: my every night is spent in long dark laps, in fitful dozes, in damp moments where you feel you're falling until a slapping pain yanks you up. The pain itself varies: it can be headaches or me grinding my teeth, or a dull deep agony which never truly shifts, but can dive and resurface at will. And that's when those special pills start beckoning, cluttering slyly in their white plastic tubs, or the wine whispers silky promises of oblivion. But this was a restlessness. An angry, escaping impatience, and I turned on the computer, just to see. I wasn't looking for bingo or chatrooms, nor forums or soft porn. I suppose I was looking for another kind of window, into the world of that boy. He was bothering my mind like an annoying Jehovah's Witness. He just kept knocking and wouldn't go away. It's like when you see, really *see* a face in a tree bark or a swirl of sheets. You can't unsee it, and once you've noticed it, you wonder how you could have been so dumb not to see it before. You wonder about all the other hidden shapes and undulations and where they live and you go seeking them out.

A window? My God, there were hundreds. Pages, pages of relentless words; reports and case studies and charities and images. Eyes like that beggar boy's and stoic shoulders and mouths all ready to speak. Through my tiny portal they came pouring, the screen blurring at me, its pixels reaching out in sleekit, twining threads, in thick black leeches, in burrowing worms. I slammed at the keys eventually to make it stop. Lay the rest of that night in the lounge, telly on for company. I'm not a stupid woman. I know these things exist. I've not led a particularly sheltered life either; I've simply led my own. I give to charity. At Christmas, I give to Barnado's, and the ones who save people's sight.

When I was a kid, I used to cry. A lot. At pretty much anything: *Lassie* films; my dad shouting; the news; seeing the rag and bone man; reading *Oliver Twist*.

You need to toughen up, young lady.

But it's not fair. Those poor orphans –

Life's not fair.

I vowed not to speak in homilies when I became a mother. And I would grow up to make a difference. I would right those wrongs, and get angry and campaign – ach, but you don't, do you? You settle for what you can grab as life pitches you on. You find your own twig or log or luxury island, and leave the currents to swirl. Until a bloody great tidal wave comes crashing over your head and –

I watch the girl in the waiting room swipe at the bee, which is clearly dying and just wants somewhere quiet to rest. It buzzes round her head, then, as I think she's about to scream – or worse, appeal to me for help – it does a body swerve and flits through the door wee Fraser left ajar. She gets up, shuts it firmly. Neither of us say a word. Then the door clatters open, almost instantly, and an even younger girl sashays in. Gold skin, lush black hair with near-white highlights on the fringe and a sari of purple and gold.

'No, I amny. I telt you – I'm on the fucking bus. Ten minutes, tops. Bloody hell.'

There's a musical cadence to her 'bloody' that's not Glaswegian. The girl winks as she removes her phone from her ear. Cracks her gum, and a silver stud twinkles from her tongue. 'Ho. D'yous know where the Ladies is?'

The bee-girl tells her it's second on the left. She has a very reedy voice.

'Cheers.' The young girl exits with an easy sway of her hips, leaving a sense of clumsiness in the room. Me and bee-wumman go back to staring at our knees.

I was drawn to the computer the next night too. I'd been dozing on the couch, woke to the hum of empty TV (we're not cable subscribers) and floury, sore teeth. Got up to go to bed, take some painkillers (white or blue, or those thick-feeling fuzzy ones?), reheat my milky drink. Bent to switch the PC off and . . . did not. Instead, I sat down. I was the most fully awake I'd been in weeks – so sharp I thought I was dreaming. Not a gradual transition from sleepy-head-stretching to blinking, but a warm steady focus which pulsed like the pain in my teeth. The pain was my metronome, it set the rhythm. I left sentiment beside my cup of hot chocolate, and moved methodically through the pages I'd saved. To tame them? Compartmentalise? Pretend I could 'do some good'? I wasn't even clear on the distinctions: asylum seeker, refugee. Illegal immigrant, economic migrant. People-trafficking, sex-trafficking, drug mules. Were they all one and the same? All manifestations of the great vast dispossessed? The sea that washed that boy here, who else did it bring?

Halfway through, I went to the window. We have a little balcony, more of a railing than anything, but it's wide enough you can put your tiptoes on the sill, lean from bedroom into air. Lovely in the summer, but this was autumn, and I was wearing it like a cool, dark skin. Just me and the navy sky. The clamping in my jaw had stopped. I could taste amber leaves, could feel flakes of paint rise like hairs beneath my fingers as I leaned out. Everything was round and curved and sparkling. Me, alone, seeing microbes scurry in circles, clouds of manic electrons binding their protons and neutrons and gluing us all to gravity. I wondered if I *had* taken the Tramadol by mistake but the feeling was too good to dismiss. Had I loosened my grip on the railing, tilted a tiny bit forwards and pushed off with my toes (which were full of distant tinglings themselves), I know I could have flown.

And I was having this conversation with myself, saying is this *happy*, you silly besom? Don't you know where you are? Who you are? Perhaps you are asleep and dreaming, and tomorrow they'll find you spread across the pavement, your skull split in a crazy smile and, my God, is that why? Have you finally decided? Stupid, stupid woman. You thought *this* was purgatory? Well, hey, that'll be nothing compared to what's coming if you jump, because He knows, He always knows the secrets of your heart, and even if you made it look so much like an accident that you believed it yourself, you'd still be fucked.

It was the swearing that drew me up. I rarely swear (well, not the 'f' word) – and never in my dreams. The anger doesn't seem to permeate there. It's more of a wistfulness, a melancholic reaching out for . . . a place that is unreachable. In my dreams – and it doesn't matter if they're the waking or sleeping ones – I imagine a shape beside me, a mote in my peripheral vision. That's where I think our memories lurk. They're not behind you at all, but perpetually dancing like sprites just outside the corner of your eye. Desperate for you to notice them, and you, blinking like fury and just getting on with life. Or sometimes they lie heavy on your shoulder, and then I imagine them as fatter entities, goblins maybe – but wheezy, old ones who mean no harm.

Away with the fairies, her.

I don't think I'm mad, though – and I did *not* imagine hearing tears. The actual smash of them striking a wooden floor, a slo-mo pause, then the elegant tinkle of hot salt specks bouncing upwards in sprays. A grief so profound that I opened wide into the night to lap it up.

★   ★   ★

The waiting room's full of leaflets. I take one, crack it like an open fan.

Our street is a beautiful terrace. Modelled on Grecian and Egyptian lines, it's a dark and leafy sleeve. Rich foliage clads sandstone walls; laurels, conifers and patient spreading beeches all jostle for position in the scraps of fenced-off gardens. Occasionally, a breeze will shift a bough and you catch a glimpse of egg and dart sculpting, fine cornice work and corbels over the door. You'll see flashes of bright tulle at a window, and know the dance school are practising for their end-of-term show, or a shiver of pink feather will tell you Mrs Gilfillan is dusting again before her home-help comes. An amazing woman, Mrs Gilfillan. Studied mathematics and languages at Oxford, served at Bletchley Park during the war. And now she wears an orange pendant round her neck, which she can press if she falls and an alarm will ring at some central location and someone will, eventually, come. I've told her just to carry a mobile, ring me instead, but she's terribly private, is Mrs Gilfillan. We all are, I suppose.

For a while, it seemed as if those private barriers were being erased, a war-spirit camaraderie melting the rigid squares and circles we draw round ourselves, just as it once melted garden railings. I definitely felt it. Between me and my neighbours, there was a brief melding of our separate lives. As they saw me lugging shopping bags and struggling with the wheelchair, when I had to tap on doors and ask if they could listen out or sit in for five minutes while I nipped to the chemist's for a prescription, when the nurse's little green car became our most frequent visitor, it seemed too ridiculous to care if I knew the woman two doors along's name before I spoke to her. All I would know is she was in and that my husband had fallen and I needed another pair of hands to lift him up. So I would go and ask. Politely brusque, not caring if I offended some hidden sensibility, upset some social more. But people were lovely, in the main. They would respond with generosity and care, they would treat him with dignity and me with genuine, open concern.

If there's anything else I can do . . .

Please don't hesitate to ask . . .

So I didn't, and they did. They did lots of things, and we would speak, animatedly, when we met in the street. Folk would touch my arm, frown and nod and it might be the first person who had spoken to me all day. Allison Black would call with her toddler twins, ask if I needed anything at the shops. Sophie, who runs the deli in Nithsdale Road, would bring in the occasional casserole. *Oh, please. We cooked too much.* Mr Patel's mother-in-law made us gallons of delicious lemonade, guaranteed to slake even the most desperate thirst.

His throat was paralysed at that point.

Yes. If it hadn't been for the part where my husband was dying, I would say it was all very jolly indeed.

And I would find myself, at eleven o'clock at night, standing in my nightie in the garden, pegging out another load of sheets and joking with Moira over the fence who'd nipped out for a fly cigarette about incontinence pads and did she know there was such a thing as the Bristol Stool Chart. Funny then how, afterwards, folk began to retreat. They would smile, but would no longer stop for a chat. Allison would hush her joyous twins, as if *I* were the actual spot where his grave lay. I was treated with kindly respect. People never know what to say, so often tend to say nothing at all.

That person crying, that raw weight I could feel as I stood on my balcony, was eloquent. They were sending their entreaty skywards, and my head kept pecking to trace the source. It was staring me in the face. Coming from a top-floor room in the house facing ours; I could see a girl behind the window, which was shut. It was shut and all the desperate miming muted noise was held inside, but I swear I could hear it.

I can hear it still.

At first, I didn't recognise her. Young girl with wide cheekbones over which her distorted skin played, her mouth shaping sobs. Possibly she was shouting, her twisted brow suggested exertion. And yet, by the way she stuffed the curtain-edge into her face, I guessed she was stifling her cries. It was too young for Naomi, the woman who lived there, and far too old for Naomi's little girls. The girl's face was in profile, and then she turned. Eyes meeting mine, and that disturbing elation which had fired me drained away.

I could have been looking into *his* eyes. His dead dead eyes when he was still alive. I knew her then, realised it was Naomi's au pair. Rula or Tula. I had seen her pram-pushing in the park when I was last out wheeling Callum; we had nodded, shyly, at our separate loads. Most mornings, you could catch her serving breakfast in Naomi's east-facing morning room, bright teeth and bouncing hair, and the children clamouring for hugs. You never saw them tug at Naomi like that. As she registered my presence, the girl withdrew, yanking on the curtains to close them tight. I finished my water, left my computer burning, and went straight to bed. Sleep came quickly, and I despised myself for feeling as comforted as I was appalled.

It's all relative
Misery loves company
You are not alone

So. This is me.

I am here because the sadness made me glad.

A faint buzzing flits past my nose. The bee is back. He has no intention of stinging. I remember my grandpa telling me: bees hibernate in the winter, they don't die off like other insects. On mild days, the workers make cleansing flights to stretch out their wings. I put down my leaflet and uncross my legs. As I do, a woman like a dollop of soft dark ice cream comes through the door, smiling.

'Mrs Maxwell. That's us ready for you now.'

But I'm not ready. It's not my turn I've changed my mind.

'Thank you,' I say meekly.

We trot to a glassed-off office. I can see wee Fraser in the next room; we are specimens on display. The door opens, two men's faces turn. I feel the lady's hand touch my sweaty back.

'Deborah. This is Abdi.'

SHE DOESN'T KNOW me. She knows nothing of the man I am or was. When she hears me speak, she hears a child, an infant who gropes for words, whose thick tongue can't translate his deep and bursting mind. I'm angry with her, and I shouldn't be. Nobody made me do this. It has been one of the few free choices I have made since . . .

Ah. I am not sure. An image comes hurtling from its cage a hand a wheel rim a hand a choice. I punch it back down. I punch it again, I keep punching it, flatter and flatter until it dies.

They watch me, those compassionate heads on stalks that bend and tilt and nod their sympathy. What do they see passing over me? Is it transient, or do I wear it like a winding cloth? This is my choice my choice a free choice. I am a free man. Free. I wonder what her word for it will be. *Day-bo-ra*. Urging my ears to focus, scooping up all these fast-flying words. They are like insects, and I am a lizard; still, then flicking, trying to catch, trying to swallow and digest each one before the next one darts by.

They screech and chew their words here, spit them out faster than gunfire, their heads crack and dart, they swagger and they duck, all of them. It will be the cold in their bones, making them fragile. These people are stooped and jerky. The sky settles damply, like the cloths we lay over milk. Even now even then when we had a generator and could keep it cool, we I we would still lay cloths over milk I will keep talking in my head and I think only of the heat I think of it I think of it until it comes, obliterating and fierce and it will sear me clean and . . . I miss it. I miss the easy heat that warms your blood, loosens you so you own your posture, own the air you walk in. Here, the cold confronts you, it demands that you draw inwards and down. That you jerk and jabber and squawk.

She's looking directly at me. Day-bo-ra.

'Does he mind that I'm a woman?'

He, Simon, my caseworker, co-ordinator, intermediary integration facilitator, also looks. 'Do you mind that –'

I interrupt them. 'No.'

I mind that I am here. I mind that I am grateful.

'Why?' I ask, then say more words.

'Why' is a good word to learn in many languages. 'Why' and 'where' and 'how' and 'when'. I learned these quickly. I can recite them in English, Swahili, German, French and Italian. As well as Somali, of course, but I've had little use for that since leaving. I learned them all; it made me useful. Made me heard. I also learned 'please' and 'thank you'.

'Thank you,' I say, as she tells me. She talks of 'giving something back' and 'it being the right thing to do'. She talks of anger and unfairness and then, when I don't respond, I hear Simon again:

'Abdi, do you understand all this?'

'Yes,' I say. 'Thank you.' What I said before was wrong. I must have said 'why is it that you *do* this?' I meant to say 'why is it that you *say* this?' Yes, it is '*dire*' in French, not English. To *dit*, to do. It doesn't matter.

She clears her throat. It's a vulnerable sound. I look up. I've noticed that, mostly, the women in this city try to emulate the girls; they wear clothing meant, I assume, for firmer flesh and daub their faces with colours. She, Deborah, is a contradiction. Her face is unpainted and relatively young. Her hair is wild wire and straw, her legs thin, shoes flat and plain. But the middle section of her is tethered into place, drapes of fine silken fabric. If I cannot grasp all their words, I doubt I can grasp their nuances, but that is my impression. If I had someone to if I was at home and talking to my mother or Az – if you were if you were talking to a friend, you would say she looks odd. As if she is either unfinished or not yet begun.

She speaks again. 'And I hope that we can be friends.'

I leave with a form on which is written a list. There are some dates and directions and a mobile telephone number. The form is headed 'Mentor/Mentee Contract'. It's another official document which I can add to my pile. I'm much better at the reading than the speaking. Oh, I'm not particularly good at either, but with the reading you have more time. You can see the shapes and repeating patterns, you can go backwards and forwards until the shapes make sense. My daughter and I read together. I want her to read before she goes to school.

It's one o'clock. *Une heure, una ora.* I never eat lunch. I have a meal in the morning and a meal at night, but I make food for Rebecca. It's important that she knows. If she sat at school with a book instead of an empty plate, they would laugh at her. And if she asked for fish and beans, they would laugh at her. So I make her reconstituted chicken threads, dipped in powdered bread and fried until hard and greasy. I don't even make them, I open the brightly coloured packet that they come in, and drop them in hot oil. She seems to like them.

I go to the grocer's shop. I can go to any shop now, in theory, but this small stretch of chip shop and licensed grocer's and bookmaker's are the shops I know. Thirty minutes' walk away, there's also a supermarket, a vast grey space full of tins and freezers which I went to on the first night. My fault. I had turned left instead of right. Eventually I came to its garish lights, and I recognised its blue and yellow sign because it was on the list for vouchers. When I got there, it felt like I had triumphed somehow. And then I realised I didn't know the words for their food. That was the only time I thought I might lose control. The cold in my hands was intense, my daughter was slipping from my grasp and crying because she was so tired, so hungry. So cold. You cannot imagine the pain of a cold that makes the blood in your fingertips go hard and die. Yes, now I know about gloves and hats, but not then. And where was I to leave my little girl? Alone in an unknown room? So we walked in the freezing night air, my daughter weeping into my neck, and me trying to shelter her inside my own thin coat. I could accept the sun had left us, but I struggled to understand where the moon was. At home, the moon and stars are so big, you can see by them, work by them through the night. Only thin glimmers here, cold specks in the muddy sky. In the shop, it was a little warmer. I put Rebecca down, but she cried so much harder. My arms ached, the burning inside made worse by how the outside was so cold. Liquid was running from my nose, I saw the same on my daughter's face. Clear and thick. I wiped it off her with the back of my sleeve.

'Take Aabo's hand, baby. Look. Put your cold-cold hand in Aabo's warm one.' Together, we trudged the aisles, overcome by coloured boxes and the huge chests of ice-bags. Were my vouchers for all of these things or just some? What were they? Was it food or drink or paper or books? Nothing I could recognise. Nothing I could touch or see the shape or smell of. Was I meant to open up one of the packets to check? Several times, I lifted up an item, then dropped it again. Impotence and hunger growing, trying to keep smiling for my daughter. For so long, all my food had been given to me. I'd forgotten how to provide. At last, a man came up to us, words spattering like oil in a too-hot pan. 'Help' was one I seized on. I tried to say what I needed, but I was so exhausted, the only words I could remember were French. He was pointing, jabbing his finger to somewhere beyond my neck, and I became terrified that he'd give up and walk away. All I could do was offer my voucher card. He nodded, fried up more words for me, but I could take nothing in. The thought of returning to the freezing building in which we had been deposited, trailing all that way back with no food, made me want to weep. Then the man stopped talking, gestured me *Sit* on a pile of tins. I did as I was told, lifting Rebecca on to my lap. The man handed me a sheet of paper and a pen. I shook my head. All of my words had escaped me, I couldn't write in any language now. He waved his wrist in front of his face – he was miming spooning food. I nodded again, frantically this time, and he pointed once more to the paper. Suddenly, I realised. I held the pen. My fingers were utterly numb, but I held it like a clamp. Drew one curved line that tapered to a point, then reversed it with another. Made the two ends intersect, flick out. Held it up to him.

'Fish,' he told me. 'Yous are wanting *fish*.'

God bless that man. We did this many times, until I had fish and milk and bread and meat. I also wanted rice, but how do you act out rice? It was enough, what we had was wonderful, and I trudged home in the biting air, carrying two bags and my little girl. Later, someone said I could have got the bus. I have learned I don't like buses. There is a train as well as a bus. I got the train today because they give me expenses and they said I could, that it makes sense because their office is very close to the station. I wonder if this was a hidden kindness. If you learn the pattern of the name of the station at which you are to get off, you can see it written on a board once you get there. Buses simply go, they jolt and swing and will not stop unless you tell them where. It's worth the long walk to get to the station near my house.

In the grocer's shop, I'm scanning the shelves before me. Long walk. I've become flabby, like my surroundings. It's only one mile, maybe two to get to Cardonald Station. I look again. We need bread and milk, cold sterile stuff that tastes thin. I buy some more of the frozen packets Rebecca likes and I buy myself a pie. It's an envelope of flaky bread-like stuff, I've had them before. This one is called Chik'n'Ham. I count out the correct money. The man behind the counter tuts at my pile of coins, tosses them in his till. He has no conception of the effort it took to learn his numbers, learn all the differentials between copper and silver, between their weights and how the smaller circles can be of more value. A woman with bright yellow hair comes in.

All right, Billy? Howzitgaun?

Fair tae pish, hen. Fair tae pish.

I am putting my milk and my food into my backpack. The man and woman begin a conversation about the *bloody polis* and *wee Gringo* and *the jail* and I wait, patiently at first, for the man to hand me the newspaper I had requested. I know I gave him enough money to pay for it, he nodded when I said the words.

'*Re-cord?*' I say again. '*Re-cord* please?'

He breaks off his animated discussion. 'Whit?'

'The man's wanting a paper, Billy.'

'Forty pee.' He opens out his hand, forms it like a cup.

'I give you money.'

He shakes his head. 'Naw, pal. You gied me a pile of snash for your messages. No for a paper. You didny say you wanted a paper.'

'Yes, I say *Re-cord* and I give you money.'

His hand changes from a cup to a fist, and then a crab. He plays his fingers one two three one two three, tapping them down on the counter. The yellow-haired woman folds her arms.

'You trying tae come the wide-boy, pal?' he says. 'Palm me off wi a load of coppers —'

'There was pound coins —'

'Aye — for your fucking MES-SA-GES! Away and piss off afore I call the polis. Christ,' he turns to the woman again, 'they'd have the clothes off your back an all.'

'I give you money,' I repeat.

'I'll no fucking tell you again.' His face is red, his mouth twists with unfettered disgust. For me. He sees a black-skinned, lying thief. I see an ignorant stupid man. Stupid can be most dangerous of all, because it is deaf to reason. Stupid people bluster and shout. Often after much shouting on their part, and you, standing still and resolute, it will end with the slow dull realisation that you, indeed all of the people watching them, *know* that they are stupid. Then, usually, they lash out: with words, fists, actions – by that stage it's immaterial, because you've both lost. They, their dignity, and you, your pride, your argument and – once – your tooth.

I say quietly, one final time: 'I did give you money,' and then I leave. Even though I let him win, I will have to go back to the supermarket in future, unless it's his wife that's here. Mah-gret. She works on Tuesdays, Wednesdays and Thursdays and, occasionally, will offer Rebecca a sweet.

The shops – I've heard someone call them a 'parade' but that jaunty proud swagger of colour and bodies and music I've seen marching through the town hardly seems in keeping with these grey concrete cubes – anyway, the shops are in a separate block from the flats we live in. Between the shops and my block, there is another concrete square called the Wally Dug. I assume it's like a *maqaahi* but I've never been inside. I imagine what it would feel like, to enter the warm blend of alcohol and men's conversation, to have the sting of drink on my lips, and the garrulous comradeship that comes from it. But women drink here too. Every night, pinched men and women cluster outside with their cigarettes. Are these women their wives? Often, people will stagger, the women too; sometimes, bodies erupt from the door in a clatter of fighting limbs. One night, from my window, I saw a man being dragged behind the building, to where they store the empty bottles. He was kicked to the ground, and then I could no longer see him. But I saw the others, I saw one with a small, sturdy paddle and I saw him swing it, several times.

To reach my home, there are more choices. I am overburdened with choices. You can climb seven flights of stairs or you can go inside a tiny metal lift. If I tried to explain this to my mother to my grandfather to who would I tell but it is a small, empty space that carries you upwards and downwards. Yes, a hoist, I would say. That's right, of course you understand. It's the same as the rope over the branch, and the nets being pulled up then lowered.

I wonder if we always mean it when we patronise; if it's always more than unthinking. If you being small makes me grow taller.

Last time I took the stairs, a man blocked my path on the second landing. He asked me what my daughter's name was and his breath smelled of beer. He stroked my daughter's hair, said it felt like a scouring pad. 'Does your daddy do the dishes wi your heid, hen?' he said. The last time I took the lift, there was a teenage girl lying inside it. Her eyes were closed, and there was a needle protruding from the crook of her inner elbow. Fortunately, Rebecca wasn't with me. What would I have told her? I knelt to check the girl was breathing, saw a spit-bubble at her lips. Should I have told someone? I should have, of course I should have, she was a girl in my village in my home in my concrete block and she would have been a daughter too. Her lips moved and I pretended she was fine. Left her there, sliding up and down in the metal cage, and crept inside and locked my door.

Always lock your door, son.

A valuable piece of advice, given to me the week I arrived, by an old lady wearing an overall and a knitted hat. My neighbour, Mrs Coutts. It was the first time I met her, it was her greeting. There are fourteen floors in this building, around ten flats on every corridor, and each floor has two landings, I think, each with two corridors running off at angles. The whole building forms a square with a space riven through its centre. So even if each flat only houses one person (and I think the one above me must hold twenty at least, although they, their dogs and their drum kit only stir between three in the afternoon and five in the morning), but even if you discount them as abnormal (which is not a difficult thing to do) and count each flat as one person, that means there are five hundred and sixty people living one on top of the other in this single tower.

There were two hundred and twenty-four souls in my village and I knew each one. You couldn't not know them; they lived and died and ate and loved and squabbled in the bleached dirt beneath our gathering-tree, on their stoops, behind straw and dung-packed walls. Oh God, I crave that sensation so much: the scratchy-smooth rub of my handbuilt walls.

My forehead rests inside my flat's front door. If I touch the walls here, they feel damp. A fine mist clings to my hands and heart. Through the wall, I hear a clatter of metal, the gradual shuffle of feet. It is a stomp and a drag, a stomp and a drag. Quickly, I move away, tuck myself behind the door of my living room, holding it before me like a shield. I hear more rattling, and belching, then the thumping on my letterbox starts.

'You still fucking there, you big black bastard? I fucking *know* you are. I fucking seen you come in. Away tae fuck back tae . . .' the voice drifts as my neighbour lurches away.

'Away tae fucking niggerland!'

I flinch, the sudden poison hitting me. And then I hate myself, even more than him. Bawbag, I think he is called; I have heard his friends refer to him as this. If he goes to his *maqaahi* he will be gone for hours. If he goes to buy cigarettes he will come back soon. Standing trembling in my hallway, blowing through my mouth. If I blow slowly, I can pretend my rage is expelled. I am a vigorous, tight-packed man, compelled to be dull and slow. Moving round my living room, I circle like a lion, circle smaller and smaller until I am calm. Selecting one of my two chairs, moving it closer to the window. Wiping nothing from my empty tiny table, setting out my things, my things.

I have things.

I am lucky; I have things.

I read the mentoring contract, slowly. My dictionary is by my side. I have a dictionary, a telephone directory and three children's books. A lady from the church gave us those ones; I think they're very old. There's one called *The Magic Porridge Pot*. Rebecca loves it. Porridge is a kind of mealie thing, it's all right. Fills you up with a heavy heat. We also have *A Child's Garden of Verses* by Robert Louis Stevenson, which I like very much, and a book called *Letterland*, where all the letters are given names and faces. At home, I used to instruct the children. I had gone to school for two years before my grandfather died. I knew so much that I wanted to share with the village, so we built an awning out from our madrassah and we would sit in the shade after work and I would teach them. Basic things, the things I teach my daughter now. But it was me, I was the teacher. Me, I would instruct and enlighten, encourage and reprimand.

Me.

The lady who gave us these books, my neighbour Mrs Coutts, put her arm round my shoulder and squeezed me. 'You mind and learn your letters, son, and you'll be fine.'

I know my letters, Mrs Coutts. I knew them all. Have you read Hadrawi, our poet laureate? Or Nuruddin Farah, or Timacade? You see. This is the measure of the man I am become. Bitter with the people who help me, humble to those who do not care.

Rebecca is with the minister's wife. I said I'd collect her as soon as I was finished and Mrs Girdwood said: *No rush. You take your time, Abdi.* I should get back to her immediately, I always want to stand over her, by her. Know her small hand is trusting mine. But today, I feel . . . I don't know what I feel. For so long I've been a plant that is dying; one whose roots are upended to the sky. Today I did two things. I met that woman, Deborah, and I secured myself a library card. It was my minister who had said how I could get more books.

All you need is something with your address on —

But he doesn't know how long he'll be here —

Kate, for goodness sake. Abdi, they'll show you the internet too. You know, computers?

He had nodded his head, encouragingly, the way I would do with the shyest of pupils. I wish I could tell him a joke. I wish he could see me at home, teaching my class. Drinking *shaah* with my friends or hauling my nets. If he could see the expert way I twist and heave, so that only the tiniest fish escape.

So. I have my library card. I have papers with my address on. I have my daughter, I have a church, and now I have a mentor. A plant that is dying will take the thinnest of soil. It will gladly relinquish its roots to the smallest, stone-strewn pot if it means that it might live.

Simon thought our meeting had 'gone well'. After Deborah left, he smiled at me the way my brother-in-law smiled the first day I met my wife so today I met my mentor I met my mentor, when I got the letter. When. OK, when I got the letter about mentoring the first thing I saw was **UK Border Agency** in bold black, and the slimmer **Home Office** words above. Overarching all of that, they place a little black rainbow. I believe the correct word for this is irony? But their irony brings fear. That familiar jolt as my stomach meets my throat, and all the acids mix. I've learned that you have to read these things. You have to try to understand it before you give in to the despair, and this time, it was a nice surprise. It said I had been selected (always a word to get you terrified), selected by RIES for a pilot integration service.

I never asked to fly. Who told them I wanted to fly? (I'm quite a funny man. I was.) And RICE is very tasty. I know that 'inter' is good, it means to weave and worm your way inside the system. The more roots and tendrils and suckers I can insinuate, the further and wider they go, is good. Then I will be stuck, adhered not just like a plant, but as the limpets are on rock, and they will find it harder to pull me off.

RIES. The Refugee Integration and Employment Service. Once you have been granted refugee status, you enter another strange new world. The country that you have been sent to, that had said it would welcome you, and then sends you to hell, now welcomes you again. From keeping you in a war-zone prison block they call homes in an area they cannot make their own people live, from giving you vouchers and prescribing how and from where you will feed your family, from *pro*scribing you from engaging in any meaningful work which would allow you to feed your family yourself, the country turns, once more, benign. And, once more, you allow yourself to engage with the possibility of hope. You sniff round it like a wary dog, you poke it with your paw to see if it will bite, then, when it lies face up and artless, looking you straight in the eye, you seize it hungrily in your teeth.

And I seize this. The letter told me that, since I had been granted refugee status, I was now eligible to access an employment advice service and a support service to assist with schools and housing – all food to help my body. But I needed food also for my soul. Buried further down the page was a line that danced higher than all the others:

'. . . will offer friendship . . .'

I read back and forth until I could see the full meaning of it, that they would match me with 'a mentor from the receiving community'. I am a package to be received. I am a gift; I could be. I want to be. This mentor will be my guide, 'sharing knowledge and experience' to help me understand the ways of this fresh-opening world. For this, they seem to want nothing in return. I wonder again about her. *Day-bo-ra*. What will be the barter? The bribe? Even the minister and his wife seek to secure something of me. I sense their watchful eagerness, their slight thrill of panic that, if not tethered firmly within the flock, I may revert to my heathen ways.

I am an ungrateful bastard. Oh yes, I know that word too. I am cynical, ungrateful, and almost spent. I concentrate on my mentoring form.

Agreed aims

We will work together to ensure that:

- *Deborah and Abdi meet regularly (ie once a month) & undertake to give each other sufficient notice if an arranged meeting has to be postponed*
- *Deborah commits to showing Abdi a variety of cultural & historic environments in order to extend his knowledge & understanding of the receiving country*
- *Abdi agrees to advising either Deborah or the 'Putting the Me in Mentor' project if his personal circumstances (eg address, employment status etc) change or if he wishes to disengage with the mentoring process*
- *Deborah and Abdi exchange mobile telephone numbers in order to make contact with one another*
- *Deborah and Abdi respect each other's privacy and confidentiality, offering only information & advice with which they are both comfortable*
- *Deborah and Abdi agree to meet over the period of one year from date of this contract, unless either chooses to withdraw from the process*

'That all seems fine to me,' Deborah had said. I had said 'Yes' although I'd not had time to read it properly. Reading it now, I'm drawn not to the list of vague things that we've agreed, but to the word 'other's'. Is that right? I try to learn the punctuation when I learn the spelling (there are five or so pages of grammar notes at the back of my dictionary. It's a good one, Mrs Coutts tells me), but whenever I think I've mastered the apostrophe or understood why a 'k' might not be pronounced aloud or how and when and where the 'i's and 'e's are placed, I see an exception to the rule. And I get even more confused.

Anyway, the point is we will meet, once a month, and Deborah will take me to different places and we will talk. About what, I have no idea. I'm not clear why they've matched us. Truthfully, I was hoping for a man, a man my age that I could observe. That is the trick, you see. That's the key to blending in. Observation. You come, you go. Place to place, an alien, a drain, a usurper. Everywhere is challenge. If you puff up your chest, you are a target. If you cow your eyes, you are a target. If you stand as an equal, if you answer a question honestly and clearly, you are dragged from the line. You are made to kneel in the hot red dirt and they beat you on the soles of your feet. They beat with switches and sticks until the resultant lattice is more blood than skin. After that, you are always mindful of how you hold yourself, where you look. I want to know if it's different here, and I think a woman cannot tell me that.

We'll see.

My free choice extends to rejecting my mentor, if we're not suited. To sniff and savour this piece of hope, then spit it, petulantly, out.

We'll see.

Deborah has arranged to meet me at Kelvingrove Art Gallery next week. 'Or would you rather wait a month, if you've got too much on? It's just – this isn't really a meeting, is it? More of an introduction.' I know from a misunderstanding with Mrs Coutts (that made her heave with laughter and raise her skirts to reveal voluminous petticoats. I don't want to talk about that, though. It wasn't pleasant) that this phrase 'too much on' doesn't mean the amount of clothes you wear; it's not literal. And I don't think Deborah is trying to be funny.

'Next week is fine. Thank you.'

Her smile was awkward. 'Would you rather make your own way there? I don't have a car, but we could meet . . .'

'Is there train?'

'Not really. Only to Central, but Kelvingrove is up by the university.'

I noticed how much slower she spoke to me than she did to Simon, the enunciation and roundness of her words. Then she added: 'There's the subway.'

'I do not know this?' I made my voice into a question. That way, you don't always have to know the right phrase, but if you frown and lilt, they usually understand your statement needs an answer.

'Clockwork Orange? The underground? The train that goes under the ground?'

'Abdi,' said Simon. 'You can get a bus. I'll give you the number of the buses that go there, OK?'

I said thank you. But I knew I'd take the train.

I fold up my contract and put it in the pocket of my backpack. The other letter stares balefully up at me. It's been in there all week, rustling to itself. I hide it beneath my contract, zip up the pocket tightly. From the big pocket, I take out my milk and packets. As I move through the hallway into the kitchen, I see a shadow at the little bubbled window in my front door. It sees me. The banging starts again, insistent pounding on my flimsy sliced-wood door. If I was allowed, I would build a fine door. Strong planks from a healthy tree, jointed with its own wood, which is best. That way the dowels and pegs swell with the same sap, they naturally graft and fit as the sun and the healing lets them grow into their own snug shape. Maybe here it would be different: the cold would shrivel the wood, the structure would collapse. Maybe here thin sheets of pressed-up fragments and sawdust bound with paste is best.

I wait in the kitchen until the banging stops, and then I go to fetch my daughter.

3 · FEBRUARY

KELVINGROVE

City of Architecture & Design, European City of Culture, UNESCO City of Music – Glasgow's artistic credentials are second to none. One of the jewels in the city's cultural crown is the internationally significant Kelvingrove Art Gallery and Museum, which sits on the banks of the River Kelvin and houses one of Europe's greatest civic art collections.

Constructed in the Spanish Baroque following Glasgow's International Exhibition of 1888, Kelvingrove is Scotland's most visited attraction, with twenty-two galleries displaying an astonishing 8,000 objects. Collections include a vast natural history display, Egyptian artefacts, arms and armour and many outstanding artworks by the Old Masters, French Impressionists, Scottish Colourists and proponents of the Glasgow School. Some of the museum's most famed exhibits comprise a full-sized Spitfire aeroplane, the much-loved Sir Roger the Elephant, the famous Kelvingrove Pipe Organ (played daily at 1pm) and – arguably

Kelvingrove's finest treasure – Salvador Dali's Christ of Saint
John of the Cross.

Entry to Kelvingrove Art Gallery and Museum is free.

★

OH. ONE OF those headswims is happening again. The cool wall offers
an upright for my spine. What have they done to the museum?
I thought it would make me feel better. I lean further into the
wall, unpackaging the scene. I haven't been here in ages. It was
my favourite place as a child; a quiet douce cavern in which to
marvel at soft-lit colours and soaring beasts. Today, it's screeching.
Chaos slaps me: bright plastic chairs spilling from the Costa outlet
on to the central marble floor, weans eating sandwiches, sketching
pictures and shouting, and surmounting it all: a flock of dangling
heads. Seriously. Laughing and girning from the majestic ceiling
(where I'm sure there used to be chandeliers). Massive creamy
things, carved in grotesque masks, their mouths grimacing. It's the
swinging and the dancing of them. Their pupil-less eyes are scary.
The place feels so . . . busy. Too many people; everything loud and
jiggling – they've stuck coloured lettering by some of the paintings.
Interpretation areas. Cartoon bubbles beside cracked oils, the hidden
genius of the painting turned inside out. They've even reproduced
sections of oils and watercolours, with the rejoinder to: *Touch the
surface! You can feel the paint!*

We shouldn't have come here. No, they haven't . . . Oh. Yes.
Good. Thank goodness for that. At least the elephant's still here; I
thought for a moment they'd ditched it too. Massive big moth-
eaten thing. Sad as well. Sir Roger used to perform in Buffalo

Bill's Victorian circus, until one day the indignities and the small, ridiculous podium on to which he had to climb got all too much. He ran, trumpeting for his life, all the way down Sauchiehall Street. They shot him, of course. If you look closely you can still see the bullet holes, the ones the taxidermist didn't manage to buff and plump out.

I'd said I'd meet Abdi by the elephant. Only because you can't really miss it. Oh God I'm nervous. Will he think I'm making fun of him, like saying *I'll meet you in the jungle*? Do they have elephants in Somalia? I have no idea, no idea at all what I'm doing and I feel so daft. I feel thick and slow and ugly. Standing here, by the elephant, I feel faintly colonial too.

I also feel shocked and mean. If I can expel my anger on to the museum, maybe that's a good thing. Maybe Kelvingrove will work its distractive magic after all. On the way here, I bumped into my neighbour Naomi, and her girls. A Thursday, she was wearing jeans, yet she still had her work expression on. You know, that clouded furrow of a mind constrained, impatient to be elsewhere. We smiled our hellos and she was almost past me before I said, 'Day off then is it?' Like that: burble burble staccato-rush.

'Oh no,' she said. 'Just working from home. And shopping,' she grimaced, holding up a damply darkened paper bag. Then we did that little two-step, where you're half-past on your way, but lingering on the actual point of execution. That next step, the decisive one, is poised and raring to go, and yet the close proximity of words and bodies makes it somehow rude to leave. I swayed fractionally and said, 'No au pair today?'

'No,' replied Naomi. And I thought she was going to leave it like that, I honestly did, and how could you recover from an exchange so blunt? I'd have to hurry round a corner when I saw her next.

'No,' she repeated, shifting a little closer. Her girls beamed and burbled. Lucy, the elder, held on to the pram while the baby jettisoned a pink rabbit. It landed at my feet, but bending to retrieve it might have broken the spell because Naomi was coming ever nearer and her face had changed. She was there, in the moment, and there was a visible softening of her expression – to me, I think, to her confidante.

'Gone.' She lowered her voice. 'One letter from the Home Office, and she's off like a bloody shot. No notice, nothing.'

'The Home Office?'

Naomi withdrew slightly. 'She *told* me everything was fine. And I mean, you always pay these girls cash in hand, don't you? They prefer it that way.'

'Do you mean the tax man? Was it from the tax man?'

'*No*. Rula told me she was a student, but it was all just a pack of lies. She was an illegal bloody immigrant. Can you imagine? I mean Duncan's hoping to get called to the Bar soon.' Naomi held up her hand. 'I know, I know. I should have checked. But her English was good, she had references.' She sighed. 'Anyway, that's me back to paying agency fees, and there's a two week wait before I get another.' A shrug. 'What can you do? So – we're playing offices with Mummy today, aren't we, Lucy?'

Lucy had retrieved her sister's rabbit, but was refusing to give it back.

'Don't do that, darling. Give Flora back her bunny.'

'*No*. S'mine.' Lucy ducked from her mother's reach, her arm

40

glancing off Naomi's paper bag which ripped immediately, in slow parting waves. A pile of fish slid to the pavement.

'Oh for fucks – *Lucy!* How many times –'

'Here, here. I've got it.' I tried to scoop up some of the fish, but it kept slithering away.

'*Christ*. Jesus fu – Just leave it, will you? Deborah! Please. Just leave it.'

Naomi's face had bricked-up again. Furious, bright bricks. 'We'll just have sandwiches for dinner, won't we, girls? Mm, Flora? Will we just call Daddy at his work and tell him we're having *sandwiches*?'

Flora's cheeks were gathering momentum, quivering wetly, and I knew she was going to scream. So we each mumbled stuff about 'having to get on', and off we went, Naomi stepping over the puddle of fish and into her house; me to do my mentoring, my badge that I am a responsible and caring adult. I'd watched a stranger disintegrate and had gone to bed. In the fishscales and dried-up rainbows, I kept seeing Rula's face. Of course I knew all the time that her name was Rula, but it makes it simpler to pretend you don't.

There's Abdi now. Punctual. I can see him coming through the crowd. It's not hard. There are not that many tall black men in Glasgow, and there are none at all at Kelvingrove. He walks with a sloped elegance. An italic, a dark defined slant through a sea of similarity. All those other faces I can see, in their bobbing and pointing bodies, all of them are comfortably anonymous. If they choose not to stand out or make a fuss, they can. Does Abdi feel conspicuous? Like when you've had a new haircut and it's much too short and you have no hair left behind which you can hide?

He does look worried. And he's got that rucksack again. Bright red. He had it when we met, a wee lost schoolboy. Long concave face. Quick, brisk licking of his lips, his eyes scanning the displays.

I am the host. I step forward.

'Abdi,' I call. 'Hi.'

He comes towards me, smiling.

'Hello, Deborah.'

His accent is melodic, not the clipped guttural tones I associate with Africa. It's nice, how he says my name with the emphasis on the second syllable. I sound exotic in his mouth.

'Hi,' I say again. 'How are you?'

'I am well.'

'Good. Good.'

He looks at me expectantly.

' Well – do you want to go for a coffee first, or have a wander about?'

'A wonder?'

'A wander – to move about, to roam?'

His smile widens. Generous.

'I know this. Yes. We can wonder. Nice elephant.' He nods at Sir Roger, and at the baby elephant nestled by his side. I'm not sure where that little one came from, but I begin to launch into the sorry circus tale, gabbling like a hyper-historian, when he interrupts me.

'No,' he says.

'I'm sorry?'

Abdi points to a little plaque in front of the display. Another new development. 'No. This says that he came from zoo. Look.'

I look. The plaque also says he was put down after he got ill and started attacking zoo staff. So. Sir Roger was the villain of the piece. Well, I like my version better.

'We have been to zoo in Edinburgh,' says Abdi. 'My church thought I would like it.'

'And did you?'

'I felt very at home.'

He's laughing at me. His head dips sideways, and he's smiling at his feet. Now I'm the conspicuous one, a beacon of flustered red.

We go first to the Scottish Colourists – one, because I want to take him up the marble staircase (and away from the damn elephant) and two, because I think, if the bright oranges and blues of Peploe and Cadell don't impress him, then nothing will . . . I tail off. Wait for him to follow, but he's gazing skywards. Grinning.

'Glorious.'

'Pardon?'

He frowns. 'Is that the word? Glorious?'

Following his gaze. Seeing those ugly faces above us. 'Glorious means, um, wonderful, I suppose. Happy and overpowering and . . . grand? You know, big, important – like the sunshine.'

I'm making sunburst gestures, painting circles with my hands. 'Do you know that word: grand?'

Abdi laughs. 'Yes, exactly. Glorious. Those faces. They are so full of . . . joy!'

I look again. Everywhere; at the light brightness of the

chequered tiles, the new old shimmers. At the wrinkly grey hide and the giant heids.

'Well. They're certainly . . . big.'

I lead him up the staircase, pretending I'm in a crinoline. There's something *Gone with the Wind*-ish about these sweeping stairs. We get to the top, I turn left. Conscious he's behind me, that I'm leading. The leaflets the Refugee Council gave me said that visiting places or learning stuff will make it easier to chat. I don't think Abdi got the same leaflet. He is content to walk in silence, as if we're in a library. But yes, the Colourists are gorgeous, the Impressionists divine. And I think he likes the Mackintosh stuff – I know I do. One of those wee pewter pitchers would look lovely on my dining table. Just one – I finger the glass case – I mean, would they miss it?

Now we're in the Caledonian gallery. Lots of majestic braes and glens, a fair spattering of mighty stags, and everything worked in muddy ochre. All that's missing is the haggis grazing on the hills. Haggi? Abdi's scrutinising one of the good ones. Guthrie's famous funeral scene: men in sombre black pressing down on their grief; the setting winter light a smear on the horizon. Tucked in a corner, two stiff chairs stand outside the cottage round which the assembled men are gathered – and it is all men. There's no room for women at this Highland funeral. One stiff drape of black velvet hides the small coffin that rests between the chairs. But it's the clench of the father; I don't think I've ever noticed that before, how he holds himself so solid. How you do that at a funeral, when you're the chief mourner and everyone's pretending not to look, but they are, they're attuned to every twitch and shift you make. The tiniest emission of breath is measured for tears. *She's so brave.*

She's very . . . controlled when all the time you're thinking, thinking I will never see this person again. I will never touch their face. They are in there, in that box in front of me and I will never hear them speak or hold them close or smell their hair. You're almost calm with the knowledge. Well, I was. Your body has been bled and you function as part-ghost. And yet, at the same time, you're giving thanks, your crumpled heart is so full of love that it pales your grief, makes it insignificant. You are saturated with love and you are deeply, deeply lost.

I blink. See Abdi raise his hand before the painting. His arm drifts closer, I think his open palm is going to skim the surface, but it doesn't.

'Hoi!' shouts a man's voice. 'You canny touch the pictures.' The curator scurries over, blazer flapping with importance. 'Ho! You! Step away fae the wall.'

Gallery-gazers turn to stare. Abdi freezes.

'Excuse me,' I say. 'This gentleman's with me. He didn't –'

'Will you tell him no to touch?' repeats the man.

'I did not touch your painting.' Abdi will not make eye contact with the curator. It makes him look like he's lying, but I know he's not. I was right beside him; it was more like he was stroking the air in front of it.

'Any mair of your nonsense and I'll have to ask you to leave.' The curator waggles his walkie-talkie at Abdi. He turns to me. 'Keep him under control, eh?'

'He's not a dog.' I jouk my face close to his red-rimmed nose. 'And anyway, what d'you expect when you've got signs every- where telling folk to "feel your paint". I mean to say –'

'*That* is confined to one specific area of the interpretation centre. And if folk canny tell the difference –'

Abdi moves between us. 'Please. I am sorry I touch your painting.'

'Right.' The curator steps back a pace. 'Right. Well, just see that it disny happen again, OK?'

'Yes. OK.'

I wait until the curator's out of earshot, until the gawkers have returned to their perusal of art as opposed to drama. 'Why did you say that? You didn't touch the painting.'

'I know.' Abdi eases his thumb behind the padded strap of his rucksack, transfers it from one shoulder to the other. Gives me a half-smile. His eyes glisten. 'May we carry on, please?'

'You want to go?'

'I want to see other paintings.'

We walk on through the museum in silence, broken by me going, 'That one's nice,' and him going, 'Mm.' Under my skin, my heart is going haywire. Maybe I shouldn't be allowed out. Abdi won't look the road I'm on – he can't be *that* transfixed with the Sioux Ghost Dance Shirt. I blether on about it for a while, telling him about its origins and its repatriation, then we leave that room and move to the next. I'm suddenly conscious this must all seem greedy. Piles of stolen property – that's what a lot of this is. I watch him gaze at all the faded glories. The Refugee Council folk tell you that you haven't to pry, you mustn't ask 'leading questions'. Well, what is a leading question? *What's been stolen from you? What do you do with your days? What brought you here; to me, to Glasgow?*

'Oh, wait. You'll love this one.' But he is already gone.

He's walking down the vaulted corridor, galleries opening on either side, and he is ignoring them. As you should. As you are drawn, intractably, along this narrow passage, by a thread of light that calls your name. I see it dawn on his face, the lines of cloud and sky and sea and cruciform arms, the billowing up and out and down of this sublime painting. Although it's iconic, although you see its image on mugs and brollies, postcards and bags, it does not purport to be more than it is.

Quite simply, it is a vision.

I let him stand awhile. I'd forgotten how beautiful this picture was. Even the trace of the tear, a jagged half-square carved by a nutter's knife, is beautiful. It speaks of visceral response. It's like the painting kisses you, every time.

'It's called *Christ of Saint John of the Cross*.' I don't know why I'm whispering. 'By a painter called Dali. Have you heard of him?'

Abdi shakes his head.

'Do you like it?'

'I do.'

His head rises a little on his neck. I hadn't noticed it was bowed. Most people look up at the Dali, not down.

'Do people pray here?' he asks me.

'Eh – no. I don't think so.'

'They should.' He shrugs. 'Maybe.'

'Maybe,' I agree. But I don't. Not really. I don't want to argue with him, though; in fact, I'm glad if he still has the comfort of prayer. To me, it just got easier to stop asking.

'Coffee?' I chirp. The word tastes bright and harsh.

We go back downstairs to the basement café, another new

development, honey-scraped from the dust. Previously this was stores. They've gouged out windows through the sandstone, broad curving windows that seem to have always been here. There's a shop full of trinkets and postcards, beaded bags and Egyptian jewellery. Actually, it's very pleasant. I buy two buns. Iced ones.

'Is this place very old?' asks Abdi, as I place the plastic tray on our table. His rucksack is locked between his knees.

'Quite old. About a hundred, hundred and twenty years?'

'Mm.' He sips his coffee. Makes a face.

'Is it not very nice?'

I think for a moment he's going to ignore me. His lips and brow indent, as if he's doing a wee calculation.

'Do you mean *is* nice or is not?'

'No, that's what I was asking you.'

'Yes, but is hard to . . . it is . . . not easy. This is how you say it? With the knot always?'

'Do we? With a knot?'

Maybe he's not used to sugar.

'Yes, you do. You say "is not far" when you mean is close. You say "not bad" when you mean a thing is good.'

'No we don't.'

I see I've flummoxed him further with this double-negative. I shake my head.

'Sorry. Doesn't matter. Is your coffee good?'

'No.'

'Oh. OK. Would you like some of my tea?'

'No. Thank you.'

Oh, this is awful. I have to say something.

'Simon tells me you have a wee girl?'

Immediately, he brightens. That smile again; every so often, a kindling radiance.

'Yes. Rebecca.'

'That's a lovely name. What age is she?'

'She is four.'

'Nice age.'

'Do you have children?'

Yes no I did I was a mum and now I'm not, if I deny my baby then he didn't exist but then he doesn't exist and I imagine each possibility with which I can respond passing like colours through my skin.

'No,' is the answer I plump for in the end.

'Ah.'

Abdi holds my gaze that pretends to be inscrutable, but is really belligerent. Do *not* feel sorry for me.

'You are alone then?'

Christ. Tea, scalding the delicate puffiness of my mouth. The bluntness of his question stinging more. *And* he made me swear again. This is going terribly badly. I think I want to leave. I make myself swallow the bitter-hot tea. 'I – my husband is dead, yes.'

He says nothing. Nods.

'Yup. Dead and buried at forty-nine. Isn't life a blast?'

The nodding stops.

'Your wife?' I figure this will be all right, since he started it. Abdi picks up his coffee cup once more, but doesn't drink.

'Apart from Rebecca, I am alone.'

For a while, neither of us speak. We each shift our buns around their plates, mine with a neat nibble either side, his untouched. It's very hot in here, and clattery. Echoes of metal through the kitchen hatch, the smack of trays on trolleys. And yet they've hung fine art on the bare brick walls.

It *is* very pleasant.

'Your English is good,' I say, eventually.

'I try. Is much better – I have been here almost one year. And I have no choice. No one here speaks Somali.' Was that his tongue, peeking from between his teeth? I think it was another hint of humour, I do, and I seize on it.

'Aye, but we don't speak English here either. We speak Glaswegian.'

A polite cough, then more crinkling round his eyes. 'You do not speak. You –' he makes a squawking noise, miming wings with his elbows.

'True,' I laugh. 'We screech. So' – and I don't even take a breath in – 'why did you come to Glasgow?'

It's not meant as a challenge, it absolutely isn't, but his smile wipes clean.

This is a minefield. Should I apologise, if I apologise will that make it worse? 'If you don't want to talk about it . . . I don't mean . . . I don't mean what happened, I mean – why choose Glasgow?'

At last, he bites his bun. Speaks with crumbly enunciation. 'I was sent here.'

'Yes, but why specifically here? What made you go for Glasgow?' He swallows. 'No.'

'So, how – sorry. I don't understand. Why Glasgow? Out of all the places you could have ended up? Why did you choose Scotland?'

'Before I come here, I do not know there was place called Glasgow. I knew place called Yookie.'

'Yookie?'

'Yoo – kay.' He says it patiently, like he is my translator. 'But not Scotland. Not Glasgow. I do not know Glasgow until they put me on bus and brought me here.'

'I see.'

But I don't, and I think he understands this, because he carries on.

'I was in camp in Kenya for many years, then they sent me to Sudan. Then Sudan sent me back to Kenya and Kenya sent me to Yookie.' Another bite. 'And Yookie sent me here.'

'So you'd no idea you were coming to Glasgow? Do they not . . . give you *any* choice?'

I thought it would be like council houses or something; you know, you get to ask for a two-up two-down with a garden, and they go: *oh, not sure about that, but we can give you a nice four-in-a-block with a back court. Would you like to see it? And you go, oh well, OK then* – and you have a wee look, but you know you get at least two or three bites at the cherry before you have to decide.

'We are told we have to get our things and go on bus. It is long enough away to sleep?'

I nod.

'And then, we wake up here. The man says to me it is Glasgow. I say I do not know Glasgow. He tells me: "You do not want to, mate," and then he takes us to where we live.'

'And they didn't say why you'd ended up here?'

'No.'

I try to think how I would feel, dumped on the rim of a city in a country I'd never heard of.

51

'But they must've shown you round, eh? I mean like an orienta-
tion? They can't just drop you in the middle of somewhere you've
never heard of and bugger off . . .'

He carries on eating his bun.

'Did they tell you where shops are and schools, and how you can
get places and what you're meant to do?'

As I'm saying it, I'm thinking of a conversation I had once, with
Sally, a fellow teacher. We often sat together in the staffroom,
exchanging moans about Garry Black in third year, or catching up
on the three-way shenanigans between the Drama staff (so *dramatic*,
they were). Chatting in that cloistered confidential way that makes
you imagine you are friends. I remember her getting quite exasper-
ated with me.

*But surely they give you, I don't know – a caseworker or something?
And you'll get nurses, like those Macmillan ones for cancer. There must be
grants too. They won't just leave you to flounder, Debs. Don't be silly. Your
consultant will know who to speak to. There must be research and support
groups and–*

And a refusal to accept that, actually, you're on your own.

Yes. There must be that, at least in the initial stages. That's what
keeps you going, the assumption that it *will* get better, it has to. I shut
up, pour a little more tea. 'Is there anything you'd like to ask me,
Abdi? About Glasgow, or . . . how I can help you. Can I help you?'

Pathetic. I am not good at . . . people. *Can I help you, sir? More tea,
vicar? How about a mealy-mouthed mentor bandaging whatever gaping
wound it is you carry?*

'Yes.' He fishes a letter from his pocket. 'Can you read this,
please?'

Punctual and practical. A model pupil. I take the letter. It's from Social Work and Education.

Dear Mr Hassan

Thank you for your letter dated 17 September.

Well, we're only at the start of the next year. That's not too bad.

Please note that registration of Primary 1 pupils due to start school in August of this year will take place in the first week of February, and will be carried out by the Deputy Head Teacher of the relevant school. However, as discussed, and following the letter we received from your GP, no decision will be made on your daughter's placement until you have first made arrangements to meet with the educational psychologist as first intimated to you in August of last year. Please note that any further delay in arranging such an appointment may result in a delay to this process, particularly as a further referral to our Pre-School Assessment Centre may be required. Thank you for your attention to this matter.

How many times could you recycle the same few words in the one paragraph? Abdi watches me, his bun forgotten. A scattering of crumbs rest on his chin, caught in whorls of curling stubble.

'This means Rebecca cannot go to school?'

'No, no, they're not saying that at all. What they're asking is . . . they want you to see a kind of doctor. Has Rebecca not been –'

'I have seen doctor. He says Rebecca is well.'

'Yes, but this is another doctor, one who'll talk a bit more to

Rebecca herself, find out if something's . . . och, I don't know – upsetting her maybe?'

When I was a teacher, this bit was always hard. Suggesting to a parent that their child might need 'a wee bit help'. I'm wondering what it is: trauma? Problems with concentration, displaying inappropriate behaviours –

'Rebecca does not talk.'

Abdi's hand is shaking as he drains his unpleasant drink. A quietly horrible thing to see. I try to look away from his shaking skin. It's too intimate when our public bodies display our private truths. Callum's hands would shake terribly. The greater his paralysis became, the more his hands would tremble. His hand and his fingers, laced stubbornly through the handle of his cup, and the brown liquid spilling. How flat and round the brownness of it was as it skittered down the edges of his cup and I suddenly remember: here, it was here in Kelvingrove, sitting by the old tearoom up the stairs and this is why the place upsets me.

It's not Rula, and it's not the stupid heads at all.

It's me, insisting that of course there'll be a lift, and how it would do him good to get out, now we have the new Zafira and the folding chair – of course no one's looking, don't be stupid. Saying it more crossly than I meant. Terrified of the power and weight and length of the car, and then there not being a lift, not then, not a proper one. Just a goods hoist, and they're very kind, the curator folk. They sling us in – Callum's chair and his knees pressed against the lattice grille, the curator talking to me, always me, above Callum's head, the awkward sliding of us out. The limitations of where we can trundle to, and what time do we want the hoist back down, because you have to be accompanied, you know. So we decide on tea. Tea and a scone in the old-fashioned salon that used to be in the museum, up on the first floor. But there are three small steps. Three shitty steps, don't you know, little ones that you would never normally notice, pointless, decorative absurd humps of stone that bar our passage and make us sit out in the corridor beside some marble statuary. I insist, *insist* that we're having tea, and I leave him there, parked nose-up to a statue (lest he pose a fire-risk), to queue for tea and scones.

I fumble with tea and plates and change, then scurry back to my husband, my beautiful fine husband encased in his shell. His neck is locked, his eyes fixed on the marble forms before him: a bereft father and his motherless child. I arrive just in time to see the tears run freely down Callum's perfect cheek. And him, unable to wipe them dry. It's me, me who spills the flat brown tea. I'm doing it now, in fact.

Funny, how I'd forgotten that.

'Honestly, don't worry,' I'm saying to Abdi, who's staring at me. 'It'll be fine. Trust me – I used to be a teacher. I know . . . I have a friend who works in special needs –'

'You are teacher!' Spontaneously, he reaches for my hand, claps the back of it, once, and then retreats. That glow is back about him. '*I* am teacher,' he beams. 'I may teach Rebecca. Can I do that here?'

I was sure Abdi was a fisherman. I'm positive Simon told me that.

'I think school would be good for her, Abdi. She'd make friends there.'

'I think this too. But if they will not take her —'

'No, they will. We'll get it sorted. Have you had other letters from Education? From the school? Has school written to you before?'

'*Yes*. And I know is in February I must go, I wrote it down, and I am to go to school next week, but then this letter comes.'

I read it again. You'd think the *Education* department would write coherent letters.

'All they want to do is check that she'll manage. She doesn't speak — at all? Doesn't speak English or doesn't speak Somali?'

He shrugs. 'It is . . . I can speak for her.'

'But she can hear OK? She hears you speak?'

'Oh yes. She hear everything. We learn English together, she is clever, clever girl.'

'OK, well, what you need to do is contact this educational psychologist — see the number here? You phone them, they'll tell you when you and Rebecca should go and see them, and they'll make sure she gets to the right school.'

'I can go with her?'

'Of course you can.'

He visibly relaxes. 'I thought they would take her . . . she . . .'

I can tell he's struggling with choosing the right words.

'She doesn't like to be away from you? Well, of course not. She's in a strange country, away from home.'

'Yes. No. With some people. If she knows them . . . I . .' He shakes his head, and I see tears there, poised on the point of becoming real, and we both pretend not to notice.

'She is good, clever girl.' He offers it up like a plea.

'Och, we're both teachers, Abdi. You know how clingy wee ones can be –'

'She was always good friendly. Very happy girl and I cannot . . .' Staring into my head. Not my eyes, but drilling into my mind, grasping through like I'm driftwood for him to seize. I have no idea what this little family has been through. All I can do is sit there, with the sugary taste of icing on my tongue. Too intense, I can't bear it, but, just as I'm about to turn away, he breaks his stare.

'I cannot help her,' he finishes softly.

'Would you like me to phone the psychologist for you?'

Is that a leading question?

His shoulders slump, and he fingers the top of his rucksack. 'I would like that. Yes.'

'OK, then. I will.'

The high planes of his cheeks slacken. I recognise a fellow teeth-gritter. Then he finishes off his bun.

'YOUR FISH IS ready!'

Rebecca gallops in from her room. There's a smudge of black on her cheek, a dash of green on her knuckles. Felt-tipped pens; a present from Mrs Coutts. I resolve to find a higher shelf to keep them on.

'Mucky pup!' I wipe my daughter with the dishcloth.

She giggles.

'Mucky pup!' I repeat, and she purses her lips up like she might make an 'M'.

Her Sunday School teacher told her she was a 'mucky pup' after craft-time, when she had glue on her hair and chin. I looked up 'pup' in my dictionary afterwards – it means young dog. She called my little girl an animal! But I've learned, so many times now, that what you have to study most is the inflection. It's how the words are given, not what they are, that forms their full meaning, and Miss Blake-call-me-Sophie is always gentle. You can tell from how

Rebecca runs to her and takes her hand. Miss Blake speaks frequently through laughter, and always with warmth. A 'pup' is just a baby, and it's striking how amusing people in Yookie find animals to be. You see that on the cards they send one another on their birthdates. You see calendars brimming with fat little kittens, and framed pictures of dogs in strange hats. Yet I also see boys throw stones at shivering curs. I still see dead meat hang on hooks and bleed on slabs.

Still, I decide that to be a 'mucky pup' is a nice thing. It makes my baby laugh. And I thought if we spoke sometimes in English . . . it is a different language. If it is a different place . . . If she thinks the past is made anew . . .

'Here are your fishes, my little mucky pup.' I slide the crisp orange slabs on to her plate. They're labelled on the packet as 'fingers' but I cannot call them that. 'And your nice green peas.' She looks suspiciously at the garish green. 'They're yummy. Look, Aabo's going to have one.'

She picks up the buttons that make the television work. Mrs Coutts calls these buttons a doofer, but then, Mrs Coutts often speaks a language of her own. I doubt doofer is the correct name. It's another word that makes Rebecca laugh. I grab it from her. 'You can have doofer when you eat your peas.' She scowls, I shrug. She eats.

Deborah will telephone the child-doctor for me. It is like stones being taken from my chest. I have heard the expression 'breathe easier' before – Mrs Girdwood said it after church, when we were sipping tea and she was talking to another lady about a robber who pretended to be from the council, and was tricking his way into people's homes. The lady had told Mrs Girdwood the police had a description, and Mrs Girdwood had said: 'Well, we'll all breathe easier when he's caught.' Often, I don't ask them to explain phrases. It interrupts the conversation, and singles me out. Plus, I like the challenge: me and my thoughts, wrestling with all the possible connotations as I unpick words like knots in my net. 'Easier' was 'more simple', so it was 'simple breathing', which implied to me breathing that had been difficult before. But I'd never thought of it as an obstruction. I had decided it was to do with holding the air inside your lungs, because you are terrified to breathe out. Like when you shake behind the thick trunk of tree, in whose branches you are perched, your face crushed tight against its bark and your head squashed low, immobile and you feel your head melt and the pressure is of underwater with the force of not-breathing in case the soldiers down below pause in their gutting of your friends – and look up to find you.

When they go, you can 'breathe easier'. That to me was the definition. But when Deborah read my letter and said she would help, I felt a lightness in my lungs. I hadn't known they were . . . congested? Being crushed? It was a strange, free feeling when she offered to help. Like a crouching jinn had been removed from me. I kiss my munching girl on her forehead, steal a bite of fish. It tastes, and smells, of paste.

Deborah and I were both 'easier' after that. I know I'd embarrassed her, when that guard shouted at us, but it did not diminish my pleasure for the Kelvingrove. The museum wasn't boastful. It made me feel small as well as full. No coins were exchanged for entry, no bribe was passed to leave. It simply stood there with its doors unlocked and its visitors passing through. Like a temple in which Glasgow kept her history. She chose what of creation to display to the world. In Somalia, people always praise the new. The higher and shinier a building in Mogadishu, the greater it is revered. You can cram more people inside, you can shake your fist at the unblinking sky and say: 'We are nearly there, beside you. Ha!' I noticed, though, that Deborah only delighted in the objects that were made, not the ones that were taken. Several times she had apologised, alerting me to signs and explanations. I just wanted to look at the art.

'You understand?' she had persisted. 'A lot of this stuff is stolen. You know? During wars maybe? Or when Britain was "pretending" to help countries.'

I think I annoyed her. 'If it was war, then much of this "stuff" would have been destroyed. At least it is here.'

'But that's not the point, Abdi,' she began. Then, immediately, she stopped. Rubbed her nose. I noticed she'd painted some of that pigment on her face, very faint, but you could see it gathering in powdery flakes where the bulge of her nostril was. I think we were both thinking the same thought. *You are going to lecture me on war?*

Even knowing so much of Kelvingrove was filled with plunder, I loved it. Glasgow is both barren *and* rich, it is poor and it is bold. In Somalia, one wealthy warlord would live here and he would put up gates and guns. Next time, I will bring Rebecca. Tell her we are having a feast. She's finished her peas and fish, has her hand outstretched for the doofer.

'You want cartoons?' I ask. She nods. I press the red button and the house is filled with noise. I go to the fridge to get some milk, pass the shelf above the fireplace. My mother would have ... I grope for the phrase I heard Mrs Coutts use. What was it again? It seemed to encapsulate all her great excitement ... *And then I seen that boy off* River City. *You know the shell-suit one? I tell you, I was fair beside myself.* Yes. To find a fire that needed no wood or flame, kept ever-ready in a home that needed no building. My mother would have been fair beside herself. I lift the picture frame that sits on the shelf, wish beyond almost anything that my family's faces were inside it.

On the way out of the museum, Deborah had asked me to wait in the foyer. 'Foyer' – I didn't know that word. She told me it was the hall between the basement and the grass outside, and that it was French. 'Sometimes we use foreign words like everyday words.'

'I do that all the time,' I said. She liked that. She laughed. A real laugh, with eyes and belly, not simply mouth, then told me she'd be 'two ticks'. I stood and read the walls; there were bricks with people's names on them. When Deborah came back, she was carrying a thin white paper bag. 'Here.' She handed the bag to me. 'I put my home number on the back, so you've got that as well as my mobile. I know the Refugee folk said we should only exchange mobiles at first, but to be honest, I'm pretty rubbish with them. I always leave it in the bottom of my bag, or forget to switch it on ... It's just that, well ... if I'm going to help with Rebecca, we should ... I wouldn't want to miss a call if you needed me, you know?'

Inside the bag was a piece of card with numbers on.

'Thank you.'

'Turn it over.'

On the other side was a picture. It was the painting we had seen of Our Lord, hanging in the bluest skies.

'It's the —'

'Dali,' I said. 'I know. Thank you.'

I've put the picture in this frame. Rebecca made it at Sunday School. The children collected strips of wood from the fruit ices they like to suck, then glued them together and painted them. Rebecca painted her frame in bright stripes of yellow and blue. Along the top, once the paint had dried, someone (I suspect the Sunday School teacher, because it was very neat) had written in black ink: 'Thank you for . . .' and then, at the bottom of the frame, Rebecca had written 'Aabo'. Before I put the Christ inside the frame, I copied Deborah's number into my phone. Her mobile number starts with 'M' for mentor, but I gave this one her name. *Deborah*. It jumps to the top of my list. I know no one here with names who start A, B or C — except Mrs Coutts, and I'm positive she has no mobile.

As we passed outside, Deborah had asked me where the camp was, and how long had I been there? She said *So* before her straggly question, as if it was a final thing, and that she had been waiting to ask it from the start. Immediately, I shrank from answering. Wished I had never said a word to her, I should have refused to tell her anything at all except 'my life is here now thank you'. But that would have been rude. And I'd already embarrassed her . . . And I had agreed to this whole — No. I had reached out gladly, to the false creation of a 'friend'. And friendship means to give something of yourself. Just something, a piece no bigger than a little picture.

I return the frame to its shelf, go into the kitchen.

I had *known* there would be this necessary exchange, but I wasn't prepared for it. Stupid. Of course I must revisit the camp. But it's so hard to sift the silt, to make bright fragments of sense and clarity from the mass and mess of those days and years. You forget deliberately how the purpose of your coming, the focus of your search, the transitory – necessary – nature of your stay eked out to weeks, then months, then years of sloth. Of hope and future seeping out and sinking through the dust. To remember means to search for landmarks, for anchors in the grinding endless time that yawns and weeps itself to sleep and yawns some more. So all of your time there merges until there are only two fixed points – the first day and the last and the last the last I will not there is not I am I will only remember the first.

'Dah-dah!' The man swept his arm back, a wide and knowing gesture like when the witchdoctor scatters bones.

'You get it?' he grinned. '*This* is the centre. Right here. This is Dadaab.'

Grinning and chewing. All the time chewing, from the moment he began to lead me through the camp, the slack khat swilling in his mouth, making his eyes too round and his speech too slow. Which was good actually – it helped me to understand him more. We don't all speak the same language. I crouched, peered through the plastic curtain and into a long dark shelter. Many men lolling there. I recognised the low murmur of madness and a quick, rising shriek that may once have been laughter. One or two turned their heads as the light drove in, but most continued in their steadfast stares, or carried on monologues with unblinking neighbours. All locked in their constant chewing. We had walked through this swarming, stinking human sea for over one hour. He had brought me to a khat house. I moved back into the light.

'No, friend. I was looking for food?' This place smelled evil. I had to get back to my wife. I had left her and the baby with a group of women, told her to stay in the middle of them and not to move. But I wasn't sure, now, if I could even find the way back. Never had I seen so many shacks, so many people. Such vast barren tribes of scattered people. Someone told me there were three hundred thousand human beings crammed here, but I didn't believe there were that many lost souls in the world. Me, who had lived in my village with my friends and my kin, who had learned from meagre books and from the generosity of my grandfather, from the love of my mother. Who had ventured from the village to the *big town*. I was book-boy, learning-boy – I had been to school. Over four hundred in my school! *But so many, child!* My mother fussed, made me patties.

From only knowing the same faces for ever, I had learned at school that there were many different shapes of nose and cheek, that there were Bantus and Cushties and a whole bubbling soup of peoples that made our little piece of Somalia. And I also learned that, in our scraps and differences, we could still be friends. But there was no sense of that here in the refugee camp. No community, no shape to the place even though it was mostly Somalis packed inside. There was nothing except stench and wide lost lakes of bodies in mud blocks. However far you looked. You have no idea how many tents and mud blocks, shored up with tin and ancient wood, how much sharp-wire fencing, camel-blood and sewers and plastic bags and long dirt roads and dust and gates and guns. Only this, and then the desert. After trudging for so long, you come to this.

The chewing man ignored me, stumbled inside the khat house. I stood in the dull beat of the Kenyan sun. I knew it was the same sun wherever it blazed, but it was no longer my sun. I hated it. It didn't grow our crops or give us joy and light. It didn't warm my sea. Just shone above all the atrocities I had seen, drying up land and bones until they could no longer be named. The heat licked the nape of my neck, puckering my skin. People thumping by me; everyone close and surly, no one with anywhere to go.

'Follow me, son.'

An old man touched my elbow. My first response was to strike him. The single belief I clung to now was that every creature might do you harm. I'd let the chewing man lead me only because he went in front. I could see him from there, and I knew he was alone. This feeble old man had come at me from the side – he might have his sons behind him, and my eyes swung crazily as I lurched away.

'You want food, boy?' He gave a toothless smile. 'Don't worry. I'm not going to eat you – far too stringy bastard for me.'

Still I hesitated.

'Suit yourself. I'm going there anyway. You registered?'

'What?' I hurried after him, before he was lost in the swirling, aimless ocean.

'Is it your day?' he shouted. 'You got your ration card?' As I caught up with him, he lifted a piece of cardboard, dangling from a string round his neck.

'Yes. We just arrived here.' I took my card from the pocket.

'Best keep it round your neck. See – make a hole like this, then knot the string tight tight tight. You lose it, you starve.'

'Won't they give you another one?'

'Who? UN? Ha!'

'Yoo-en,' I repeated. 'Is that who the soldiers are?'

'Some of them. Right – see there. That's the ice house.'

We had come to a kind of a marketplace. I hadn't expected to see anything like this. There were even shops, like in the big town. Dirty, rough shops, but they had real walls of metal and mud. The old man pointed to a tin shed. 'In there, ice. OK? You got any dollars? That one next to it is where you can change money.'

'Dollars? No. I need dollars?'

'It all helps. Especially if you lose your card.'

There was so much to assimilate. But I was young, strong. I had survived. Even this decrepit man had managed. He'd come here, old and confused, and he'd found his way. In a week or two I'd be doing the same.

'How long have you been here?' I asked.

'Sixteen years.'

I laughed out loud at his joke. Then I saw it was not a joke. His tree-bark face, crumbling. He wiped his nose with the back of his hand, then poked me with the same knuckles. Snot on my shirt. Old-man snot, which I doubtless deserved.

'You keep all your papers close, boy, you hear me? Then maybe you'll get out of here. Every time they give you something official, a paper, a stamp, a name – you guard it like you guard your sister. Understand?'

I felt my knees give under my weight. He wasn't to know.

'I don't have a sister any more.'

He'd touched me, twice now. He was the age of my grandfather and I just thought . . . I had thought in the shock of the moment that he should know. In giving him this knowledge, I'd be giving him trust. Trust and my ration card were the only commodities left.

'Well, fucking guard your papers better than you guarded her, eh?' He sniffed. A deep, long gurgle. 'Right, we're nearly there. Stay with me; watch what I do.'

The momentum started to build, tramping feet growing more purposeful, arms swinging as the crowd I found myself within became a complex body, a giant, undulating centipede. You sensed that, at any given moment, if one of these many, many feet were to fail or trip or, worse, begin to run, then the whole beast would implode in a bloody, rampant burst and all thoughts of my sister were swept away as the crowd carried me towards a wooden build-ing. It was no bigger than the schoolhouse I was taught in, and the walls were swathed in razor-wire, yet people were reaching to it, clinging like it was God inside. The soldiers separated us into two lines, men on one side, women on the other. Bright hijabs and quivering hands. A silence falling.

'They let the females in first,' whispered my companion. 'They don't push so much. You got a wife?'

I nodded.

'Send her next time.'

I would never send Azira here. I watched the women shuffle forwards, holding up their cards. Their colours shining, wrapping their heads, concealing their arms, beautiful and garish in the midst of all that dust. The soldiers checked each card against lists they held. Sometimes, you saw a head-shake, heard a mournful keen as pleas were ignored and a weeping woman sent away. No one went after these rejects. Each queuing woman, each queuing man, gazing stoically ahead.

'What's wrong?' I whispered.

'Not on the list.' The old man shrugged. 'It happens.'

'And what do you do then?'

He spat. The man in front of us shifted his heels as the spittle hit the dust. 'You make sure you're on the list.'

Once the queues had been culled, the doors to the food store were opened. I could see the shed was divided up, the way animal pens are, and the women were being shoved into one of several lanes. There was no need to push – all they wanted was to be inside the space into which they were being man-handled. After that, I couldn't see much, just the steady swell of people moving in and out. In and out, in and out. Rhythmic as the throw of my nets. Steady and wild as the sea washing my boat. Eventually, I stopped worrying about Azira. I had no energy remaining. The old man was called forward, disappeared into the throng. I had been standing in bare sunshine for hours, but I was numb beyond discomfort. Until the surge frothed up again and I found myself at the front. It was my turn. All the saliva dried in my mouth. It felt like a paper-moth was dying there, its fluttering death-throes trapping my voice. Mute, I held up my ration card. The soldier moved his pen across the page. Moved it again. We had one heel of bread and some water left. I had three mouths to feed; milk was no longer sufficient for the baby, Azira said. Or she told me to say that when we registered. A smart – and beautiful – woman, my wife.

'OK,' he said.

And that was it. Granted access with a blunt-nosed nod. I entered my allocated slot, was pushed with all the others into one of the runs. Then the run processed me into a darker space, where there were many wire cages. For a sick-lurch second I thought I was trapped, that they were going to kill me, until I saw men in the cages. Flour-coated men, dragging out sacks and cans. I tried to watch the man next to me. 'Keep moving!' roared a soldier. My elbows, steadying me against the heave. We each had to take a sack, then reach through a hole in the wire for each sack to be filled. I scrabbled with the rest of them, hearing rumours that the cornmeal had run out. It would be two more weeks before I could come back here, and the panic in me grew, the bestial clamouring filling up my head.

'I'll kill you!' shouted a man. 'Give me my cornmeal now!'

The soldier laughed.

I felt my sack being tugged away from me, but it was only a worker taking it. I reached further in, ensuring my grip remained fast. Wire biting into my crushed-up cheek. I felt the pull of the sack increase as it filled up with food. Cornmeal and flour. Vegetable oil, salt. Stuff we could make lumps of solid nothing from, but I didn't care. After my father died and before my grandfather took us home, my mother sometimes fed us camel leather to chew.

At last, I was released into the sun. Scorched. My sack dragged, satisfying with all its lumps and bumps, and I was desperate to take it straight to Azira. I used to do that with my fish. No matter what I sold or bartered, I always kept the finest silver for her. But how to find the way? Screwing my eyes up from the sun's bleak glare. If I could find the market square again, and from there to the khat house . . . Ahead of me, I saw a breeze of shadows, leaping in the sun. People were jumping from the thin dust road, backing themselves into doorways, straddling their robes and hems over sewers. Then a shout, and a truck rolled by. It was open-topped, driven by a soldier, and it was full of people like me. Not parched with the dead-eyed acceptance I saw surrounding us. No, there was life in those faces. Joy and fear and a sense of reawakening.

'Where are they taking them?' I asked another man. Wherever it was, I wanted to go there.

'Being resettled, probably. You pay good dollars, you get out. Cut your hands off and you can even get to America.'

'Cut your hands off?' His glibness made me sick. To even make fun of that, when so many of the rebels and militia used it as a brand.

'Yeah. Disabled. Be deaf or blind or lame and you get to the promised land.'

As the truck lurched by, I saw a little boy, staring from his mother's lap. Or possibly his aunt or elder sister. Or perhaps a kind deep heart had plucked him from the side of a corpse. On his own lap he clutched a red backpack. New and impossibly big; he had to pitch his head to the side like a little bird in order to see past it. It was his eyes that hurt me. Unbearable. Huge in his sunken face. Then the truck made a sore, grinding noise, came crashing into a pothole, and immediately, people started to move closer in. Like ants teeming on a hill of dung. Men jostling, girls running. I saw a woman offer up her child, her cries for mercy beaten off by another soldier on the back. He pointed his gun at the growing crowd,

72

shouted angry words to his colleague, who revved and revved the engine until the truck groaned and shot forward. From the basket of his arms, the little boy's backpack was thrown. It soared into the air, a red square in a blue sky, and I could hear his screech of desperation. I don't think anyone else noticed. Most people were still trying to waylay the truck. I ran to where the bag had landed, snatched it up. The truck was picking up speed now, but I ran after it. The boy could see me, he was leaning out, his mother yelling at him to sit down, wrestling with him as he struggled forward. Faster and faster, the truck rattling further from me, but I could reach it still, I thought I could, even with my heavy sack and the clattering of it on my legs.

And then I saw the soldier again. Levelling his gun.

I stopped running, and the truck sped away. In one hand, I held the child's backpack. In the other, my sack of food. The crowd had deflated, crept back to their shiftless shambling. But I noticed the man I'd been talking to, edging nearer and nearer to the backpack.

'Give that to me,' he menaced. Fist gripping a large, flat stone.

I jerked my chin above his pitiful head. Taller, broader than he was, and not yet desperate enough to lose everything I had.

'You touch me, I will rip off your fucking stinking skull.'

He paused, still holding the stone.

'That bag is not yours.'

'Says who?'

'You stole it. I saw you.'

'You calling me a thief? Fine. Let us call the soldiers over. Will we?' I raised my voice. 'Is there police here? I have plenty dollars.'

'Fuck you.' He threw his stone in the gutter.

'No. Fuck you.' I bowed politely.

'I will find you,' he said through uneven teeth.

'Good luck with that, my friend.' As I spoke, I pressed my body forward, entering the flow of human sea. This time, I was glad of the limbs and trunks that propelled me, because my legs were crying with fear. But I held on to the red backpack, much tighter than the little boy had.

It was mine now.

5 · MARCH

LOCH LOMOND

Scotland is rich with beautiful scenery. Only fourteen miles north of Glasgow, the 'Bonnie Banks' of Loch Lomond are known the world over, thanks to the popular melody. Interestingly, the 'low road' referred to in the song actually comes from Celtic mythology. When someone died far from home, the ancients believed fairies would provide a 'Low Road' so his soul could return to his kin. Majestic and mysterious, it does seem possible this place could be the gateway to another world!

Twenty-four miles long and six hundred feet deep, the loch – nestling in the shadow of Ben Lomond – is the largest expanse of freshwater in the UK. Flanked by several Munros and the West Highland Way, Loch Lomond is also open to every kind of watercraft including canoes, jetskis and speedboats.

The National Park Authority seeks to accommodate both land-based tourists and loch users, with environmentally sensitive areas subject to strict speed limits. The rest of the loch, however, is open to

speeds of up to 90 km per hour. Whilst entry to Loch Lomond, along
with walking and climbing, is free, there are charges for some activities.
Of course, you can always bring your own boat.

★

A STONE SCATTERING sparks. As it lands fully and punches through the water's face, it will blast circles up and out. The process has begun already, but they are caught, these circles. Framed, they have become suspended hoops, suggestions of themselves made flat. Tones of brown and green, of creamy-gold and purple-blue rustle and call you in. Yes, I think. That's it. We'll go somewhere that's alive. In the foreground, a heron preens its plumage and the mountain preens itself in the water.

The computer screen glows green with the shimmer of the loch. Slowly, pointlessly, I spell out my name. You rarely get the same person twice when you phone here, but I'm finding people like the security of it. If you give your name to them, it's an anchor they can hold.

'That's right. Delta, Echo, Bravo. Debs.'

'Thank you, Debs,' says the thin, tired voice. 'I will remember you.'

'Good luck,' I reply. I sound as exhausted as she did. A minute to calm down. I'm fine while I'm talking, or doing. It's afterwards . . . My nails gleam in the artificial light. My sister Gill persuaded me to get a French manicure. *Resistance is futile*, she beamed. *You want to look all smart!* The girl did a lovely job on me, but no one really dresses up in here. Including me. I just bought my first pair of leggings. Worn with a baggy top, mind, to offset their clinginess.

Beneath the desk, I circle my ankles. They *are* very comfy. But my new bra is chafing. Absently, I rub the side of my breast.

A large brunette leans over my workstation. On my side – so she must be someone that works here. Either that or a revolt is underway and we're being raided by our clients.

'Ooh. Did I hear you using the phonetic alphabet?' Her breath is nicotine and coffee, her scent is crisp and old. *Charlie?* Do they still make that?

'I always find it's better to use words like "Dog" or "Egg".' She's got a little dab of lipstick on her teeth.

'Really? I find it better not to patronise folk.'

Gamu, the volunteer next to me, snorts a little, then dips her face in her coffee mug. The brunette lady hoists the rim of her spangly jumper down over her tummy.

'You're new, aren't you?' Her question is rhetorical; she extends a hand in welcome. 'I'm Mrs Winters. Senior Project Officer and Campaigns Manager? I'm just back from my holidays.'

'I'm Deborah.'

'So I gathered. Hello, Deborah. You can call me Caro – we're all very informal here. Well, didn't mean to interrupt. I'll no doubt see you later.'

A nasty flush burns up my neck and face. I want to go after her, say *I'm sorry. I don't get out much!* But the damage is done. She looked about ages with me, too. We might have gone for lunch together. Gloomily, I inspect my keyboard, small puffs of fluff flying up as I breathe over its smooth black lines.

I have a keyboard!

I've started volunteering at the Refugee Council. Just the odd day here and there, when they're really busy. No, make that 'short staffed'. They're always busy. It was Simon's idea. We'd had our second meeting, the one where the mentor is brought in and asked: *So. How d'you think things are going?* And you either say: *Fine* or *Well* . . . and then launch into a big long guddle of reasons why it's not really working.

'Fine,' I said. It felt odd to be speaking about Abdi, actually, as if it were private, or I was talking about him behind his back.

'Good, good,' said Simon. 'And you're enjoying the whole process, then? Any problems?'

I searched my mind for problems. Me, who is nothing but a little ray of sunshine.

'Nope.'

And it's true. Practically. Abdi is my friend-stroke-project-stroke-good-deed right now. We're learning, slowly, about what we want from each other, what we share and what we can share. No different from any other relationship.

'No. I think we're getting on fine. I'm hoping to meet his daughter soon –'

I stopped. So keen to get Brownie points for how well we're bonding that I didn't think. Did they know about Rebecca's not-speaking? Did I just break a confidence? Was I even allowed to meet his family, because, to be honest, I hadn't read all the bumph they'd given me from cover to cover. It was all a bit earnest, with lots of SHOUTY TEXT!!

'Yeah, well,' I backtrack. 'At some point it would be nice to meet her. Rebecca, she's called.'

Of course, Simon had the file in front of him, but it was

important to me that he knew that I knew. 'I used to be a teacher you see . . .' It was a lame tailing-off, made worse by the slightly creepy: 'I like kids.'

'That's why we thought you'd make a good pairing,' he said.

'Because Abdi used to be a teacher too?'

Simon smiled. 'Did he tell you that? That's great.' Then he smiled a bit more. 'And are you enjoying the whole "interaction" thing, Deborah?'

Yup, he did make wee air quotes as he said it. Nice chap, Simon. Late twenties, beginning to bald – and I suspect his mum picks up his jumpers in Asda when she's getting the messages. But you can tell his heart's in the right place. Tucked right behind the three neat biros he keeps clipped in the dip of his V-neck. Bless.

'You mean "talking"?' I did the air quotes back at him. 'Yes, I do. Abdi's a fascinating person.'

Fascinating? A puzzle to be solved? A sop to my need to 'help someone' and fill my day? I bet Abdi's had the same interview. We're not allowed to ask what our mentee said about us. I wish I could. I'm not sure if we are 'getting on fine'. We've only texted twice since Kelvingrove, once to confirm our next meeting, and the second time for me to check what dates suited for the psychologist. His answer had been instant – and very vague:

R school sorted. No need. Do not wory. A

Was I no longer to contact Education, then? Had Rebecca started talking of her own volition? We were way into March, the deadline for her school enrolment was past, and I'd had no more word on what Abdi wanted me to do, despite me texting 'Why?'. But I must 'respect our distances as well as our differences', it says in my mentors' handbook. Also helpfully vague. Me being me, I keep thinking: *maybe he doesn't like me*. Was he more upset by the curator shouting at him than he'd let on? Did I not defend him well enough? But then, he'd told me about Rebecca afterwards . . . or was that the shock? I'd thought we'd bonded over it, och, not bonded, but I thought . . . I thought I was thinking too much. This monthly-meeting framework is too impersonal. More rigid lines to trip over. Texts are impersonal too. But a trip to the Bonnie Banks would give us plenty of time to talk. Although, if I didn't get my backside into gear and hire a car, we'd have to hike it there and back. Loch Lomond in March? Och, it would be a breeze. (Considerable pun intended.)

'Now, you're not actually working at all at the moment, are you?' Simon continued.

'No. Like I said before, when my husband took ill –'

He'd held up a hand. 'Oh, no, no, I'm not . . . what I'm thinking is, well, you're clearly a "people person".'

'Am I?'

'Oh God yes. Abdi . . . if he's talking about his daughter and his teaching in the space of two brief meetings . . . well, you're obviously the type of person who . . . you seem like a good listener, Deborah.'

I knew he was buttering me up for something, drizzling me with oily sentiment before he popped me in a hot oven, but, regardless, I allowed myself a bask. Because I *was* a people person, once.

Before Callum's illness took hold ... ach, before lots of stuff, when I still believed in happy endings, in positive thinking and all that guff, I was quite good fun. But bitter bindweed has taken hold. It's where they get widow's weeds from. Doesn't refer to garments at all. No. These weeds are constant green tendrils of restless despair, trussing you. Always.

'Thank you,' I said. 'And you're telling me this because. . . ?'

'I was hoping you might get a bit more involved.' Simon folded his hands neatly beneath his chin. 'Here at the Council, I mean. We're always looking for volunteers – even if you could only do one day a month. The Helpdesk in particular, it can be pretty ... well, you saw for yourself how busy the waiting room was when you came in today.'

It was manic. Babies in pushchairs, old men in tattered coats, dark-eyed women flapping hands, shrilling tongues, and a bank of phones that rang and were answered, rang and were answered, rang and rang and abruptly gave up. Those were the ones I worried about most. Did they ever ring back? Was that their one and only cry for help, lost in a vacuum of nobody there?

'Oh ... I don't know,' I said. But I did. 'OK then. Just the odd day.'

Simon undid his fingers, shook my hand. The false neat smile slipped away and a person grinned at me. And I wondered if he found it as hard to ask for help as I found it to offer.

Behind our workstation, another phone rings. A toddler howls.

'Oh-ho. You and the boss lady were bonding well!' Gamu is grinning at me. 'Coffee?' She waves her empty mug.

I shake my head. She's lovely, Gamu. She was one of the first people I met at the Refugee Council. It was she who took me through for my mentoring interview with Simon. I'd thought she was an employee, but it turns out she's a volunteer like me.

'Oh Lord no. I do this just for love, Debs.'

'So are you an asylum seeker too?'

'Tch, no. I'm a nurse.'

Another of my presumptions. While the employees might reflect that necessary diversity, all the volunteers, I assumed, would be white-middle-class and all the clients would be ... not. Take Geordie, for instance (I'm sure that isn't his real name). A slim and neat gentleman who hails from Iraq and is the perpetual bearer of a battered briefcase – even when he goes to the loo. Talks to himself a bit as well. I'd thought he was a harmless waif who'd wandered in and been permitted house room. It transpires Geordie is a celebrated professor and mathematician, who volunteers daily, is particularly good with the spreadsheets and has been in asylum limbo for nearly seven years. He carries his life's work in that briefcase, because the hostel-hovel he lives in has been firebombed twice and his room is ransacked on an almost weekly basis. On his neck and wrists, he bears quiet twisted scars.

So I shouldn't have been surprised at Gamu's revelation.

'I was *invited* here, my darling.'

This was on my first day; we were stuffing down a quick lunchtime sandwich.

'Yeah You Scots were so desperate for my skills you begged me to come live here. Heh–heh–heh!' She'd slapped my back, causing a piece of cheese to go down the wrong way. 'OK, OK. Tiny white

lie. But I did come here to study, you know? Few years ago now
– I'm talking two thousand four, two thousand five? And you had
this wonderful scheme. We were called "Fresh Talent" –'

'No – that's what they called you up the dancing,' said Len, the
most un-PC politics graduate I've ever met.

'Button it, big boy!'

It was fortunate we were in the staffroom.

'I tell you, Debs, it was a marvellous thing. You guys didn't have
enough nurses, so they say we don't need a work permit, we can
stay, you know? We have proved we are smart, we are working hard.
But the best thing is – you *need* us.' She had lowered her voice, even
though it was only us and daft Len in the room. 'That's what's so
bad about those poor babes who bowl in here. Don't nobody need
them, you know?'

At the Helpdesk, helping was your job. By definition, every soul
who entered your portals (or stood at your slightly shabby counter) was seeking assistance. Choosing to volunteer here meant I
wouldn't risk mortifying myself like I did with that poor boy in
the street. With Abdi too, I was finding it awkward to know my
boundaries. Working at the Helpdesk was foolproof. Deborah-
proof. It would provide that warm, fuzzy glow I was so desperate
to ignite, and it would be a preordained exchange, so no one
could get hurt.

I've just finished dealing with a destitute mum of four when
my phone goes again. You're telephone-based as well as front-
facing (I'm learning new jargon by the second), so the whole
place is going like a fair pretty much constantly. There's an

urgency that could frighten you if you let it. Abdi is quiet, reserved, with the occasional glimmer of humour. He's had time and distance to repackage himself. Most folk that trundle in here are on their knees. They are as raw as it is possible to be and still keep walking. But there's a thrill in it too. Each time I pick up the phone I am tested. Faint, dusty lobes of my brain will cough, I can feel them come to life as I field an enquiry, punch in a number or tug a colleague's sleeve for help. Not sure about the fuzzy glow yet, mind.

The phone's still ringing. I give my chair a wee twirl as I reach out.

'Hello? Scottish Refugee Council.'

'Aye, this is Baird Street Police Office here. We've got a young man at the front desk, claiming to be an asylum seeker.'

'OK. Do you have a name for him?' I flick over to my keyboard, fingers poised. Beside the glass door which leads into the foyer, I can see Gamu put her arm round a little girl. The child is Chinese, tiny and round. I doubt she's even in her teens. From here, she looks pregnant but she can't possibly be.

'Naw,' says Mr Charisma at Baird Street. 'No name.'

'Right. Eh ... d'you get the impression he's just arrived here?'

'Looks like it. He's ... well, he's minging, to put it politely. Disny speak a word of English other than "asylum".'

'Well, what we need to do –'

'Look, I'm up to my eyes here, hen. Can you no just send someone up to get him? He keeps greeting.'

'I'm afraid we don't have any vehicles ...'

He sighs. 'You're in Cadogan Street, yes?'

84

'Just off. Cadogan Square.'

'And you *will* deal with him?'

'Well, we'll do our best. Once we've worked out where he's from we'll –'

What? I run through my mental checklist. I need to arrange an interpreter. If he's already claimed asylum, we'll have to think about emergency housing, check if he's on his own. I got my fingers burned the last time – arranging a hostel for one, then finding out it was a family of five. And, if he's not claimed asylum?

Well.

Computer says no. There is no alternative, and no way we can help. He must present at Liverpool; that is the law. All we can do is point him in the direction of the bus station and give him the money for the fare.

'Right, I'll tell him to come down to you lot then,' says Constable Charisma.

'Wait!' I say.

The Chinese girl is shuffling into the waiting room. Gamu seems to be holding her up; she is shivering, soaked. Thin snakes of hair are flattened to her brow.

'Sorry?' The policeman does not sound happy.

'Are you going to make him walk? Baird Street's miles away.'

'You're just after saying you havny got any cars.'

'But you must have. Surely.'

There is a little pause, and in that pause I see that the Chinese child *is* pregnant. Gamu helps her to a chair and the wee soul won't let go her hand. Gamu's telling her she's going to get someone but the girl is weeping and shaking her head.

'Can I just tell you, *madam*, we are extremely busy. We've no got time to run a taxi service –'

'Look!' I yelp.

Isabelle, the caseworker on my other side, raises an eyebrow. She's my de facto supervisor. But as she doesn't bodily seize the phone from me, I carry on. Actually, I don't think I could stop.

'You have a distressed, destitute asylum seeker, who by your own admission doesn't speak a word of English. Despite whatever horrors he's had inflicted on him – quite possibly by people in uniform – he's come to you for help. *You*. Baird Street is away at the back of beyond – I don't think *I* could find my way to Cadogan Square from there. In the time it's taken for us to argue the toss, you could have just stuck him in a passing patrol car and dropped him off here.'

'Listen, hen. We're no a charity.'

'Aye, well we are. I mean, for God's sake, what if it was you? Can I just tell you – I am an unpaid volunteer, as are many of my colleagues, this charity is seriously lacking in funds, but see if you put him in a taxi, I'll pay the bloody fare myself. How's that?'

I hear him clear his throat. 'Eh, there's no need for that.'

Here we go. Time for the complaint. Isabelle's looking at me like I've sprouted horns.

The policeman's voice is flat. 'I'll get one of the boys to bring him down. How's that?'

'Thank you,' I say, still watching the Chinese kid. She's refusing to take her seat. I hang up the phone. Gamu's half-dragging the girl, trying to get her to stand up or sit down, but she's curling up on the dirty floor. One of the other women in the waiting room goes to help. I leave the desk. Now Gamu's crying, and Isabelle's shouting at her, telling her that the way she's holding the kid is 'client assault'. Mrs Winters-call-me-Caro emerges from her eyrie to join in the fray.

'Hey, there.' I kneel down on the lino with the little girl. 'Hey, ssh now. It's OK. Nobody's going to hurt you.'

'Hut you,' whispers the child. Her eyes are sealed, she's in a trance.

'Hey there.'

'Tere.'

'Hey there. Ssh.' I keep repeating nonsense, she echoes it back, no longer moving apart from her blue-tipped lips and small scrabbles of her hands. Caro Winters butts her butt in.

'What on earth is going on?'

'The child is kidnapped.' Gamu shakes Caro's arm. 'I've seen this before at work. She says she been kidnapped. *Men* did this to her. They keep them, use them – I have seen this before at the hospital. I'm telling her we will get the police.'

'NO,' shouts the girl. She starts to stir once more, her feeble body struggling under the heft of her pregnant belly.

'OK. No police. NO POLICE.' Caro holds the girl's face, makes her listen. 'You hear me? No police. Can we move this out of the public area, people? Gamu, Isabelle, you help me get her into my office.'

Just like a leaf, the girl is swept up. Her drama has flurried us all. We, the waiting room, are changed and ruffled. In one corner, a teenage mother dabs her eyes. Two men frown and look away, and a granny scolds a wailing child. It takes a moment or two for us to settle, before the space the girl was in is filled by someone else, and we recalibrate, move on.

I turn my head from Caro's office. Raise my voice. 'Next –' Three phones ring at once. I lower my gaze, pick one.

I'm learning how to be a refugee.

WE ARE LATE, late, late. Blood pounding as I jog, then slow, then jog again. Backpack bouncing, Rebecca's arms are round my windpipe, snake-tight. A black circle bursts inside my eye. She's there, she's still there: Deborah is standing by the car, arms folded, her face drawn. Her ankles are crossed; she is tight and crossed. I should have got her to pick us up outside the flats, save this mad hurrying down streets we barely know, but I'm ashamed. Smashed glass every-where, it would rip the tyres off her car. Litter and dog-waste, rude words on the walls insulting each visitor. Each inmate.

Yes, inmate. That is how I feel and I can tell her none of this. I cannot say why I'm late, or why my daughter is with me. I should have said, texted, phoned. All these various ways in which we can communicate, and I choose none of them. I don't even tell her how hard it is for me to understand her time, that my one o'clock is your seven o'clock. It makes no sense, but it is so. The fact exists and, daily, I negotiate it.

I set Rebecca down on the pavement, feeling the ice-wind on my neck. Her clinging has sheltered me; she has been the substitute for my scarf which is wound tightly round her neck, the edges tucked inside her coat, across her chest. My beautiful baby is my reason and my excuse. I hope Deborah understands. I watch the pavement, watch my daughter's booted feet. My brain feels light and transparent. I am a jellyfish.

'I am sorry we are late, Deborah. This is Rebecca.'

Deborah unfolds herself. Her long coat is open, flapping, and her legs are clad in some tight, green material like the sprites in Rebecca's library book. I pray Deborah sees the tear-stained eyes, that she knows. A good teacher knows. She walks to where we are, sinks down on long, slim haunches.

'Hello, Rebecca. How are you? My name is Debs. D-e-bus. Can you remember that?'

Amazingly, Rebecca nods.

'You all wrapped up cosy then? Because we're going on an adventure. You like adventures?'

Again, Rebecca nods. Deborah stands up. 'Oof. My old bones are stiff.'

Rebecca smiles.

My friend Debs feigns astonishment. 'Wow! What a beautiful smile. You got teeth in there too?'

A giggle, another nod.

'Good, because you'll need to bring your teeth as well, so you can eat all the nice food I've brought. And guess what – we're going to eat it outside! It's called a picnic. Pic-nic. Yes? Does that sound good?'

Rebecca considers. Looks at me. This time I'm the one to nod. 'That sounds very good, I think. Thank you, Debs.'

I call her this to see if she notices – is the contraction too familiar, meant only for children? – but she is busy opening doors. We get Rebecca in the back seat of the car. Debs sits her on a folded blanket, then fusses with the seatbelt, eventually placing part of it under Rebecca's arm. 'We don't want to hurt your neck, eh?' To me, she says: 'I could have hired a car seat too. If you'd said.'

'I'm sorry. We had . . . no time.'

We speak over Rebecca's head, one of us either side. Our faces are too close. Debs suddenly stares at me. 'Abdi! What happened to –'

My jaw hovers, loose. Useless as my fists. I grope to find some words, but she slides over the space I've left, refocuses her attention on the seatbelt.

'There you go, missus. That's you all tucked up safe. Right, come on. Let's go. Abdi, in you get.'

I drop into the front seat, put my bag between my feet. The chair is cushioned to hold my body much more generously than train seats do. Smells better too. A tiny blue tree swings from the mirror. The gentle bounce of it is hypnotic. In here, with the warm air purring and waves of fragrance breaking, I let myself relax. As we drive off, the car begins to ping. A melodious single note that's quite pleasant. Debs, though, taps the dials before her, turns her head, searching for its source. 'What is that? I hate new cars. They're far too fancy for their own good.'

This makes no sense at all. Fancy is special, pretty. How can it be too much?

'Ach — it's you,' she says at last. 'Abdi, you need to put on your seatbelt.'

'I'm sorry,' I say again. 'I did not know.'

Heat rising on my face. My clumsy fingers, pulling on the length of webbing, unsure of where and how to fasten it. Even the simplest things. I cannot do the simplest of things. Driving appears hugely complicated, so I leave Debs to mumble and fuss. We move through the crowded city's streets, passing domes and spires. A mighty religious place. Broad dark rows of apartments, lower and more attractive than mine. Each grey and sand and rosy glitter of stone is substantial. Bright shops and bustling people, who move with purpose and intent. I would like to live in this separate city. We move through greener areas, where the houses stand apart, are bigger. We stop and start, spin circles, scale water, cross other roads. Debs tuts at every junction. The roads are so busy. Frequently, the car makes another strange noise — which I know is not my fault. It's a grinding like bones on rock, or my boat-hull as it finds, and rises on, the shore. *Get into gear, you stupid thing.* She shoves and forces, hisses a word that's painted on our foyer wall, and we jerk into the flow of vehicles beyond. Her knuckles are pressing through her skin as she wields the wheel before her.

Deborah is scared. My heart makes a fist: I'm touched she's made all this effort for me. Embarrassed — again — that I can't repay this, and angry, angry, angry that I am here and she is here, being kind. What will we talk about, on this imbalanced journey? She has forced herself to drive because of me; we are late, because of me; we are silent, because of me. And if I speak, it will distract her. She is a woman fixated on being kind.

I turn to check Rebecca. Lulled by the motion, she's drifted off. Probably exhausted too, after our ... siege this morning. I don't want to think about that, so I keep looking, looking deeply at my girl although my neck is twisted and pain shoots round my skull. Soft in sleep, Rebecca's face is ... her mouth is. Her mouth is her mother's. The fist makes a dagger, and I let it tear me. Just a little or I will bleed to death. The pain makes me quick and alive, it splashes over me, reminds me who I am. Look forward, I must look forward. Glancing across at my driver. The fringe of her hair is damp; she pushes it away. Quick snap, heel of hand, and the image is so familiar as I see her, see Azira standing next to me, the fly on her brow, the cloth of her blanket falling as she flicks it it is my wife alive there is nowhere for me to focus. To run.

She is calling me. *I'm here, Abdi. Can't you see me? I'm here.*

And if I don't answer? She is so clear. Feeding my longing. What if she goes and does not come back? I have never seen her so clear, here in the warmth and safety of this car. My daughter sleeps. My driver drives. I sink into the bitter memory. I close my eyes, and I let myself bleed.

Only Azira was there. Stripped to the waist, sluicing herself from our broken basin. Washing was a luxury; I knew she would have saved the water from cooking or some other chore. Here was not fresh sea with the salty bite of life, nor was it shallow scoops of muddy water discovered after rains. Here in the camp was barren air and plastic jugs and drips from grubby, rationed tanks. All my Azira wanted was to be quiet and clean. Being alone was a luxury also.

The man who ran the schoolhouse had been talking to the children about his God, and about Hell. I helped there some days. We'd no paper, no books, but we could teach the little ones songs. One day, I showed them how to make woven nets from scraps of wire and straw. I had to walk quite far to reach the school; it was near where they kept the Christians – which made some people stay away. Not me. To escape into learning was a pleasure. The schoolhouse was just another concrete frame of open walls, sheltered by a ragged tent, but inside, the man – Paolo – had pinned up a map and some pictures. He was a priest, a *mzungo* imam. He put fresh, leggy straw on the floor most days, and nailed a sheet of silvered glass to one of the dowel posts so it captured the harsh white light from outside, made it bounce around the tent. A soldier had come and made him take it down – in case of fire, was his reason, but I think he wanted it for himself. Anyway, I listened to Paolo talking about his Hell, and it seemed to me that Hell must be a place of mirrors, where all the badness you'd ever done was shone directly back at you. But not just that; the mirrors would reflect every thing and every one you had feared or despised the most, those horrors you would spend your whole life running from. My Hell would be a place so full of people that their limbs slithered over you like fish, a huge shoal of fish that eddied and copulated and ate and bickered and lay flap-flap dying, but never dead in the net that held them all, swinging far above their sea.

I didn't move any further into the shack. Didn't want to disturb Azira, or interrupt the sight of her working herself clean. The spread of her muscles flexing as she dipped and rose, as she brushed off flies and held her blanket. How long, since I had held my wife?

Unless you wished to rut like animals, how did men and women ever love in this teeming sewer? I stood watching as the water pooled in the twin wings of her collarbone, as it beaded her breasts and navel, making webs of spun sunlight across her body.

'Oh!' Azira's breath was sharp. 'You frightened me!'

I came nearer, conscious our baby was sleeping on a mat in the coolest corner. There were no cool corners, really. Tin and plastic bake in the spite of the sun.

'You're frightened of your husband?'

'No, silly boy. Not you.' Her smile I can't I cannot bear her smile I cannot bear the loss of her smile . . . ahh . . . Am, am I'm sorry I'm sorry, so think, think yes.

Yes, I can do that. I can remember the feel of her smile. Slender and curving, like her body.

'It's shadows I'm scared of,' she said. 'Why were you lurking there?'

I was against her. One thumb falling on to her bare nipple.

'Ah. Oh, no, Abdi.' Her eyes darted to the thin and fluttering door-cloth. 'No, don't, Abdi.'

'Where are the Mursais?' My thumb traced widening circles, my other hand taking her by the edge of her blanket-skirt. We shared with the Mursais, a garrulous family of five.

'Oh. She is . . . she is taking the children to the doctor again. They still can't keep anything down. A-a-a.' Like she was sipping boiling water. 'Oh, that's nice. They can't keep anything inside either,' she sniffed. 'The little one never made it to the la –'

'And Dires?' Moving my mouth along her neck. Her head tilted to accommodate me.

'With his miraa-mates, I suppose. Chewing khat like a dumb cow. Adbi, I don't like it when he – Abdi!'

Then my mouth was on her breast, both hands clamped to her blanketed buttocks. A pearl of milk glistened at her nipple, so sweet to taste that it made me crazed. My hands drove up the length of her skirt folds, and she was seizing me. My modest, shy Azira, who loved me so much she couldn't help it, and we were inside one another's minds as well as flesh. Skin and bone and muscle and brain, we were all one creature and our son slept his beautiful sleep and I loved my beautiful wife.

'We can't – have – anotherbaby.' Panting the words into me. Me, licking her nipple and her, clutching my head.

'How can – we –' I couldn't find my breath '– when you're still nurs – oh. Ohzirazira. Oh.'

I know she felt it too. Not the push and the press of us, but the love, how we were perfect. Since our son was born, the few times we'd been private, oh it was wonderful. I wasn't hurting her any more, she was open, we fitted as we should.

I didn't know. Older boys joked about it, of course they did. The joy of a nice tight wife. They talked of opening their gift, but it didn't mean we knew.

What man would want to tear his wife?

I hear my baby stirring.

What man would let her die?

Rebecca snuffles, her anorak rustles. I hear Debs speaking. 'Hiya, sleepy head. We're nearly there, you know.'

What man would let his baby die?

★　★　★

Forcing my eyes awake. Limbs heavy. A rhythmic beating in the space above my aching nose. My dull, conniving brain leaves the mists of one world to creep into another. It is a wounded animal; I should leave it to rest. But I can't. There's too much pressing on it.

My bag crinkles with the sheaf of letters I've brought. I know Debs will ask about the school; she must think I brought Rebecca to distract her. And maybe I did, a little. But we were late. If I'd taken Rebecca all the way to the minister's house before I set out to meet Debs, that would have been another thirty minutes. I think, then, she might have driven away. Complained to Simon that I was 'unreliable' or 'not committed' and that would be a black mark, privileges withdrawn, my name on a list.

I don't know.

So do I tell her? Tell her I was late because I was hiding behind my own front door? That my daughter was hysterical, that the old bastard in the next flat was threatening us again? Actually, he is not that old. Grey, yes, and hunched with the anger of poverty and disappointment. But not particularly old. I think, however, that he is a bastard. Yesterday, he put a leaflet through my letter-box. Of course, I never saw him do it, but I heard him. I know his cough, his shuffle. He shuffles when sober and clatters when drunk. The leaflet was from people called the Scottish Defence League. I guessed what it would contain, but I read a little of it anyway.

Refuges, assylum seekers, migrants.

This country, this city, this scheme is awash with them. They live in houses you could have, they take your benifits but pay nothing themselves. We pay for them to live in lugxury, while we loose out.

Ask yourself how they got here? If things are so bad, how did they get out? Can **you** *afford to fly abroad? Criminals, scroungers, liars and cheats –*

That was as far as I got. I have it here, with all the other letters, but I do not think I will show it to Deborah. It will only make things worse, because she'll want to 'do' something, like with Rebecca. And what is done cannot be undone.

Today, when I was getting Rebecca ready to go out, I heard him again, scrabbling at our door. Rebecca heard him too. We went very, very still. She was holding her breath. Last week he had shouted at us on the stairs, called her a fucking monkey. He was above us, we were walking down the stairs and I told her to keep walking. Making too-bright smiles and talking loudly about the sweeties I would buy her and all the time he's bawling down: *Haw! Err a perra fucking monkeys.* So, when I heard him sniffing at our door and I felt my child solidify in the place we had made safe . . . I could not bear it. I might be a refugee, a humble-grateful shadow, but I am still a man. I marched to the door, flung it wide.

'What is it that you want?' I may have raised my voice, a little. His face is always ugly, but today it gleamed like greasy metal. There was a shine of fury on him and a stink of stale alcohol. Blind hate: this face is universal; I should have said nothing, closed the door. My daughter was watching me.

He swayed on my doorstep, blinking his yellow-rimmed eyes.

'Who-a fuck d'yithink you're talking tae, ya fucking monkey bastirt?'

'I am talking to you.'

'Away tae fuck, yi cheeky cunt. I'd my way, yous'd aw be put doon like fucking dugs. You no take a fucking hint? Stealing our money, our fucking jobs –'

'But you do not have job, I think?'

While he was frightening, he was comic too, in his ill-fitting shoes and his leering gait and I had a cold desire to show him this. My mistake. For all he was drunk and disgusting, I suspect my neighbour had been a fighter in his time. His action was more of a reaction, it was an impulse separate from his brain. Before I finished speaking, his head flew down and forward, crashing into the bridge of my nose. Unprepared, I struggled to keep my balance, was aware of Rebecca screaming as I fought to blink away the starbursts and keep my footing and push him away from me, my child. He dipped back to come at me again, and I slammed my body against the door, using all my dizzy weight to force it shut. Hearing him howl as the wood caught his flesh, his foot? I didn't care, just kept pressing and pressing until the latch clicked and we were safe again.

Safe. There's a fine word. Solid and flat. It opens softly, closes definitively. We make many sentiments out of language, but I find, often, they are lies. They don't mean to be, these supple, helpful, laden words, but what *you* imagine and what I imagine from the weight of a single word – well, it may be very different. I hear an ss in 'safe'; the sibilant hiss of snakes who blend like grass and strike when there's nothing there. I knew the man was lurking outside and I knew, when he finally shuffled off, that he would pounce, spring, bite, be back. Telling Deborah this will only diminish me further. When beggars wait outside our church, Mrs Coutts always says: 'Och, that's a wee shame.' I am nobody's shame.

My daughter is watching. Her brown eyes study me in the little mirror that sits above the windscreen.

'Hello, baby. Did you have good sleep?'

'Huh! Ask your daddy if *he* had a good sleep, Rebecca. I don't know, all this lovely scenery and there's you two, snoring away.' Debs widens her nostrils, snorts like a pig. Is she insulting us? Rebecca has a fit of giggles, Debs joins in. No. I think she's laughing with us.

'Anyway, Hassan family. You'll be glad to know – that's us here. Forty minutes door to door. Not bad, eh? Having this on your doorstep?'

Surprised, I refocus on the world outside. The real one. Grey-pink sky, gentle green fields and hills on my left side, a flash of liquid through dense thickets on the right. Debs slows, turns the wheel so we swing sharply there, to the right. The car crunches over grainy stones. Dark trees curl their bare knuckles at us, part their arms to show us . . .

This.

I'm too inarticulate, but I think Deborah senses that, because all the tension of the journey falls away. The brittle air between us dissipates and we smile. She stops the engine.

'OK, gang. Wee walk first, I think, then lunch, yes?'

We get out. A searing, healthy cold rinses out my lungs, and I tuck my daughter's scarf tighter in her coat. My red bag swings forward as I bend to her; I've hung it loosely from one shoulder. Not secure at all. I am growing casual – and that means careless. I slip my other arm through the flapping strap. Look and look and look again. We are the only car parked here. It is as quiet as desert sands. Rebecca beams at me. Tugs my hand in her urgency to get to the water's edge.

In my life, I do not think I've seen anything so beautiful. Quiet water lapping land, the beach a steady slew of wide flat pebbles. So many rich greys, blues and greens, and sparkling red-brown-pink. They are all the colours of the earth, and the silky water licks them and makes them shine. The sun is low in the sky – I can see it though I cannot feel it. But it is the power of this brown and amber and pale green water that makes this whole place luminous – not the sun. Ha. Today, you know what it means to be weak. You are insipid, you futile mass of dying fire. Today, overpowered by Loch Lomond, the sun is liquid pale. It is curds, the top of a bowl of milk. Strange birds keen above the water. *Skraw, skraw* in lonely, wheeling dips. Beyond the loch, the mountain rises in bands of green and blue. Shadows roll across its face. It smiles. It is a low, comfortable hill, not the fierce dry mountains of my home. I sense the essence of it, humming. It lends all the colours of the earth so that they saturate this beach, that water, this sky.

The mountains in Somalia bleed life from the land, not into it. I know; I have lived by the Karkars as a child. We are, we were, a nomadic people, moving with the rains. Rain means grass, grass means grazing, grazing means food and trade. When the rains begin, for two, maybe three months, the desert becomes a garden. Flowers, tall grass and water are abundant, almost too lush. It hurts your eyes to see it so full and rich and temporary. Our people come to life as well. When we have only drought, we dry up inside. Our lips parch and our blood slows, thin and thirsty as it is. But something happens also to our hearts, I think. When it is *gu* and the rains come, we unfurl our faces and dance in the rain. We meet, make poetry, make friends, make love. Our ages are calculated by how many *gu* we have lived through. By the lour of the Karkars, it is never temperate, always harsh. In December it freezes, in July in bakes. When the rains come, the mountains suck them dry, greedy for moisture. My mother told me and my sister: *Look up. Look up at Mother Rain. She will fill the earth with good things*. But, after the initial deluge, when you think you will drink your fill, you still see bare, steaming earth. It breaks in parched clods as you pick your way over dry beds of streams, while up on the mountain will be a twist of stunted green, or the tantalising drip of faraway rivulets through fissures of stone. Eventually, as Mother Rain keeps battering down her bounties, the mountain is sated and we're allowed our share of rain.

Rebecca hops. Stands on my toes. In the distance, a small craft shrieks like an angry spirit over the smoothness of the water, and Rebecca cuddles into me. The speed of the boat is amazing, but your nets would snarl instantly – I can't see how you would fish from it. So narrow too – room only for one man to perch. Idly, I pat my baby's head. 'Ssh, mucky pup. Is just a boat.'

'Bloody jetskis,' sniffs Debs. 'That's why I brought you in March. Come summer, the place is teeming with them.'

*Jet*ski. I know jet plane, so that makes sense. Ski? It echoes the cries of these drifting birds, and the shape is thin-necked, so maybe ... but there are so many other sights for me to focus on, I let the question whip past quick as the boat. These strange trees, for instance. Some of them have no leaves, while others are full and strident, like spiky bushes grown too high. We have frankincense trees. They are the scent and shade of my childhood. You can eat the roots, inhale the resins, rub bark on sore skin or chew leaves to ease your pain. It is a haunting smell; spicy-rich. This faint sharp tang I'm breathing now, that reminds me of being older. Not the scent of trees at all. I taste in great long pangs. The smell of bright and moving water — whether it's fresh like this loch, or salted sea — fills my mouth. It slides over me, in me, setting tiny sparks alight. The top of my cheeks are tight, my nose aches, tingling with the liquid underneath. When my father died and we moved to the coast to live with my grandfather, it was humid. The rains were milder, the sea was full, and fish lived in the sea for ever. Silently, I thank Debs for bringing us here. When I turn from the water, she's watching. Nervous, I think. Her shoulders are drawn. 'You like it?'

'Oh yes.' I stroke the little hand that rests in mine. Our palms pat thickly; we're both wearing gloves. 'Don't we, Rebecca?'

My daughter nods, first at me, then, more shyly, at our companion. I can feel the press of her little body huddled in my legs. The jetski has frightened her.

'Wait, wait. There's more!'

Debs skips as she says this — I know she's a middle-aged woman, but she does, in fact, skip — over to the back of her car, pulls on the silver handle. The back of the car swings up like a lid, and she leans inside.

'Take that, will you?' Emerging, she hands me an orange plastic box with a thick white lid. Embedded in the lid is a handle, which

I raise so I can hold it with one hand and reclaim Rebecca with the other. The space is so vast out here; I worry it will make her more afraid. Or maybe I'm afraid I'll lose her in it. But the box is heavier than I realise. I almost drop it.

'Whoops! Tell your daddy to be careful, Rebecca. That's our lunch in there.'

Debs wrinkles her nose at me. I think she is a far more expressive woman than she realises. 'I know. A coolbox, in this weather. Daft, isn't it? But we . . . Callum and me, we always used to bring this on picnics.' She leans further inside the car, resumes her task.

'Can I help you, Debs?'

'No, nope. We're fine.' She tugs at something long and thin, pulling and pulling on its whip-length until she sets it free.

'Woo-hoo!' She is a warrior, brandishing her assegai.

I smile, politely. Why is she excited by this? She unfastens the black casing, revealing a wooden stick, which she presents to me. I lay the orange box on the earth, carefully unwrap my other hand from Rebecca's grasp, so I'm free to receive this stick.

'Thank you. What is it?'

'It's a fishing rod!'

I roll the stick in my cupped palm, testing its weight. Light and loose. It trembles. A wisp of transparent twine glimmers and waves, glimmers and waves.

'I thought we could do some fishing,' says Debs. 'If you like.'

'I've never used fishing . . . rod? *A* fishing rod.'

'Oh.' She claps her hands in front of her. 'Oh, of course. Hey, well, neither have I. It was my husband's. Far as I know, you just flick it back and wheech it forwards.'

'Wheech?'

Rebecca has let go of my hand, is fingering the rod.

'Tcha-tcha. *No.* This is not yours.'

'It's fine, there's no hooks on it. I thought you'd know how ... och, look, never mind. I'll stick it back in the boot for now.' Debs holds out her hand to Rebecca. 'Ok, missus. How about that walk?'

As we walk, I tell Debs about the letters. The first was months ago, from the Housing people. Since I had been granted leave to stay in Scotland, I could not stay in my house. Does that make sense? I would have to leave my flat because it was for asylum seekers, not refugees. In my sad hierarchy, I was no longer at the bottom. I did what the letter said: made a homelessness request to the council, and started applying to local housing associations for help with a new home. Or I could also buy my own house, the letter said, if I had the financial resources. Hmm. I wonder how many of my fellow refugees tick that box first?

Another letter came. *Yes, we find that you are homeless.* Why, thank you. I was given temporary permission to remain in my flat, while another home was sought. I met with a nice lady who said, 'What are you looking for?' I said, 'A house with a garden would be lovely,' and she said, 'You won't get one of those.' I said, 'A small flat with a garden'; she said, 'Oh, I doubt you'll get one of those.' I said, 'Anything please, but can it be near my church and my daughter's school?' (At that point, I still thought Rebecca might go to school.) She said, 'We'll see what we can do.'

She told me I did not have to accept the first place that they offered. Added darkly *but always seek advice before you refuse.* I was given extra leaflets and a computer address. More phone numbers, another department of this council or that charity or . . . I'm never clear who all of these people are, but to ask would suggest it matters. All that matters is a nice lady will help us find a house. Except the nice lady is no longer there. She does not answer her phone; when I ask on the other telephone number, they say she is ill. When I ask about my house, they say she is dealing with it. That I must use her telephone number, not theirs.

My sore head mocks me, I hear my voice whiny like a child's. We are sitting on large boulders by the side of the loch. Warm now, with all that walking and a fine tired sense of achievement. A good ache in my legs. The *pic-nic* is still in the orange box inside the car. Rebecca has the fishing pole, which she refused to relinquish, and has been parading like a mighty staff for all of our walk. My love for Loch Lomond has intensified with each new vista. *Here*. If I could, I would live here. Build a shelter from some of the leafless trees, learn to use this pole and fish.

'The new letter,' I bring it out to show Debs. 'It says my application has not been processed and I will need to start again. But I *did* meet with that lady, and she said I would be on a list . . . No! Rebecca, no!' My daughter sulks at me, withdraws her hand. She has been pushing the pole into the water, stirring up silt.

'Well, that's just nonsense.' Debs takes it, reads. 'Sounds as if the right hand doesn't know what the left hand's doing.'

'Pardon?'

'Your woman. She's probably disappeared off on the sick and no one's been picking up her workload. But that's not your fault, Abdi – you shouldn't be penalised.'

'No.'

'It's just not on.' She's scowling at me. 'I mean, I had a lady last week, at the Refugee Council. Exact same thing – everyone dyking it, and she's back to square one.'

A *dyke* is one of those layered walls, built with stones like the ones littering this shore, but they are not square and I don't know what she means is on them. As my mind catches her next words, I let these words slide. Their sense is indignation, and purpose and a plan, so that is all good, I hope. I stretch down, take a handful of the flat stones from the beach. Outside the water, their colours are chalky. *Just push me over this wall, Debs*. Please. I cannot tell the height and breadth of it any more; it seems to move and shift, as though the bricks are made of living, netted fish. I *want* to be independent. To sort these things myself. I want to build my home, not beg for it. A roof and roots and work. I have not been allowed to work for so long.

Deb's speech is becoming compressed. Spiky. 'Honestly, folk have no idea. It's like a bloody labyrinth and you're left to . . . Look. Why don't we ask for a meeting, eh? I'll come with you, kick up a stink. Or I could speak to your councillor. You know about them? They have surgeries, and –' She stops, her frown increases. 'Sorry.'

'Why are you sorry? Rebecca – no!' Rebecca has slipped from the boulder, is inching towards the creeping fingers of the loch with her rod outstretched. It is twice the length that she is. 'You will have no *pic-nic*! Debs, why are you sorry?'

She has gone into herself, face pale like the sun. 'I don't mean to interfere.'

'But I asked you . . .'

'Yeah, I know. But you asked me –' she looks at Rebecca, whose tongue is stuck firmly out as she inspects a cleft in the rock, 'you asked me to help with Rebecca, and then you just went . . . cold. So, you know. Maybe it's me. My fault, I mean, if I come on too strong . . .' Her voice goes very quiet. 'You've got to realise, for years it was just me, my husband and his illness. I had to fight for everything, and then . . . it was just me. You get tired. You close off, you know?'

'Cold? I mean to be respectful. Polite.'

My indignation is ignored. She continues like I am invisible. Perhaps I am. Perhaps I remain in my other world.

'Closed off, self-contained. You get like that, don't you?' With the white rim of her varnished thumb, she picks dirt from another nail. 'My husband died ten months ago. But he was ill for years. A wasting disease. Atrophying his body, bit by painful bit, while his mind remained intact. Years and years of dying from the outside in. There's days still when I just want to punch the world, you know? Just kick the –' She pulls her hands across bent-up knees. 'How long since you lost your wife?'

I have a thickening of saliva; I do not possess all of Deborah's words, but we share language and she must know, she must know that she is smashing me inwards, to the closed-off cold where I will not go.

But I did. I let it visit me today and it was beautiful. Although it rests on me now like these stones. I make a decision. Numbers drop into my sparkling breath-cloud. One year, two months and eleven days. But I cannot say them out loud, they come as a coughing *Longer*. By the loch, my daughter wheels with the shrieking birds. She has her mother's grace. Her face is light, she holds the rod out to the water, laughing. I take another gulp of water-air. It is good. Here is good.

'I *did* want your help with Rebecca. But then I thought I could not lose her too. She will be ready when she is ready. Like we all are.'

It was remembering that young boy from the camp. The way his face rushed away from me, fast and dragging all at once. How lost he looked, and how my daughter's face would look if I deposited her with strangers.

'So what did you tell the Education Department?'

'I say I make a mistake with her birth year. That she is not yet four.' I shrug. 'It is the only time I have found a lack of papers advantageous.'

Debs laughs. I like that she recognises my joke.

'You should laugh more like that. Big laughing.'

'You forget, though, don't you? How to laugh.'

I shake my head. 'You must not. My grandfather told me: Be glad for the life God has given you. If he gives you a different life from that which you already had, be grateful for that also. To carry bitterness will drag you down like stones in your net.'

'I take it he was a fisherman too?'

'He was.'

The very, very best. An elder and a philosopher as well. He always spoke the truth. I cannot carry rocks. I must leave them where they fall or I will not be free to live the life my daughter needs. Rebecca is tottering on the edge of the loch again. She is trying to fish for something on a boulder, a slick strip of green. 'Will you come away from there!' I shout.

'I'll get her.' Debs slides down, hurries over to my daughter. I hear her say, 'What is it you're after? Is it that? The pretty tree?'

Next thing, she is shrugging off her long coat, is scrambling on to the boulders. Sleek heads rising from the lapping water, she steps on one, then the next, until she is close to her prize. The thing bounces up against the rock, is drawn back by the water. It is merely a severed branch; a wand of bushy spikes. 'Is only leaves,' I call. Debs turns her head towards me, but not her body. Caught off balance, she slips. Her mouth a perfect O as she falls, splashing into the shallows of the loch. Rebecca screams. And screams again. I run to her, get there just as Debs's head emerges from the water.

Rebecca is hysterical. I cannot stop the scream.

'It's OK, baby. Look, Debs is fine.'

'Hey, Rebecca! REBECCA!' Debs bawls. 'Hey, look at silly me!'

Deliberately, Debs throws herself backwards into the water, then jumps like a frantic star. 'Wheee! Look at silly Debs in the water. Isn't that funny? Wheee!'

She splashes water at us, tiny droplets striking our skin. 'Oh, oh, oh . . . nooo. Here I go again!'

Once more, she flops backwards into the icy loch. Utterly sodden, pushing through water to grab the stupid green weed that's draped over the rock. Her saturated jumper clings to her breasts. Her whole body shivering. 'Ta dah!' she jumps. 'Look what I got! But you can only get it if you give me a lovely big smile.' Her teeth chatter with the cold, but she doesn't leave the water until Rebecca's laughter replaces her tears.

'Yay! That's better.' Debs waves the branch behind her like a flag, comes out in a flurry of running and spray. I place my jacket round her shoulders.

'There's your lovely ribbon, madam.' With a flourish, she presents the glossy weed to Rebecca. In return, Rebecca hugs her.

'So you want to get all squishy-wishy wet too, do you, missy?'

To me she whispers, 'I can't feel my toes.'

I untangle Rebecca's arms from Debs's waist. 'Why don't we fetch Debs's coat and all get into the car? Then we can have our pic-i-nic!'

'Pic-i-nic!' whoops Debs. Her skin is sheened pale blue. 'Hot coffee! Quick!'

I lift my laughing daughter in my arms. I am buoyant with the swell of water-tipped air and a rising hunger. Today is a good day. One that I will keep.

7. APRIL

THE TENEMENT HOUSE

Adequate housing is at a premium in any city, but a distinctive benefit of the Industrial Revolution sweeping 19th-century Scotland was the growth of the unique tenement apartment block, as city fathers sought to house the rapidly swelling population. Built in red or honey sandstone, tenements – still hugely popular today – are three or four floors high, with two or three flats per 'landing', providing homes for a variety of families while minimising land use.

Run by the National Trust for Scotland, the Tenement House is a wonderful example of city living at the turn of the 20th century. With a bedroom, parlour, kitchen and bathroom all opening off a central hallway, it's the home of an ordinary Glaswegian – and that's what makes it so special. Miss Toward, who moved there in 1911, made few changes to the décor and contents over the years. Lit by gas lamps, furnished with late-Victorian furniture, and decorated with original fabrics and paint, the Tenement House is a treasure trove of social history.

Step inside and enter another world – you may find it's not so different from your own!

Please note, an entry fee applies. Concessions are available.

*

There's a high, black-lead grate with white washing strung across. On the scrubbed-wood table lie baking bowls, worn spoons and a set of creamy scales. For all the high ceilings and long windows, it's very dark. Faint, fuzzy gaslight hisses, wavers nauseous yellow over antimacassars and Abdi's hand touching them and a loudly ticking clock. We glide on brown linoleum, library-quiet, and I recognise the dark-green woodwork from my own grandma's house, the metal doorplates where sticky fingers must be placed, on pain of . . . well, pain. Administered via a reedy switch which Grandma kept on a nail in the hall. I don't think I ever saw her use it; I don't imagine her paper-thin fingers would have had the strength, but it hung there, laden with omniscient potential, and my cousins and sister and I would shuffle by, awestruck. Each secretly hoping that one of the others would incur Grandma's wrath and we could *see* the switch in action. But we never did.

There's the hall press, into which coats and boxes, a carpet beater and – latterly – a lightweight Hoover were crammed. At my grandma's, I mean. The one in the Tenement House has artfully arranged shelves of vintage linen. My cousin Jessie and I would nestle into the press with an old torch and the *Jackie* magazine, hiding from Gill and the boys. Jessie was my best, best friend, and I haven't seen her for . . . I loosen the belt of my coat . . . ten years, it must be. Apart from the funeral, of course. Everyone came to the funeral, but I saw none of them in my faint fuzzy gaslit gaze. You know when you hold in needing the toilet for so long that your kidneys ache? You're jittery-sick and think your eyes are swimming in toxic pee? That's the only way I can describe the product of my deeply compressed rage.

Why come now, when I needed you then?

There was no line-up afterwards, no purvey, because I knew that was precisely what I'd spit at them all. Fine, pay Callum all the 'respects' you like, but don't come anywhere near me with that word, because I'll shove it up your arse. Maybe I did used to swear more than I think. Maybe I *do*. I experience a sudden, horrible thrill of self-realisation. What if I'm one of those women who shouts at bins, waves my fist and screeches profanities at passing dog-walkers and cars – *and I don't even know I'm doing it*? Who would tell me if I did, if I walked around outside without my skirt on, just in my jumper and my slippers and my vast crazy hair?

I remove my coat altogether: it's very warm inside the Tenement House. Abdi appears transfixed by the piano in the parlour. He's reading the sheet-music that he cannot possibly read. Or maybe he can, maybe he was a concert pianist in Somalia as well as a teacher and a fisherman. What would I know? I stop traffic in my pants. Ach no. I consider the reality of where I live. My street has a very (*very*) active Neighbourhood Watch. I'm sure some discreet phone call would have been made to the authorities by now. My secret's safe.

Abdi strokes the rosewood lid, lights up this mustardy room with his smile. 'You can play?'

'No.' I shake my head, not clear on whether he's asking me or asking permission.

No doubt the curtains were twitching this lunchtime, when Naomi from across the road arrived at my door. Since Callum's death, I *never* receive guests.

'Deborah. Hi. Have you got a minute?'

'Em . . .'

I already had my coat on to come here. 'Sure, come in.'

'No. No, I won't stop. Duncan's just away to fetch the car.'

Our street's hopeless for getting parked, as I'm rediscovering for myself. You can trawl for that elusive space for ever, crawling up our road, down the next, until you find yourself several squeezed-in streets away and you abandon both car and hope on the double yellows. Still, I think it's been a good decision. Buying a car, I mean. Just a wee hatchback for getting to the shops. And I thought we . . . well, the Hill House in Helensburgh's lovely. Then there's Edinburgh Castle. Or Stirling. Plus, car hire's extortionate when you add in the insurance, the damage waiver. Absurd excesses. Their gearbox was clearly faulty.

Naomi seemed edgy, her delicate kitten-heels kittenish on my step. 'Look, I really need to talk to you. How about this evening? Could you call in after eight? I'd come over, but I can't leave the kids and Duncan's out . . . We've only the nine-to-five nanny at the moment . . .'

'Yes . . . I guess so.'

Was she going to tell me why? Naomi's not a committee type of woman – or churchy, I don't think. I once accepted Mrs Gilfillan's invite for drinks and found I was spending the evening – along with a squad of Women's Guilders – making wedding fudge for the local minister's daughter. Yes, *fudge*, not favours. All wrapped in greasepaper and coloured tulle. As far as I know, favours represent fertility, so I'm not quite sure what fudge meant. But it was a salutary lesson to always check.

'Is everything OK?'

'Not really.' Naomi was continually surveying the street as she spoke. I imagined she would do that at parties too; scan the room as you tried to engage her attention with witty banter. But I hadn't *asked* her to come and chat.

'Bugger. That's him back already.' We both watched Duncan creeping his Jag through the narrow strait left by the 4×4s and jazzy little sports cars parked either side of our road. 'Don't say anything to him, OK?'

I doubt Duncan and I had exchanged more than *Merry Christmas* or *Nice day, isn't it?* in fifteen years.

'OK, I won't. About what?'

'Rula,' she whispered. 'See you later, yes? Got to go – lunch at Rogano.' And she was gone, in a puff of citrusy perfume and camel coat.

Poor, lost Rula. I don't know how Naomi thinks I can help. Either someone reported her to the authorities – and you'd be surprised how many anonymous do-gooders *do* – or she was already in the system and her claim had been refused. *Your application for asylum has been declined . . .*:

Heads or tails

Stay or go

Life or death

One thing I know since volunteering is, the moment you get that letter, your ship begins to sink, tilting you slowly, inexorably down. And, as the sea waits blankly to receive you, the powers-that-be nudge you further on your way. They withdraw your meagre benefits, take away your accommodation. Only when you've been made destitute and are literally sleeping on the streets will they consider letting you apply for emergency support. And all the time, the threat of detention hangs above your head. Then, subtly cruel to the very end, they posit the tempting notion of your 'voluntary return'. *If you are interested in finding out more about help returning to your home country . . .*

The faux-chatty brightness makes me think of the gleaming posters Callum and I would be faced with at hospital: *How to Manage Your Pain!* set alongside cartoon graphics and amusing speech bubbles; the physio exhorting us to try relaxation tapes and, *if all else fails, Mr and Mrs Maxwell, you know, it really helps the endorphins if you can have a good laugh.*

Laugh? I nearly cried.

Yes, that's the spirit. Dear failed asylum seeker . . . Laugh! Or at least be civilised about all this. You can either be dragged screaming back to the country you fled from, or . . . we can do this the dignified way. *Good God, man – you wanted to be British, didn't you? Well, here's your chance. Let's see that stiff upper lip. March proudly on to that plane of your own volition, and thank Britannia you learned a little of what makes us great.*

That was the thing with Callum, the worst of it wasn't the illness; well, of course it was, Deborah, you stupid heifer. OK, take that as a given, because there are insufficient words in all this universe to describe observing – uselessly observing while you rail and pray and search for uncreated cures – your husband set within the carapace that was his quick, lively body, the body that held you and made love to you and must now be fed and wiped. So. *Deborah* of the slipshod thoughts. Given it's riven through your marrow that the illness was the worst thing, what you're trying to say – as you sweat inside this sombre, ticking room – is the ancillary stuff compounded it utterly. All those changed appointments, the mobility aids that didn't fit, new doctors with old questions, interminable waits in waiting rooms when time is one of the many presumptions you no longer have. Trying to get benefits for his increasing disabilities: we'd to go to a medical for that one. Oh, that was a fun day out. All appointments took place on the second floor, and there was the lift not working and there was a disabled man in a wheelchair. Ah, but was this the first of the tests? How crippled are you, really? How desperate are you to ascend to the place of power and distribution? *Pick up thy bed and walk*. Jesus was a DWP assessor. When we finally got there, we were given a ticket, like the ones for the deli queue at Sainsbury's. Had to wait until our number was called. All us junkies and shamblers, fat women leaking weans, old boys with sticks, young men with limps and a girl who laughed hysterically and swigged from a paper-wrapped bottle. Strange noises distressed my husband, he couldn't turn his neck very far. I knew how vulnerable he felt when we ventured from the house, although Godknows I tried to make him do it. Fresh air, some other faces, a remnant of life still living through our walls. Now I wonder, was I just being cruel? But at that point, he could still walk a wee bit, and where there's life there's hope and every day brings a new dawn and all that shite. His walk was a swaying hobble with the aid of me and sticks. After a few near-tumbles, though, we decided he was safer in the chair. *But I'm choosnit. It'shnot choosin me*. He smiled his lopsided smile and I kissed his lopsided head.

Too long sitting, though, and Callum's shredded nerves begin to scream. He-we needed to move again, raising and shifting buttocks. He hated this; it drew attention to him. Callum, my erudite witty professor, exposed as a sack of limp bones and fluids. One hour late, we were summoned to our medical. The entire interview was conducted by a male nurse who refused to look at the notes I'd brought from Callum's consultant. We all quickly formed a rapport: in answer to the long list of questions, Callum would slur *schomtimes*, I would say *he can at the moment, but in a month or so he won't be able to* and the nurse would say *but he can now*, and tick his little boxes.

When the letter arrived some five weeks later, I was proud to learn that Callum scored consistently highly throughout. Apparently my husband – who, at the moment I was reading this letter, was lying on his side in bed unable to halt the passage of liquid shit that was trickling down his thighs but I was too busy reading this fucking letter to notice – had been *found capable of work*. We could appeal, of course, it said. As long as it was within one month, and, by that time, Callum had been hospitalised with a bout of pneumonia and I no longer had the capacity to care about anything except his lungs not drowning him.

That is how they do it. Pick, pick, picking at your bones. Grinding you down and goading you on until all the fight in you dies. They'll do it with Rula too, wherever she's hiding. I shake out my coat before putting it back on. 'Ready?' I ask Abdi. We've been in all the rooms of the Tenement House – twice – and visited the exhibition space downstairs.

'This is fascinating.'

'I know. How we used to live, eh?'

I'm thinking how spartan it is, how cramped.

'Yes! To have so many possessions, such comfort. Only two women lived in all these rooms?' Abdi smooths his hand one final time along the rosewood piano.

'Yes, but some places could have families of ten or more, no inside toilets. This is more . . . middle class. And I don't think you're meant to touch.'

Mentoring is far closer to teaching than I realised. Mentally exhausting. Depending on the route you take, the words you choose, a random question can lead to a chain of further questions, a lesson, an entire journey into an area for which you haven't prepared. And we haven't even got to where we're meant to be this afternoon.

'Middle class?' he says. 'Like in a school?'

'No. More like a . . . caste? A group with more money, more status?'

'Hmm.' He nods, thoughtful. 'Still, I think your Industrial Revolution must have been a wonderful thing. Did people realise what it brought them? In my country, a home like this would be far beyond most people's reach. Even in the cities.'

'Well . . . there was a lot of upheaval.' I button up my coat, aware of the April wind that blustered us up the hill when we came here, and will still be prowling outside. 'Folk being made to leave their homes in the country, coming to a town they didn't know . . .'

'Yes, but –'

'Speaking of which, we'd better shift our butts. We've to be at Housing by three.'

The Homeless Unit have agreed to a meeting. I decided to go straight to the top – the local office Abdi's been dealing with is where the problem emanated, and I'm too jaded to give anyone the benefit of the doubt. We move outside the tenement, begin the long descent towards the city's centre. The wind is behind us this time, which is cold but helpful, until it catches my hair, blowing it up and out. I must look like I'm being electrocuted. Abdi, ever-sanguine, pulls on a red woolly hat.

'Ooh, very smart. Matches your bag. Knit that yourself, did you?'

'No. My friend Mrs Coutts made it for me. For my birthday.'

'It was your birthday? When?'

'Last week. On Wednesday. I did not know my real birthday, so Mrs Coutts decided that would be the day.'

'You should have said.'

'But why?'

'Well . . .' I make it into a joke. 'I could have knitted you a scarf to go with it.'

'Ha! No, I fear Mrs Coutts may already be doing that. She is a demon with the needles.'

'An old lady, is she?'

'Yes. Very old.'

'So how do you know her?'

We're passing the doorway of BHS. *I could buy him a scarf in here*

I'm thinking as I skirt both the man selling the *Evening Times* and a *Big Issue* guy who jinks with the wind, thrusting his single magazine at customers while offering to open the door for them.

'She is a lady in my church,' Abdi says. 'But I met her before – that is how I know about the church. In fact, I found her in my flat.'

'*Inside* your flat?'

'Last one, hen. Err a last *Big–*'

The *Big Issue* seller waves his magazine at me. 'No thanks,' I say, upping my pace until we're out of his plaintive reach. I always say *no thanks*, I don't ignore them. I'm still trying to process the fact that Abdi's said 'church'. We've never talked about it, but . . . well, his name is Abdi, he's from Somalia. How could he not be Muslim?

'Yes.' Abdi's half-laughing. 'It was very first night we have come to Glasgow. There was . . . we had no food or milk, so I had gone to shop with Rebecca. We were away long time . . . When we are back and I open door of our flat, there she was! Ancient grey lady, sitting on mattress we had been left. *That you back, son?* she is saying. I didn't know what to do; I thought maybe we were to share flat with her? But she stands and is offering us paper bag. *Does the wean want a wee sweetie, son?* Of course, I know *now* what she is saying, but then, I was so confused. I am circling one way, she is coming after! Before I know what goes on, she is shoving red shiny sweet in Rebecca's mouth. I made her spit out – well, I didn't know what it was, it could be poison! Then Rebecca starts to cry, and Mrs Coutts is patting her, trying to quieten her and I am backing away!'

We're both laughing now. I think he's deliberately crafting this into a funny story. His exaggerated movements as he describes the scene, his clever parody of this old Glaswegian granny's accent – it's brilliant. That animation in him again, suffusing his mild smooth face; it's like he's thrown off a hood and I'm seeing him clearly as bundles of shoppers stream by us and the spring wind worries and whoops.

'She keep wagging finger at me, and then I think she is cursing us! But now *I* am facing front door and she is retreating, and all I want is get her outside and away from us, so I follow, make sure she leaves. At door she stops, is pointing always at the handle. Clicking the little . . .' Abdi mimes a tiny pincer movement.

'The snib?'

'She called it "sneck", I think?'

'Yeah, snib, sneck, it's the same thing. The lock, really.'

'Exactly! That is what it was she kept repeating. *It wisny locked, son! I waited here till yous came back. You hear me? Aye mind and lock your door, son!* She was rescuing me, God bless her – not cursing me! So now, we are great friends, her and I –'

A gang of youths are bearing down on us. Boys, really, they skip and jostle like gazelles, but their language has no grace. One screeches *Haw, ya fucking nig-nog!* as another strikes Abdi on the face, an insolent slap with the back of his hand, I'm shoved to the side as they whip the red hat from Abdi's head, run squealing with their trophy and we stand, dazed. Reeling from the assault, the world all slow and distant. Abdi is dusty-grey but his first concern is for me.

'Are you all right? Did they hurt you, Deborah?'

'Oh my God, are you all right?'

We speak in unison, touching each other's arms.

'They hit you – Jesus Christ!' I pull out my mobile. 'Jesus, in broad day – I'm going to phone the police.'

'No!' he shouts, galvanised once more. 'No police, please.'

'But, Abdi! They assaulted you. They stole your hat. Christ! You have to stand up to these people –'

Abdi pulls away from me, starts marching down the street. 'Do not tell me how to fight my battles, Deborah. I am not your child.'

Folk are gawping; I run after him, yanking on his arm. I swear to God, when he bowls round, dips his shoulder, I think he's going to strike me.

'Just leave me. Leave me!'

'Haw! Haw. 'Scuse me there, big man!'

In my panic, I think the gang have returned. My arm lashes backwards, connecting with yielding fabric, then denser flesh.

'Ho! Cool yir jets, doll! I'm no the enemy, by the way.'

A thin man is panting at us. I don't think I hurt him, but he's stooped slightly, catching his breath. In his outstretched hand, he brandishes the red hat.

'Err you go, big man. Err your bunnet back, pal.' It's the *Big Issue* seller.

'My hat? You found –'

'Did they drop it?' I am raw and furious and shaking. The safe air round us; ripped away, my skin with it. I am raw and furious and shaking.

'Naw.' The man stands upright. 'Fucking decked the wee shite, so I did.' He grins like a wizened pixie, presenting stained-brown teeth and a set of grazed knuckles for inspection. 'Just weans, know? But you canny go round daeing that tae folk. So, err you go, big man. One hat and nae harm done, eh?' He pats Abdi on the side of his arm.

'Thank you!' Abdi grabs his hand, shakes it vigorously. 'Thank you.'

I turn my fury on our saviour, because he is part of it; all the shitty city street-crawlers are complicit in the stash of blades and crap and piles of steaming spew that is my home town. 'You can't just go round punching folk! What kind of a message does that give out? Abdi's not from here –'

'Nae shit?'

'Well, he's not. And you can't solve violence with more violence. We need to get the police. What if those boys come back?'

A fluid shift; it's not the wind, not even actual breath or motion, but I feel as if a sliding door has brushed quietly shut, where I am on one side and these two men, who are entirely strangers, cultural, geographical strangers, are on the other. A small nuance passes between them, erasing me.

'There is no need for police.' Abdi folds his arms. Regenerates. I could argue with him, I know I'm right. But I don't.

'Here, I'm no getting caught in some domestic.' The *Big Issue* seller slaps Abdi's back. 'Stay well, big man – even though yir stuck wi Greetin Teeny here.' And he ambles off, his satchel bumping from his hip.

Abdi turns to me. 'Who was that man? Do you know him? Why did he call you Teeny?'

'No, I don't bloody know him. He's just some *Big Issue* seller –' My breath is catching in my craw, too-fast bubbles caused by my too-fast heart. *Broad bloody daylight* and they just –

Abdi's frowning.

'He's homeless,' I say. 'The man's a beggar. Sells these magazines as a kind of a job —'

'Wait!' shouts Abdi, running after the man. I follow, at a more sedate pace. Puffing out until I find my rhythm.

When I reach them, Abdi has his rucksack off, is unzipping the top pocket.

'May I buy your magazine, please?'

'Naw. Yous had your chance — but your burd there gied me a dingy.'

More puzzlement from Abdi. I'm going to buy him one of those *Glesga* dictionaries.

'He means I turned him down.'

'Aye, in your dreams, doll.' The man indicates his empty satchel to Abdi. 'Only joking, big man. I wisny lying. That really wis ma last one. They're all done.'

Abdi is crestfallen. 'Oh.'

'You can gie me ten pee for a cup of tea if you want, but.'

'OK.'

'Here.' I get in first, thrust a pound coin at the man. He considers it, shakes his head. 'Naw, you're all right, doll. I havny got change.'

'I don't need change. Just take it.'

'I'm no wanting it, fuck. I didny jump in for a reward.'

'Indeed. Thank you again. Anyway. I am . . . My name is Abdi.'

The man nods. 'Dexy, pal. Pleased tae meet you.'

'Decksy?' I say.

'As in "sexy", but wi a D. D for *dong*.' He gives a leery wink and taps his forehead. 'Be seein ya, folks. That's me away tae get pished now.' Nudging my elbow as he goes.

Abdi and I walk the length of Sauchiehall Street, down towards George Square. Neither of us speaking. If we were a machine we could reset, but we are just two bruised, surly people. Why? Why them, passing us, right then? If he hadn't worn that hat . . . Abdi has his God. Perhaps he's thinking how lucky he is, that God sent those boys to him. In absorbing their blows, Abdi has saved some other, weaker soul, while all I am thinking is I hate this bloody city. I hate it and I love it. When its vital, raging energy is channelled well, it's a wonderful place. Maybe Abdi's thinking how he met the nice *Big Issue* man, how God made it so that they met and maybe I should be thinking not to judge a book by its cover because I am a teacher and LESSONS MUST BE LEARNED! I flex my fingertips. A flurry of wind sends a newspaper scudding by my feet. The updrift scatters the pages, each leaf rising in various directions. Tattery birds in flight. I think there's no sense to be made of it at all. But we insist on weaving a narrative.

Beside me, Abdi clears his throat. Gruffly, he says he's sorry, and he doesn't think I treat him like a child. I say I'm sorry too, that we got a fright. He agrees. Makes a joke about his hat being so desirable, and we're fine, fine, fine again. I need to be fine, because I'm dreading this. Another bout with officialdom. The Homeless office is quite close to Marks and Spencer's. I've told Abdi I'm going to buy Rebecca a pair of wellies after. Apparently they're going fishing this weekend, although he's a bit vague on the 'where'. I gave them the rod to take home when we were at Loch Lomond, gave Abdi all the hooks and flies and stuff – he said he'd work out what to do. I'm glad it's going to be used again. I think it was Callum's dad's.

When our son was born, and the nurse went: 'It's a boy!', Callum leaned his face into mine. I can remember the rasp of his cheek on me, the two-day stubble of our two-day labour, his coffee-breath, eyes glazed with tears and delight. 'It's a *boy*, Debs. A boy! I'll be able to take him fishing! God, I love you.'

'I love you too.'

Him passing our son into my unreal arms, the three of us, holding each other in a heart-shape. My husband was bright with joy and I was blessed. When it becomes too much, when the loss runs through me like a burning wire, I remember I *was* blessed.

'Debs? Are you all right?'

'Yes! Yes, I'm fine.'

Abdi takes my arm. His face is grave. 'Are you sure? You look like you might cry. I am sorry, very, very sorry. I should not have shouted at you.'

'It's not –'

'Is it those boys are still scaring you? Do you want me to go to the police? I will if you think I should.'

'No, don't be daft. I was just in a wee dwam.'

'*Dwam?*'

'Daydream. It's Scots for daydream. Reverie?'

'Ah. *Di-wam.*'

Mouthing it, considering it like flavour. I like when he does this. Weighing the word, or computing it. I picture a flashing wheel of words inside his head, where he stores new treasures, cataloguing them alongside his existing selection.

'Your Scottish words are much more descriptive than the ones in books. That word sounds swoony and sleepy –'

'Swoony!'

'Sorry. Is that wrong? To feel faint?'

'No. It's perfect.' Without realising what I'm doing, I reach up and pat his cheek. My skin on his, another boundary blurred.

'Oh look,' I burble gladly. 'That's us at the Housing.'

'Good.'

We stand outside the pale stone building, united in our cause. Abdi unzips his rucksack. Removes a notepad and pen.

'You don't have to write anything for them, Abdi. Don't worry – I can do all the talking.'

'No.' He hoists his rucksack into place. 'It is for to take notes of what they say.'

Good on you, pal, I think.

AN APOLOGY! I have never had one of these before, I don't quite know what to do with it. Do I hold it like a baby, or slam it down and demand another, better resolution? 'Sorry' they have said – I counted three times. 'Unacceptable' was another word she used, the homelessness lady, as she was scrabbling in my file and tap-tapping her computer keyboard. It seems that I had fallen through the mesh, slipped like a silver fish to be lost again in the waves.

'This should never have happened; we have systems.'

Debs glances at me, eyebrows raised. What a terrible word is 'system'. It is all rigid, inhumane structures, much like the building in which we live. But all is well, I am back on the housing list. At the top, where I should have been, she says, before *Belinda* went off sick. Belinda's name is mentioned in the hushed regretful tone of a woman already dead. The lady started doing this when Debs first raised her voice. They spoke very rapidly, many jagged splinters I couldn't follow, and I wondered if Belinda really was so ill, or if the lady was using her sickness as a cudgel to silence Debs. It didn't work, though, Debs insisting: 'That's all very well. However, your job is to manage your staff and maintain a proper service. Irrespective of how under the weather they – or you – might feel.'

My head down low; I wish I had not come. These people have power – you cannot speak to them with so little respect. Soon, the order will come to throw us from the building, and maybe Debs will offer cash and the guards will go and we will start again. Or maybe we will be beaten.

Both women are speaking in a curiously polite and brittle way. I keep my focus on my shoes. My one foot is dancing all by itself, small insistent jerks which makes the toecap flap. I need new shoes. Rebecca needs new shoes. I am on the list; can we not just *go*? They might have rooms in here, places where they put you, to wait. And it is in the waiting that the torture begins. They make you wait so long, you are begging for it to begin, for a clean slice of pain to cut through cloudy terror. But they will not beat us here. The lady has said 'sorry'. Sometimes, though, people say 'sorry' crisply, as an interrogative, or it can be the 'sorry' which is not all at, but which arrives to preface 'I absolutely disagree', or to suggest the finality of discussion over and the guards being called. The old man at reception, in his braided suit and white peaked cap, is not a threat. There was a sign there, I noticed, and it is replicated in this interview room:

Our staff aim to provide a courteous and helpful service at all times. However, we deserve the right not to be intimidated, abused or threatened. Such behaviour may result in clients being asked to leave the premises. Failure to do so may result in police being called.

To call the police, however, would be a great threat. And maybe they *will* beat us.

Maybe it will be like when I tried to strike that policeman in Dadaab, and they took me and stood me in the sun. My arms tied with wire above my head, then they swung me round so I was upside down. Laughing, laughing as they beat me with wooden poles and cut my feet, scraping red earth from the ground and rubbing the grit of it into my wounds. Leaving me strung in their station yard.

'Mrs Maxwell, I appreciate what you're saying, but you have to understand –'

'No. What *you* have to understand is –'

I watch my shoe flap as if it too wants to add to the conversation. They were Kenyan police; the UN soldiers rarely ventured inside. I think it was three days I hung there. Each time I drifted, they would burn me with cigarettes. Tell me that they were fucking my wife; I would writhe and scream and they would burn me some more. *Enough*, I screamed. *Enough*. If I had known Azira was hiding, I could have borne it all. Mrs Mursai had helped her and the baby to get away, passing them to her sister, and from her sister to her uncle and his wife, who were in another part of the camp. Suspended in the bastard sun, I did not know. All I knew was what had happened, what they were *telling* me was happening.

'Look, Mrs Maxwell. Are we broadly in agreement?'

'Apparently.' A note of lightness enters Deborah's voice. One could almost call it smug. (This is a recent word to me, but a very fine one, combining as it does the ugliness of the 'uh' with a thuggish 'g' and the slyest of cat smiles.) I relax a little in my chair, but this is a mistake.

Compressed, it rushes at me; a long fine filament of light. I shut it out, the fierce brilliance of her eyes, blinking a thousand crystals, cut, cut, cutting through.

She had been crying. She tried to hide it, but I could see. Azira had been gathering firewood. Usually I went with her, subjecting myself to catcalls and comments.

You lost your dick, Abdi?

Come kiss my balls while you're at it, pretty chick.

But it wasn't safe for her to go alone. Being in the midst of Dadaab was frightening enough, being at its lawless borders was horrific. Men gathered women as women gathered wood and water. Stealing from them, raping them. And it wasn't just local Kenyans who came to harvest the dispossessed. Some of these men were my people, gone crazy, I suppose, with the waiting and the lack. If you have no form to your life, what are you? An animal, it would seem. That day, though, I had to stay behind. Our baby girl was very ill, sick with the fever the Mursai children had had the year before. The fever that had killed our son. His little body would hold nothing inside it, not food, nor milk, nor faeces. Every half hour, we would feed him water on a spoon, but it was in vain. I had held Azira, and she held our boy, and we watched him pass from this life. Our firstborn. For some minutes, I had shielded them both, hushing Azira's sobs, but then Mrs Mursai heard and began to wail, then it was the other women gathering, and the separations of women and men, the ritual washing. Of all our friends and neighbours, it was Paolo, the man from the school, whose kindness struck me the most. He brought us meat and a stolid cake. He understood our need to celebrate death the same way we celebrate birth, even though it was not his way. It was a hollow festivity. Neither Azira nor I could thank Allah for very much.

'How will he be judged, Abdi? When he is so little? Such a tiny, tiny leaf.'

As Muslims, we believed each person would be judged in the afterlife. We believed, then, that a tree representing all Muslims grows at the boundary of Heaven and Earth. Each of us is a single leaf on that tree. At Muharram, when the angel shakes the tree, those whose leaves fall will die within the coming year. My boy must have been very special to live less than two years.

This little one before me was even younger. How could she fight the same fever? I watched her tiny mouth pout and struggle for its air, the fist that clawed to dissipate pain. But this time, I was wiser. I knew a man who knew a man who said he could get us medicine. Crystals that would firm up my baby's stools and replenish the vitamins she was losing. The medicine would cost us money, of course, money we didn't have. Tucked under the straw on which we slept was a woven reed box. Inside was hidden my mother's two remaining bracelets; intricate carved work, fit for the elder's daughter she had been. For these, you could get money. I was hoping we could negotiate, man to man. Khadra would never deal with a woman, Dires said. I had only spoken to Khadra once before, years ago when we had just arrived. Striding imperiously through the main square, followed by his several wives. 'You!' he called to me. 'You are new here, yes?'

'I am.'

'Good, good. I am Khadra. Whatever you need, I have. You understand?'

Khadra means lucky or fortunate. Seeing him in his clean white robe with his wives and his comfortable belly, I thought, yes, you are well-named, sir. But I didn't understand *then*, not really. When my son took ill, Azira queued for hours, waiting to see a doctor. If only I had known about bribes and favours and how you circumnavigate the tides.

Anyway, Khadra was late, Mrs Mursai was out, and we needed wood to boil the baby's water. Azira said there was a group of women going, and one of them kept a fruit knife inside her wrap. *For the firewood,* Azira smiled. So I let her go. When she returned, Khadra still hadn't come and our daughter was barely moving. Her whimpers had ceased, her eyes were glazed in a netherworld of neither shut nor open. I thought at first Azira was crying only for the baby, and then I saw grazes on her cheek. The collar of her dress torn.

When you are unprepared for the arrival of your most buried fears, the full violence of them is terrifying. I think I seized her, was shouting over and over *What happened?* And her, sobbing at me and reaching for our baby: *Has the man not come? Has the man not come?*

The man never came. Perhaps he would have if I hadn't done what I did next. It was police, Azira told me. Police who demanded a fee for the wood.

That is Kenyan wood, bitches. We can charge you with theft, you know. We were lucky up until then, we had avoided their attention. The Mursais had been waylaid before they even got to the camp, made to hand over all their money and every possession they owned before police would allow them passage. They told Dires Mursai they would imprison him for 'unlawful presence' if he didn't pay. Then they whipped him and said he was an Al-Shabaab terrorist, that he would be executed. Until then, Dires had been a doctor who thought he was rescuing his family. Now he smoked khat all day and beat his wife.

When the border at Liboi was open, us refugees were safer. That was how Mrs Mursai's uncle arrived here. The Liboi transit centre was where most Somalis first sought refuge in Kenya. From there, the UN would transport us to camps. But when Kenya closed the border, the transit centre closed too. Without it, the only way across was by smugglers. That is how we arrived, that is how I had only two carved bracelets remaining. Thousands of us, creeping and crawling and seeping into Kenya, and the police take advantage of this. If we are clandestine, we have no rights, and we are rich-pickings for extortion and demands.

Until then, we had been lucky.

'Have they . . . did they hurt you?' I could not say it, the thought of another man. Hurting her flesh. She was shaking me, sobbing into my face.

'We need to go, we need to go. I got away – he only hit me. Oh, Abdi, when is the man coming with the medicine? If we hide, we won't get the medicine.'

Mrs Mursai came dashing in then, shooing her brood like chickens. 'Aie! What did you do? I hear the police are after you, girl.'

'Did they chase you here?' I shouted.

'I think so. I ran and I ran but I could hear their boots behind me. Abdi, look at my girl! Did she take her water?'

'Hey, Abdi, man. Don't be stupid!' yelled Mrs Mursai. 'You'll get killed and your wife will end up a *dhilo*!'

But I couldn't hear them. I was pushing past, driving myself and my fury out. On and on I ran, searching for policemen in the filthy ribbons of streets. Any policeman would do. At last, I found one. A smug leather-skinned beast who walked with a swagger. He was in front of me, lagging behind his two colleagues. I fancied he was out of breath with the thrill of chasing my wife, and I launched myself at his back, dragging him to the ground. Wild bug-eyes and his forehead laced with ritual scars. They heal them open with ash. Twice I managed to hit him before the others descended. And then ...

I will not revisit this. I am alive.

I am not in Kenya.

I am in the office of the homelessness lady, and, as I wait to be evicted, I repeat this incantation. *I am not in Kenya. I am not in Kenya*. Part of me is. Kenya is very far way, but it inhabits me, always. My blood is in its soil and its soil is in my blood. Buried in the soles of my feet.

'I'm sorry,' says the lady for a fourth time. 'Rest assured Mr Hassan's case will be monitored very carefully from now on.' And then she addresses me directly. 'You can expect to hear from us within the next three weeks, sir.'

'She called me sir!' I say to Debs, when we get outside.

'I know she did.' Debs knocks her elbow into mine. 'Dream Team, eh?'

'I'm sorry?'

A lurch of discomfort over me, like when the sea swells inside your belly. Is she telling me this is not real? I thought I had understood enough; that I was to be given priority consideration. I check my notepad again before putting it away. Yes. That is what the lady had said.

'You'n'me,' says Debs. 'I do the talking, you take the notes –'

My notepad is nearly empty. 'Oh, not so many, I'm afraid. I couldn't follow all that you were saying.'

'Was that me screeching again?'

'A little bit.'

'Still, you managed to get your oar in a few times. You must have got the gist of it, eh?'

'Gist' and 'oar'. Neither of these words make sense, but her intonation is approving, she nods to include me in the sweep of her words, then says *well done*. My contribution has been approved. Yes, it is true, I could speak more freely with Debs at my side. Without her, I doubt I would have requested a letter of confirmation, or ask that they tell me an actual date when I will next hear from them. There was a confidence in having Debs there. When you are hunting and there are two of you, or fishing with your friend, and the weight of the planning and the circling, the hauling and the trapping is shared, you become bolder in your attack. You can measure your performance by your companion's actions. Judging, observing. Sharing the lead. The thing I like most is that you do not feel alone. When we are alone, we lie small and quiet to hide our weaknesses. I don't like who I am then.

'Would you like a lift, Abdi?'

We are walking on the ground, on the street. Ah, I see – she means to be a passenger in her car. Debs has bought herself a vehicle, bright blue and squat. The woman who is scared of driving has decided she will drive again. I am very pleased for her.

'Yes thank you, I would.'

We go first to buy the wellington boots for Rebecca. Debs insists on paying. And so, when we arrive at the apartment block, I feel I should ask her in. To see Rebecca, of course, who waits for me in Mrs Coutts's flat, but also to repay Debs's kindness. I have cost her a bus fare and a pair of shiny pink boots. At least I can make her coffee.

'Would you like to come inside?'

Debs shuffles in her seat, the moment's hesitation before she speaks is damning and I retreat and bluster to make the awkwardness not there.

'You do not need to –' My hands lie upturned on my lap. The gleam of our joint victory goes dull. *Stupid refugee.* Who would step inside here unless they had to? The building next to ours is fenced round with wire, and bears a sign saying: *Condemned.* Under this, someone has scribbled *Fucking right.*

'I'd love to. But . . .' Debs's nose wrinkles, her mouth goes square like the hole in a pillar box. 'I'm not being funny, Abdi, but would the car be all right here?'

We are parked beside a grubby van and a car which has no wheels. Broken glass abounds, but it is from bottles, not cars. The lightness in me returns. I too would protect such a bright blue, happy car. In the window Debs has hung a sunflower, which emits the same astringent smell the little tree did in our hire car. Her hire car.

'Here is fine. For now. Later, children drink here and they smash and spit, but now is fine. I think.'

'Great. I mean, I would like to see your house.'

'Is not my house, Debs. Is where they put me.'

'No, of course. But I'd love to see Rebecca again. Is she–?'

'Yes. She is here. With Mrs Coutts.'

'Ah-ha. The hat lady.' As she speaks, she blushes and we both remember the feral children from before. I *could* have stopped them, I could have done what Dexy did for me. *Easily*. They were pallid youths who have no conception of what a human will do to survive. I hope Debs knows it was strength that held me in. Not fear.

She is still a little dubious as we lock the car. When she thinks I'm not looking, she pats its roof.

'From my window, you will see your car. We can watch it, just in case.'

'How far up are you?'

'Eight floors.'

'Oh. Right.'

We step over a discarded nappy and four squashed beer cans on the step. Inside the foyer, more words have been painted over the words that were painted out yesterday. 'I'm sorry. Is not very clean.' Pressing the button, expecting the interminable wait, and instead – magic happens! The lift doors open. This is a rare good omen. Two good things in one day. I have been heard, and my elevator is waiting . . . three, if you count Debs coming in. Four if you count her driving me to my door. My cup is overflowing.

'At least the lift is working.'

Neither of us mention the smell. Cramping in, trying not to touch the wall or the foetid air. We each pick a spot to stare at as we bump and drone our way up. I don't think I would have asked Debs here before today. This tower is nothing to me: I can invite her because I know I'm leaving. It's official. To be here was never my choice; it is a receiving centre, like the camp, and I have intimated my desire to leave and the lady has said it will happen. I am choosing, it is not being done to me (although it is, of course). And when I have a house I can get a job in a school that is closest and Rebecca will come with me. She will be fine if I'm there. Somewhere, a new home waits for me and my little girl.

If we do move far away, I will be sorry to leave Mrs Coutts, but I'll see her still at my church. We can travel. The city is not so wide – even after my Loch Lomond journey with Debs, when we travelled through its varied vastness, even then, I could see its limits too. Glasgow is a finite place, unlike Dadaab. And the homelessness lady said they would aim to keep us on the same side of the Clyde at least. We will walk or find a train. My church is a root I don't wish to sever. I sense Debs does not like to talk about religion. I'm being very unChristian, I think, because I should ask her. I should be sharing God with everyone. It's one thing to profess your faith with friends, another to justify it to a brittle woman who has already drunk from the well of the spirit, swilled it fully in her mouth – and spat it out. At least, that's what she makes me think she's done, with the little bitter comments and tosses of her head. She did that postbox face at the Dali when I talked of prayer. A true Christian would not care, they would testify and spread the good news, swirling all the doubters high with exultation. My faith is a new one, and should be all the more exuberant for it, but we are shy with one another still. It is quiet, it calls up my mother's arms and my wife's breast and my baby's scented head. It is my refuge and I its refugee.

I confuse Debs by stopping at the seventh floor.

'Is it stuck?'

'Mrs Coutts lives here.'

'Ah. Will I wait outside?'

'Why?'

'No reason.'

I chap the door. I don't think Mrs Coutts was ever a teacher, but she sees my education as a priority. *We don't knock on doors, son, we* chap *them.* God bless Mrs Coutts. I will never fit snugly here, but she insists on trying. Just as she insisted that the knitted sweater which goes with my hat will 'loosen up' with wear. The sleeves reach my elbows.

'Mrs Coutts, how are you?'

I give her my finest smile, but I know it won't come close to dazzling her. What she is instantly interested in is Debs. Although the chain remains on her door, restricting her vision to a two-inch slash, she homes in on this stranger.

'Who's this then, Abdi?'

Debs steps forwards. She is very smart today, with her hair pulled back and a swinging, sea-coloured coat. 'Hello, Mrs Coutts. I'm Deborah.'

'Hmm.' The door closes, then opens fully. 'Sarah, did you say?'

'Deborah.'

'Aye, just as well. Never liked that name. Ma mother-in-law was a Sarah, and she was a right old besom.'

I see my daughter running into the hall. Imagine her shouting *Daddy!* But I content myself with her joyful skip. 'Hello, mucky pup! Have you been a good girl?'

'Och aye. She's been nae bother at all, have you, Rebecca?'

Rebecca shakes her head, then hugs Mrs Coutts's knees.

'Oh here, you'll have me over on ma bahookie, lass!' But you can tell she's delighted.

'Mind and take that cake for your daddy, hen.'

'A cake?'

'Aye. We made you a cake, didn't we?' She shuffles into her kitchen, returns with a lopsided loaf. It is greyish-pale, and sagging on to the plate. 'There you are, son. You and your lady friend can have that wi a nice cup of tea. Just mind and gie the plate back once you're done.'

We walk up the single flight of stairs to my flat. I notice Deborah reaches for Rebecca's hand. It's an unconscious touch, she doesn't look as she does it. Neither does Rebecca, whose own small fist slips happily into place. The germ of a wonderful idea grows in me. I unlock the four separate bolts on my front door and we step inside. Debs stands in my hallway and takes off her coat. She hesitates before removing it fully. What does she see, that we are inured to? Dull yellow walls I presume were once white, the paper curling top and bottom. The fact we have no carpet in the hallway – but there are mats I made from offcuts the Somali Centre was throwing out. The cold, unloving air which meets us? This is not a home.

'Would you like some tea? Or coffee? I have African coffee, if you like.'

'Tea would be great, thanks. Milk, no sugar.'

Debs sits on my couch, pulls the carrier bag on to her knee. 'Now, Miss Rebecca. Your daddy tells me you're going fishing. So I've got a wee present for you. Have you ever heard of welly boots . . . ?'

I leave them to make the tea. On the stained fawn worktop, Mrs Coutts's cake glares reproachfully. This worktop is a healthier colour than the cake. I give it a little poke. Very eggy in the centre. I'm no baker, but even I can see it's not been cooked for very long. I decide to ignore it and hope it goes away. Get out mugs, check we have some milk left. Kettle on, teabags in the pot. *In a pot, son, a pot. Dinny just dunk the bag in the cup.*

Schlump. Schlump. The noise of a hog slurping mud heralds the arrival of my daughter and her wellies. In the centre of our tiny kitchen, she twirls then stomps.

'Wow! Those are lovely. Did you thank Debs for your present?'

Rebecca nods. Points at the cake.

'Oh no, baby. I don't think the cake is ready.'

Nods more vigorously, then grabs the plate from the counter.

'Rebecca. I really don't think you will like it.'

Giggling, she runs off.

'Don't you run when you're carrying a plate!'

As I finish stirring the tea, I hear first one 'Yeugh!' then another, coming from the living room. The second 'yeugh' is an exact replica of the first sound, but faint as it flows in fluid light from unused lips, and the blood in my fingertips goes soft and hard.

Spoon slipping from me. Clinking silver on the floor.

I cannot move, am holding in wisps of a delicate fear. Debs arrives into the kitchen.

'Well, I don't think we'll be eating that.' She slides the cake directly in the bin. Now *I* have no words. I clear my throat.

'Did Rebecca just say "yeugh"?' It comes in the faintest whisper.

'She did.'

'Is that a word?'

'I guess so. Oh! Abdi!' Debs grips me by the shoulders. 'You mean that's her *speaking*?'

I feel sick. 'I don't know. But she has never said . . . I don't know, Debs. What should I do?'

'Do nothing,' she says. Decisive.

'But I need to –'

'No.' We are both whispering. 'Don't make a fuss in case you scare her. Just be very normal, and if she says anything else – you respond, OK? Calmly and casually as if it was no big deal.'

'Are you sure?'

Hope like dripping water; I want to dig it all out, make it pour and pour so that it never stops. I want my daughter's chatter to fill this house and fill my head, my thirsty, thirsty heart.

'I think so,' she says slowly. 'Look, let's just play it by ear for now, OK? Take our time and see if she comes out with anything else. If needs be, we can still take her to that child psychologist –'

'I want you to teach her!' It is out, blurted and crass, with none of the careful arguments I was planning. 'Please. You made this happen, she trusts you. And you are a teacher and she should be at school, you are right, I know that, but I cannot pay you . . .'

I lose momentum; in any case, it is all said. Debs keeps her face sincere; it is calm, but slightly pained as if I have asked for some of her spare blood when all I asked for are the wasted skills she chooses not to use.

'I want to be her friend, Abdi, not her teacher. School will give her so much more than I can offer.'

'But she can't go to school like this. Who would play with her or try to speak to her, a child who does not speak? Debs – our skin is black, our hair is like Brillo pads –'

'Who said that?'

'It doesn't matter. We smell of goat, apparently, and young boys strike me randomly for sport. I need to make this life better for Rebecca.' A glaze of tears obscures my vision and I blink and I blink and I blink.

'What age is Rebecca really?' she asks.

I shrug. 'I think five years. Four and then a half? She was born in Dadaab, in the camp. But we do not mark our birthdates like you do – or the years. This hat I get from Mrs Coutts is the first birthday present I have ever.'

Debs presses my hand and then releases me. 'Let's just take this one day at a time, Abdi. Have you got some eggs?'

'What?'

'I said to Rebecca I'm going to make her pancakes. But I need eggs and flour and milk.'

'Maybe,' I say. 'Try that cupboard for the flour.'

There is some, from the time we made dumplings. I watch Debs move around my kitchen, finding bowls and spoons. My worktop becomes busy and the sickness in me grows.

'Go, sit with her,' Debs says. 'Talk about the wellies, talk about fishing.' She shoos me out like a chicken. 'On you go.'

Rebecca is sitting in front of the television, pink wellies drumming on the sofa-edge. Around her, the air is crystal. I'm afraid of my own daughter. I sit beside her.

'What are you watching, mucky pup?'

She doesn't answer, but blends into the side of me. Cheekbone to rib. We watch the coloured animations leap and flicker on the screen. *Do* you think, if you don't speak? One of Rebecca's arms creeps slowly round my middle. Of course you do, we live always in our own head, it is the one sphere where we present ourselves fully and entirely: no false fronts, no delineated areas. And we can make it into a comfortable, drifting mush. Rebecca is wrapped inside soft silence. Who am I to rip this away? Do I know those actual things I think before I have to say them? Can I define my experiences beyond a fleeting sensation? As soon as I use words, I give my fears substance and diminish my joy. And the vast scope of my imagination can no longer conceal my revulsions.

This is what my daughter will not do.

Rebecca sighs and snuggles deeper. I smell the coconut shampoo in her hair. I hear Debs singing, smell the pancakes as they cook. It is a sweet warmth of eggs baked with flour, of milk lapping in a bowl and the steady pound of women grinding flour.

It smells of my mum.

PART TWO

LOST

9. MAY

SCOTLAND STREET SCHOOL MUSEUM

A Scottish education is renowned for its vigour, breadth and integrity. As early as the 15th century, Scotland had schools for girls as well as boys, and, by the 17th century, there was a school in nearly every parish, with the population largely literate – putting the Scots education system well ahead of any in Europe.

By the early 20th century, schools were, and continue to be, run by local councils. Scotland Street School was built in 1903 for the children of Tradeston shipbuilders, and is the only school ever to be realised by the famed Glaswegian architect and designer Charles Rennie Mackintosh. Particular highlights include exquisite glazed tiling and a pair of windowed Scottish baronial-style tower staircases which let light flood the inner hall.

Functioning as a school until 1979, Scotland Street is now preserved as a museum of education. Play peevers in the old Drill Hall, see what school days were like during World War II and climb

to the top-floor cookery room for a panoramic view of Glasgow, before
you sit up straight for a lesson in Miss McGregor's Victorian class-
room. And don't worry – we no longer use the belt!
  Entry to Scotland Street School Museum is free.

★

'I MET HIM in the library,' I say, in response to Debs's surprised
Where from? As in 'where-do-you-know-Geordie-the-Iraqi-from?'
We're sitting on the low wall in the museum that acts as a form
of gallery, separating the open corridor from the large main hall,
which is also the foyer of the school. Rebecca is skipping on the
hopscotch squares painted on the floor. *Peever,* Debs insists. *We call*
it peever.

'Yes, the library!' I am quite short with her, actually. I can hear
the bite of my voice, see it take effect. I've been what Mrs Coutts
calls 'gey frosty' since the pancakes episode, ignoring Debs's calls,
waiting days before I text her back. The kindly smell had soothed
me. Fooled me. I had let her serve up her cakes, let her appropriate
my daughter – this child she will not teach – on her knee for a
story, then tuck her into bed. Let her clear up my kitchen, clattering and chattering without pause, then sit by my side and firmly
take my hand.

'Maybe we should start again, yes? I'm here to mentor *you*,
Abdi, not Rebecca. It's all got a bit confused since I said I'd help
with her school. I meant to say I'd help *you* get it sorted, not that
I'd take over.'

Me, fumbling for a phrase such as 'Forget it' or 'Doesn't matter'
but my real words and my learned words had become a nest of

152

vipers; the sharp ones I needed slithering from my grasp. Then she said: 'It might help if you told me a bit more about the two of you. Or about Rebecca's mum, maybe? Abdi, believe me. I know how hard it is to lose a loved one.'

Again, I cringed as she tried to dig out my past. Recoiling sufficiently until she left me alone, making vague promises to phone me soon. The space we make round our losses is not for others to invade. My life is my story to tell, as and when and how I choose, not as a payment for kindness or a sop to make things smooth. I want Debs to recognise this, and to know why I am so angry, but she refuses to do so; apart from one very brief allusion to Rebecca when we meet today. *Well? Any more words?* which is a trite and stupid question and to which I reply, truthfully: *No*.

This 'play it by ear' – I looked it up on the computer in the library (which is how I met Geordie, incidentally, but that is none of her business). It means 'the playing of music without reference to printed notation' or 'to handle a situation without applying predetermined rules'. It also means Debs will not bother her backside. (Perhaps I *should* appoint Mrs Coutts my official mentor.) Does Debs know what a terror it took, to ask her to help my daughter? *Stupid refugee.* I want a big pile of dictionaries for her, ruled paper and coloured inks. Not *peever*, whatever that might be.

My rant continues. 'Where else would I furnish myself with books? How else will I learn more words and ideas? You have idea of the "noble savage", don't you?' (It would be nice to say I had been reading Dryden, but the truth is a patrician old lady said it on the train when I stood to give her my seat, so I searched also for it on Mr Google. Next time, I will remain seated.)

'Abdi, I didn't mean –'

'No, no. I understand.'

If I do push too far and she drives off without us, there is an underground train station right outside the school. Undergrounds, I have discovered, are even better than the land trains, because they have a picture of every station on them, telling you which one is next. Plus they run only in a circle, so you can never get lost. 'I don't mean you personally,' I say, 'it is collective "you". French *vous*.'

I append that deliberately, to show her the scope of my education. French, Italian, poetry – if she were to ask. Mathematics, science – everything useful except English, which my grandfather forbade me learn. The British were an occupying force in Somalia for many years, as were the Italians. I was never allowed to ask why, but he hated the British and loved pasta with tomato ragu. 'Why should not Geordie visit library? Geordie was professor in Iraq, a man who said the wrong thing at wrong time. Now he is stripped of his country and profession, and all he can do is live in Refugee Office as another of your ghosts.'

'He's not a ghost, Abdi, he's a person with a history. And that history's scarred him. He talks to himself – haven't you noticed?'

My brain is clear on what I want to say. I want to tell her that all the *yous* see all of us as ghosts. We are shiftless shapes at the limits, and when or if the *yous* are forced to speak to us, they see an inarticulate fool who has no initiative, no breadth of feeling or understanding. Our future is bleak and to be managed; our past is a multi-authored file (and, if we are lucky, some supplementary medical reports to augment our case). Every time I am asked for 'my story', I am packaged up a little more. But all of this must remain inside.

'Are you saying I should not speak with him because he is "damaged"? Geordie is very brilliant man. My Rebecca may be brilliant woman. Who knows how many great leaders, artists, *mathematicians* there could be in world – the *whole* world, Debs, I mean my world also – and yet they never will be – because of where they live. Here, you have much wealth and excess, but your youth are indolent. *Fat.* They consume but what they create? *Do* they create?'

'I think that's a little unfair.' She rubs at her nose with her fist. 'Anyway, I'm glad you know Geordie. I think he needs a friend.'

She is *determined* not to engage with me in argument. To her, I am happy, simple Abdi. I have layers, yes, she thinks, but they are merely chronological, and once she has leafed through them to her satisfaction she will have read me. Knowing a person's past tells you very little. 'Layers' suggest a skin that is complete and sealed and built upon, and that is absurd. People form like fish-scales, who they are fashioned in overlaps of light and shade. This month I am grumpy, last month I was grateful. As a boy I was bright, as a youth I was brave. Tomorrow that shopkeeper may be rude to me again and I may laugh it off or the sight of a golden-scarved woman may remind me of my wife and I will go home to curl up and weep.

'So do you like this place?' Debs asks.

'Is all right.'

'Rebecca seems to be having fun. She liked the old classroom, didn't she? The one with the inkwells and the gas masks?'

'Hmm.'

'I thought it might be good. I love it here – and not just because I used to be a teacher.'

I stiffen. Is the subject of Rebecca's education to be raised now, or is she waiting for me to ask again? I will not ask, and I will not respond. I wish we were speaking properly, though, because I know precisely what she means. I love the liquid-green tiles on the walls and the asymmetric janitor's house; the fact that the same care is lavished on carving cupboards in the kitchen as there is in the azure droplets of glass. You sense the spirit of the place – I think that is what made me snap about ghosts. The echoes in this hall could be long-gone voices, not Rebecca's slapping feet. (How I have grown to hate these welly boots, the molten pink and rubber smell, the tight screak of them as I prise them off each night when she goes to bed. One day soon I hope they become too small.)

'The architecture's stunning, isn't it? Says a lot about how they valued education, giving kids such an airy space.' Debs looks upwards, eyes following the bevel of the long gridded window. 'Yeah. So, one, I brought you here because *everyone* who comes to Glasgow should see a Rennie Mackintosh. Two, I wanted to show Rebecca what the inside of a school is like – albeit an empty, preserved-in-aspic, designer-handbag of a school. And three, I thought, as a fellow teacher, it might put a smile on your huffy bloody face.'

'What is huffy bloody?'

'*You* are huffy bloody. Or bloody huffy, I suppose. Either way, you've had a petted lip on you since I picked you up. So come on, out with it. What's wrong?'

'There is nothing wrong.'

'Is it the Housing? Have you still not heard from them?'

'No, I have not.'

'Well, it's only been three weeks. Give it one more week and if you haven't heard anything, I'll give them a ring, OK?'

'Fine. Rebecca,' I call. 'Come. It is time to go.'

Debs glances at her watch. 'No rush. Is it work? Are you worried about work?'

She must know I had a meeting with my caseworker – on the same day I got the train and was baptised a 'noble savage'. Do they discuss me at the Refugee Council? Do they say 'Oh poor Abdi needs a job' like 'Poor Geordie needs a friend'?

'I have no work to worry about.'

'Not yet, no. But I heard you were thinking about college?'

'My caseworker says now I am refugee-status I can apply to go in September time. Learn more English and exams in mathematics and science. Things I already know, but have no paper to say that.'

'That's great. I think you'll really enjoy college. And what about Reb –'

Her phone trills reedily, bouncing on the low wall where she has placed it. Unusual for Debs, to be so overtly attached to her phone. She swipes it up. 'Damn. Sorry, Abdi, I need to get this. Been trying to get hold of her for weeks. Hello? Yes . . . No, slow down, I can't understand what you're –' A pause in which she nods. 'Yeah, yeah. I know it. Out – no, *inside*? Are you sure? It'll be quite dark then.' Another silence, another nod. 'All right, that's fine. I'll see you then. Bye now. Bye.' A click of the plastic scallop cover and the phone is shoved in her handbag. 'Phew!' she says. 'What a palaver.'

'Is there problems?'

'No, no. Just a friend ... well, it's kind of ... it's nothing. Sorry. We were talking about your work? So what are you going to do from now until September. Get a job?'

'What I wanted to do is teach. Right now. But I do not have your qualifications.'

'You say that like I'm greedy or something!'

'Rebecca, come down from the stairs, please. Not greedy, no. But wasteful?'

She sucks on her breath, the way I would eat up noodles. I am ashamed of myself. This woman is not my saviour. I invest too much in her, then I punish her when she doesn't meet my needs. But *this* is about my daughter, not me. Debs pulls her knees to her chest, fixes again on the lustrous window. Its insistent light dominates the hall, bouncing back from gleaming tiles to land in dapples and wavery squares. Reminding me of water rippling.

'So, tell me,' she says. 'What sort of books is it you've been getting in the library?'

'Is hard for me to choose.'

The first time, I borrowed nothing. Where do you begin in a room crammed with foreign free books? Stacked linear planes and towers of books, most shoved in sideways with only a single strip of text and colour to entice your hands to touch. I sidled like a thief, scrutinising with my head on one side, moving back and forth then out. The next time, I asked the man at the desk: what is a good book to read, please? He said, *well, this is very popular*, passing me a book about a blonde woman who is famed for having very large breasts. The third time, I recalled a book the priest, Paolo, had in the camp. It was by an Irishman called Lewis, with a lion on the front. Paolo's copy was in Italian, but he said it was read the world over. 'It is a Christian allegory,' I told the man at the desk. 'Try the kids' section,' he said.

'Well, what kind of stuff do you like?' asks Debs. 'History or novels? What about the war – men always like war books.'

'Do they? Which war is that?'

The jaggedness in my voice is beginning to harm me too. I need to stop, but how? 'Rebecca!' I shout. 'Come down from there at once.' My daughter ignores me.

Debs is chewing her lip. 'How about some Scottish books? Would you like me to recommend a couple?'

'I like to read poetry.'

'Poetry! Oh, OK. Um . . . have you tried Norman MacCaig? He's very good. Lots of landscape stuff.'

Despite my rudeness, she continues to appease me, which makes me more ashamed, and thus more belligerent. Why am I doing this, should I not be grateful for the efforts she *does* make? She is nominally kind – we have established, I think, that she will only offer what she can – and I must accept that. I can talk to her. I learn, I enjoy her company. Without her, I would have Mrs Coutts, my church and my television, with all its brash cartoons. Even the programmes for adults are mostly like cartoons. And I want good books, am greedy for them.

'Thank you, yes. I will try him. And also novels. I would like to read a book that tells me what it is to be Scottish. Please.'

The basket of her hands unlocks, letting her legs go free. She stretches them long, is wearing the green leg coverings again with high brown boots. I think her hair is different too? A richer brown, made luminous inside all this light. She is very pretty today.

'That's a tall order. OK, let me see . . . well, *Sunset Song*'s an obvious one. You might end up doing it for your English exam anyway, but it's a brilliant book. All about how the land endures, no matter what folk throw at it. Tells you a lot about rural life too, how it used to be. It's not contemporary, of course, so you'll need one that . . .' she chews her lip. 'I know. James Kelman. Either *The Busconductor Hines* or *Kieron Smith, Boy*. If they don't take you inside the head of the Scottish male, nothing will.'

'Thank you.'

'So.' She nudges me, whisper-light. 'Are we friends again?'

'I am very grateful to you,' I say, before standing up to fetch my daughter.

We take the underground train back to Cardonald. I tell Debs it will be an adventure for Rebecca, and it is. She laughs as the trains whizz past us; I let her watch a couple rush by before we get on the next one. As long as she knows about the noise and dark beforehand, we are fine. It is *unknown* dark that scares her. We make a game of counting stations. Well, I count, she listens. But she is absorbing every drop of information I give her. When we get home, I make dinner (Chic'n'Stix: a combination of those breaded chicken threads and very thin potato chips. It is disgusting) then give her a bath. There's a musical night at the Somali Centre this evening. If things had gone well today, I was going to ask Debs if she would sit with Rebecca for a while. Mrs Coutts doesn't like to venture out at night, even up one flight of stairs, and I would have liked the chance to hear some *qaraami*. I rarely go to the Somali Centre, it is on the other side of the city, and mostly it is just talking and chewing and reminiscing for what you cannot have. Plus I am no longer a Muslim and that can cause . . . difficulties. Nothing overt, we are all brothers in God, but it makes me 'other' there too. After we get the *Abdi mans, good to see yous* over, and the familiar beautiful babble has washed me clean, there are always lot of *whys? Why are you reading that book? Why you turn Christian? We have Somali women here – why do you not take another wife?* Then I respond *Why do you not learn English? Why do you not let your wife go to college?* And they shake their heads, or whistle. *What is the point man?* and I tell them: *We are not going back, though. This is where we are; we are here to stay.* And then they look like I have punched them and I go home.

Hard as I scrub the surface of this bathtub, the ingrained grime remains. A grey streak along the bottom and some orange stains of rust. It long pre-dates our arrival in the flat: dirt compressed by another person's buttocks. We make bubbles with Miss Matey so the dirt is hidden. You never get white dirt.

'OK, mucky pup. Clothes off.' Obediently, Rebecca holds up her arms for me to remove jumper and vest. Steps out of her pants and trousers, carefully manoeuvring so she retains the wellies.

'Hoi! Boots too, please.'

Rebecca shakes her head.

'Boots off. Now.'

Defiant, she sits on the edge of the bath, little pot-belly thrust out. I bend to grab a boot.

'No!' she says firmly.

I rest there a while, my lips and forehead inches from her shin. Resisting the compulsion to hold her close, to paint her wonderful face with kisses. Praying quietly in my head. *Do not take this away from me, Lord. Do not take this away*. Feeling my body pause and hold like the instant before you land a catch and a single wrong movement could lose you that week's livelihood. Only this is far more precious and fine. A huge breath in and I say: 'No boots off, no bath. Now quick, before the bubbles pop.'

She complies! I am amazed! At her, at the smooth soap-scented air and the thrill of my blood. I am amazed that we are here, that both our lives are whole and here. That we have hope! And the first person I want to tell is Deborah. We make it a quick bath, a sluicing, so that I can scoop my baby out and swaddle her with towels, swing her high and kiss, kiss, kiss. My face is wet from bathwater, that is all! Into the living room, quick, quick, quick – *the hall is cold! Brrr*. I blow on her neck to wordless giggles – and as I pass from the front door to the living room I hear a clang. A letter at this late hour? Perhaps it is about my house, because today is a day of wonderful surprises! Putting my girl down on the couch, returning to see and to fetch her slippers and there is a smell, an acrid smell of burning and I begin to shake, am shaking it is the smell of burning as my village burned as the flesh of my friends and family charred, there is burning on my floor. Twisted newspaper belching flames and I stamp on it, stamping and yelling; it is soft beneath the paper. Something squirts. Hits me on the hands, the face. Warm and stinking like body-bloody-bursting-red — they burst like sausages — dear Christ, I keep stamping, stamping out the pain in my burning feet. 'Go back to the living room!' I yell at Rebecca. 'Is OK, is OK!' She is standing behind me, sobbing. Her eyes black and wide, her clean face filthy with little brown drops. I bend down to her. With my thumb, I wipe her tears.

On her face is spattered shit.

I touch my own face, smell my hands. Hear a cough of laughter through the wall and I'm out on the landing, at his door, at the old fucker's door. Pounding it with fists and feet, another kick, another, at the flimsy fake-wood door. The door jerks open like he is waiting, like he *cannot* wait. I fall inside.

'Get the fuck away fae ma door, ya fucking black bastard!' My neighbour is before me, in a vest and striped pyjamas. I push him in his grey, weak chest.

'My daughter is covered in shit!'

'Well, she'll smell better than she did before then.'

Then I am bawling at him and he is bawling at me, but my voice is louder, mightier.

'Why do you torment us?'

'Get the fuck oot ma house, ya darkie cunt.' He tries to strike me, I slap his face, he lunges and we tumble back on to the landing. He is smaller, but fleshy, I could kill him, I could hit him and hit him and never stop, my back strikes something which moves and swings, and we fall in a heap through another door. Hard head crashing on hard floor, his arm falling backwards and away as his fat body is carried by its own momentum to teeter at the top of the stairs. Hanging for a heartbeat that is fast and slow before he plunges, arse first, down the staircase. I hear the clatter, hear his anguished yells. Cower until the noise stops.

Like a noble savage, I crawl back to my own house.

'Police! Open the door, sir.'

It is happening again.

Azira and I had been living with the priest for nearly a year. *Forgive us our trespasses*. Alas, I had made a mighty enemy. It wasn't as if the police actively sought us out, but if they were bored or simply passing, they would come inside our house. Kick things over, take our food. Sporadic but systematic, over and over. Four times also, I had been arrested for theft (of what, I was never informed); four times in the eighteen months since I hit that policeman – that is nothing, I know – but the last time it took me some weeks to recover. On each occasion, Azira was spared. I didn't know why, but I told her it was a good jinn, that's what protected her.

'Jinn bring only bad luck.'

'That's not true. What if it's a good spirit? *You* have a good spirit, baby, so it makes sense you have good jinn protecting you. That and God.'

'Well, why doesn't he protect you too?'

'But he does. Look at me – I am still alive!'

Physically, I was. But there was always the blank and solid fear of waiting, then the terror–spikes each time they came. Sometimes the tattooed one would be there, but he was a generous man, he liked to share sport with his friends. That last time, they'd taken my backpack, made a totem of it by throwing it in a tree. My Azira rescued it for me, later.

'That was him,' I said, when she presented it to me (and when I had washed a lot and slept a little and my mouth had ceased bleeding). Dirty, scuffed but essentially intact; me and my backpack both. 'Yes? The one who threw it? He was the one who tried to hurt you?'

'No?' She was puzzled. 'Why do you think that? It was a young idiot who chased me. Pale, pale eyes: very ugly. Not that old leather man. Huh – I could have *easily* run from him.'

Ah. To the uniforms then, I am just a random madman. I almost understood their chagrin, if not their enthusiasm. Paolo had insisted we move into his home. 'You are my best teacher, Abdi; it's an investment. Whoever is doing this to you might not stop at a beating next time. Can the police not do anything about it?'

I hadn't told him it was the police. Why would he believe me? And he might think I had brought it on myself. It was so important to me that he believed I was a good man. So I lied. Casual robbery and brutality was an everyday occurrence in the camp; I let him assume I was the victim of some tribal 'bad blood'. The Mursais were desperate that we leave, especially Mrs Mursai. It was her home, too, that was being violated. 'I *told* you, Abdi. I told you not to go after them.'

Azira loved it at Paolo's house. There were real walls and a generator and a big white fridge, into which she never tired of putting jugs of milk and water. All still covered in damp muslin, of course. She planted a garden, growing *khajaar* and straggly beans. Our little girl grew stronger every day, and we had changed her name to Rebecca.

'It is from the Bible,' I told my wife. 'I should like you to read the Bible. I am going to teach you letters.'

'But why?'

'So that when Paolo talks to us about the Bible, you can form your own opinion.'

'Oh, Abdi, you are such a sweet man. I am allowed to have an opinion?' Gleaming with suppressed laughter. Her tongue moistened her lips, and she came closer to me.

'Yes,' I said, grabbing her waist. 'To go with the many, many you already have.'

We talked a lot about becoming Christians. It was a gradual certainty, if that makes sense. When Paolo told me all the stories of Christ, showed me how he was not a prophet but the Son of God, I believed him. Wholly and absolutely. The certainty permeated me until it was not a separate sense at all. Azira was less sure. It didn't help that Paolo and I talked sometimes in Italian. He could speak sufficient Somali for the classroom, but when he was seized with an urgency of explanation or exaltation, he lapsed into his native tongue. *These* were the times he transported me with his convictions.

'All we know is what we have known,' I told Azira. 'What our parents and our grandparents instil in us. When do we *choose* what we believe? This is simply another path to God; it's a path that tells me I should follow it. Don't you like to learn?'

There were a few Christian families in the camp, and we talked of their relative freedom, how their daughters were schooled alongside their sons. Azira was scared, I think, that she wouldn't see our son again. Then Paolo talked to her, and we prayed. A great peace was in the room that night. In the smoke and lamplight I felt the spirits of my grandfather, my mother and my father. They were holding our boy and smiling.

'Strathclyde Police! Would you please open the door?'

A steady, steady thump. Me lying on the covers on top of Rebecca's bed with one arm beneath her, the other over her shoulder, moving my hand to cover her ear. She sleeps on, exhausted from her tears.

When the police came inside Paolo's house, they never said please.

Carefully, I slip my arm from under my daughter and wriggle from the bed. A raw pain resonates as foot connects with floor. That's right: I am burned. I had forgotten. Slowly, I hobble to my front door, open it.

'Yes?'

'Can we come in, sir?'

And, if I say no . . . ? Wordlessly, I stand aside. Two young men in black uniforms enter my house, one of them wiping his feet on the mat outside before he does so. I made that from an offcut as well – brilliant purple flowers dulled with mud. But it is the mat inside that they both notice. Charred and filthy. I was going to throw it out, but it is too late now. It stinks and smoulders in a badge of shame. The taller of the two doesn't look at me. He's too busy circling the toe of his boot across my ruined mat, although he's not wiping, like the other policeman did. He's examining. 'Mm-hm. And your name is?'

Is that not what I should be asking you?

'Name?' he says again.

'Abdi Hassan.'

'Right, Abdi.' He has a large mole beneath his left eye, which stretches and shrinks as he speaks. 'We're here about your neighbour, Mr Bullmore. Boo-ool-more? Just nod or shake your head. The man next door?'

I nod. 'Yes.'

'He says that you threw him down the stairs. DOW-WIN THE STAIRS. Is that right?'

'Excuse me, Mr Hassan.' The smaller man steps closer to me. 'Can I just establish something. Are you able to understand English OK? English? *Ou vous préférez français?*'

The tall one sighs – at me, his colleague? I'm not sure.

'Yes, thank you,' I say. 'I speak English well.'

'OK, good. So, the reason we're here is that your neighbour Mr Bullmore is currently in hospital. He's alleging you broke into his flat and engaged him in a stand-up fight. Now, I see that there's been a bit of damage to your doormat here. I wondered if –'

'We wondered if you'd be able to answer a few questions,' says the one with the mole. 'We can either do this here, or we can go down the police station –'

'My daughter is sleeping.'

'I see.'

The small one tips his hat back from his face. 'Look, all we want to do is try and clear this up. So maybe you can tell us your version of what happened?'

'Am I being arrested?'

'No, no, of course not –'

The taller man folds his arms. 'No yet, pal.'

I lower my head. 'I am a refugee. I keep quiet, I want no trouble.'

'Did Mr Bullmore provoke you in any way?'

'To do what?'

'To push him down the bloody stairs.'

Mr Mole is getting angry. As am I, but the anger is leavened by blind fear. It seeps through everything else, gathering its authority. My leg quivers. Aches swell in my bladder. From the bedroom comes a thin wail.

'I think you have woken my daughter. Can you stop shouting, please?'

'Look, pal. You sure you know what being a refugee means? It means you're here on trial, aye? You start beating up old men and that's the fast track to a one-way ticket home. You understand?'

'Mike, keep it down, eh?'

Rebecca, bleary-eyed, is shuffling towards us. A fierce tug in my heart. She is my miracle.

The smaller one bends down, removes his hat. 'Hello, wee yin. What's your name?'

'She is called Rebecca. And she is very distressed.'

'Want a shot of my cap?' He hands her his hat. 'Whoah – nice wellies there by the way. You go to bed in them?'

Rebecca sidles into me, and I reach to touch the top of her head. 'Ssh, mucky pup. It's OK. Everything is OK.' I wink, stick out my tongue. She hides her face in my thigh. The hat drops to the floor. 'It's OK. Aabo is just talking to the men.'

The policemen are conferring in the corner of my hall. 'Well, I think we should get the gaffer. This is a racial incident, we've a wee kid involved –'

'Gonny step into my office, eh?' says the mole one. They move into my kitchen, so I can only hear fragments of conversation:

Obnoxious old bastard – Christ, I'd of chucked him down the stairs . . .

That's no the fucking point, but . . . assault . . . concussion . . .

Aye but where's your corroboration? No witnesses . . . old boy's a piss-head . . .

They whisper some more, then re-emerge, the small one talking into his collar. There is a pause. Another, tinny voice responds, the small one says: 'Roger. Noted.' He turns his attention to me. Sees his hat dishonoured on my piecemeal carpet and comes over to retrieve it. 'OK, sir.' Moving and sweeping me through my own hall, we are corralled like cattle towards Rebecca's bedroom. For one terrible pace I calculate how many seconds it will take to run and seize a kitchen knife. But the policeman does not go inside her room, only stands at the open door.

'What we're gonny do is leave you now, so you can get the wee one back to bed. OK?'

'Thank you.'

'But our sergeant's on her way to speak to you. If needs be, she'll decide if you've to come in for a formal interview. If that's the case, we'll make provision for Rebecca –'

'No! You cannot take my daughter!'

'Abdi, calm down, you hear me?' He lays his hands on my chest. Not hard, but the pressure is full of potential. Under his touch, my heartbeat is magnified. 'Just calm down. Nobody's going to take your daughter. You can get someone to come and sit with her. But you must let our sergeant in when she arrives, all right?'

'Aye, and we'll no be far,' calls the mole one. 'We're just going to interview your other neighbours. See what *they* can tell us.'

'All right, Abdi? We'll speak to you later.' The smaller one replaces his hat, goes towards his colleague. 'Goodnight then.' My front door is closed on me. Severing the air, pushing foul smells upwards.

It is a jinn, a bad jinn swallowing us.

I 0 .

'I CANNOT BELIEVE you've got me into this.'

'Oh shut up and quit looking suspicious.'

'Does it have to be in the middle of a park?'

'Well, you say I never go out any more. You should be glad we're on an adventure.'

'Bloody wild-goose chase, if you ask me. Are you *sure* this is the right place? We've been here forty-five minutes already.'

Gill is shivering beneath a beech tree. Her slim fingers are wrapped across her trenchcoat, her boot-heels too pointed for the soft, cloggy mud. Dusk has brought shadows, and the faint rising moon bleeds white across the park. Unearthly, bone-coloured narcissi point skinny trumpets skywards. There is not another soul around.

'So why couldn't your pal come again?' says Gill.

'She's not my pal. Naomi is just a neighbour. And she couldn't come because she doesn't want to be "seen in suspicious circumstances". Her husband's a judge or a QC or something.'

'Big wows – and what about me? I'm a bloody headmistress. I don't want to be caught with my pants round my ankles either.'

'What a lovely turn of phrase you have, dear.'

My wee sister Gill. Two years between us, and she's been striving to erase the gap ever since she could breathe. Followed me round school like a cullie dug – *but* why *won't you play with me, why?* – followed me to uni, then followed me into teaching. Got married the spring after my summer wedding, got pregnant four months after I did, moved into a house *slightly* nicer than ours then . . . whoosh. One day I looked round and she wasn't there. Behind, I mean, in her rightful place. All of a sudden, my wee sister had overtaken me. Headmistress of a *very* good state primary school, mum to two beautiful teenagers, possessed of a chic bob, svelte hips and a floaty, elf-like wardrobe. Gill is what you would call petite. Everything that is dainty, neat and groomed, while I am a shapeless bag. And somewhere along the way, Gill has developed elder-child syndrome.

'It's too cold to hang about – you should zip up your jacket. And your Russian spy can't be that desperate if she's not even bothered to turn up on time.'

'Rula's Chechen, not Russian – and she sounded pretty desperate when I spoke to her earlier.'

Today at Scotland Street had been the first time I'd succeeded in talking to Rula since Naomi nominated me her download-buddy.

'I mean, you deal with these migrant people every day, don't you?' Naomi had said, once I was ensconced in one of her velvet armchairs, being plied with G&T.

'Well no. I do an occasional volunteer shift at the Refugee Council.'

'*Exactly*. The thing is, Rula sounds like she's in a bit of a pickle. Since she buggered off –'

'You mean since she had her claim for asylum refused? Is that what actually happened?'

Whenever you saw Naomi, not actually conversing with her, but when she passed by the window or you saw her in the car, her default expression always struck me as one of barely-contained impatience. That evening, it was considerably more overt. I like to think I bring out the best in people.

'*Since* Rula left us in the lurch, I'm not quite sure what she's got herself mixed up in. But the upshot is, she appears to owe rather a lot of money, and I'm getting utterly sick of her telephoning me.'

'Have you asked her what it's for?' I said. 'Maybe we could get her debt counselling or advice with repayments? Has she launched an appeal against the decision?'

'How would I know?' Naomi uncrossed linen-clad legs, reached for her tumbler. 'No, Debs, this is the problem. I don't *want* to know. I just want her to stop annoying us. So much so, I'm prepared to help her out – on the proviso she leaves us alone. I mean, Duncan's in a very delicate position –'

'That's good you're going to help. But you could maybe also say to her –'

'Now, this is where you come in, Debs. I can't say anything at all, that's the thing, because she doesn't have a bloody mobile. Just calls me from a payphone as and when the mood takes her. And I absolutely can't get involved in any meetings with her, not when I haven't a clue what she's up to. So …' ice-chunks clinking as she took a sip of her drink '… ah. You just can't beat a G&T, can you? Yeah, so how would it be if the next time she calls, I give her your number? Then you could arrange to meet her and hand over … well, like I say, I don't mind helping her out. A *little*. As long as you stress that she must never phone us again.' She set the glass down, was all bright smiles. 'And you can give her all the refugee leaflets and helpline numbers you like, if you think that'll help. Oh, Debs, it would be such a relief to have a proper professional helping Rula.'

Good old Naomi. I can see why she's such an effective business-woman. So that, in a gullible nutshell, is why I'm loitering in the middle of Maxwell Park with my wee sister Gill as bodyguard and £500 in my purse. And maybe there's some creeping sense of atonement too, but we won't go there. It's not my fault Rula ran away. I did nothing *wrong*. Fair enough, I did nothing at all. What is a sin of omission but a slipping instant which you could have caught, but didn't? My bodyguard stamps petulant, neat feet. 'Fecking May? Did nobody tell the weather? Och, c'mon, Debs. Can you not just phone and find out where she is? I've left Richard in charge of dinner –'

'She doesn't have a phone.'

'Brilliant.'

'Look, you go on. I'll give it another half an hour.'

'No you bloody well won't. I'm not leaving you here on your own. We'll give it ten more minutes then we're going home. Right?'

I nod meekly. 'Yes, miss.'

'You're too bloody soft, that's your problem.'

'Soft?'

Me? Me that is a wreck of flattened-out humanity, grinding my weary way on? Me, who can't see beyond bitterness and regret? *I don't think so, little sis.* When was the last time I was soft? When I wept at a roadside don't don't don't when I held my son, oh yes, for a glittering perfect instant soft was the finest of all things I could be. When I nursed my husband, reeking stoic fortitude?

I have to say, Debs, you're just so brave.

A couple of Callum's work colleagues had called to visit. That was the last time anyone called me soft. I remember because it was also the last time Callum would let anyone except closest family see him.

Soft hands too. Mike, kissing my hand as he said goodbye. He was a sociology professor – and a little bit creepy.

Och, you know – hands that do dishes . .

We had laughed, a dry rasp neither of us meant. The other chap, Gregor, was ostentatiously patting Callum's shoulder, telling him in a too-loud voice THEY WOULD SEE HIM AGAIN SOON. Callum, staring at the fireplace in a huffy trance as the dribbles carried down his chin, bringing with them the last of the biscuit he'd insisted on sooking. While he'd alternately gnawed and choked on the mushy Hobnob I held to his mouth, I'd engaged his colleagues in conversation, skirting over all but the most mundane of our trials. We had tossed words back and forth like a desultory ball, none of us keen to hold the responsibility for very long. And then it was time for them to go and me to stay. *I don't know how you do it.* Mike, all breathy, his quick hands pressing down on mine as my husband hung ape-like and inert. Both Mike and Gregor had been visibly shocked when they'd come in; it had been a few months since they'd visited last. Even then, Callum's trembling mouth and limbs had been alarming. Now the spasms were held in check by his atrophying body, his thickened slurs incomprehensible. Communicating with desperate eyes. It could not be, would not be borne that these were the same eyes which laid claim to me twenty years ago in a trendy bar. When I could, I avoided looking into them.

Och, you just have to get on with it, don't you? I had moved to rescue Gregor, who seemed incapable of taking his leave.

Right, my love, time for a wee nap, I think, yes? It was an innocuous, if insensitive, phrase and I'll never know if he spasmed or it was a purposeful act, but Callum's arm jerked furiously over the tea tray, the plate of remaining Hobnobs smashing on the wall.

I suppose if I'd ever gone to the Carers Support Group (never enough time, a fear of mass emotion and the wilful lack of apostrophe in the title ensuring I *did not*), there may have been some kindred spirit there who could empathise and explain that yes, familiarity *did* breed contempt, and it was gruelling routine which made us so, not cruelty. That when anger spilled as our loved ceded to their illness, it was justifiable, because every so often the delicate contortions of balancing more than our fair share were bound to send us spinning, and that dreams of pillows firm-pressed against the coming of another light were merely that. Bad dreams.

Och aye, a total soft touch, me.

'Hoi! Dozy!' Gill is smirking. Always a bad sign. 'Earth calling Deborah! I said how're things with your big black man then?'

'*Gillian!*'

'I'm joking! But when are we going to get to meet him?'

'You're not. For God's sake. He's not a prospective boyfriend.'

'Hey, I wouldn't be complaining if he was! Do you no harm at all to have a wee bit fun.'

'Gill, just shut up, will you? God, I can't believe you think –'

It is May. One year this month since my husband died. I haven't been to the grave. I think if I did, I would climb in beside him. And then where would I be? One year. It's for ever, and it's nothing.

'I don't! I don't! Calm down. I'm not disrespecting you, or Callum – or Azerbaijani . . .' Gill's annoying pointy chin comes to rest on my shoulder, arms arched behind her like a coquette.

'His name's Abdi.'

'*Abdi*, then. Aah-b-di.' Mouthing it in my ear. Then louder. 'Abdee. Ab-i-deee! Time for bed, Ab-i-dee!' Pretends she's bouncing on a spring, twirling her fingers round an imaginary Zebedee moustache.

'Christ Almighty. You are so immature.' This is why I hide from her in cupboards.

'But can I be the bridesmaid? When you get married?'

With anyone else, the heat in me would rise and I would – whilst not actually saying a single word – rage about their insensitivity. Luxuriating in the burn, and possibly ending with a big fat side-order of tears. That's why people hide from *me*. I punch my sister on the arm. 'Piss off. Anyway, I think the wedding's off. He's barely speaking to me.'

'Ooh, gossip! Howso?'

'Och, he asked me if I'd tutor his wee girl, and I just . . . I kind of dyked it.'

'Why?'

179

Panic, I think. Simple panic. Not false modesty or reserve; it wasn't me getting my own back because he refused my help before. Saying no was my first and visceral response. After all that effort to have Abdi 'open up', I got to see his insides torn and gaping, and I ran away. A kneejerk to the desperate rawness. It's one thing to offer yourself in rationed measured doses, where you plan out how much and where and why you're doing it – but it's another to be seized. You can't escape from that, and I know, I know all about great meaty mouths of need: they trap you. They *slobber* and sook till only your bones are left. And what if I couldn't do it? Rebecca, that damaged wee soul relying on *me*? Wholly me to fix her? That kind of need can kill you. The damage I might make of them both. I'm not a teacher any more. I'm shapeless, pointless. Foolish, ugly, cowardly me – that's what Abdi would find if he got to see my insides.

My sister's waiting.

'Och, loads of reasons . . .'

'Scrape 'em off, Claire!' Gill flares her nostrils, turns sidey-ways to creep like a pantomime villain. We both laugh. It's a line from that film *Scrooged*, the one with Bill Murray. Our father (also Bill) was a ferocious Tory, much given to writing letters and shouting at the TV, and *scrape 'em off, Claire* was a phrase he readily deployed: at Mum's request for extra housekeeping, whenever Gill argued about politics, the time I wanted to volunteer abroad for a year. He meant it in an ironic way, I think. Gill does not. The way she sees through me is chilling.

'No! I mean, I was a secondary teacher, for one, not primary. And the wee one – Rebecca – has got communication problems –'

'Deaf?'

'No. Just doesn't speak. Nothing physically wrong with her, as far as I can see.'

'And you blame the dad?'

Do I?

'No, I wouldn't go as far as that. But I don't think Abdi pushes her, put it that way. And I don't think it's healthy for a kid who's indulged in her "not-speaking" to be shielded further. She needs to be in school.'

'Where's she down for?'

'That's the problem. She's not.'

Gill opens her mouth and I can see a lecture coming on.

'Just leave it, OK? I'm not going to teach her, but I'm not going to abandon her either. Let me work on it, and if I need your help, I'll ask. *Ask*. Got that?'

She rolls her eyes. 'Fine. Right, Mata Hari's a no-show. Now can we *please* go and get some dinner?'

My head aches, I want to go home, stuff Naomi's five hundred quid through her letterbox and pour myself a big glass of wine. But Richard's making us steak.

My brother-in-law is a bluff and jovial chap, five years older than me, and with the flushed face of a rather naughty child – the kind who misbehaves in such an endearing way you can only laugh. He winds me up atrociously.

'Deborah, my darling!' Birls when we come in, wafting a spatula.

'Richard! It's the cooking fairy! Love your wand.'

He blows me a kiss as my sister takes my coat. 'You're looking scrumptious. How are you? Secret delivery all sorted?'

'No, she never turned up.'

'Good, good.' Bowling on in his pinny and not listening to a word I say. 'Sit down then, sit, sit. So. Still hard at it with the asylum seekers? Many of the great unwashed have you adopted this month?'

I pretend to count on my fingers. 'Well, that'll be six now – no, actually, twelve if you include the family of Iraqis in the back bedroom. Oh, and a camel.'

'Excellent. Camel milk's very good for you, apparently. In fact, I'm sure we're trialling it down south.'

'Yum.'

Richard is the regional manager for a supermarket chain. Started as a Saturday boy at college and worked his way up to the company car and a 15 per cent staff discount. A very handy ally if you're planning a party and need a lot of booze. Which I think is how his and Gill's courtship began. Gill returns from the hall, closes the door to her massive kitchen so we're all wrapped up with the sizzle of meat and onions. They have a dining table and a couch in here, a Welsh dresser tumbled with books and pottery and a French armoire containing linen tablecloths. I could live in Gill's kitchen. There's a pile of books on the table, a Bohemian centrepiece in place of flowers.

'Wine?'

'Just a wee glass. I'm driving. Where's the kids?'

My nieces Iona and Lisa. I don't possess them like Gill does, but they're easy and content with me. Both students now, they don't *have* to visit Auntie Debs, but they do. We text and email and they wander in for dinner occasionally, or we meet in town for coffee. OK. My life's not always as bleak as I make out. My sister and her family love me, consistently, irrespective of the rebuffs and sulks and the time Gill used her key to find me sobbing in the bed I'd refused to come out of for three days. But sometimes your situation is predicated on how you *feel*, not how it really is. I shift the books so I can read their spines.

'Iona's at her boyfriend's and Lisa's rehearsing.'

'Rehearsing? Ooh.' I look up at my sister. 'Can I borrow this one, please?' I hold *A History of Scotland* aloft. 'Rehearsing for what?'

'If you want. Rehearsing for the concert. The one I told you about. In the Royal Concert Hall? You have a ticket?'

'Oh, yeah. That concert.'

'It's for Breast Cancer Awareness.' My wine is placed before me, gently.

I cross my arms. 'Well, I'm not wearing a pink bra, I'll tell you that for nothing.' My wee sister ruffles my hair. Glasgow Uni Big Band. With Lisa on trumpet. Canny wait.

'Gill tells me you're going out with one of them now.' Richard shouts above the drone of the extractor fan and the exuberant gush of the water he's draining from his boiled potatoes. I wanted chips. Everyone knows you have chips with steak.

'One of who, Richard?'

'Your asylum seekers.'

'I'm not going out with Abdi and he's not an asylum seeker. He's a refugee.'

'Same difference.'

In with a big bloop of butter. Good. We're having mash.

'No. It's the exact opposite, actually. An asylum seeker's someone who arrives in this country looking for help – appealing to our better natures to let them stay. A *refugee*'s already been told they can stay. And you have to go through a hell of a lot in between. Medicals, interviews, all sorts to prove you're a victim of persecution. Thank you.' I take the glass of water Gill's offering. 'The deal is, if you can persuade us your life was *so* shit before you got here that going back will kill you, you might, just might, be allowed to remain.'

'And contribute to our economy by becoming *Big Issue* sellers?' Richard dollops the mash in an earthenware bowl. I shudder. It's the one I brought from the Transvaal. Eighteen bloody years ago and not a chip in its mud-ochre skin.

'I tell you, there's one stands outside our Giffnock store, looks like Gypsy Rose Lee.'

'Economic migrant. Totally different again.'

'Debs, he's only winding you up –'

'I am not. I'm thinking about the bigger picture. I'm a business man, Debs. And we don't have enough jobs and resources for ourselves any more. So why should it be *this* country welcoming all and sundry? We didn't cause their wars or their famines, why should we be the dumping ground?'

Gill pours herself more wine. 'OK, Richard, you're not even funny any more.'

'But if we don't, who does?' I want more wine, not water. Want the easy slurp and slide of warm lubricant which will polish my words and relax my neck. Above me, Richard twinkles, and I know he doesn't mean it, but to not rise to the challenge is like laughing at an old lady falling, or a joke about handicapped kids. Even silence is complicit. Four months ago, my world was sleeping pills and sitting in my nightie.

'Richard, you're an arse. At least we live in a country that's prepared to do *something* for our fellow man. And, for your information, we only take about two per cent of refugees worldwide, so we're not exactly Mother Teresa.'

'I love you, Debs.' He drops a paternal kiss on my head, starts dishing out the food. 'Sirloin steak for you, my darling wife. Sirloin steak for me, her masterful husband and – ah, yes, here's some dry bread for our champion of the poor. Tuck in, Debs, it's fab. I unwrapped it myself.'

'Ha, ha.' And we're back in the pleasant hammock of banter in which our relationship rests. 'Can I have my steak, please?'

'Well, I thought you might want to take it away for the home-less –'

'Don't mock. But that's something your bloody supermarkets could be doing, for starters: giving away food. All that past-its-sell-by stuff . . .'

'Eh, for *your* information, madam,' he passes me my plate, 'we've just launched a new initiative, whereby we earmark a percentage of our apprenticeships for homeless folk.'

'Oh, aye. Apprentice shelf-stackers?'

'*No.* Butchery. Bakers. Fishmongers –'

'Seriously?'

'Yes, seriously.'

'*Fish*mongers?'

Gill winks at me.

Just as we finish dinner, my mobile goes. I snatch it, expecting it to be Rula, have judiciously nursed my little half-glass of wine in case I've to dash back to Maxwell Park. But it's Abdi.

At least I think it is. I can barely hear him, his voice a shaky whisper.

'Please, Deborah. I need your help.'

I am there in twenty minutes. One front door, ajar. One police-woman, stern. Her arm acts as a hinge, preventing entry.

'Yes?'

'Can I come in?'

'Who are you?'

I hear Abdi's voice, thin but steady. 'She is my friend.'

'Excuse me, please.'

I squeeze past the policewoman as politely as she steps back. A performance-piece of studied movement, where both unbend but neither concede, and I really don't care about any of that as I take in the scene in the hallway.

One doormat – 'Don't!' says the policewoman. 'Eh, I wouldn't stand on that' – one doormat, soaking underfoot and emitting a stink that can only be described as shitty.

One refugee, stooped. His fists balled by his sides, he has the sly furtive movements of a dog that's just been whipped.

'Are you all right, Abdi?'

'Yes.'

One little girl, sitting bolt upright in her bed. You can see her through the open door, face patterned gold by the nightlight on her wall.

'Hey, Rebecca!' I do a little star shape with my hand. Her mouth opens slightly, eyes stay wide.

'I'm Sergeant Heath,' says the policewoman. 'Jenny Heath.'

'Deborah. Abdi's mentor from the Refugee Council. Eh, can you tell me what's going on exactly?'

'I was just leaving.'

'What's happening with Abdi?'

'Nothing.' She has a sharp, pretty face on her, and too much eyeliner.

'Nothing for now, or nothing at all?'

They are thoughtful eyes, in amongst all that blue and black. She touches my elbow, positions and deports herself so I find myself propelled down the hall. It's not threatening, in fact it's quite hypnotic. We take ourselves off to Abdi's living room, leave him standing there.

'Abdi, you go and check on Rebecca,' I manage to say, before the door between us is firmly shut.

'I take it Abdi asked you to come over?' she says.

'Yes.'

'So what did he tell you?'

'That he's been accused of hitting his neighbour.'

'So the neighbour says. You know him?'

'Which one?'

'Old boy next door. Bullmore?'

There is a beat of hesitation, then I go: 'Oh, *him*.'

'Mmm. Now, at the moment, it's his word against Mr Hassan's. Mr Bullmore says he was pushed down the stairs, Mr Hassan claims he fell. Judging by the amount of alcohol Mr Bullmore has consumed, falling is certainly a possibility.' Her stern, painted mouth has an upward tilt. Up close, I don't think it is so stern; more a trick of the light and the uniform. 'Unfortunately, we've no witnesses to corroborate either side of the story.'

'I see.'

'My problem is, I've a feeling if we don't intervene in some way, then this is all going to escalate. I mean, I don't know if you noticed the doormat ...'

'I did.'

'And the fire damage.'

I swallow. Nod. 'Yeah.' *Fire damage? Bloody hell.*

'Well, Mr Hassan claims it was Mr Bullmore did that. And that there's been an ongoing campaign of harassment. Now, I realise how hard it can be for refugees to integrate into the community ...' She pushes bleached hair behind her ears. 'Tell me this. Is Mr Hassan settled here?'

'Yes!' My stomach lurches, drawing itself in and up. I feel it pressing on me, am conscious my breath must smell of wine and meat. They couldn't send him back for this. Surely? My voice rises and speeds when the effect I need is calm. 'Absolutely!' I squeak. 'He's going to go to college, he's got some job opportunities lined up –'

'I don't mean Glasgow, I mean this flat. Don't get me wrong, I'm not in any way condoning ...' Sergeant Heath sighs, then smiles. It's a stunt-smile, one to leaven, not to warm. 'In my experience, when an asylum seeker or a refugee starts getting a hard time, things often get out of hand. And it's usually the asylum seeker that ends up worse off. Of course we can investigate both allegations ... but ...' she looks at the ceiling, 'I just wondered if a fresh start –'

'Move him away from here!' I seize her arm, realise what I'm doing; drop it. 'Totally! That's what we've been trying to do. We were at the Housing three weeks ago, they're supposed to be finding him another flat. But we've heard nothing.'

Jenny Heath arches fine-plucked eyebrows. 'Yeah? Well, let me see what I can do.'

She returns to the hallway. Quiet murmurs, Abdi nodding with his head down, her saying words like: *no further action* and *this time, you understand?* She shakes my hand before she leaves, promises nothing. Shakes Abdi's hand too. There is something straightforward in her gestures, they are clean and overt and I think I trust her. When she goes, I read Rebecca a story and Abdi makes some tea. Rebecca's thumb twists into her mouth, she's asleep before we get to the end, but I stay on, stroking the little forehead. It is soporific. I have made a spell, and if I move, I'll break it.

'Your tea is coming cold, Debs.'

'Going.' I look at my watch. Eleven thirty. Ach, I've time for one cup of tea.

We drink quietly, accompanied by a ticking clock and the dull clamour of someone else's telly beneath us. Only one lamp is lit, casting a single pool of light. Abdi is in shadow.

'Why didn't you tell me about your neighbour? That he's been hassling you?'

'Hassling?'

'Being unkind.'

'Is my problem. Deborah.' He is very calm. 'Will I go to prison?'

'No! The policewoman said no further action, didn't she? That means the matter is over.'

'Police say many things.'

'Trust me, Abdi, it's going to be fine.' I'm assuming the sergeant didn't mention housing to him, so I don't either, in case I got my wires crossed. We sip and think a wee bit more. Neither of us mention the neighbour being in hospital – or Abdi's involvement in putting him there.

'You know, tea's not a good drink so late at night.'

'No?'

'Nope. Keeps you awake. You should try hot chocolate. Rebecca would love it. That's what Callum and I had most nights before we went to bed.'

'Callum is your husband?'

Have I never used his name before? 'Yes. Yes it is.'

I wonder that he's never asked. But then Abdi's never really asked anything about my life. I never know if he's being disinterested or scrupulously polite.

'Hot chocolate is a good memory, I think. You are smiling.'

'Am I?' Can he see behind my eyes, to where I am lying in bed, belly aching, full of insomnia and Callum is stroking my hair? Can he see Callum's body lying behind mine, supporting it, him raising the cup to my lips, then stopping. *Wait*, he breathes, blowing over the mug. Taking a sip to check, returning it to me. So my lips don't burn.

'Well, yeah. I have a lot of good memories of Callum. They're just a bit – clouded, I suppose. Because he got so ill. And he was such a . . . he was really – lovely. And kind. Smart as anything – he was an economist at first, then an academic. Looking at money, how countries spend it, move it –'

'I know what an economy is.'

'Yeah? Sorry.' I sook in any hint of retort; don't want to go back

190

to that frostiness of the last few weeks. Abdi shifts forward in his seat, face moving through the edges of light. He wears a mild smile.

'You can go anywhere as an economist. Even rule the world. Our First Minister's one.'

'Now, First Minister, I'm not so clear on. Ever since I am in Glasgow, I try to watch the television news to understand. You have rulers in London and you have rulers in Edinburgh?'

'Kind of.'

'So is Scotland a country or a state of England? On this I am not clear.'

'Oh, we're a country, all right. We're a nation – with our own money and laws and education system. Some of the world's most wonderful inventions have come from Scotland, don't you know? The TV, the telephone, the bike, penicillin –'

'I think I've upset you?' But he's laughing. 'You are very proud of your country within a country, yes?'

'Damn right I am. Here,' I take *A History of Scotland* out from where it lies forgotten in my bag. 'That reminds me. You read this and *then* we'll talk.'

'Is this my homework?'

'It is. And I'll be testing you on it after.'

Abdi examines the uninspiring cover – a spindly lion rampant, pawing at air. 'So, teacher, tell me this. If I am able to vote, who should I vote for? In your democracy, did you not vote for your rulers in London? Are they imposed on you?'

'Abdi, it's really complicated.' I'm tired, my head's sore. The tannin-tasting tea is sticky in my mouth, and Abdi's had the police out to him and there's a wee lassie out there waiting for money I was supposed to give her and an even wee-er lassie through the wall. Who is sleeping in her starry bedroom and will not speak a word.

'But you are a free people, yes?'

'Depends on how you look at it. We have devolution, not independence.'

'So London are still your masters?'

'At the moment. Some folk feel it's . . . I dunno, safer.'

'I understand. When warlords came to my village, we fled. But the land outside was . . . hostile?'

I nod encouragement. Abdi has told me so little of his home. I'd like to be able to visualise it.

'You mean like no water, no food?'

'Yes. It was very dry. We were fishermen, not hunters.' He shuffles, sinking again so all I see is his outline. 'So, we tried. But then we got sick . . . some of us eventually came back. Our village had been taken, other families there. We crawled back like dogs, and we lived outside the homes that once were ours. I begged a man to give me employment on the boat that was . . . that used to be mine. *My* boat, Deborah, that I had built myself. But it was too hard. Every day, they wanted more from us, more pleading, more work. More of me, you know?'

'I do.'

'But some of my friends, they had never left. My mother, sister, my grandfather. The village elders, they stay although everything is taken from them. *I am a guardian of this place*, my grandfather told me. He didn't think any man could own the land, only walk on it. I tried to tell myself it was better here than not here, but then more warlords came . . . more men with guns.'

Abdi stands up, walks to the window. I want to put my hand on the hard square of his shoulders, but I know when I talk about Callum, I can't bear someone touching me. It feels like infidelity, and I have to focus on their touch instead of the effort of selecting and making words. Abdi sighs. A dreadful, cleansing heave. I don't know if I'm ready for this. If his secrets are worse than mine. I don't move, do not breathe for fear I ripple the air.

'They killed them.'

A tremor in the concave of his cheek. The silence drags at the end of his words, but I can't fill it. I can feel it with him, feel his family's absence as the heavy presence it is. If he wants to, Abdi will tell me more. Or I'll put the kettle on and we'll drink more tea.

'I was out fishing. When I returned I found . . . it was the whole village. Little children . . . My mother and my grandfather both dead.'

From the window to the couch. But he doesn't sit. He is watching his knuckles and how the blood progresses up the veins of his unquiet arms. His wristbone ticks. Tight wrinkles move over the drumstick of his thumb, his cooried-in, pumping fingers.

'I found my mother first. She was right at the far edge of the village, face down, with great gashes on her back. They had torn off her clothes. She was . . . her body was lying outwards, like she had been fleeing. I couldn't understand it . . . I couldn't understand that she would leave my sister or my grandfather. No matter what. Or that my grandfather would leave them. He was a lion, but too old to run – and then . . . then I found him. He was hanging from a tree, with the other men. I think she had been running *to* him when they hacked her down. My sister was . . . she was not yet dead when I found her. She had hidden in a cave by the sea. Or they took her there ...'

Now. I take his hand now, feel his spent skin, his wasted wanting bones.

'Abdi, I'm so sorry.'

He sits beside me. Rests his head upon my arm. I think he is crying, a little. I know that rasp, it has the same dry quality as bile, when you've nothing left to give but the reflex insists your body still performs.

'Is this also when you lost your wife, Abdi?'

Caught up in the live wire of emotion that sings between us, confusing intimacy with equality – and I'm duly punished. He bolts upright. 'I did not know her then.'

There is an awful silence. It clangs on and on above the telly-drone downstairs, above the loudness of my heart.

'I'm sorry, Debs. You must go. Is late.'

'Abdi, please. I'm sorry.'

'For what? For my family dying? Where is your coat?' He's up and out, scrabbling through the mess and tangle of his hall cupboard for my jacket. I follow him, stand in the doorway of the living room. Speak in whispers so as not to wake Rebecca.

'For asking about your wife again. It's absolutely none of my business.'

'No.' His frenzied searching slows.

'I have no right to pry about your life. I ask only as a friend ... it is difficult, Abdi. It is hard to be someone's friend when you only know little snippets.'

'Snippets?' He glances at me for a clue.

'Wee tiny pieces.' I make a scissoring motion. Stop half-snip. It looks too violent.

'That is how you become a friend, surely? By taking time and getting to know a person in small pieces?'

Despite the sump we've slipped into, I laugh.

'What?'

'Nothing. You've described me perfectly. A person in small pieces.'

He leaves off his search for my coat. 'That is a nonsense, Deborah. You think you are broken, that you are dead inside, but you're not. You have a *vitale* that shows you alive? Is that the right way I am saying? You make laughter in spite of yourself.' He shakes his head, returns to fumbling in the cupboard. 'The will to live runs like sap – even inside dry wood. But if you keep tearing and breaking to examine what is there, it *will* die. Accept only that you live – and be grateful for that. Here. Here is your coat.'

His tired hand flops out to reach a hook right at the back.

'Please, Deborah. I am not angry. Just very, very needing of sleep, OK?'

'OK.'

'I need to sleep now.'

'Fine.'

'But thank you. For coming when I asked.'

'No problem.'

I take my coat and go. Out on my dry-wood legs. I think we've both had enough for tonight.

11. JUNE

THE SCOTIA BAR

Glaswegians love to party – and everyone's invited. A huge array of pubs, clubs and bars allow you to sample legendary hospitality in this, Scotland's friendliest city.

Situated on Stockwell Street, one of Glasgow's four original roads, the ancient Scotia Bar has been home to poets, musicians and real Glasgow folk since 1792. When the inn first opened, the Clyde was a vibrant waterway, making the Scotia a popular port of call for sailors. Being so close to the Tolbooth Gaol and the Gallowgate, the inn was also frequented by soldiers, prison visitors and cheery souls off to see public hangings!

Along with food and friendly faces, the Scotia now offers a lively selection of musical evenings, specialising in folk bands and traditional singers. Popular with Scotland's literati, the bar also hosts storytelling sessions, poetry readings and the Scotia's own writers' group, where all are welcome to read their own work or simply listen to the work of others.

And, if you listen quietly in the shadows, you may also hear voices
from the past, come back to enjoy another dram at the Scotia. Or are
those spirits just the ones in your glass?

★

I ARRIVE AT the Refugee Council with a bunch of roses. Creamy-white and full, they hint at summer. I want to surprise Deborah with my gift. Everything is fitting together, my life is taking on a momentum I've never known before. Happiness bubbles at the surface; the trees I pass are fixed and steady, pauses in traffic are deliberate, designed to time with me. I cross building-shaded roads, flit smoothly between high glass office blocks. My movements are focused and my direction is clear.

I have a new home!

The flat is near to where we are now, we can still go to church, we can still see Mrs Coutts. But the building will be lower, smaller, and there is no pub-and-jaggy-glass in the front garden. In fact – there is a garden! Or a park, you call it a park where there are swings and slides. Deborah knows all this, because I texted her last night. Apologised, too, of course, for my recent sharpness, mediated it with the news that Rebecca has three times said 'kew' after I have given her things.

This is 'thank you', yes?

Oh Abdi, that's wonderful.

But I want to see her expression when I say, 'Oh and by the way, I have a new job too!'

The roses are irresistible. I bury my nose in their faint scent, straighten my tie. I have a tie! The doors to the Refugee Council lie open, haphazard as if people have just run in or out. Inside, too, there's an air of confusion, of hurriedness that's different from the usual shuffling-through. It is busier than ever, there seems to be less patient explanation going on at the booths, but many static, worried faces – on both sides of the counter. Perhaps it's a hunter's skill, to sniff the air and know a change is coming. Perhaps it's a trick I've gleaned from all those years in the camp. Like impala who can turn and flee on a single hoof, you learn when air is tainted and it is time to run.

A haphazard door is all it takes.

My meetings with Debs are opening too many doors, I think. Good ones and bad ones. All with Azira behind them.

Father Paolo had sheltered us from the police, the first time they came to his house. Had I truly thought it would stop? Nearly a year had passed in quietness at the priest's home; me teaching at the school with Paolo, Azira growing a garden. Rebecca growing strong. Until, one day I had been returning from the school, turned right instead of left. Collided shoulders with a uniform, my red backpack swinging.

'Forgive me,' I said, with my head low. Do not meet eyes with the uniforms: I was, belatedly, following Mrs Mursai's advice.

'You,' said the voice. 'What's in that bag?'

'Books. For the school.' Humbly, hurriedly, I opened my bag. Kept my face averted.

'You steal them?'

'No. I work there.'

'You work there, huh? So you got money?'

'No, sir, no.'

To say 'sir' made me wish to vomit. It was not a voice I recognised from any time before. But the uniform was definitely police.
I know that khaki green. There was a clanging in my head. I braced;
to cower or sprint or punch. Or pray. I watched the uniform's feet
shift. He had fat black legs. A goat bleated, was answered by other
bleats. A heavy smell of dung.

'On your way.'

Amazed at my good fortune, I sped home. With my bright-red
backpack flashing. But that was enough. I suppose even uniforms
talk.

Paolo refused to let the policemen enter when they came,
demanded to speak to a superior officer. None appeared. But the
next day, Paolo was summoned to the city. The charity he worked
for had an office there. We stayed inside all that day, sniffing the air.
Azira worked hard to make a meal with the bad bananas and rice
Paolo had in his kitchen, and then I read her some of the Bible. All
of us were learning the Bible: me the words, Rebecca and Azira the
stories. Azira was also learning alphabets: Somali first, then Italian.
There are four different scripts for Somali, but I taught her the one
I knew best, based on the Latin.

'It makes more sense to learn these letters, rather than Arabic.'

'But why? I know some of these ones.' She pointed at the Waadad
curls in one of the books Paolo had let me take from school.

'I know. But if you're going to read and write in other countries,
these letters are better.'

'What other countries?'

I felt her fierce breath, the quick look of disbelief and hurt gathered there, ready to fly at me if I said the wrong thing. Azira and I had met on the long road to Dadaab. She was fleeing with her village, I with the remnants of mine. I'd recognised her brother-in-law, vaguely, from some gathering. He was struggling to drive on his children, his pregnant wife, a single goat and his wife's young sister. My Azira. It was easy to fall into conversation with them. Easy to sink into her wide brown eyes and secret smile. Easy to offer to protect her, to lie beside her in the shifting, bumping vehicles that smuggled us over one mountain or border to the next. Unaccompanied women rarely arrived at the camps unscathed. Many married ones met the same fate. I heard the screams, once, of a husband forced to watch his wife I did not nothing nothing nothing you cannot hear that you can never hear that. So.

Yes. So. Azira and I fell in love, as simply as falling into water. I suppose I loved her before I knew her. Knowing her, though, made me love her more. Such a quick, bright intelligence. So funny. So hungry for learning and debate. That is one thing I will thank my brutalised country for. Without our wars and troubles, Azira would have been shackled to a fat old man instead of me. But, lacking parents, dowry, roots, she was allowed to become a boatless fisherman's wife. And oh my God, how I loved her. Was consumed by her.

Still am.

'The other countries we might move to,' I said in answer to her question. 'This place is not our home.'

'Where is our home, Abdi?'

'I don't know. But here is good for now.'

At Paolo's house, we had flourished. We, who had known no

stability, were able to work and learn and laugh and raise our beautiful daughter. The day Rebecca was baptised, I was baptised also. Azira didn't want to be, but that was fine, because she was still deciding: I had a wife who was not commanded, who decided things. Very odd, I know; I was seen as an object of derision – yes, but by men who'd never known a freely given kiss, nor a woman who would reach for them because it was her choice. So I didn't care.

It was three days before Paolo returned. He was quiet, drawn. We shared some *shaah*. Even Rebecca sat up at the table with us, to drink a cup of milk. A table is a European thing; at first it was awkward to be so high and straight. Food took too long to drop down to my belly. But then I liked it. The table became a place to study and to share. To have a table was to be . . . was to have some impetus, I suppose. To be higher out of the dust.

When Rebecca was in bed, we ate the food Azira had prepared and Paolo told us about his meeting. His job was pastoral, educational, he was advised. It was a valuable role, to be shared amongst many. And, as such, it was important he be seen as an 'impartial resource'. Consequently, his employers had warned him that he was not allowed to be directly involved with any individual or specific family's welfare.

Azira had made spaghetti. It was cooked too long, and there was very little sauce. We struggled on, all of us chewing and sucking, Paolo talking haltingly in Somali.

'What they really meant is that they cannot – or will not – guarantee my safety within the camp if I'm seen to be "taking sides".' Paolo's fingers made little pounces in the air when he said that. 'They say . . . Abdi, they say you are a thief. And that you assaulted a policeman.'

'Father, that is not true! Abdi was protecting –'

'Have we to leave?' I asked.

'No! You're my assistant schoolmaster. I told them it's vital to my work that you're available to support me. And I *know* you wouldn't ... But I don't know how ... I'm not sure if I have a strong position any more.'

'You mean the next time the police come to bully us, they might not leave. Ugh,' Azira pushed her bowl away. 'I'm sorry. This is disgusting. We'd none of that tomato paste you like. I thought this would taste all right.'

'Azira, please. It's fine,' I said.

Paolo speared another forkful. 'It's delicious.'

There was a moment's pause, each of us caught in a little arc, before we started laughing.

'Father Paolo,' said Azira, pulling his dish towards her. 'Today I learned the word "patronise". There is a good way to patronise and a bad way, yes? You must only do the good way!'

I was so proud of her that night. Her wit and her courage. Paolo told us his plan. If Azira was to convert to Christianity also, he might be able to argue that we were being religiously persecuted in the camp, that our lives were at risk.

'But they *are*,' said Azira. 'They play with us, pick us out. Three times in a row, I've been refused my rations. They say my papers are wrong, but they're not.'

'Yes, but police harassment isn't a recognised category. It does not exist, you understand? If I could get you away from here. To some other country. At least to another camp.'

And he did. Eventually, we were moved to a camp in Sudan. God bless him, Father Paolo arranged a teaching job for me there, said I was working with his Christian charity. But we were still stateless refugees. We stayed there ten months, until the school was burned. Anti-Christian sentiment. Those bloody Muslims . . .

Azira was still a Muslim. Every time I raised the subject, she would brush it away. Mutter about jinns and bad luck and I'd say: 'Don't be stupid. Look at me – I'm still here. We got away from Dadaab, yes?'

'Look at your stupid school all burned, huh? Where was your baby Jesus then? Shows how much use a *nunu* God is.'

Rebecca was almost four by the time we came back to Dadaab. All Christian families were being moved out of the Sudanese camp, there had been too many bouts of 'sporadic' violence. Ach, the sick slump of us as we trundled back through those gates. Dust more bitter, the stinging, thirsty, knowing sun burning up our steps. I imagined its voice like sing-song children chanting rhymes. *See you come; see you go. See you live; see you die.* But I couldn't imagine God above it, watching us and doing nothing.

Father Paolo had gone from Dadaab by then; no one at the school wanted to know me. I wrote to him, though, to say we were back. The tin church he'd preached in was gone too, but I sent the letter to the charity headquarters, in case it might reach him. I'd no hope he could do anything more to help us, I just wanted him to know. *Keeping in touch*, you call it. We were given an even worse hut than before, this time in the Christian section. Beside an open sewer; the hut stank day and night, but I think we were immune to bad smells by then. Our nostrils knew little else. My Rebecca had never tasted the sea air, never stood on a hill and breathed crystal sky. I missed my table. At least we were far on the other side of the camp. Anonymous and small – that way is safest.

And it was. Until the day of the haphazard door.

I found it swinging on its barbed-wire hinge. The three of us had been for rations; me to queue, Azira and Rebecca to gather any leavings from the ground. I'd fashioned our door myself, from scraps and splinters, but it was good. Strong. It would take tough boots to break it open. Inside our hut, everything had been smashed. Clean clothes were trampled in the dirt, the little blue pot Paolo had given Azira when we left was in a thousand pieces. A dead chicken, its belly slit, lay in the middle of our bed.

'Ah well, at least we have a good dinner, huh?'

There was a lilt to Azira's voice, but her eyes held fear. And rage. She had made Rebecca a dolly out of rags. It too had its belly slit.

The cycle began again. Spitting at our feet on the way to market – but this was fellow inmates, not police. No rations, papers wrong. Being stopped and searched by police as we left the Christian area – Azira as well as me. *Your neighbours say you are thief,* gaal. *Well then my neighbours are liars, sir.* Slap. Being made to stand one day in the heat with my hands on my head for six hours. Each time, we surfaced full of anger and despair. Each time, we did nothing. Except I prayed. What way is there out of chaos? The tattooed uniform was gone; I do not think my fame was so great it had preceded me. And it was not only us; other of my neighbours suffered in similar ways. But there is no solace in that.

A month after our chicken dinner, I received a visit, from a white lady. She had worked with Father Paolo, at his new mission in Malawi. I was delighted he'd sent us greetings, and from so far away.

The tight kernel of my heart relaxed a tiny, tiny breath. *God never gives you more than you can bear.*

'Is Father Paolo well?'

'He is better. He had a little fever, but he copes better now.' Even though she'd come with her own armed guard, her every move was uneasy. Furtive, you might say. We spoke in Italian, although her accent was very strange. 'I understand you've had some . . . trouble here?'

'How do you know?'

'That's not important.'

'Please. I am not a troublemaker. If you ask Father Paolo . . . before . . .'

'Mr Hassan. No one is suggesting that you invited this. We . . . the charity, I mean, believe it's because you're Christians. When the . . . If there is trouble, do they say you are hyenas?' She blushes, hugely. 'That you *eat* people? Do they call you names? Christ-lover? Infidel?'

'*Gaal?* Yes, sometimes.'

'You're *all* Christians, Father Paolo tells us. Is that right? Even the little one?'

'Oh yes. She and I were baptised together.'

'And your wife?'

'Um . . . she believes what I believe.'

'But she is not baptised?'

'No. Not yet.'

'Ah. That might be a problem.'

'For what, please?'

The lady was a Catholic. She was arranging a transfer of forty

Christian refugees, a hurried, rushed affair because they had intelligence a raid was being planned.

'We can make no formal application, as that would implicate our source.' All the time, this stilted, formal Italian, and her head dipping back and forth like a nervous bird. 'But there is evidence to suggest raiding parties have been granted – or paid bribes for – access to other camps. Especially to areas at the periphery, like this.'

'But why?'

'There's an unfounded belief Christian families receive considerable alms and support from the Church, which makes them attractive to robbers, as well as fundamentalists. Now, we can't suggest that the Kenyan police are complicit in this ... but they certainly seem powerless to prevent it happening. And it's happening far too often. I mean, Christians are supposed to be housed in with the other vulnerable groups –'

'Ma'am, we are all vulnerable in this camp. Irrespective of our faith.'

Azira arrived back then, with Rebecca. She offered the lady coffee – a good wife. I should have thought of that. In clumsy Somali, the lady said thank you, then, reverting to Italian, told me she'd no time. I couldn't translate in case our neighbours heard, but Azira knew some Italian by then.

'We leave the camp tomorrow evening. From here, we plan to go to Mogadishu, and then get a flight to the UK. Father Paolo was very keen that you come with us.'

Azira gasped, then busied herself with pots and water, telling Rebecca to fetch some beakers. A good wife. Then she had to tell her again: Rebecca would not stop staring at the *mzungo* lady who was in her house.

'I'm sorry,' the lady continued. 'This is all very cloak and dagger. The UN know . . . But,' she shrugged, 'we can't set any precedents. I can take only Christians.'

'I am Christian,' said Azira, in Italian.

'You are?'

'Yes. Every night, I read Bible. You ask me, ask me any story about Bible.'

'You *read*?'

'Hm. My husband teach me.'

'Well. That's very . . . but you're not baptised?'

'You do. Make me now.'

'Oh no, dear, I'm not . . . I mean. Well, you –'

'You bring me priest. Or take me go to one, now.' Azira fell to her knees, pulling on the lady's sunburned arm. '*Please*, lady. Please.' Weeping openly, all the frustrations pouring out of her like brown water in our sewer.

The shock gathered in me, swinging in bolts, in punching fists. Since the haphazard door, we had been light and evasive, saying little and laughing lots. Strung together in tender wires. I hadn't realised her desperation to get out of here was even greater than my own.

I knelt beside her. 'Azira, baby. Don't.' Holding each other hard, her face wet in my chest. Then Rebecca was pushing at my armpit, nuzzling to get in too.

'Please.'

On my head, I felt the pressure of the lady's hand. Her hand, my daughter's hands, my wife's hands. All pressing on to me, me, me. And a feeling like communion. 'You are a Christian family. We will take you all.'

The atmosphere inside the Refugee Council is flat, yet buzzing. Sad gossip lingers behind hands, my roses wilting under the scrutiny of frowns and pursed-up lips. It feels like someone's died. I can see Debs at one of the booths. She's on the phone, but she waves me over. A fat woman in a mighty kaftan tucks her hands under the folds of her breasts and tuts.

Debs mouths: *Hiya.*

'Hello.'

I take a seat. Today Debs is in a brown, short-sleeved dress, sprigged with little creamy flowers – ha! My flowers match her dress. I'm smiling at her with irrepressible pleasure, I know I am, and it feels too bright in this sombre room. But I can't help it. She finishes her call.

'These are for you.'

'Thank you! For why?' She sniffs them, her eyelids lapping shut. 'Mmm. They're gorgeous.' Then she looks at me. 'Och, Abdi, I told you, I'd nothing to do with you getting your new house. It was that Sergeant Heath.'

My smile widens. 'I think you both helped. And I don't think she would like the flowers.'

'Nah. She'd probably eat them. And you. But we should send her a wee note anyway, eh? So, you all ready for the big day? And the painting party – we'll do that the week before you move, OK?'

'Debs — I have to move by this weekend.'

'What? Why?'

'They need the flat we are in now.'

'You're joking!'

People say that a lot here, usually after you've said nothing funny at all. And they often follow it up with 'by the way', which is *via* in Italian and makes no sense to me whatever.

'No. It is no joke. It is real.'

'Aye, well, I wouldn't be so sure about that.' She tapped some keys on her computer. '*Shit*. Still nothing. Actually, you probably are better to grab it now. Quick as possible, after what we've heard this morning.'

'What? What has happened?' The knot in my tie seems to tighten, I am swallowing, swallowing. Of course I will not get this house. Of course I will not get this job.

Stupid refugee.

Debs twists her chair away from her computer. The swing of her is assured. She looks as though she fits here. Behind her looms a stack of files, which she begins to dig through. 'Sorry, Abdi, I need to . . . Ah.' She pulls a sheet of paper from the file. 'Sorry. Yes. Well, the UK Border Agency and Glasgow Cooncil've had a major fall-out over who pays what to who. They've just terminated their accommodation contract with the city. Boom. Just like that. We're waiting for them to put some kind of a statement up on their website, but everyone's going crazy. Hundreds of folk are going to have to move, this place'll probably shut.'

'Shut?'

'Well, if Glasgow isn't housing asylum seekers any more, there'll be no need for the Refugee Council, will there? At least, not here.'

Flashing pictures of gates, of clanging, dull barred doors. Of Debs being lost in a sea of struggling faces. To her, all is casual speculation. The Refugee Council will close and she'll go back to her smart house and her memories, her visit to the poor complete. She dipped her toe in, did her best. Do I sense relief in there with the smooth movements? Shaking us off like troublesome drops of water. But what about *me*? What about me?

'Hello there.' The wide-hipped kaftan woman shimmies into Deborah's space. 'Debs, check your PC again. One of the news agencies is running a story. Try PA first.' She bares enormous white teeth at me, leaning forward until I can see the twin peaks of her cleavage. 'And who is this *fine*-looking gentleman?'

'Gamu, this is Abdi.'

'Ho, so *this* is Abdi. You kept *him* well-hidden, girl.' She offers me a fat, firm hand. 'Hello, Abdi. And you bring flowers too? Now don't waste your time with her, my love. Come talk to me. I'll sort all your problems.'

'No, no problems,' I smile back. 'Only good things today.'

'Yeah? Well, that *is* a nice thing to hear, my love. Especially today. You keep your good things close, OK?' And she gives me a huge long wink, in case I'm too slow to sense the dripping innuendo.

I wink back. 'I will.'

Debs is very quiet. She can't be jealous, surely? I smooth out my tie, look over to see what she's doing. She's frowning at her computer. 'Here, look, Abdi. See for yourself. *Jesus.* Thank goodness you've got that flat. They did confirm it, yes? You've definitely got the letter?'

'Yes.' I squint to read the screen.

'I mean, it shouldn't affect you at all. It's the asylum seekers that're going to suffer.'

Together, we read the news website.

Over a thousand asylum seekers in Glasgow will have to be rehoused after the government terminated its contract to provide them with accommodation.

The UK Border Agency has failed to reach an agreement with Glasgow City Council over charges for asylum seeker accommodation, which it states are already the 'highest in the UK outside London'.

According to the Scottish Refugee Council, concerned asylum seekers have been 'pouring' into their offices for help. A spokesman for the charity said: 'Many of these people have fled traumatic situations involving persecution, torture and violence and have already faced a great deal of uncertainty while waiting for the outcome of their asylum claim.'

Glasgow Council has been providing housing and support services for asylum seekers for 10 years. An insider commented: 'It's a matter of great regret that UKBA has terminated its contract for the council to receive asylum seekers.'

A spokesperson for the UKBA said, in the face of current cuts to government budgets, it could not continue to pay Glasgow Council's high charges: 'We will work with other providers to ensure all asylum seekers currently housed under contract with Glasgow Council continue to be properly accommodated while their asylum claims are considered and their appeals to the courts are concluded.'

Charity groups have expressed doubt that other housing providers in the city will be able to offer enough accommodation, and speculation is now rife that Glasgow's asylum population may be dispersed across the UK with only a few days' notice.

Readers' comments (1) There are to many on the waiting lists to house people coming in from abroad like this. There are to many local authoritys homes tied up in this way. There are plenty of cheap providers – let them do it.   Anonymous

'Och, don't look at that rubbish. They can't even spell.'

Debs tries to pull the screen away from me, but I hold it steady until I'm finished reading.

'Do you think these people know who we are? What we come from?' My head is getting heavy. A thickness building in my nose; it's the flowers. 'Is there a way to talk to them? I would like to talk to them. Ask if they had to flee their nice houses and jobs, snatch up their children and run from men with guns, run from their own government who beats and robs their people, where it is they would go. What it is they would hope for.'

Debs is shrugging her jacket on. 'Och, Abdi. Folk who make comments like that can't empathise. All they know is what they read in the tabloids – which would make you a mad pirate as well as a job-and-house-stealing mugger of old ladies. But,' as she stands up, she gently tugs my tie, 'a very smart one, too, I must say. Now, are we going for lunch or what? And by the way, if you're all dressed up because we're off somewhere posh, you can forget about paying for it, OK?'

'Why? Will we run away instead?'

For a long blank second, Debs looks horrified, until I add: 'When they bring the bill?'

'Ha, ha, very funny.'

I'd said in my text I'd take Debs for lunch. That is what friends do. I hear them on the television, there is even a programme called *Friends*, and, always, always, they are meeting for coffee or lunch. Problem is, I don't eat lunch. And I don't know where to go. So I asked my friend Geordie. Geordie is a cultured man.

'You like poetry, Abdi?'

'You know I do.'

'And you like the oldness of this city, the history? Yes?'

'Yes.'

'And you are no longer good Muslim, so the alcohol won't matter?' He had waggled lush eyebrows above his spectacles.

'No. I am a fallen man,' I laughed, although I've never tasted alcohol. But I suppose the potential's there. Geordie closed the book he'd been reading. We were in the library, of course. Rebecca was enjoying Story Corner, I could see her listening intently as the librarian read to a cluster of children. Occasionally, her mouth would form circles and slants. Practising. I'm still not sure where it is Geordie lives. He sighed portentously. Took off his glasses, dabbed his moustache. 'Yesterday, Abdi, a man handed me a lucky ticket. He was tourist. American. It was for open-top bus trip round the town. Very good, he said. Very, very good. And he was finished with it, and would I like it? Is not like half-eaten fish supper, you know? Half-used bus ticket is OK, so I said yes. Up on the bus I go. Oh, Abdi, it was mar-vel-oos. You should take the little one, you see the city most different. They give you little plugs, too, for your ears, and a commentary in several languages. And, fortuitously for you, we pass the very place. Ancient hostelry, nestled on the banks of the mighty Clyde, and home to folk club and poets' retreat.'

'Sounds good. And do they have lunch?'

'Oh yes. Very very best of Scottish cuisine.'

And it's in the city centre too. We checked it on Mr Google. So *that* is where we are going. Debs and I walk into the sunshine. She's left her flowers out of water, on her desk, but I don't mind. I am bursting, bursting to say about my job, but walking, I can't keep sight of her face. It bobs and weaves below me. We go through streets teeming with people, most of them eating from paper bags, walk past Central Station, with its big grand hotel rising over it. A curious statue of a man in a face-mask stands outside the door. A miner? A fireman? He is big and sturdy and blank.

'Where is it we're going?'

'The Scotia Bar,' I say proudly.

'Really?'

'Yes? Why? Is that not good? Geordie said it was a very good place –'

'Geordie? Our Geordie? Iraqi Geordie?'

'*Yes.*' I sound defensive.

'I wouldn't have thought an old man's pub would be his kind of place.'

'Old man's pub? It is a folk club and poets' retreat.'

'Oh, OK.'

'Do you not like it, Deborah?'

'Well, I don't think I've ever actually been. It's the one in Stockwell Street? With the black and white beams?'

'It is.' I have seen the picture on Google. I will recognise it, I'm sure.

We pass the department store where we bought Rebecca's wellington boots, carry on down Glassford Street and into Stockwell Street. Wait for a gap in the buses, then cross the road, the bulky glass dome of St Enoch's shopping centre to the right of us. Ahead, a lone black-grey spire reaches up to the sky. It seems to jut straight through the roof of a lower, paler building which is adorned with curlicues of fish and coiled serpents. The steeple is like a tree growing through a crack. An optical illusion, surely. I would ask, but it's been some time since either of us spoke, and with each quiet step we take, it's harder to start a conversation. One more crossing, and we are outside the Scotia Bar. It's further than I realised, and I worry that Debs will be late getting back to the Council. She must mean to go back – she left her roses there.

In front of us, the slow brown water of the Clyde slips by. There was a ford here, once, so Geordie says. Medieval Glaswegians would wade, or paddle coracles, to move from north to south. Now, many iron and marble bridges traverse the river. Turn your head left, turn right, and all you see are spans of bridges, some squat, some graceful. There is one stringed swinging beauty over there that looks to me like a harp. Only people walk on it. Most of the bridges are thunderous with traffic or trains. What would my mother have thought of these speeding, roaring hulks that eat you up and carry you off? I'd never have got her inside one, that's for sure. *It is an evil jinn, child. Do not trust the evil jinn!*

We stand outside the bar. The walls are rugged dirty-white,

panelled with black strips. Each panel outside bears a painted board, with the legends:

Pool and Beer
Mince and Tatties
Real Ales and Real People

Two men contemplate us through blue smoke. Their faces are weathered and tracked with broken veins. One is gangly, his mouth fallen in on empty gums. The other is small, wears a cap. The one with no upper teeth clicks his tongue. 'All right, folks?' A little flurry of spittle accompanies his words.

'Well,' sniffs Debs, her hand on the brass doorplate. She pushes, and a waft of warmth, of dark polished wood and live bodies and malt rushes out. Inside I can see long red benches and glittering brass. From somewhere hidden, a curl of music rises thinly. It is a fiddle, I think.

'Well,' repeats Deborah. 'I'm sure it'll be fine.'

IT IS FINE, actually. The food, I mean. I have steak pie, Abdi has the fish. We're pretty much done now, but he pokes the remainder of it with his knife. Our table is a play of intersecting sun and shade, four neat squares reflecting from the window behind Abdi on to the surface, slicing dark smooth wood with bouncing light.

'Why is so much orange? Your beer is orange, that fizzy stuff you drink is orange, every food you eat is crispy-fried-and-crumbs orange.' He holds up a piece of fish, screwing up his eyes as if he's examining it. 'Hello, Mr Fish. Yes, all nice fruity colours – and yet, you people never eat fruit.' Grinning widely as he gabbles. My fault; I suggested we have some wine to celebrate. Mentoring Abdi in the wicked ways of the west. Well, we were both getting a bit gloomy thinking about the Refugee Council. *Shit*. Oops, pardon me. I check my watch. I should really be getting back, but you feel a bit pointless, sitting there behind your desk, with not a clue what to tell those desperate faces. So many lives about to be turned upside down. *We'll sort it out*, I've assured him. *There'll be marches, protests. Don't you worry*. But I know it's taken the shine off Abdi's excitement. God love him, he even asked if Geordie could come and live in his new flat. So, if a wee drop of cheap white wine can get his fizz back, then where's the harm? He's a big boy, he doesn't need to keep drinking it. And we're pals again, proper pals having lunch and sharing a laugh.

'Don't forget most of our women are orange too.' I nod towards a skinny blonde who's propping up the bar. I say blonde, but she's really platinum, with skin so tanned I'm not surprised she's wearing sunglasses. Abdi sloshes us both another glass of wine.

'A toast!' His voice is a little too loud.

'Another one? What for now?'

He clears his throat. 'Today, I have very good news.'

Not again. I lift my glass. 'And I say once more: To your new hoose. Lang may your lum reek.'

'Ah, no, not my house . . .'

'Old Mr Bullmore's deid?'

'Deborah! As you know, Mr Bullmore and I no longer converse. Since his return from the hospital he has been most subdued. I believe Sergeant Heath may have visited him again. But I do not wish him to be dead. No. *Dear friend*. Today . . .' he is bouncing in his seat. The tie, loosened by now, veers slightly to the left and the dip of his collarbone is glistening. I watch him lick his lips. His every move is taut with concentration. 'I have also got a job!'

'Oh, Abdi!' I clap my hands, foolishly like a little girl. 'How? Where?'

His finger waves admonishment. 'Do not pretend, my dear, dear friend. Before I come here, I have the interview. The interview your dear, kind brother has made for me?'

I had completely forgotten. At Gill's that night, at dinner, I'd given Richard Abdi's details, asked if there was anything he could do about the apprentice scheme. But the sneaky bugger had not said another word. I notice the blonde girl staring at us. At Abdi, to be fair. He *is* a handsome man, but it's not his face. There is lightness about him, a luminosity that's striking. It's not gaudy, or brash. There's a dignity to him I've never seen before. He is a bright patch of satisfaction. The woman smiles at him, and he gives her a steady grin.

Aye. *Buggers*. Plural. 'Is that right? And why did no one tell me?'

'Pah. We are men together. We talk, we decide. Why should a very un-orange woman be consulted of manly things?'

I find myself rising in my chair, planting a kiss, hard on his cheek. The scrape and the soap-smell, dizzying.

'Well done you!' I arrange myself back on my chair, pulling it further from the table. 'That is just fantastic. Tell me all about it.'

'I start in one month's time! Apprentice fishmongerer.'

'Mong*er*.'

'Mong-ger then!' He rolls his eyes. 'We have training and college, and we work with supervisors. At the end I will get a certificate and –'

'Fish college? What about going to study English?'

'I can do that too. My work college is only one day, my training is for two. It is very, very excellent. They do it so for people with benefits, they can still train.'

The more wine he consumes, the looser his sentence structure becomes. It's quite sweet. I forget to be annoyed that Richard never consulted me, or that Abdi never cracked a light. I am a *good* mentor, so I am. My little mentee is flying the nest . . .

'And they have part-time work when I am qualify, so even if I train to be a teacher, I can still make money.'

'What about Rebecca?'

'I know, I know.'

'If she was going to school this year, it would make it so much simpler.'

'Yes. Well, she is not. I have speak –' he frowns '– spoken to Mrs Coutts, and she will watch her one day. The college has a crèche, so she can go there when –'

'Abdi, I've been talking to my sister. She's a teacher too, a headteacher. And she told me about this special language unit. We might still be able to get Rebecca in it this year. She'd need to go to a place called a child development centre first –'

'At a crèche she will play quite happily. Is no assessments, I do not think. Just water and sands. I will tell them she is very, very quiet . . .'

My hand is tingling. It's adamant it wants to thump him. 'Abdi, you have to face up to this. It's great you're moving on – but what about Rebecca? You've lost your wife, but she's lost her mummy.' I hear my voice quaver a wee bit as I teeter, then dip on wine-soaked rails into . . . I dunno. A rollercoaster of prim self-pity, a Hollywood speech? 'Believe me, I know what it feels like when someone who's your whole life just isn't there any more. It tears you apart –'

'Thank you, Deborah.' He takes my hand and kisses it. Refusing

222

to let me upset his equilibrium. And I know what he's going to ask me now, and I know I'm going to say yes. I want to.

'From my heart. You have made so big changes to me. I trust you. I hope you trust me.'

'Mmm.'

I wait for the request, smooth out my poker-face. *Please will you watch Rebecca on the other day?* But it doesn't come.

'Why do you think we were matched? Is it because you have lost your husband and I my wife? Did you ask for this? For a lonely man? Because sometimes I think it is that you project your emotions on to me.'

'Project my emotions?'

'Yes. Like I am your mirror. If you feel a certain way you think that I will too. I am grateful for my life, Deborah. I do not want to look backwards, only forward. Rebecca will do the same.'

'Well, that's just bullshit.'

'Is it?'

I am furious. 'Why? Did you have a choice about me?'

'I had a choice to say no.' He takes a sip of wine. 'And then I met you, and I said yes. But you have not answered me.'

I am in a dark beer-stained tunnel whizzing far too fast. This insistence on honesty, who started it again? 'No, I did not ask for a lonely-hearts date, if that's what you're implying. In fact, do you want to know how I got you? Do you really bloody want to know?'

'Yes.'

'OK then. I asked that it could be someone from Africa.'

'Why Africa?'

I change my position. The light's shining directly in my eyes. The sly wine gleams in my glass as I lift it, see the greasy slide of it up and down, up and down. *Push-me, pull-you.* Suddenly I find it very *vitale* to do this, to be horribly, plainly honest.

'Some of my husband's family were from Africa . . .'

Abdi's eyes widen. I imagine his chest expanding, poised to welcome me as one of his own.

'*South* Africa. White, not black.'

He makes that eloquent *Ah* that he does.

'Yeah, so. I spent some time there when I was younger. Just a month, you know?' I drain my glass. At the bottom, in the dregs, fragments of my steak pie rest.

Know the worst of me, then see what's left.

'I didn't like what I saw.'

The woman flourished her feather wand, and all her clothes fell off. Nothing but a golden G-string to cover her modesty. The crowd clapped furiously, even Callum and his pinched, prudent mum, but I was embarrassed for the poor soul up on stage. She had a lovely voice, had pretty much been the star of the show, while all around her topless girls danced and pranced the night away – a plume of ostrich feathers each and the spindliest of heels giving them their stature. The woman's nipples were also clad in gold, and I wondered what she felt as she painted them on in her dressing room. Was this, for her, the grand finale, or the denouement she'd been dreading? Gold tips waiting under that gorgeous dress?

'Wow, what a show!' Callum beamed at me, and I at him, conscious his mother was watching.

'Well. Shall we go for suppa now, my boy?' Myra cut between us, stroking my husband's cheek. 'Fatten you up a little, hu? They do terrific steak here. Oh, isn't Sun City marvellous?'

Callum saved his broadest smile for her. I took his arm, squeezed until he returned his attention to me. That was one of the very few parts of Callum that stayed, right until the end. His smile. On our good days, I'd call him my Cheshire Cat, and he'd elongate it further, till the tilt of his cheek met the droop of his eyes. But then, there, it was strong and full, it was lips that searched mine and pushed in hard and I loved them. Just the look of them, knowing they were mine, what they had whispered to me last.

'Can we just head home, Ma? I think Debs is a little tired.'

Immediately, Myra's eyes slid from him to me. 'Oh. What a shame. We'd planned to make a real evening of it.'

'But we still can, Ma. How about we go home and you make us some of your fantastic *vetkoek*?'

'Honestly, I'm fine,' I said, squeezing ever harder. Why were men so stupid? *Vetkoek* were greasy dough balls that she insisted on stuffing with some kind of curried meat. I think it was beef, but I was scared to ask.

'You don't like my *vetkoek*, Debs? Shame. I was going to show you how to make them for my boy.'

'No, I love it.' *I've had them twice already since we got here.* 'It's just – everything makes me feel sick at the moment.'

Going for the sympathy vote here. You too were a woman once, Myra.

'Ach. Everyone moans about the sickness. Me, I was fine, fine, fine. You just have to get on with it, Debs. That's what life's about, you know.'

Callum returned my squeeze. I think he thought I was being affectionate. 'Remember Debs isn't used to the heat, Ma.'

'Tchu.' She clacked her tongue. 'You should be here when it's really hot. My! Even my house-girl scuttles into the shade, but me, I just keep going.' She jiggled the cheek of Callum's father, who had returned from the cloakroom with a pile of jackets. 'Someone has to run this family, eh?'

'What's that, darling?'

An apparently absent-minded, mild man, Callum's dad seemed to float through life, his wife tethering him to the world. I liked him, hugely. Even Myra mellowed when he came close. He'd been very kind to me since we'd arrived – suggesting we all take things easy, limiting Myra's mad schedule of braais and excursions to no more than one a day. The odd conspiratorial wink, or an arm offered as we strolled round the garden, suggested that he was actually far more present than absent. He'd clearly decided that, since retiring to South Africa to placate his wife, he'd bob gently on the surface, while she swam with the sharks. Well, it was her natural territory.

'Family, Angus. We're talking about family.'

He kissed the top of my head. 'And what a beautiful family we have. Soon to be even more beautiful, thanks to this clever girl. Shall we head for home, dear daughter-in-law? I don't know about you, but I'm all spangled out.'

'Oh but look – there's the Swanepoels. Oona!'

A blonde woman returned Myra's wave, but kept walking. 'Ach, just one drink, Daddy, then we'll go. Oona! Oona!'

One drink turned into many. When the Swanepoels learned

Callum was the Maxwells' son – that we were Scottish, just like funny old Angus! – they insisted that whisky be fetched to join the wine and beer. And when they realised I was pregnant (not simply fat), well, champagne was called for too. I sat and sipped my Coke, but I didn't mind the lack of alcohol. Callum and I had tried so hard to have a baby ... I find it hard to remember, even now. To *remember* – what am I saying, it's carved into my pointless gut. I remember each and every cell. Four little lost people.

Four.

But now it seemed that this one was here to stay, I would have happily sipped plain water for the rest of my life. We'd never told Callum's parents about our troubles, nor my mum and dad. I let them think I was selfish for making them wait. I don't know why. Because it was better than letting them know I was faulty and should be returned to the shop? That my womb was as inhospitable as an Afrikaner mother-in-law?

The Swanepoels were nice people. More folk joined us – Mrs Swanepoel's sister and her husband, plus two of their friends. The friends, both older men, were a bit more raucous, the type who think it funny to tell jokes about *kaffirs* as black waiters bring them drinks. But it was fine. We laughed and drank, ate some nibbles (chewy leather on a stick, anyone?). Then Mr Swanepoel started talking about going to a 'duck shoot'. All the men laughed, except Callum.

'What do they mean, Dad?' he whispered.

'Och, it's just an excuse for a piss-up, son. Erik's got a wee outhouse on his land. Men only, pool table, darts. Got a nice big fridge an all.'

Erik Swanepoel leaned over to our wee huddle. 'You coming, son-of-Angus man?'

Myra answered for him. 'Of course he is, Rikki. Let my son see what he's missing by not coming to live in Africa, hu?' She patted Callum's knee. 'Miss you, baby boy.'

'Och, Mum, we need to get back –'

'Nonsense.' She downed another gulp of wine. 'Erik has a great big Land Rover, don't you, Rikki?'

'I do indeed. Boy!' He clicked his fingers at a passing waiter. 'Get me my car keys. Quickie-quick, yes?'

'So. You and Daddy go have some fun. I'll take poor Debs home.' Myra smiled wanly at me. 'She's finding all this *so* hard, aren't you, dear?'

The baby did a little kung-fu kick. *Kill Granny, darling. Kill her!* He'd only begun to stir in the last few days, and we guarded each movement jealously. As soon as I went 'oop', Callum would know junior was shifting, and he'd rush over to cup my belly. But not here. I wasn't sharing *here*.

'I'm fine.'

'No, no. You're looking very . . . grey. I shall miss the duck shoot and take you home.'

'You weren't even invited to my duck shoot, lady!' said Erik.

'Is that so?' His wife pretended to smack him. 'Well, just for that, I will come also, Erik Swanepoel.'

'Never! A woman in *my* clubhouse . . .'

'Tch. Clubhouse! I mean, it's just a little shack. Well, as I am your driver for the evening, darling,' poking her husband's belly, 'I think you'll find that I will decide. So, I will have the ladies back to the house, and you lot can go and play at being savages.'

There was a lot of laughter at this, especially as a young black boy dressed as a Masai warrior had just brought Erik his keys. I tried to make Callum look at me, but he'd been swallowed into the beery belly of camaraderie, was earnestly explaining the difference between blended and malt. Even my saviour Angus was entering the fray, growing more pseudo-Scottish by the minute. 'Ach away, ya daft gowk. You canny whack an Islay malt.'

Beside me, Myra struggled to get out of her seat. Her skinny arms folded in on themselves as she tried to push up from squashy suede.

'Can I give you a hand, Myra?'

She slapped me away. 'Don't fuss, girl. This stupid couch is slippy.'

I put on my jacket and waited for her to rise. Noticing she finished her wine first.

'OK,' said Mrs Swanepoel. 'All the men in my car please. I shall drop you reprobates off somewhere in the bush. Um – Myra – do you have room for Monique in your car?'

'Sureoona.' The affirmation, Mrs Swanepoel's name; it all came out in one word. 'You'll come withus, Monnie, yes?'

Mrs Swanepoel's sister Monique was slumped in a corner of the banquette. At the mention of her name, she giggled. 'S'long as there's more alcohol, I'll go with anyone!'

'A woman after my own heart,' said my mother-in-law.

'Myra,' I said quietly. 'Please let me drive.'

'Nonsense. You're not insured, girl. And it's very, very dark – you're not used to our roads.'

'But I think you've maybe had too much wine . . .'

Myra Maxwell fixed two deep and glinting bayonets on me, and I think the truth of our relationship revealed itself right then.

'Who are you to lecture me in front of my husband and my son? You are a guest, you are a –' she stopped abruptly before the final thrust, perhaps conscious that her voice had risen, or that once she really started she wouldn't be able to stop? It didn't matter. No one else appeared to have heard. I shrugged, tried to fight back tears. The Maxwells had retired to South Africa before we even got engaged, but I know she saw me as the reason she was irrevocably parted from her son. Without me, he'd have joined them in her beloved Jo'burg, and her family would be complete. And if this holiday was meant to convince me to move here too . . . no, I don't think it was, I truly don't think Callum was ever that duplicitous. But even in the space of a few short weeks, I hated the way he'd subsumed himself, subtly altering his speech, his manner, himself, to suit his mum.

We all trooped outside – men at the front, women to the rear. Our cars had been brought round, of course. It gave the black boys the chance to drive a big car, and the white folks the excuse to clean up the steering wheel. Seriously, that's what Myra did. She opened up the glove box, took out a pack of baby wipes and slid one round the grip of the wheel.

'There. Everybody comfy?'

From the back seat, Monique groaned. I said nothing, just stared out of the window, into the grasping night. There were layers of black and blacker, humps that uncurled and moved as we drove through the compound's gates, following the red eyes of the Swanepoels' tail-lights. The humps were children, begging by the roadside. Myra had explained to me before we left that we were going to a different country. 'Well, kind of. Sun City is in

Boputhatswana. They don't allow gambling in South Africa, see.' I don't know if Sun City still exists, but the way she told it, the casino was an act of benevolence; it brought jobs and money to this poor and scrubby piece of homeland.

'Aye. How much of it stays there, though?' That was Callum, but he said it, quietly, to me.

As we bounced over rutted roads, the red chips of light in front would disappear, blink, then disappear again. Each time we caught sight of the tail-lights, the distance between us and the Swanepoels' truck was wider, until eventually the lights disappeared entirely. In the back seat, Monique snored. In the front, I clutched the padded arm-rest of my door, focusing on the jittering beams of our head-lights, which pointed the way like two arthritic fingers. Just a strip of barely-there asphalt, then layers and bands of black-grey-black, but, beyond that, there was nothing. Of course there were many nothings: the black rustling trees that lunged at the windscreen, a distant, animal ululation, the thick unpleasantness that sat between me and my mother-in-law. The low, seeping sky that was everywhere.

Even in ink-thick darkness, you could tell sky from land. There were no clouds, no moon that I could find, but I'd never seen so many pale stars. From some muffled, nearby place, a creature leapt – not at us, but to the side of us. Myra cursed, fumbled her gear change. Again and again, grinding up and down until I was sure the transmission would fall out. Then she found her slot, moved smoothly into gear. Began to pick up her speed. I sensed she was panicking without the guiding lights of the Swanepoels' vehicle; there were moments when I'm sure she lost the road entirely, and we swung and clattered on to rock or scrub. When this happened, her shoulders would dip and, with an apparently languid pull, she'd guide the steering wheel back to where it should be. Never acknowledging her near-miss – or me. The grim inevitability of her movements was terrifying. I, too, kept my eyes ever-forward. If I could just concentrate on the road, I thought, I could keep our cargo steady. The force of my will alone would prevent us from veering into the bush. Faster and faster – was she goading me to speak? Well, it worked, because I ended up yelling: 'Will you slow down, Myra?' Then: 'For Christsake!' when she contin-ued to ignore me.

'What is wrong with you, girl? I thought you wanted to get home?'

I didn't answer, but my shouting seemed to have slapped her out of it, because she did slow, a little. Her damp lips pursing, dropping her rigid elbows closer to her sides. We were coming to a clearing, you could make out lighter shadows where the bush had been cut away and that was how you could see it all: you could see the two dark shapes, you could see the graceful curve and the balanced basket. You could even see the swinging V of hands being held as mother and child walked by the side of the road and then you could see the skittering sky. The stars and the shapes and the dull, dull thud. The rise of the vehicle as it surmounted and drove on, drove on and the dull, dull distant wailing and you shouting, screaming. *Myra! Go back! We need to stop!*

I feel Abdi lift up my hand. 'What happened? Were they hurt? Were you hurt?'

I take my hand away. I can't have him near me. I am filthy with sweat. 'No. I wasn't hurt. But the child was. I'm sure he would have died.'

'It was not your fault, Deborah. The hospitals in Africa, the poverty. It is –'

'The child never got to hospital.'

'Ah.'

'The child never got to hospital because we never stopped.'

It doesn't matter how many times I relive it in my head. How often I prove to myself that I screamed, that I shook her, grappling with her wrists until she slapped me, hard. And she was screaming too. 'It's an ambush, you stupid girl. You're pregnant – do you want to be slit from groin to neck, because that's what these people will do?'

'But I saw you hit him!'

I had seen his little face turn to stare at the fancy car. His small hand raised to wave as we smashed through the side of him.

'It's just an act. They train their children to fall beside the car, then when we stop –' Myra struck the steering wheel – 'you are robbed, you are raped. And you – you would have your unborn child torn from you even as they cut your throat. This is where I live, Deborah. I *know* these people.'

'Get out and check your car, Myra! You'll see if you hit him –' My lungs were raw with screaming.

Finally, in the back seat, Monique stirred. Her head appeared in the mirror behind us. 'What's happening? Whatisit?'

'Nothing, Monnie. You go back to sleep.'

All I can see is the little smiling boy. Smiling, big eyes, smiling then he drops. A skin closing over my throat. My double-heart beating too hard, my pitiful hands protecting my belly. So full of tears I couldn't see. And still we were driving, ever further away.

'An ambulance would not come out here,' Myra hissed. 'And how could they pay for a doctor anyway? They will have medicine men, that's all they use. They don't trust the white doctors.'

'But we have to go back, Myra.'

'And what? You want me to go to prison? You want to tell Callum that you put his mother in jail?'

Tyres thrusting forward, each second and minute moving us on. I curled on my side in the front seat, nursing my cheek where she'd struck me. When we got to a phone, I would call the police. And I'd call an ambulance and I'd send it to – where? The car bumped over a pothole, my stomach swilled into my mouth.

'Now look, here we are.' Myra patted my knee. 'This is the entrance to the Swanepoels' land. See? We are here now, and none of this ever happened.'

A massive floodlight shone on electric gates. Silently easing open as we rolled towards them, then through and into a long bright drive. White pebbles and white urns and white light scourging my eyes, shining on an ornamental stream.

'And what would you say to Callum now, even if it was true?' Myra's voice was sugar-soft. 'That you saw it and did nothing? You have come all the way here and done nothing? What kind of a woman would do that?'

Carefully, she drove our car off the clean white pebbles. Aimed it at where the water met land, and drove swiftly through the stream's shallow breadth. A loud volley of ducks rose up in protest.

★ ★ ★

I unclench my eyes. Abdi sits across from me, saying nothing but his hands are flapping crazily, the heels of his palms are drumming and drumming on the table edge as if he is pushing it away to a rhythm I can't comprehend.

'Did you hear me? I said we never stopped.'

The drumming ceases. 'Ah.'

He stares at his hands, which are safely returned to his lap.

'I was scared, Abdi. She told me it was an ambush. I didn't know what to do –'

'Did you believe that you hit the child?'

'Yes.'

'Then you should have stopped.'

Sometimes his English is too blunt. Its directness is strident and rude. If I turn this back on him, if I blame his ignorance, then I will not . . . I haven't weakened. I've been honest; I have offered my dishonesty truthfully, let it slither out of me like a half-dead child.

Oh.

Oh.

Crying would wash this all down, it would ease it out. So I need to stay dry. I want it to hurt me as hard as it can.

'If I could go back. If I could change it . . .'

His neutral expression can't mask his disgust. And it doesn't really matter what he thinks of me, because I think it all myself.

'I was scared for my baby, Abdi. Do you understand that? You have Rebecca – you'd do anything to protect her, wouldn't you? That's why you won't let her go to school.'

Only now does he raise his head. 'Your baby?'

'I was pregnant at the time.'

This is my story. I can tell it how I like.

'I thought you had no children. Many times now, I am not sure what it is you say to me.'

'My baby was called Stephen. He was born three months after we were in Africa. And he lived for seven hours.'

In each of those seven hours I had willed him on, and I had thought of that mother by the roadside, doing exactly the same.

On my glass there is a smear of light, a brilliant translucent streak that runs halfway round the rim, accentuating my lipstick. In the bottom, there are the crumbs from my mouth, on the side a finger-print. All the places I have touched, and, if I move it, the light will go. I rub my thumb across the surface.

'So. There. Now you know. That's why I wanted to help some-one from Africa. And I couldn't . . . I never told Callum. Or anyone. Only you.'

Abdi's head is down again, he's looking back in his lap. Knee jigging at the same speed his hands were – he's texting on his bloody phone.

'Deborah. We need to go. Geordie's been detained at Brand Street.'

13. JULY

THE GLASGOW TOWER

Once the second City of the Empire, Glasgow is still Scotland's largest city, where thousands of people live and work in an ever-developing cityscape. Walk along the Clydeside and you can chart Glasgow's proud industrial heritage: from the Tall Ship Glenlee *and the glory days of sea-borne trade, past the Finnieston Crane – a mighty relic of when Glasgow was the world's shipbuilder – to the shiny new media and financial districts, there's proof this adaptable city will always seek new ways to thrive.*

Key amongst modern attractions is the Glasgow Science Centre. This glittering glass and titanium dome is a fascinating complex for curious minds, with its Planetarium, Imax, Science Mall and the Glasgow Tower: Scotland's tallest freestanding building.

Thanks to its aerodynamic design, the tower is the first building in the world able to rotate 360 degrees into the wind. Five hundred spiral steps (or a nice quick lift!) will take you 127 metres up to the viewing pod, for panoramic views north, south, east and west.

Combine this sky-high thrill with science workshops, shows and interactive exhibits and you have the perfect day out for schools, families; anyone, in fact, who wants to be challenged and inspired by thoughts of a brighter future.

Please note, admission charges apply.

★

WE WERE TOO late to save him. By the time I'd got back to the Refugee Council and tried to organise a lawyer, Geordie was gone. Patient, trusting Geordie, who'd sat quietly in the room they'd put him in at Brand Street, who had walked without fuss through the outside door, had said nothing when a uniformed arm gripped his elbow, and, when another slid open the door of the van, had mutely stepped inside. Only then did he ask if he could use his phone. He rang here first, the Refugee Council. What with the accommodation contract being cancelled that day, all those clients coming in or phoning, petrified they were going to be moved, the press demanding comments and spokespeople, me late back and the Refugee Council a volunteer down . . . Well, Geordie phoned. And his was one of those calls that rang and rang, then stopped. Another phone started just two rings before and the girl who would have lifted his and heard his frightened voice took that call instead. I guess he texted Abdi before they took his phone away. They're not meant to take your phone away. Of course, we thought he'd be taken to Dungavel but, amid all the confusion, and the fact he never turned up there, and then his caseworker making some calls that evening and into the next day, it transpired he'd been moved down south. Straight to Yarl's Wood, do not pass go. He had it coming, you see.

Geordie was one of the legacy cases. One of the keep-your-head-down-and-don't-make-a-fuss-and-we'll-let-you-live-in-limbo cases. In the first influx of asylum seekers coming to Glasgow, the established systems had been unable to cope. Places like Brand Street, the UK Border Agency's outpost in Scotland, had been set up to speed the sifting. Overwhelmed by new applications as well as old, it was inevitable that some fell through the cracks. Geordie was one of them, just another piece of paper gathering dust at the bottom of the pile. Except, one day, eventually, the bottom gets to the top, and they call you in and off you scurry, thrilled at last to be brought into the light. Or maybe I'm . . . what is it Abdi accused me of? Projecting my own emotions. Maybe Geordie wasn't thrilled at all. Maybe he went, knowing this was it. That the length of time this country had taken to pay him any heed at all would finally count against him. *Iraq, you say? Times have changed. Things move on. What 'evidence of torture'?*

As the law requires, they left five days between his detention and Geordie boarding the plane. We tried to get him a visitor. There was a lawyer, too, someone nobody knew, and who never knew Geordie. I don't think there was anything much they could have done. Geordie didn't struggle. He passed through Heathrow Airport as humbly as he passed through here. His quietly living and scribbling out mathematical proofs and troubling no one had not been enough.

'He'd got so close.'

'I know.'

Abdi is still shocked. I am too. How precariously we're balanced. I know this is a trite thing to say, but it's *not* a statistic when it happens to an actual face you can see. It's not our borders one step safer from assault. It's just shite.

That's something else. I'm swearing more. It's like a boil has burst in me and all this filth's coming out. *Goes with the territory, baby doll.* Or so Gamu tells me. *You start to care, you get angry, yeah? And, man, does it feel good.* I'm not sure it does. Like the creep of Abdi's need – the need I invited – plus the where-the-hell-did-that-come-from rupture of my pub confession, it scares the shit out of me. But I can't unknow what I know. And Abdi can't either.

Beyond that manic beating with his hands, Abdi's shown no reaction. South Africa hasn't been mentioned again, and it doesn't seem to alter how he is with me. Or how I feel about myself. It's simply there, hanging like the sky. It is what it is, and I can't change it. There's no sense of relief, absolutely none, although I've never told a soul before. It is entirely uncathartic. As it should be

From up here in the viewing pod above the Science Centre, you can see the whole lazy stretch of Glasgow. Rising towers and spires, the grey blocks, the green parks, the sandstone tiers and terraces. The River Clyde is a slothful worm, oozing and burrowing on its way to meet its estuary. Largely ignored by the city that built herself on its banks, it's too silted-up now for the big ships, too skanky to sit beside. Off to my right, I can see the creamy pavement of the north bank walkway, its concrete bandstand daubed in raucous graffiti. Nice idea to relax by the river, listen to a band. But only jakies sit there of an evening, polishing off their meths. Amazing view all the same. Amazing, too, that this thing's finally working. Since its inception, the Glasgow Tower's become infamous for faults and closures, its sleek and clever design too tricky for the sullen Glasgow weather. But, at last, they seem to have it sorted, and it's a slender silver marvel instead of the white elephant it had threatened to become.

We've finally finished off the painting in Abdi's new flat. There's a cracking view from there too; the block's not as tall as the high-rise he was in before, but this one's on a hill. You can see birds swooping past the windows, see the long parade of Mosspark Boulevard, the green of Bellahouston Park, the darker green of Cardonald Cemetery. This symphony in green is lovely outside, but a bit oppressive within. The previous tenant must've been a Celtic fan, either that or a rampant naturalist, because every wall and a fair helping of the woodwork was various shades of green.

Do I have to keep it –

No!

We'd settled on white – a blank canvas, we agreed – and I'd donated two huge tins of emulsion. Promised I'd be back at the weekend to help him get started, but, oh no, Abdi had tried to do all the painting himself, armed with a single roller. The gap between ceilings and walls was a muddle of patchy blobs.

'Did you not use a brush at the corners?'

'I don't have a brush. The man in the shop said a roller was quicker.'

'Yes, but you still need to do your edges. And you'll need two coats at least. Look, I brought brushes, turps. Here.' I opened my bag of treasure, handed him a paintbrush. 'And I got some nice blue for the bathroom.' I peeled off the plastic lid, so he could see the blue in all its blueness. 'See?'

'I have done the bathroom already.'

'Och, Abdi. I told you you'd to use the waterpoof stuff. Why d'you not wait for me?'

Lamely, Abdi daubed at the gaps on his wall, making pindots of rough colour while resolutely ignoring me.

'Och, give it here.' Tossing my head, mock-chiding. 'For goodness sake, man. Have you never painted a wall before?'

The moment I said it, I wished it back.

'No.'

His ceilings weren't like mine, all lofty and full of their own corniced importance. Abdi's ceilings were low, practical; you could stand on the carpet (also green) and reach the top corners without effort. I eased out the paint, nudging dried blotches into neat lines, pretending my concentration was such that I hadn't heard him, or I needed to keep my tongue poking out between my teeth. Or something like that.

'Wall,' said Rebecca softly. I turned to see her little hand imprinting on the spread of wall below me. Without either of us noticing, she'd managed to get her hand inside the paint pot I had opened. A perfect blue hand waved at us about six inches from the windowsill.

'Wall,' I repeated, my insides tingling. Abdi didn't move. I knelt down so I was eye-level with Rebecca. 'And are we meant to paint the *wall* with our hands, mucky pup?' I lifted up her sticky fingers. 'What is this, madam? Is it a paintbrush? No. It's a *hand*. *H-A-N-D*.'

'Hand.' Glee uncoiling on her face, the irresistible measure of a cheeky grin. Challenging and fearless. A normal, naughty kid. I covered her face with kisses, each kiss provoking a shriek, then I turned her upside down and Abdi tickled her and we bawled and cackled until our bellies ached.

Later, when Rebecca had finally gone to bed – *B-E-D: bed* – and we'd finished the Chinese food I ordered, and Abdi had unwrapped his housewarming present (a set of cream towels and a blue glass vase – *Ha! I bring you flowers and you bring me a vase*), he closed his eyes. He must have been exhausted, but there was utter peace about him; that striving, watchful edge had gone. His features fell in comfortable folds, and I thought he was sleeping. Then he spoke. 'This is a good house, I think.'

At home that night, I counted all my rooms. Lounge, dining room, morning room. Basement/kitchen – with French doors to the garden. Bathroom, en suite, bedroom, spare room. Box room. Walk-in cupboard that's bigger than Abdi's kitchen. My floors are rugs and polished wood, my curtains thick brocade which slide on padded tapes to muffle me from the world. My bathroom sparkles, my windows gleam. My furniture is old and solid, not one thing I possess comes from IKEA and yet I bought Abdi a foldaway table called Klunk or Flumf or some aggressive spit of a word. You take your house for granted. The fullness of it. The fact of it. Yes, you could argue that I worked hard to get my house, but did I? Did I really?

Down below us in our viewing pod, Glasgow breathes and settles. Abdi steps away from the glassy wall that holds us in the sky. 'We should go now,' he says, as he's done every ten minutes since we got here. Rebecca is spending an hour at the college crèche, to 'orientate' her, the letter said, before she starts there properly next week. And we've agreed Mrs Coutts will do a Monday and I'll do a Tuesday – well, of course I was always going to do it. I'll drive over first thing, bring her back to my house. We can go to the park, museums, we'll draw and practise our words (we're up to about ten words, which is just fantastic). I feel stupid, now, that I got so scared about the teaching thing. I mean, he wasn't asking me to marry him, just educate his child. What else do I do with my days, other than a twice-weekly stint at the Refugee Council? I had forgotten the deep satisfaction teaching can bring. Not the jaded going through the ropes and requoting poems you can scan in your sleep, while shouting *keep the noise down* and planning what you'll have for tea, but proper teaching. The magic stuff. When your placing of words and patience makes a spark in another person's head, and you see it, you *see* it ignite in them, form from chaos. And you are *in* their head, with them when the jumbled dense text becomes brighter and more appealing than a TV screen, or an interpretation (although I think they call it close reading now) becomes literally that, an interpretive mediation where you consider and weigh and unlock the sense of a piece, you break through the impossible thickness of it all and it is there – your clear slim thought – and it broadens and broadens and the chaos becomes overlaid with planks. Strong, shining planks beckoning you on and in. Brave enough to say 'wall' like you mean it.

The first time you do that for a child . . . well, you think you can walk on water.

Rebecca looked very smart today. They give them a wee red tabard to wear over their clothes, which she loved, and I'd bought her a pair of gym shoes in the hope she'd relinquish her wellies. That didn't go so well.

Noooooooooo.

She'll be fine, smiled the nursery nurse, shooing us out the door. Abdi looked like he was about to greet, and I thought, let's *do* something, let's not just sit in a café and watch the clock. So we came up here. Further to the right and up, up, up, you can make out the onion dome of the City Chambers, where we held our protest march about the housing contract. Mill, really. Can you have a protest mill? Despite the posters and articles and Twitter appeals and posts on Facebook decrying the decision to axe asylum accommodation in Glasgow, all we got was a few hundred folk. Is that good for an ad hoc protest? I don't know; it was my very first time. To be honest, it didn't feel like we were storming the barricades. We were a hubbub of earnest do-gooders shambling before the seat of civic power, waving our homemade placards, shouting slogans. It was really hard to think of a snappy chant for 'don't send all these asylum seekers away from the homes they've struggled to make'. It was Gamu who finally came up with: *Don't Go from Glas-Go!* Which segued into: *Our home is Glas-Go,* topped with several choruses of: 'We belong to Glasgow, dear auld Glasgow toon!'

But I think it was a catalyst. Some of those few hundred folk were the asylum seekers themselves, visible as scared, angry individuals, and the media picked up on the human-interest angle. With perfect timing, UKBA then issued a letter to all the city's asylum seekers, informing them they might have to quit the city with five days' notice – and that they could take only two pieces of luggage. Then another, bigger protest was held outside Brand Street, statements issued from Glasgow's Archbishop, from Scotland's First Minister – shocked, indignant, sorrowful. Crisis meetings were convened between housing and Home Office officials. Within a week, the decision had been reversed. Glasgow's asylum seekers would stay, the contract picked up by the strew of other housing providers and charities in the city. *Storm in a teacup*, cried the press. But it wasn't.

'C'mon then, Mr Impatient,' I say. 'Let's go and get Rebecca.'

Abdi sticks his tongue out at me. The tower stutters and bends in the breeze. How precariously we're balanced.

Later that evening, I'm sitting having a cup of tea and the doorbell goes. I decide to leave it, *The Book Show*'s started on Sky Arts and it's rare to get a programme devoted to only books. Abdi's never told me how he's getting on with his reading list. Maybe Kelman and an omnibus edition of *A History of Scotland* weren't for him. The bell rings again, one of those strident finger-digging rings that goes right through you, so I drag my weary carcass off the couch (the combination of paint fumes and strenuous bending has conspired to make me sleepy. It's nothing to do with the massive plate of pasta I've just eaten). Naomi my neighbour is standing there, and, behind her, a policeman. He's wearing his hat, which is usually a bad sign, and my heart seeps into the hollow of my chest is it Gill the girls Abdi Rebecca but as I'm thinking it I'm thinking no, why would they go to Naomi's door and then Naomi says 'It's Rula' and, God forgive me, I relax.

Only Rula. What has she got herself into now – and why am I being included? Not a single word from her since she failed to turn up for the cash. I doubt Naomi's overly exerted herself to find out why. Out of sight, out of Naomi's hair – and her purse.

Naomi speaks first. 'Oh, Deborah. Glad we caught you in. Listen, there's been some bad news –'

The cop removes his hat. He looks old-school, ex-army perhaps. Very neat and clipped, as are his sonorous tones. 'I'm afraid a woman we believe may be Ms Kadyrov has been found dead. We need someone to identify the body, and Mrs Houston felt –'

Naomi is fair dancing in her need to physically wedge herself between and get in first. 'I mean, of course the police traced her last address to me, but I explained I'd only let her stay a while, as a favour to you. Because she was one of your refugees.' She simpers to the policeman. 'Deborah works at the Refugee Centre, she's always bringing home strays!'

'Mrs Houston thought that you might be better placed to identify her. And possibly help trace any next of kin?'

The pasta in my stomach has twisted in a lumpen knot. Rula is dead? Beyond this fact, I hear my telly, and the husky voice of Mariella announce the publication of another political memoir; hear Naomi prattle on and on, her nervousness spilling on to me in sharp stinging drops and why am I getting worried and what is it she's saying? That *I* was Rula's friend, not her?

'I'm sorry, but –'

'Well, we both knew her, of course we did, so we'll both come. But for your records, you know I – didn't really have that much to do with the girl . . .'

'How did she die?' I ask.

'Gosh, yes.' Even Naomi must realise her giggle, here, is inappropriate.

'Suicide, I believe.' The cop says it plainly, without emotion. 'Do you have transport? She's in the mortuary next to the High Court. In the Saltmarket.'

'Yes,' I say. 'I have a car.'

'OK. I'll let them know. Someone will meet you there.' Then, as an afterthought, he adds, 'I'm very sorry.' The snide way he says it; he's just seen us vie to prove how little either of us knew her.

'That's Rula.'

There is a face made of wax, on which someone has painted blue shadows. The shadows run across her lips and under her eyes, where they become green. Bloated. Her hair is tangled-damp from the water, from the Clyde where they fished her out.

Suicide, no doubt.

Because a lady and her wee boy saw Rula jumping in. Nobody pushed her, just as nobody saved her. The lady hid her son's eyes as she phoned the police, a passing bus driver stopped and clambered out of his cab, found a lifebelt that hadn't been vandalised and chucked it in, but the current and the depth and Rula's determination to die were too profound. They found a cross round her neck and stones in her pockets. The cross sits in a see-through bag, along with her other effects. She had placed her handbag on the stone balustrade, carefully zipping it up before she swung her legs over the side and was gone gone gone. That was how they found Naomi's address. From a piece of headed notepaper on which was written an old shopping list.

On the way to the mortuary, in the car, me driving and fuming, Naomi continually going 'Oh God, isn't this terrible?' and 'How was I to know?' until I burst and shouted: 'What the hell was all that about, with the police?'

'Oh, Debs, please. Just say I knew her through you, will you? If it comes out we were employing an illegal, that's Duncan's career over, you know it is.'

'But you *were* employing her.'

'Oh Christ, Debs. That's hardly the point. Please. What difference does that make now?'

'Tell me the truth. Did you know what she wanted the five hundred pounds for?'

'No. Not really.'

'Not really?'

'I think she might have owed some money.'

'To who?'

'I don't know. People. Digs money or drug pushers? How the hell am I meant to know? She chose to run away. She chose to lie and say she had a work permit. It's not my responsibility.'

The mortuary technician told us Rula also had a broken leg. He probably shouldn't have said anything, but Naomi was crying and going: *We didn't know where she was. Oh, if only she'd come to see me,* and I think he thought he was being kind.

'Don't beat yourself up, dear. I doubt she'd have been able to go and see anyone. Looks like she was out of action for quite a while. Left knee's been smashed up pretty bad. Some time in the last two months, the doc thinks. Could've been a car accident, or a bad fall, who knows? It's healed no too bad, mind.'

Or maybe it was administered deliberately, by whatever shitey scum Rula owed money to. And maybe that was why she couldn't make it to Maxwell Park that night. And maybe, ultimately, that's why she died. The policeman who meets us at the mortuary takes a couple of desultory statements, but his every tut and headshake suggests this is all 'for the files'. 'Tragic, isn't it?' he agrees, when Naomi reiterates that I work at the Refugee Council and how terrible it is when these poor souls have no hope. 'What happens now?' she asks, once she is assured of his sympathy.

'They'll hold a post-mortem.'

'But after that?'

After that they hope Rula will be able to go home. There is a father called Vlad, perhaps, in a town called Tsentoroi in Chechnya. It's Naomi that knows this, but me that pretends to. Why? Well, she briefed me in the car and she's right: what purpose would it serve now to drag Naomi in? To punish her would just be vindictive. And it was me who saw Rula through my window. Me who has learned nothing from my past.

Me who did nothing at all.

14.

MY NEW SHOES creak. My belly is coated thick with porridge and my arms swing loosely by my sides. I have plenty of time. Over my head, a green canopy rustles; hundreds of tiny fingers waving me good luck. Birds preen and coo between the leaves – the fat grey ones are pigeons. Mrs Coutts calls them 'rats wi wings', but if you look closely they have iridescent necks of green and oil-swirled blue. And it is warm, still warm, and has been all this month. Last summer, my first in Glasgow, I remember only rain. It rained so hard I thought the streets would wash away, was glad for once that we didn't live by water. Rebecca and I spent the days huddled by the window, searching for a patch of blue. I thought the seasons here would be consistent, like they are at home, but this summer is bursting with juice and warm light; it kisses my skin like a welcome friend. Mrs Coutts has made me a piece – *a piece of what, Mrs Coutts? Just a piece, son. A piece and cheese.* Rebecca and she waved to me from the window, waving and waving and me turning and waving until the blur of their hands was a pindot. This morning Mrs Coutts walked to ours, *because I'm aye up at the cracka dawn, son. And it's such a bonnie day*. In future I will take Rebecca to her flat. It's a fifteen-minute walk in the wrong direction, but this is nothing when your limbs are as quick and long as mine.

She is a good friend, Mrs Coutts. And so is Deborah, no matter what she has done. How to say this without invitation? Any words of consolation I might have gathered up for her were lost in the flurry of Geordie's detention. She has been very unhappy since then. I thought, when she called last week regarding babysitting, that she was ill; her words were monotone and bereft. I should have asked *what's wrong?* For sympathy only; for if she were to raise the subject of the little boy, I would say *remember the stones* and we would say no more. Gladly I will say no more. I would find it very difficult to offer convincing platitudes, an absolution for abandonment. Maybe one day I will tell her . . . nononot today I look at the birds the sky the ground. Maybe one day I will tell her about my little boy. Women are easy to be around: they listen, but do not try to solve. I unwrap my 'piece' – the slippy bread-wrapper in which it's twisted is undoing itself as I walk. Sniff it. Ugh – vinegar. The sandwich is full of little onions, which make hummocks in the soft white bread. I put it back in the bag and lay it on one of the park benches. Perhaps someone else might like it. I can get something at work.

My first day at work! Five words that make me taller.

And breathless. For a year, I lived in limbo. Then I got my letter and they believed me and my life began again. Granted refugee status in December, given my mentor in January, a new home by

May and this job by June. My college application's been approved and I will begin there in September, to study for my Higher examinations. Without these, I cannot go to university and be a teacher and start to dig my own furrow for my roots. Proper, wholesome roots from which we can grow and grow and grow. For the first time in . . . I don't want to count it, but I do, as I walk each step closer to my new job I count from the first time our village was taken over, to hiding on the edges of my old life and scrabbling and stealing and coming back and seeing . . . and running, running away and trekking to Dadaab and all those wasted years, not wasted for I saw my son born, saw my daughter born, and Sudan and back to Dadaab and and and – my pace is quickening, I realise I am running, that my hands are crunched and angry there is sweat on my back. I breathe, I slow. Not today, Lord. Please not today.

I am back to being a fortunate man. The early swelling light is warm, my belly is full. I walk with purpose. Slowly.

For the first time in eight and a half years, I will not have to beg for my life. I do not think it's possible for them to know the humiliation when they *look* at you. The gatekeepers. The people in the offices, immigration, housing, jobcentre, the handers-out of benefits and rights. They endorse or refuse your continued existence in so many ways, and you are powerless against them. You stand or sit with sloping back as they run their eyes across your face, your clothes, your carefully written-out form. Who is one human to judge another? And you see it in their small tight eyes; the assumption that we are there to cheat them, every one of us has come with the sole desire to exploit and lie and scrape our future on begrudged sand. How do you think a man can live like that? Do you think if

I had any other option I would beg for scraps? Would you? It is not *your* money you give to us. It is the money society, in its kindness and wisdom, has decreed we may have. It is called 'humanity'. Do you know this? When 'humanity' is a concept, it is fine, but when it is one human being deciding on another's right to *be* human, then it's petty and unkind. One day, I want to be like Debs, moving through the city in which I live so successfully and well that I have room for others too. I want my benefits to be self-manufactured, not given by the state – although I am so, so grateful that they were.

In front of me, I see an old man stooped over. He is sheltering by a tree, curled in on himself, and is puffing, puffing as if it's his dying breath. I deviate from the path, go over.

'Are you all right? Can I help?'

He jerks, then straightens.

'I've nae mair fags.'

There is dank fear in his expression and I see that he is trying to light a cigarette. I cup my hands either side of his. 'Try now.' He hesitates, scared, I think, to be vulnerable, to lower his head in my presence. It is a thin, spindly snap of a neck that he has; his jaw is weak and grizzled. But the desire for his cigarette is stronger than his fear of me, or maybe, up close, I am not so bad, but anyway, he puffs and I cup and he puffs and I cup, and suddenly we have ignition!

'Cheers, son.' His eyes flicker briefly as he inhales, then, quick with the need to be always on guard, he opens them wide. Checks left and right and touches his cap before he shuffles off. As he passes beneath the trees and into the sunlight, his posture alters. There is a dignity to his walk, how his shoulders are braced to face the world. His gait reminds me of Geordie, who reminded me of my grandfather.

For a moment, I lean my spine against the tree. Watch the shadow of the leaves dance patterns on the earth. Then I push myself off and continue on my way. I am begun again as a fish seller, but I hope this won't be the end. As you drop stones, you can also find them. It's how you cross rivers, standing on one, then the next, testing the weight, feeling the breadth and tilt with your feet. It may take time to get your balance before you can safely move to the next, but then you do. You must.

The trees on either side of me become lampposts. I am out of the park, and nearing the supermarket where I am to be inducted. My supermarket! This job is a mark of another human's faith in me. It is a fine country, this, it is generous and sound in principle, if not always in the practice. At first, when I said about my new job, the lady in Housing told me my housing benefit would stop, that I should not take the job. I said the supermarket people told me I would keep my benefits because this is a scheme for those who have nothing. They have made the hours, the pay, the training such that it should not affect what little income you have. The lady sniffed and shook her head. Then she also *thought* – although it was not her place – that my Jobseekers Allowance would definitely be stopped if I were to go to college in September. So I should not go.

'You seem annoyed that I want to escape,' I said and she called her supervisor, said I was 'giving her cheek'.

I turn the corner – and there it is. My supermarket! Many windows, a black and yellow frontage, a long sloping roof and a little turret built to look like the kind of clock-towers you see on old halls and churches. But it's the vibrant black and yellow that dominates. It is modern and traditional and I love it! I love this generous, unpredictable, light and dark and beautiful city. My shoes make a lovely clipping sound as I walk past the cars scattered in the car park. Maybe one day I will drive and have a car and drive in here like Richard and be their Regional Manager but I am going to be a teacher but I could be anything now! I suck another breath of bright morning air, swilling it to every pocket of my lungs. The door is cool and clean on my palm, I push it inwards, show my badge to the uniformed man as he says *we arny open yet. Oh. Right. Away you go through to the back.*

Is the back at the top? I assume it is, make my way to the rear of the store. On every side of me: shining towers of food. Huge rows of bottles, tins, whole pyramids of eggs. Refrigerators that are longer than a truck, full of different types of milk. I see goats' milk – *they have goats' milk in Scotland!* – and resolve to buy some and am pulled on by the smell of fresh bread and my excitement, past the floury piles of rolls, past the buzzing cabinets of – I pause – *dips and hummus?* – until I reach a wide door masked with plastic sheeting. It is positioned between a counter heaped with fish and sea-smells and another of garnet-bright meat. As I hesitate, because to go inside will mean going behind the actual counters, a florid man appears in the gap. Red hair, red face, red arms visible beneath the rolled-up sleeves of his overall – which is white with pale-red staining. He nods at me.

'All right, pal? You the new start?'

'Yes. I am Abdi Hassan.' I extend my right hand towards his. Each time I do this is fraught – once a man refused to shake it because

Nae offence, pal, but yous wipe your erses with your hands, don't you? This man wipes his hands first, before he clasps mine.

'Maloney. Kevin Maloney. Pleased to meet you. I'll be your supervisor when you're in the store.'

'Thank you.'

'Come away through, Abdi. Come and meet the boys.' He pushes the plastic strips back and we go in. 'Have you been at the college yet, did they gie you an overall?'

'Eh . . . no. I go to college on the Wednesday. This Wednesday it starts.'

The room we enter is broad and echoing. It contains silver metal tables and silver metal shelves. Silver metal doors with vast spear-shaped handles line two of the walls; every wall is tiled in white, is shining, scrubbed and dazzling in piercing artificial light. Other lights – round blue lights – hum, spaced at regular intervals near to the ceiling. There are people in white coats and hats working quietly at one table, precise movements of weighing and wrapping, while a younger man sweeps left and right, left and right methodically across the floor. It is cleaner than any hospital, but with the same faint smell of blood.

'Nae worries,' says Mr Maloney. 'We'll get you kitted out here then. A white coat's a white coat however you get it, eh? Only don't say that to a doctor!' He butts me with his elbow. 'Aye. We had one of your lot last month.'

'My lot?'

Yes, I do mean my voice to be that way. Clipped, but not yet discourteous. I aim for a tone of censure, the way I would warn Rebecca that this is her last chance before Aabo gets cross. I am only following orders – good ones, I think, if this is really to be my rebirth. As Mrs Coutts was foisting my piece on me, she suddenly frowned. Pinched my cheek with her finger and thumb. *Now, don't you take nae snash the day, son. You hear? A bit of banter's fine, but don't let them talk down to you, right? You're a fine handsome lad, and you probably know mair about all the fish in the sea than they do.*

'Aye,' continues Mr Maloney. 'Another boy on the apprentice scheme. Didny stick it, but I'm sure he left his overalls and his knives, so you're welcome to them. I doubt the college charges you much, but if you can get them here for free, so much the better, eh?'

'Thank you, Mr Maloney.'

This good man takes my jacket, gives me a locker and a white coat, then escorts me round the room. Each stop along the way is punctuated with names and introductions. There are six, maybe seven men and a couple of women, but only two others who seem to be working with fish. I am shown where they – we – prep, where they store, where they receive, where they create.

'Aye, I encourage the lads to experiment a bit. You canny sell the fish right if you don't know what to do with it, know? And the boss loves it if we do something a wee bit different from the other stores.' Mr Maloney raises his voice. 'Local, distinctive and –' pausing, lifting his arms to conduct the response which is shouted from all quarters:

'*Quality guaranteed!*'

The boy with the brush gets carried away, flings his white hat in the air along with his shouted refrain.

'Right, you, pick that up. Oh, and you'll need a bunnet an all, Abdi.'

He is giving me a small cake? I search my brain for where I've heard this word before, see the boy scoop up his hat and remember the man with the magazines and those boys and the chasing. It is a hat, of course it is.

'So, if you've any ideas for marinades and that – gies a shout, aye? Wee Cammie there came up with a stoater, didn't you, pal?'

Is a stoater like a bloater? I have been swotting up on my fish.

'Aye. Salmon steak with ginger, lime and chilli.'

'Magic, so it was. Anyway, Abdi, that's for later. The now we'll be concentrating on the basics – your hygiene, your safety, your customer service, the produce we sell, how we prepare it. I mean, you'll no actually be on the shop floor for a while yet.'

'I understand.'

Mr Maloney speaks more quietly, so it is just him and I in the conversation again. 'Aye, I'm sorry about that. We have to go through all the hoops: it's company policy, particularly with this new scheme. I think they're shiteing themselves that some home-less laddie'll cut off his fingers cause he didny get the "knives are sharp" input. Mind, I'm expecting great things from you. I hear you're a fisherman.'

'I was, yes.'

I am surprised he knows this. And pleased.

'Kind of fish you deal in?'

'I'm sorry?'

'What sort of fish did you catch?'

I reel off the most common: tuna, sardine, swordfish, marlin, mackerel, lobster. I have prepared for this: looked at pictures on Mr Google, learned the English names, and no, I did not catch all these fish as a matter of course. Indeed, I've never fished for lobster, but occasionally they curled inside our nets. Outwith the coastal areas, few Somalis eat fish, far less spiny great crustaceans. These things go for export, and we were subsistence fishermen. What we didn't eat, we'd sell, so we fished for what would sell quickest. My friends deemed me arbiter of this. Coming from a nomadic tribe, to my mother's coastal homeland, I'll admit I was disgusted at first. To eat fish is to show that you are not a good herdsman, yet here was my *hooyo*'s family gorging themselves on everything slimy and rank. I soon learned. Firm flesh, good colour, no smell. That's what sells best.

'So, you'll have filleted plenty?' Mr Maloney asks.

'Of course.'

He gestures to the pale-grey fish that lies on the marble slab beside us. It looks like mackerel with its mottled belly. 'Show me.'

I stare at the fish and its extinguished eyes. *Come on, Abdi. Do your worst. I will feel nothing anyway.*

My fingers contract. They are cold, cold, cold. I flex and I swallow. Today is an *induction*. This action I have done a hundred thousand times becomes a clumsy horror. What if I forget; fail this simple test? My job, my stability, my stature as a newly working man is predicated on my memory of tiny bones. The fish pouts its disdain. It is obvious: neither it nor Mr Maloney think I am capable of the job. Often, on the beach, we would use the razor-edge of a seashell, or a thin sharp piece of rock. The knife which rests beside my little dead friend is silver as the fish. It is slim and light, with a fine sleek blade to it. I think it could do the task itself.

First, I wash my hands. I suspect this part is also my induction: do

I think like them? Am I clean? The two other men have ceased chopping. Watching me, quite openly. A trace of fishscale smears the bigger one's chin. I dig my nails into the fish's tail, lift it to eye-level and slit the belly with the little knife. Hook my finger inside, a gentle tugging twist and there – the skeleton laid bare. I present it to Mr Maloney.

'Aye, very good. Probably better if you keep the produce on the board, though. Health and Safety, know?'

I do not, but I will go on to hear much about Health and Safety from Mr Maloney.

'What about salmon? You can do the pin bones and that?'

'I do not know a pin bone.' There's no point in lying; the next test may be to point one out. Debs has given me much advice, but the most useful – seeing as she knows very little about fish – was when she told me: if I don't know, I should ask. *Ask once, Abdi, that's fine. Everyone's got to learn. But when someone's shown you or told you – make sure you don't have to ask again.*

'Here, watch Sam. Man's a master with the beast.'

'Aye, shame he's shite wi the burds, though!' calls Cammie.

'Your wife wisny complaining last night.'

'Piss off.'

Mr Maloney taps a knife on the counter. 'Right, lads, that's enough.'

'Aye, that's what your wife said and all, once me and ma mate had ridden her raw.'

'Sam, I said that's enough.'

'You huvny got any mates, so I know you're lying,' says Cammie, returning to his mullet. At least, I think that's what it is. I can't expect them to teach me all the names, I must pick it up as quick as blinking.

The big man – Sam – hefts a whole salmon from the fridge. I hear his knuckles crack as he prepares himself, massaging the meaty length of his hands. Hundreds of tiny brown marks on the back of them. *Freckles*. I like how that rhymes with speckles. Mrs Coutts says they are a Scottish affliction. The freckles are speckled between gingery tufts of hair. Very clean hands, clean, clipped nails, but there is something grubby about the spattered brown.

First, the knife goes in the back of the neck, a deft twist and the head goes, then Sam slices wide, halving the fish. Another flash and we have fillets.

'OK, so you lay it skinside, you take your tweezers –' he takes a metal pincer from a hanging rack. 'Grab here – see how they run along the length of the fillet.'

'Ah yes. They are floating bones. Not attached to the skeleton.'

'That's right. Put one hand on the fish – firm, but gentle –'

'Aye, like *your* wife said . . .'

'Oh, gonny fuck-up, Cammie? Right, tweezers in other hand, and pull in the direction of the grain. See? Easy.'

'May I try?'

He hands me the pincers. 'Sure.'

I work my way briskly down the bright pink body, catching all the whiskers of bone.

'Like that?'

'You got it, pal. A natural.'

'Well.' Mr Maloney beams at us. 'Abdi, pal – we're a man down the day and we're way behind. Plus, I need to nip over to our

Newlands store later. So. I think we can dispense wi the formalities, eh? After all, this is on-the-job learning. But best no to mention it at college. Or the Big Boss either.'

I have no idea who the Big Boss is, but I nod and smile my agreement. I am a little boy and I am new here and it smells of fish and I seem to fit. Behind the metal doors with their spear-handles lie the cold stores. Mr Maloney takes me into one, points at boxes and rattles off instructions. Health and Safety prefaces each one. A box at a time, I drag the fish through, lift them on to the silver-topped tables. Crushed ice, the familiar jangle of scales running through my hand, the cutting of lemons and the trimming of parsley. It is better than wonderful. All morning, we work side by side, me and Sam, while Cammie serves in the store. At lunchtime, Mr Maloney says they will swap. Not me, I am to stay 'in the back' and – if the Big Boss comes in, *for Godsake put your knife down. And put this hat on, eh?*

'So,' says Sam eventually. 'Where is it you're from then?'

'Cardonald.'

'Aye, very funny, big man.'

He thinks *I* am a big man? I am tall, yes, but he is *huge*.

'Somalia.'

'How come you ended up here?'

'I needed a job.'

'Naw. I mean Glasgow.'

I know exactly what he means. But what do I say? However I phrase it will define me. I will wear my label as jauntily as I wear my netted hat.

'There was a war.'

I wait for the next round of questions, before I say *my family died and I had to leave.* And then he will say *how did they die* and I will say . . . How much of myself must I expose before I am satisfactory?

He says, 'Shite, eh?'

'Yes.'

'I like war, so I dae. Reading about it. War stuff, know? Any war really. I'm reading a book about a Japanese prisoner of war the now. Old boy fae up north. Unbelievable what he went through.'

'Yes.'

'But you know the strangest thing – here, gonny pass me that knife there? The big one? Ta. Aye, the thing I didny get was how he coped. It wisny like they make out in the films – all heroic and that.'

'No.'

'Naw.' Sam plunges the knife into the belly of a . . . trout? Is it trout when they are nut-brown and rainbow underneath? 'He reckons the only way he got through was by looking out for number one, you know? Don't carry anyone with you. If your mate coups over, just leave him where he drops and don't look back. Fucking brutal, eh?'

'Yes.'

'But he says it was the only way he could survive. In his heid like, you know?'

'Yes.'

I lay my fillets skin-side down. I pincer-tweak and pull and focus on the translucent flesh. It is too pink. I have never seen a fish so pink.

'So do you read yourself, Abdi?'

'Yes. I am reading a book just now. By James Kelman?'

'Oh aye. Is he the one writes stuff about the LAPD?'

'I don't think so. This one is about a boy growing up in Glasgow. But some years ago – when you built ships here.'

'Oh aye. Like a razor-gang one? Is it like that film *Neds*? What does he dae, this boy?'

'He grows up.'

'Is that right?' For a moment, Sam stops gutting the trout and examines me with cool, cool eyes. Then he carries on. 'Sounds like a riveting read.'

'Yes! I like it very much. His words are ... clean and honest. When I read it, it is like I am growing up with the boy – if you understand.'

'Oh, aye.'

'There is one bit, though ... Well, I am not sure what it means.'

'What's that then?'

'The boy and his friends go to a football game and it is all like tribes. They are screaming and so angry and the boy begins to get angry too.'

'I bet it's an Old Firm game. Is it? Is it Celtic and Rangers they're watching?'

'The Glasgow Rangers – yes! He says that, and he says another word called *Fenian* and then they are shouting "No surrender". But I don't understand what it is they are not surrendering.'

'Oh man!' Sam's shaking his head and laughing. 'Half of them don't get it either. See ... well, it's a bit hard tae explain. You know Catholics and Protestants?'

'No.'

'Fuck. Look – have you ever been tae a church?'

'Oh yes. I go every Sunday.'

'Well, you must know then. Is it a Proddy one or a chapel?'

'I don't know. It is Christian.'

'Aye, but . . . Oh man. Look: if you're a Proddy you're for Rangers and if you're a Catholic you're for Celtic, and the reason how they aye hate each other is . . .'

He rubs the back of his neck. 'Ach, see tae be honest, it's like a war and all, Abdi. It's all a loada shite. I mean, have you seen them with their stupit flags?'

'No. I have never been to football.'

'You've never been tae the football? Fuck me; how long've you lived in Glasgow?'

'Um . . . one year and a half.'

'Right. You need to get to a game. How about me and the boys take you sometime?'

'I would like that very much. Thank you.'

'It's no the season yet, mind. But see when they start back –' Sam breaks off to shout: 'Ho, fuck off, Frankie. Butchery's over by.'

A youth lumbers towards us. He has black symbols on both his arms, and on his shoulder is half a cow. 'Aye, but we've a massive big delivery in and yous lot are nearly done and Talking Baloney said I could use this space.'

'Fucksake. First they tell us we've to cover the meat counter when it's busy, now we've to chop up your fucking cows and all.'

'I'm no asking you to chop up ma fucking cow. Just gie it a wee bed to lie on. All right, pal?'

The youth, Frankie, nods at me, flings the carcass on to a slab at the adjoining table. There is no head, no tail, no hooves, no skin.

The way it lands, flank up, it could almost be human. The naked body is curled, one foreleg hangs limp over the edge of the table. It looks exhausted. My legs sway.

'I was saying to Abdi here we'd take him to a game sometime. Boy says he's never seen a match.'

'Oh fuck, aye.'

Frankie heaves the body over, so the ribs are exposed. I can see into the belly of the animal, see all its crude brightnesses. It is white against red, it is blue muscle and the pearly cling of its half-cleaved organs. It is a pungent smell of metal that overpowers our delicate fish.

'Abso-dutely.' He seizes his cleaver. Whets it against the sharpening block. 'I mean, you're no really a Glaswegian till you've went to the football.'

He lifts the blade high. The cleaver catches the light. Yellow light. Sunshine. A crack of blade through bone

the blade

the blade is a machete the light is flooding me. It is blinding my eyes and the smell, the smell is shit and terror and I look back. She is running I look back and I see Azira running and Rebecca is in her arms and I am running and we are on the truck, I am on the truck and the blades are flashing –

'You a Gers man then?'

People pull me on and I reach for Rebecca –

'Ho, Abdi, man – you a Gers man?'

'Well, I'm assuming he's no a Tim.'

There are voices like flies, obscuring my vision. 'A *Tim*?' I hear an echo, weakly, and then they are gone, they are entirely gone and

I am on the truck in Dadaab, with my hand reaching out for my daughter. I seize her and pass her on as we pick up speed and I am screaming 'Wait!' and we are getting faster. Azira is still running, others run alongside her. Her golden scarf is rocking. The flesh on her face rises up and down. Her eyes are all white, her teeth . . . I can see her fingers, her beautiful perfect fingers. My hand is out, please God this time I will touch her . . .

My arm is out, the other clinging to the shuddering framework. They will not stop now and if I jump we will never get back in. Over and over, Rebecca is screaming *hooyo*, her small legs kicking mine as she struggles to free herself from the woman who is holding her. Azira is slowing, or we are moving faster. A blade sweeps down beside my ear. An animal roar, a body falling. Warm blood spattering on my cheek. *Christ, Frankie. Watch what you're daeing.* More men on horses break from behind, in front.

'Grab my hand, baby,' I yell, my body rupturing. The sinews in my shoulder snap, I fall too far, the dirt road rearing.

Wān ku jecelahay! Abdi!

She says my name and I am tugged back in.

The road rears higher. Recedes at a tremendous pace, it is years and miles as it streaks away and the men on horseback surround her and the others and it is happening as close as the skin over my eyes. I see their blades as they rise and rise, Rebecca screaming *hooyo Mama hooyo* until all I can do is crush her face into my chest, absorbing the violence of her and me and them and my weeping. *Close your eyes, baby. Close your eyes*, I whisper to Azira.

I love you too.

Lips pressing down on my daughter's sobbing skin, praying to my God, to my fucking God forgive me, to my God I am praying to my God until my daughter goes crazy, punching me in the face. *Madax! Her head!* I turn, see an arc of blood flung high and a golden scarf that flows and twines and the blades and the blades if I close my eyes if I open my eyes I see the sun and the light and the blades and the blood you must open your eyes you must open your eyes and there is the blade and the blood and a man who is hacking and a man who is staring and a man who is screaming.

Who is screaming and screaming in falling red layers.

15. August

The Dale

The NHS in Scotland is split into health boards, of which Greater Glasgow and Clyde has the biggest budget – and its population the lowest life expectancy. In a city endemic with poverty and unemployment, provision of mental health services is key, particularly given that one in four Scots will experience mental health problems.

People in deprived areas, children in care, black and minority ethnic groups, homeless people and prisoners have a greater risk of developing problems such as depression, panic attacks, low self-esteem, drug or alcohol problems, self-harm, eating disorders, bipolar disorder and episodes of psychosis.

Although many conditions can be managed in the community, on occasion patients may require to be admitted to hospital for a period of assessment and treatment. Usually, this occurs on a voluntary basis, but there are provisions under the Mental Health (Care and Treatment) (Scotland) Act 2003 to allow for emergency hospital detentions of up to 72 hours, or short-term detentions of up to 28 days.

Leverndale Hospital, on Glasgow's southside, has facilities for acute adult mental health care and an intensive psychiatric care unit. Low-security forensic mental health in-patient services are also based here. Originally called Hawkhead Asylum, Leverndale was built for the Govan District Lunacy Board in 1895 on lands once owned by the Royal Stewarts, and the asylum's central 120-foot tower is a well-known landmark on the Crookston skyline.

Visiting times available on request. Access to NHS services is free at the point of need.

★

'OPEN WIDE. BIG, big wide. Come on, we need to get a move on. It'll soon be visiting time.'

I zoom the spoon in aeroplane whorls. Rebecca's too big for this, but we're in a rush, and it makes her laugh. Anything, really, to make her laugh. I've been singing Madonna songs into a hairbrush (not 'Like a Virgin', obviously), letting her 'style' my hair with kirby grips and lurid ribbons, and — I'm not proud of this one — last night we had a burping contest, to see who could rift all their vowels the fastest.

I know. Amusing *and* educational. I should have stuck in at the teaching.

Rebecca and I have developed a routine: Weetabix, bit of reading in the morning, then we work on our hand people (who began as drawing round your fingers and are now morphing into felt realities), then *one* episode of *Scooby Doo* or *Dora the Explorer* during lunch. Sums or stickering in the afternoon (each implement in my kitchen is now labelled and defined), an hour at the park – or soft play if it's pouring. Then tea, bath, more reading and bed. Today is very different, though. For the first time in nearly three weeks, Rebecca is going to see her daddy.

Me too. Except I've seen him already, of course. The day they took him in.

I'd been on my way to the supermarket of all places when I got the call.

'Is that Debs?'

'Who's speaking?'

'It's Sam at Morrisons.'

'Who?'

'I work with Abdi. You're a pal of Abdi's, right?'

'Yes. Is everything OK?'

But it wasn't. The supermarket called me because I was first in Abdi's phonebook. Took me twenty-five minutes to get there, head buzzing with: *Just went fucking mental. Chibbing butcher-knives an all sorts.* By the time I arrived, an ambulance was there too. As was a police car. Me, wedging through the slow yawn of the automatic doors, running past startled shoppers, on into the back-shop. Calling Richard on my mobile as I ran, because he was the boss of them all, and could stop this. When I didn't even know what *this* was.

Abdi was cooried under a metal table. Bloody hands nursing his head. I could see an empty wooden knife-block, its contents scattered and a cleaver grinning. I think he was still holding one knife at that stage. By the blade. A grey-haired cop was on all-fours, pushing his nose right in, while a paramedic crouched behind him. Full in his vision, all Abdi would see was metal and knives and uniforms. The place went quiet as I barrelled in. Just the hum of the fridges and Abdi keening.

'What's going on? Is he hurt?'

The cop looked up. 'You the girlfriend?' Wary as he said it, not waiting for my answer, but swivelling again to fix on Abdi.

'No, I'm Abdi's mentor.' I went to move forward, but the paramedic straightened. Raised his hand, John Wayne style. 'Whoah there, lady. I'd keep your distance if I were you.'

'Abdi,' I called. 'It's me, Debs. Are you OK?'

No reply.

'Is he hurt?' I asked the paramedic.

'He'll no let me near him, hen.'

'Will someone tell me what happened? Has he hurt anyone?'

'It's like he canny see.'

'He's a breach of the peace for starters.'

'Oh, for God's sake. He's terrified.'

I doubled over, trying to see Abdi's face. Or let him see me, at least.

'Just stay back, please. Liaison Psychiatry Team's been alerted.'

'What?'

'We canny get near him,' said the paramedic. 'How long you known him? Has he a history of mental-health issues, d'you know?'

'Of course he hasn't.'

A voice outside shouted: 'You canny go in –'

A suited man pushed through the plastic sheeting separating the back-shop from the store. It looked like he was carrying a laptop case. 'Can I help? Dr Gallagher.'

'You from Psychie, doctor?'

'No. My surgery's across the street. Saw you guys'd been in here a while.'

'Dr Gallagher?' The cop was still on his knees, but backing slowly in the direction of the doctor. 'I'm thinking we maybe need to –'

While they were talking, I started shuffling a wee bit closer. Kicked a blade by accident, and it slid and struck the table leg, and the clunk reverberated, became roaring, Abdi roaring, spewing and screaming insane phrases: '*Isk gotta! Itsgatah!*'

'What's got who?' I raised my voice, not shouting.

'ISKA DAA!' His spine bucked, the table rose. The cop scrambled to his feet behind where I had sneaked in.

'Right, we're gonny have to use the CS spray.' Hauling me away, reaching for his belt.

'NO!' Me, pushing the polis who was pulling me, and my arm kept going, was seized, twisted.

'Enough! Now get back!'

Did I mean to rugby-tackle him? I don't know what my body intended, but I fell on the fronts of my thighs, my belly coming with me, and we went for a slither across the manky floor. Boot-scuffs and mud, splats of gore. A gobbet of bone joint. No. It was the white of Abdi's eye. I held out my hand.

'Here you, come on. Come on out and see me.'

Keeping it to a murmur, noticing the doctor was prepping a syringe. I'd rather have a dopey collapse than Abdi screaming his face was on fire. What Sam had said was true, though. There was no blink to him, no register. Me, the black boots, the hard beige floor. We were ghosts. My inching hand was simply not there.

Clean and soft, the needle entered him. A vague pucker on his face, as if his finger had caught a thorn. I crawled out again, let the doctor do his job. The policeman was on his radio.

'I'm sorry,' I said when he was finished.

'It's OK,' he said. 'You've ripped your tights, by the way.'

'I know.'

They got Abdi strapped on to a stretcher, the kind where the torso's propped upright. Blanket whipped on and round, deft fold beneath the knees. His poor head lolling, all the pinkness of his gums spilling.

'Can someone please tell me what happened?'

Sam, the guy who'd phoned, spoke first. 'Christ, I don't know. Frankie here was butchering up some silverside and Abdi just fucking flipped. But it was the cow he was punching, no any of us –'

'Naw, he wisny,' said Frankie. 'He was cuddling it, so he was. So I couldny cut it.'

'Miss?' The cop had his pen out.

'*Mrs* Deborah Maxwell.'

'Mrs Maxwell. You say Abdi has no history of mental health issues. Does he have a history of violence, then?'

'No. Absolutely not – sorry.' The paramedics, two of them now, were wheeling Abdi's stretcher past. 'Sorry – where is it you're taking him?'

'Southern General. A&E probably, take a look at they hands. They're all cut to shreds. Then Psychie'll want . . . well . . . maybe a – I dunno.' The medic turned to the cop. 'Are yous planning on jailing him?'

'Wait, please. Look, before anyone does anything: this man is a refugee, OK? He's come from Somalia, where he lost his wife. He lost his whole family in really violent circumstances. Frankie: you said he was cuddling the cow?'

'Aye. That's what it looked like.'

'And he was fine till you started cutting it up?'

'Aye. Brand new.'

Addressing myself to the policeman. 'This is Abdi's first day in this job. He's been in the UK for nearly two years. He's a lovely man – got a wee girl –'

'A wee girl? And where's she at the moment?'

'With her childminder.'

'Excuse me interrupting,' said the GP. 'I'd better get back to surgery – you've got my details. I'll phone the Southern anyway, speak to the receiving team. You can get a statement from me later, yes?'

'Sure. Many thanks again, doctor.' The cop, shifting from the doctor to Frankie and Sam. 'You say he wasn't directly aggressive with anyone?'

'No really.'

'He was fucking swinging a bloody great machete at me.'

'Was he fuck. He was waving it round his head – high up, know? Like he was stopping stuff falling on him.'

The babble of conflicting accounts got louder, another man hurried in – Maloney, who seemed to be in charge – then Richard appeared, colliding with the paramedic who was packing up his bag, Abdi rumbling past me –

'Can I come with him?'

'No,' said the cop. 'I need to get a statement.'

'Can you not take it later?'

The paramedics were trundling out the door, the fragile slump of Abdi, shrinking. He was going to fade, disappear if I didn't keep a hold of him. Richard took the cop aside, vouching for me, for Abdi, I'm not sure, but he gave a kind of wave, like a shoo, and I disappeared after the ambulance guys.

' 'Scuse me. EX-cuse me! Can I –'

'Best no go in the back, case he gets ... you know.'

'Can I follow in my car?'

'Sure.'

We were ages at the Southern. They took Abdi off, while I sat in a draughty space. He was waking up, there would be a psychiatric assessment later. When later? Nobody knew.

Is he talking yet? He'll be very scared.

He's fine.

I didn't want to leave him, but it was past five by this time, and I'd no number for Mrs Coutts. I phoned Abdi's flat, on the off-chance she'd be there, and she was, she was, which was just as well, because next minute the same policeman turns up, muttering about 'child protection issues'.

'Are you stalking me?' I said.

'What if I was?'

Pleasant-looking guy, when he turned down the dourness.

'So is a mentor like a sponsor? Does he have many "issues", your pal?'

'No more than the rest of us would, if you'd seen your family hacked to death.'

'Point taken.' And he bought me a coffee, and then he left.

Eventually, Abdi was admitted here, to this place we are visiting today. Leverndale. He came on his own. The doctor, psychiatrist?, was an identikit of the many composite *chaps* Callum and I used to deal with: bools-in-their-mooth when they mumbled their name, a dollop of jargon in place of a prognosis. But it was made very clear that Abdi needed no distractions.

'Best he gets some rest just now. Are you his wife?'

'No.'

'Next of kin?'

'No.'

The most they would tell me was that he was displaying signs of a 'dissociative disorder'.

'They tend to be quite common following traumatic events. I think what we may be seeing is a fractured presentation between the past and present events – what you might term hysterical psychosis.'

'Like post-traumatic stress, you mean?'

The doctor had smiled benignly. 'Something like that.'

I park the car beside the dustbins. Rebecca and I climb out. Low modern buildings, and the housing scheme beyond; there's not much left of the old estate but the tower which dominates, vaguely Italianate, a pointed spire above its cupola. *Leverndale.* Just the name gives you the willies. Say it to anyone in Glasgow and watch them shiver. It's a universal for 'the loony bin'. Same as Bedlam. Dark, uncompromising. Leverage, doom. Castles and dungeons; there'll be a grey lady hidden in these walls. I've told Rebecca that Aabo's been staying at a nice place, to *get a wee rest cause he was awful tired.*

Smart sloe eyes that do not buy this. But she colludes with me, placing her hand in mine as we leave the car park to search for Abdi's ward.

Rebecca has been amazing. On the day of Abdi's admission, she followed me home, uncomplaining after I sat her down with Mrs Coutts and asked if she'd like to stay at mine. Just for the night, I promised. Then the next night, then the next. Unblinking, she watched as I took the damp sheets off her bed each morning, put them in the machine, made her lunch. I explained I'd love to make some cakes, but I wouldn't know what kind unless she told me.

'Chocli.'

'Yeah? Well, how about we walk to the shop and buy some *Buttons*?'

' 'K.'

At first, she hardly spoke at all. Followed me everywhere, though, copying my movements as I read the paper, did the housework. Coming a wee bit closer every day. I was careful to be quiet and steady, telling her what I was doing, offering her a wee shot of the Hoover now and then. I know, child labour. Social Work would have a fit – and they were actually monitoring me. Was I a fit and proper person? According to my respectable sister, and the Refugee Council – and that steely-grey policeman – I was. I bought her a dolly at the corner shop; a cheap, plastic fashion doll, but we were sticking close to home at that point, so it would have to do. Found it in my garden the very next day: clothes off, head planted, arse on show to the world.

'Lovely. OK then. Would you rather do gardening?'

Her wee face had screwed up.

'Planting? Digging? Would you like to plant some nice bulbs instead of Cindee?'

I'd a load of snowdrop bulbs rotting in the shed. A friend had suggested I might like to plant them in memory of Callum.

'Yes, Debba!'

That then led to a trip to the garden centre, to buy a mini-trowel, and some carrot seeds, and lettuce and – basically everything Rebecca could tell me the names of.

'Uh-huh. No pointing. You have to say what it's called or we won't buy it.'

The flowers got ignored, it was the packets with the pictures of vegetables that she went for, sometimes saying the name in what I assume was Somali, sometimes English. She knew her plants, this girl. I hadn't gardened since Callum had gone in the wheelchair, had forgotten the scent of earth cracking, its gritty friable soil and the good damp underneath. We spent hours digging furrows – I don't mean we dug acres, just that it was a slow and laborious process. You have to pause, you see, whenever you find a worm, or when a thrush pours out a song, or a squirrel bobs across the wall. Apparently they have *very* comical tails. Mornings became a quick drink, then out into the garden to see what had appeared. Were there slugs? Had the foxes come? Rebecca began to hum wee tunes, potter by herself while I got on with stuff in the kitchen. And – in the space between the patient ploughing and the rush to get outside – the bed wetting stopped.

There are no gardens at Leverndale. Construction work is taking place at the perimeter, the clink of scaffolding and mixers churning, and the ground is pitted with tyre-ruts, filled with muddy water. Before I can stop her, Rebecca charges for the biggest puddle, jumps in with both be-wellied feet.

'Yaaaaay!'

It is an unbridled shout of happiness; I can't quell that, not even as filthy water drills her cheeks. It hits her new coat, joins the fine rain falling, the mild sky padded out with clouds. Shaded ochre, the clock tower is actually quite beautiful, in a sombre way.

'C'mere, you!'

She shrieks as I chase her, pink boots flying. Then stops. Jumps again and taps the ground with her heels. Does it again, to confirm the noise emanating from the wet rubber really is that rude. Compressed air, I guess, working against the friction of her feet.

Rebecca beams at me. 'Like jobbies comin'!'

'No, not like jobbies! Who told you that word?'

That's the downside of parks and soft-play. Other people's weans. The bogies and the bad words, the boy whose exuberance is too big for the ball-pit. But the upside is seeing her chatting, sometimes even laughing as she copies them and dives head-first down the chute. On the way home last week, we met Mrs Gilfillan, out in her strip of front garden. She was gathering hydrangea heads, gone fawn and lacy, but still with tinges of desiccated blue. As we approached, she stopped snipping.

'What a beautiful child you have there.'

A silly puff of pride about me. I could take no credit for the line of Rebecca's nose or the nascent cheekbones that would be high and fine once the babyfat dropped away. The haze of hair I sympathised with, and struggled to contain. I couldn't make it neat the way that Abdi did. But the wellies and the chocolate-smeared chin were all my own work.

'Who does this belong to then?' Mrs Gilfillan raised her spectacles above her nose. 'Or have you stolen her?'

'This is Rebecca. Say hello to Mrs Gilfillan, Rebecca.'

' 'Lo.' Swinging on my trenchcoat as she said it.

'Rebecca and her daddy are friends of mine. She's staying with me for a wee while.'

'And where are you from, Rebecca?'

'The flat.' Twisting the loose edge of my belt. The snap of an elastic band going off inside me.

'She lives in Cardonald now – but from Somalia originally.'

'Ah, Somalia, of course. Very fine features. My best friend was a Kenyan, you know. Well – you must bring her round for tea. Rebecca – stand up, don't slouch. You have lovely long bones. Now. Have you ever had Dundee cake?'

The wee soul was rigid to attention. 'No.'

School. She was so in need of school. The more Glaswegian she got, the less obedient she would become – *which is no bad thing in a child, reveals ex-teacher in shock admission.*

'Well,' said Mrs Gilfillan, 'I make the best Dundee cake in all the world. So there.'

'Debba makes nice pancakes.'

It was the longest, most structured sentence she'd ever said.

'Oh really? Tell you what then, you bring the pancakes, I'll supply the cake. How's that?'

'Good!'

It was. Delicious actually.

'This is it,' I tell Rebecca. All the wards at Leverndale have sturdy Scots names, like Balloch and Balmore. We press the buzzer, step inside. It's tepid, dim, with odd whorls of abstract art, and the pale slop of half-moon lamps illuminating the canvases. Don't be fooled by the swirly bits – they clearly run a tight ship here. There is a canvas, then a door, a canvas, then a door; five of each, on either side. Designed so there really is light at the end of the tunnel, the corridor stretching bleakly, coming to rest under a single, high window. In hospital, light is time. It passes and dims and wakes and falls. How cleverly they've blanked this out. We are in a wipe-clean womb.

'To see Mr Hassan?'

A bright nurse waits to escort us through. Abdi's in a single room. He is sitting on the edge of the bed. A moment of bewilderment when he looks up, then it's blasted as Rebecca hurls herself up to his lap. Her little feet kick my shins, not meaning to, but they are blind and desperate.

'Aabo! Aabo!'

She bends herself to Abdi's shape. He corresponds, so they are head-to-head. Big hand, little hand. Kissing. Crying. It's not my place to . . . it's just not my place. I go back outside to wait.

Even with your eyes no longer smarting, once they've read-justed to the gloom, these paintings are simply splodges. Angry blue seas of nonsense; I do not understand modern art, the slap-dash random self-importance of it, there's no concession to the casual viewer, it makes you feel ridiculous, a bystander who's not in the gang because you don't get how a pair of dirty knickers and half a shark are –

'Debba!' Rebecca's shouting on me. 'Debba! Aabo is awake!'

Does the wee soul think he's been sleeping for three weeks? I must not be so literal, must . . . I'm scared to see that blankness . . . if he's gone what do . . . my bum is being shoved forward . . . no, yes . . . I've to hug him too. She's trying to make me sit: *no, darling. Not on his knee. I think I'd squash him.* Abdi stands, before I'm forced to straddle him. We're permitted an inch between us. He holds up his hand, not salute, not touching my face.

'Deborah?'

I echo his spread-out fingers, tip against tip. His bigger hand engulfs mine.

'Hello, you.'

'Hello, Deborah.'

I get the Abdi half-smile. Shy and soft and slow and lazy, but it's his own. He is neat and firm inside his head. I'm sure of it. More gaunt, certainly, but he is strong. I think it's safe to ask.

'How are you?'

'Tired.'

Rebecca shoots him an anxious glance.

'Did Rebecca give you her card? She made it herself.'

'Hey? No. Let's see it, mucky pup.'

She drags a crumpled envelope from her coat pocket. It too is splashed with mud. The card inside is perfect. It's a drawing of a spreading tree. It has a thick trunk and blossoms; each blossom is a series of red petals, joined like grapes on a vine.

'Isn't it beautiful? Rebecca spent ages on it.'

She did, she spent meticulous hours drawing and shading, so that all the strands of colour are contained within the lines.

'Put it here, Aabo! Put it here!' She pats the windowsill, scattering the other cards already propped there.

'She sounds all Scottish!'

'Sorry.'

'No, it is . . . good. It is her voice.'

'Nice cards. Did you get one from Mrs Coutts? She asked me for the address.'

'Yes. It is the one with the kitten.'

'Oh, yes. Pretty. Ooh – you got fruit too?'

A lavish basket with a purple bow offers oranges and grapes and tempting, rosy orbs. Mangoes maybe?

'From Mrs Girdwood, my minister's wife. Yes, you may have an apple, Rebecca. They send me a card also. So did Mr Maloney. And I got this one. He, he. Read this one.'

There's no flowery couplet inside. Instead, three different hands have penned their own messages on the white space. In order:

Mine's a pint when you're back on your feet, pal

Still on for the football whenever you're up for it. Take care x

Baloney says you're on the mince counter when you get back!

This scrawl's accompanied by a wee smiley face. I look at the front of the card. It's a cartoon of a grizzly bear with an axe, chasing a lumberjack.

'It is from the boys at work.'

'So I see.'

'Should I laugh?'

'If you plan to keep living in Glasgow, then yes. It's what we call gallus banter.'

Rebecca's rearranging the cards. I lower my voice. 'How are you really, Abdi?'

'Like a bloodletting,' he whispers. 'Sometimes, we drink from camels? Not kill, just drink, you understand. When you cut them, they struggle and go crazy. Then it flows, and they calm. They just wait.' He closes his eyes.

'Knock knock!'

A doctor pushes the door. You know the term a shock of hair? Well, it really is; it's big and white and woolly. Like someone's stuck a daud of cotton wool on when he wasn't looking.

'Ah, Mr Hassan. May I come in?'

'Please. This is my friend, Deborah.'

'How do you do?' The doctor's voice batters round the room. 'Ah, you're the mentor lady I spoke to on Monday?'

'Dr Boon? Yes, that's right. With the Refugee Council.'

'Excellent. Excellent. So. How are we today, Mr Hassan?'

'I am wonderful. Look, sir. My daughter is here.'

He nudges Rebecca forward, who is suddenly bashful. It's the whiteness of the man's coat, I think it scares her. Or, more probably, his bouffant hair. Says me.

'This is Rebecca.'

'Pleased to meet you, Rebecca.'

She clings to Abdi's waist.

'Ooh, is that an apple? Is that to keep me away? Ha!'

I laugh a wee bit too, so the doctor doesn't feel lonely.

'So. Well, we've already discussed the nature of your care plan, haven't we, Mr Hassan?'

'Yes, sir. Rebecca – excuse me, please.'

Rebecca has let go of Abdi's leg, is now tunnelling beneath the bedclothes. A train, a ghost? I'm not sure. But every so often she goes 'Woo-woo!'

I leave Abdi to grab her, which is fine because I think it's me the doctor's actually speaking to, half in and out the door as we've positioned ourselves. Doctor Boon leans in close, bringing sandalwood and pipesmoke with him. 'We're talking about a mix of collaborative interventions. Therapeutic and physical. He'll have his medications, of course – that's all included in the care plan, but our clients are encouraged to engage in a holistic, individualised approach to ... well, recovery, ideally. There's a good project specifically for refugees which I'm referring him to. COMPASS. Damn good people there. I was at a conference with ... um. Doesn't matter. Horrific, though, just horrific.'

'Is there likely to be a recurrence? You said it was a flashback started this.'

Abdi is letting Rebecca name all the fruit, all their shapes and all their colours. She is even setting them out in order of height, and I can hear her chatter about our garden. Flinging this out at Abdi, who strokes her hair, blinks and listens.

'Hard to say,' says the doctor. 'The fact that he was able to function well enough up till now, and it was a specific trigger that ... well, we'll just need to wait and see.' He's already explained to me about patient confidentiality. What Abdi has said in the confessional is sacrosanct, and how I must never press him. *Leave that to the professionals, my dear!* But he reiterates it, obliquely from the side of his mouth as we watch Abdi with his daughter. 'Trouble is, conventional talking therapies don't always help. Trauma involves part of the brain not accessible through language. So our experiences get trapped where the brain controls emotions. Which means they don't get processed. Instead of being filed as a memory, they persist as if they're happening now. That's why he'll continue to have a full programme of professional support. Ongoing counselling, CBT . . .'

'What can I do, though?'

'Listen if he wants to talk, but don't initiate a conversation. Accept that he may be tired or withdrawn, seem agitated or depressed – these are all emotions he's been repressing. Obviously, if he displays signs of aggression . . .'

Abdi is biting into a pear, presenting each heart-shaped morsel to Rebecca, so she can access the white flesh. She loves pears, but doesn't like the 'chewy' skin.

'You know Social Work will continue to monitor the situation? What with the wee one.'

'Of course. But I promise you, he'll not be on his own.'

'No.' Dr Boon smiles at me. 'So, you're with the Refugee Squad, eh? You must see a lot of this type of stuff. Tell you, I don't know how much they pay you people, but it's not enough –'

'I'm a volunteer.'

'Oh. Well.' He plays with his stethoscope. *There's* a doctor who's not been on his hand-hygiene course. 'I take my hat off to you, young lady.'

Young lady. I want to hug him. He's like a jolly polar bear.

'So.' The good doctor strides full into the centre of the room. I saw him coming, but even I jump at the loudness of his hair, his voice, his walk. 'What do you say, Rebecca? Will we get your daddy ready to go home?'

Rebecca considers this, still unsure of the booming Mr Boon. Finishes chewing her pear and decides to respond.

'Ma wellies fart.'

16.

I CLIMB FROM the car. I have the bones of an old man, the brain of a child. But my lumberings are forgotten as I stand, look up, look up. Deborah's house is dazzling. So tall, mountain-stone tall for one person to live – I count three floors of windows which are hers alone. My new shoes ring on the staircase, in the hall which is laid with tiny stones. A repeating pattern of triangles. On a table below a wide mirror is a silver bucket, in which Debs has put white flowers. We take tea in the lounge room, on pillowy divans, then I am led upstairs. Rebecca was going to give me a full tour, but I am tired, the house is vast – and she is transfixed by something loud on television.

'This is your room. I thought you'd want to be on your own – Rebecca's just down the hall. But if you'd rather, I could move a camp-bed in here.'

I sniff in the dark polish of the place, its heavy furniture and half-closed curtains. The outstretched breadth of bed. 'No. This is fine. Thank you. We should not be taking so much of your time –'

'Rubbish. You stay as long as you like, Abdi.'

From downstairs, the wail of the television is trumped by Rebecca cackling with laughter. 'To me, to you!' she is shouting.

'Here. Why don't you have a lie-down? Once I shut the door, you'll hardly hear her –'

'I want to hear her.'

'Of course. Sorry. Can I get you anything? More tea?'

I shake my head. Sit on the bed and take off my new shoes. Ridiculous, wearing them to gut fish. What was I thinking of? I will need to go back there. Apologise. A heavy slab comes down on me. But I must. I must. I confront, I process, I accept. No, the other way round. The doctor lady called it CAP. Her patented method, she said. Tapping on my skull. EFT, that one was called.

'I think I will sleep for a little while. A wee while, just.'

'That's fine.'

'Deborah . . . I cannot thank you enough. For your generosity to us, your patience.'

'Ach. Away and bile your heid.'

In my monastic cell, I have been reading the history book she gave me. The Scots are stern warriors, even the women. It spills into their speech, how they brush off praise with made-up anger. I know 'bile' is boil and I know she doesn't mean it.

'You must bring me a pot.'

Her hand goes to her mouth. 'Oh, God. Abdi, sorry. I should have shown you. There is a bathroom two doors along –'

'Debs! I am joking with you. A pot to put my heid in?'

It is weak and stupid, but she laughs kindly. I saw her do the same with Dr Boom. Boon, I mean Boon.

'What are you like?'

I grab her wrist. 'What was I like, Debs? You saw me. I cannot remember anything, it was as if I was . . . I was not there. The smell, the taste was . . . I was in a different place.'

'Och, you were . . . you were upset, yes. But the ambulance came and —'

'Please. I need to know.'

She sits on the bed beside me. 'OK then. Honestly? You were hiding under the table. You know, the big metal one?'

I die and die and die again.

'Go on.'

'That was it really. You were just huddled underneath it. Oh, and you had — well, you know about the knives? You'd gone a bit . . . that's how your hands were cut.'

'Yes. Dr Boon explained. Anything else?'

'What does *iska daa* mean? You kept shouting it.'

My mouth is stuffed with paper. A CAT in a HAT, I see the cat with its cap this is how I do do it acceptaxxeptexcept. Swallow down the paper. Accept that it is in my mouth and process it away.

'*Leave her.* It means "leave her alone".'

'Oh, Abdi. Christ.'

She takes the weight of me, stroking my brow. The smell of her is sweet and sharp. I want so badly to be clean.

And so.

Don't go.

I breathe her in.

And so.

And so I tell her everything. I tell her how much I miss my

mother, my sister. How my grandfather's dead face looked as it leathered in the sun. I tell her I had a son and how he died. I tell her I had a friend called Paolo who gave us a home and how there was a *Light of the World* and the language keeps bleeding from me like I've cut a vein. Thick weak words flung out into the wind and noise that roars inside me. Or maybe it's a jinn, and he's laughing as I select and offer the very best of my words to describe –

To describe.

To describe this.

Everything is burning away. It is the burning bush of Moses, there to purge and cleanse. I firewalk and feel the pain and I feel no pain and I must ... the word is 'process'. I must be calm and *process* how I saw my wife beheaded as I fled.

And so.

'We were loading up when the raiders came. Everyone was running, literally trampling over each other to get on to the trucks. There were two guards with guns, but they did nothing ... I don't even know if they had bullets.'

The flats of my hands are drumming on the bedsheet, it is uncontrollable but I have to finish this and I talk louder over the independent noises of my hands, over the wails and shrieks and slicing noises. Have you ever heard a machete slicing air? It is a wicked shivering hissing swoosh and then the sickening clunk and thud and I keep talking over it all, because this is not real, it is the fear centre of my brain on fire and I am here and I am here.

'The first truck began to go, before it was even half-full, and it became a proper stampede. I saw one girl climb on to another woman's back, an old woman. She used her as purchase to get up on the lorry. People were fighting to get on, the people in the truck were fighting to push them off, then the second truck's engines started, and I screamed at Azira to run. I had our baggage, she was carrying Rebecca and I dropped it to get to her, but the flow of bodies was too strong. It was like a river, you know? Like a sea?'

Debs nods. She is crying now, so I carry on over the noise of her crying.

'I hit people, I punched people to get to Azira, and she was yelling *Get the baby on the truck!* We were like wild animals in a herd, being swept along by pounding feet – I was lifted off the ground, all the bags gone, trampled – except my backpack – and then I was banging into metal and I was alongside the second truck, so I grabbed it, I just grabbed it when I should have reached behind me and grabbed my wife.'

The crying is too loud to continue. It is so loud it is thickening my lips and making my breath come in sobs. These are parts I had not even remembered; but I push through this pale cold ache: the more I talk, the more there is to say, far more than I said to those counselling people, who take notes and capture you and will never let you go. But I will say it, and I do. And Debs listens quietly, beside me. By the end, I am nothing. Not even a shell. And then I sleep. I sleep the longest, deepest sleep I've ever had. I sleep for all of one night and all of the next day and there are no dreams in any of these hours. I don't even have the light on. I wake when it's dark. The red numbers on the clock say four, but at four it should be light. A strange curtain lifts in and out; there's a gentle smell of grass and woodsmoke. Dawn smells. Soon the women will begin to grind, making meal for *anjara*. I listen for the syrupy birds in chorus. Hear none. And then comes a plaintive yicker. Hyena? No, a fox.

Stupid refugee. I am resting on a feather bed a million miles from home. It must be night-time – my belly leaps: Rebecca will be starving! Shoving the spongy bedclothes back, my feet on thick, thick carpet which slips as I stand, stumble, my legs wide and then the shock of cool wood. Furniture spins around me, I cringe, waiting to be hit.

Ah.

Debs will have fed Rebecca. I catch myself, hold the bedpost. Tap my forehead, like the doctor lady did. And breathe. The wardrobe squats in its place, the dresser has not moved. I get my legs straight. Their energy is shaky, apprehensive, as if they do not know me and they want to dissociate themselves from the weakling above. *Get some rest,* Deborah told me. Now my body is telling me too. Climbing back into bed, the blissful sinking-in of bone and muscle, the brain that curls back over on its side and goes to sleep.

Aabo. A barely-there whisper. A hand patting my face, brisk shrshh and flow of light; colours fading behind my eyes from blue to yellow-pink. Smelling coffee, smelling toast.

'Aabo.'

'What have you got for Aabo, Rebecca?'

'Aabo. Toast!'

When I open my eyes, Rebecca is there, her chin inches from mine. 'Aabo!' Her fingers pulling at my ears; she's hauling herself on to the bed by yanking on my ears. I sweep her up high in the air, enjoying the muscled obedience of my arms, my solid, squealing daughter, us being strong and alive. She's on my chest now, her hands twining desperately with the fabric, scrabbling under to feel my skin. The urgent absolute press of her: there, I will say, to anyone that asks. There. That is love.

Debs puts my breakfast on the side table, tumbles Rebecca's hair. 'Give me a shout when you want more coffee.'

Then she leaves us to ourselves and I touch Rebecca's fingers, counting them one by one. Each time, she repeats the number, then tells me solemnly *finger*.

Later, I have a bath. Debs fills it with silly bubbles; they go in my nose and reek. But they feel nice. I cup them in my hands. Inhale their woman smell. Squeeze slow and compact until their lacy resistance pushes back. I think my resistance has gone. For endless months I have been as desperate and cunning as a hunted *swalla*. Swerving, hiding, doubling-back, sprinting too fast for my heart. My capacity to run from Azira's memory has driven me demented. My will, my drive, the fierceness of my resolve.

It is shite. I am a simple coward.

'*Shite.*' I utter the word aloud, relish its firm conviction and the little pop of relief the expletive gives. I say it again, elongating the vowel until it yowls in a satisfactory Glaswegian *iye*. Mm. That is a good word. At the end of it you actually feel a little as if you've emptied your bowels.

For dinner we eat vegetable soup at a table in the kitchen. Debs's kitchen is down below her living room, has creamy wooden units and a white china sink. It is more modern than the rest of the house which is full of old furniture and ornamentations. *Antiques*, she calls them. Strangely, she has labelled a great deal of her possessions in

297

here – her kettle, her refrigerator – her wall even. The walls are cream and blue tiles, the floor is polished wood. On the far wall, which is not tiled but painted, there are two glass-paned doors, propped open so you can see pots of spiky purple flowers outside, and the garden stretching beyond. A blue plastic paddle with holes in it lies on the threshold. You wouldn't get very far in that boat. Would*ny*. The shouts of children playing rise from distant gardens, along with the tinny chatter of a radio, and, again, I smell that woodsmoke.

'This is very much soup, Debs. Very good, but very much.'

'Tell the chef, not me.' Debs winks at Rebecca.

'Rebecca made this soup?'

'Well, we both did. And we made so much that we took some to Mrs Gilfillan, didn't we?'

'Fillan,' Rebecca intones. Then she turns to me and makes an O with her mouth and a circle with her fingers. I think she is mouth-ing 'chocolate', but I can't be sure.

'Who is Mrs Gilfillan?'

'She's a bit like your Mrs Coutts – only posher. Which reminds me. Mrs Coutts was on the phone earlier, wanting to know when she could come and see you.'

'Will she not see me tomorrow, when we are home?'

Debs flushes red. Gathers up our bowls. 'Yup, sure. If you think you're up to it.'

After the soup, we have chicken cooked in a white wine sauce.

'Even for Rebecca?' I say doubtfully.

'Ach, Abdi. It's only flavour. All the alcohol gets burned off. Hearty food, you're getting – to fatten you up.'

'I am not a cow.'

298

Debs serves the chicken with crushed potatoes, roasted carrots and luminous peas.

'Rebecca won't eat pea —'

Rebecca spoons a great mound of peas into her potato, mashes it all neatly, then pops it in her mouth.

'Dogshdinner!'

'That's right. You make a dog's dinner for a mucky pup.'

Rebecca nods, then mashes up some more. She finishes before I do, and presents her plate to Debs.

'Clean plate? Well done! OK, missy, you know where the stickers are.'

Slipping from her chair, Rebecca marches to a drawer beneath the china sink, takes out a roll of waxy paper. On the paper are circles, round pictures of coloured flowers. She deliberates for a while, then picks a purple one and carries it over to the wall with the glass doors. There's a poster there I hadn't noticed before, lined with columns of these sticky flowers. She goes to place this latest one on the end row.

'Uh-uh,' chides Debs. 'Look for the one that says *Clean Plate*. Curly cuh. That's right. That one.'

Rebecca sticks the flower on the second column, then lifts the plastic paddle from the floor.

'We do swingle?' It is a hopeful pout.

'Why don't you have a wee practice just now, eh? Then you can play your *aabo* and beat him.'

I don't know what swingle is, but I can tell Rebecca likes the thought of beating me. She and the paddle skip into the garden.

'Is there a fence outside?'

'Don't worry. The garden's all enclosed: there's a big high wall and a wooden gate. Which is locked. Look, Abdi – would you like a glass of wine?' Debs reaches for the open bottle.

'I'd better not. These pills they have given me . . .'

'Ach, pills, schmills. Personally, I find the one complements the other.' A brief laugh as she pours. 'I'm *joking*. You're quite right: you shouldn't mix antidepressants and alcohol. Cheers.'

'Is that what these are? Say again? What is it that you call them?' I turn the packet over in my hand. My new friends, courtesy of the NHS.

'Antee-depressants.'

'Ah. Of course. To stop you being depressed.'

'Aye. That's it. To un-depress you.'

'Well, that would be just to press you, surely?'

'Or repress?'

'Yes, yes it could be that. Or maybe just the opposite, huh? They are to inflate you.'

'Then you'll need diet pills and all!'

I blow my cheeks out in an impression of a bullfrog. Debs grins, raises her glass. 'Here's to you, Abdi. *Slàinte*.'

'Pardon?'

'*Slan-ji-va*. It means good health in Gaelic.'

'Ah, yes.' I raise my magic pills. 'To my very good, very well-managed health.'

'Will you do me a favour?'

'What?'

'No matter what the doctor says – or doesn't say to you; don't stay on those things for too long, OK?'

I don't ask why. Already, I sense a muffling in my clarity, which I don't like. There was a window where I could see so clearly, where I knew I was passing through one place and had come out into the other side and it felt cold and clean, the way water does when it splashes. But that window is obscured. I feel warmer now, yes, but a little slow and fuzzy. Debs pours me water instead of wine. Thirsty too. The pills make me thirsty but I don't think I said and I don't think she asked. I like that. Our silence resounds in generous laps. I am so comfortable here, with Debs. She is an extra eye for Rebecca, an extra hand for me. Did I ask for her? There are times when God hears me, many more when He doesn't. But my need for Him to listen never leaves me. Father Paolo's description of God is that of a parent who knows what's best for us. I lift my water glass to God, who knew it was best to have Azira die. Paolo says our human brains can't comprehend His greatness. Perhaps this is the fault of the designer.

'Will you tell me about your husband, Debs?'

She starts as if she'd been sleeping, shifts higher in her chair. I mirror the movement. Is asking disrespectful? I want only to ... I am hungry for – would perspective be the right word? No, I don't know what I want, my fine brain is woolly. I am a stupid refugee. But her lips part, and there is a fond curve to them. 'Tell you about Callum? Well, he was the love of my life, I guess. We met at uni – he was a wee bit older, but I think he'd always've seemed older, whenever I met him. Even if we had been the same age. You know what I mean? He was very ... serene.'

'*Serene.*'

I see Azira's eyes before me, in the full low quiet after we have made love. 'You mean like Loch Lomond is?'

'*Yes*. Exactly that. He was this calm space at the centre of all these frenetic students getting pished and debating the meaning of life and stuff. He'd just sit there, you know? Absorbing it all. But see when he finally spoke, everyone would listen. He wouldn't have to raise his voice, he'd just say something slow and considered and eminently sensible and they'd all fall silent – usually whatever he said had folk nodding in agreement.' She pours more wine. 'A born professor.'

A song drifts in through the window. *Wayhooway*. It's a simple hum that catches in my throat and ignites a flare of memory, of swaying in a dark smoky room . . . Debs has her arms folded tight across her body. Protecting it from contempt or pity? She is eyeing me intently, demanding I pay attention.

Hoowa hoowa.

'He was only thirty-five when he was diagnosed. I was thirty-one. We'd lost . . . we'd lost quite a few babies before our son died and we'd decided to wait before we tried again. We'd wait a year and then we'd . . . but then I ended up not being very well. Had to have an operation.' She grips herself so hard I'm sure it must be uncomfortable. '*Anyway*, I was fine. But not long after, Callum started to get sick. Really tired all the time, and he was dropping stuff and falling . . . Oh Abdi – I was so angry, you know? One bad thing after another. I felt so cheated we weren't going to live the life we'd planned. I don't just mean angry, angry, I mean like my insides twisted to a bitter crisp. I know I pushed folk away, folk that were only trying to help us. I couldn't bear seeing people being happy; people in the shops, at the pictures. My own sister. I'd be thinking: who the hell do you think you are? You bastards. And the

302

worst of it was —' she hides her mouth behind her hand, 'I got angry with Callum, too. Because he was meant to look after *me*.'

Hu waaya hu waaya.

There is a bubble in her nostril, she is going to cry and dull panic rushes in because I don't think I could cope. But she composes herself. Wipes the bubble with the back of her hand.

'After Callum's death — after my son's death, really — I felt I was dangerous to people. That I did them no good. Ever since . . . you know. It was all my own bad luck — I had made it, but it was the people I loved who suffered.'

My heart aches for her, and for the music that is rising over everything. For an instant, I glimpse Debs as she was when she was little: I see the five-year-old her, shy and searching, and the twelve-year-old who is blossoming and has her arms folded tight across her breasts.

Hu waaya hu waaya.

'Yes,' I say. 'And you feel guilty that you have kept breathing when they are not, and over and over you see them only at the point when they are dying. You forget all the liveness of them that was good.'

Hu waaya hu waaya, hooyadaa ma joogto.

I get to my feet. Too much sleep has made me stiff. 'I'm sorry — but what *is* that?'

'It's Rebecca. She sings it all the time.'

From nowhere, the music shines through competing rumblings, pulsating, coming so close I can feel . . . can see it, taste it: high and flat and shimmering. Azira sang that lullaby to Rebecca. I shuffle to the open windows, each step stretching me, releasing my cramps.

My bare feet finding the floor more firmly, more firmly. Toes gripping like a monkey on the little step. Debs is at my side. Together,
we watch Rebecca dig with the handle of the paddle. She makes a
hole in the earth, the loamy smell breaking upwards as she grinds
the handle down. She's working hard, there is a whole drill of holes
in a straightish line behind her. Humming now, to the same tune,
she walks along the line, squatting at every hole to drop something
in. There are two holes to go, when she stops and turns back.
Tramps across the garden to a patch of unkempt soil, which is
dotted with jagged leaves and cloudy globes.

'Uh-oh. She's found my dandelion patch,' whispers Debs.

'Are they good to eat?'

'Actually, you can eat them, but we don't usually. They're just weeds.'

'Too wee?'

'No, *weeds*. What we call rubbish plants. Plants in the wrong place.'

Rebecca picks one of the globes and holds it to her mouth.
Then she blows, so all the seeds float into the air. A fine grey haze
of them dancing round her head, lit by evening sun. Her hand
pinches the air, capturing some seeds, and she returns to her toil.
Even at five, I can see Azira in her. It's there in the patient bending
and planting, in how she pats and smooths the earth.

'Abdi. Did Rebecca see it all? All the stuff you told me?'

'Not my mother and sister and my grandfather. But . . . Azira. Yes.
She saw everything. More than I did.'

'Will you please let her see my sister's friend? That assessment
centre I told you about, Lara's a psychologist, she works there. But
it doesn't have to be official, she can just —'

I'm drumming again, drumming, drumming, but I have nothing

to drum on so I seize the top of Deborah's arm and knead and knead and whisper: '*Mummy's head*. That is what she saw. That is what she told to me.'

The air darkens, and it is pushing into my mouth but it's not air, not air that will fit into my lungs. I am breathing mud not mud; my face is in Deborah's sleeve.

'OK. Ssh. OK, Abdi. Deep breaths.' She breathes with me. 'All right? Do you want to go back inside? You want your medicine?'

'No.' I shake my head too vigorously. Dizziness smacks. I tighten on Debs's arm. 'See? If I have any more of my inflating-me pills, I will fly up in the air like those seeds.'

Back at the dandelion patch, Rebecca turns to wave. We wave back. A lazy bee glides through the cloud of spores.

'*Bee!*'

'That's right,' calls Deb. 'Bee.'

Again and again, Rebecca blows her seeds. It gives me an idea. My father's people were nomads. When we buried our dead, there was no coffin, only perfumed *adar* then a shroud. We would make a parting in the shroud near the right side of the face, so it could touch the earth, then we covered the body, first with grass and leaves, then wood, then soil. Before we placed the wood on, we would retrieve some of the leaves from the grave, and scatter them on the wind. So the nomad soul was free to roam.

Debs has linked her arm through mine. 'Abdi. You know how hard this is for you ... and Rebecca's speech is coming on in leaps and bounds. I just think if she was able to express how ...'

'How she feels? How does that work, Debs? Does it give her her mother back?'

'I just worry she'll be storing up more problems for the future. Lara's very professional – I've spoken to her already.'

'You've spoken to her? About us?'

'Abdi, I promise Lara will be very discreet. Just an initial chat – not an assessment, no recommendations. No intervention if you don't want it, I swear to you.' A little squeeze. I stare at her hand; her wedding ring glints as her fingers move. Milk skin pressing on my black skin.

'Your counselling *is* helping a wee bit, isn't it?'

'It is pick-pick picking away. I suppose.'

'Then give Rebecca that same chance. Before it gets as bad for her.'

'I don't know . . .'

'Just let me try. *Please*. Lara won't force her to say or do anything she doesn't want. But maybe she needs to talk to a person that isn't you.'

'You will go with her then? I cannot listen . . .'

'I will go with her. I will stay with her if she wants or sit right outside the door. And I'll bring her straight back to you.'

I nod and the nodding slips and in one swift movement my chin is at the top of her head, and I am kissing her there. Her hair smells like the bubbles in the bath. It is so very warm and soft. It is earth and undergrowth, it is spring-packed moss and safety. I have slept in a place like this. Debs goes rigid beneath me. Have I offended her? But I needed to.

'Come,' I say and take her hand. We go over to Rebecca.

'Hey there, mucky pup. What you up to?'

'Fairies,' she says solemnly.

'Fairies?'

'They're like, little spirits? Magic creatures. I told her these were fairy flowers ...'

'Well, that is perfect then.' I stoop to pick two globes, pass one to Debs. 'Close your eyes,' I say.

'Why?' There is an edge of panic there. That kiss was not a good idea.

'Trust me. Close your eyes and hold your flower. Now. I want you to think of your happiest memory. With Callum, I mean. Think of him when he was at his finest and you loved him best.'

In my heart, I do the same.

'OK? Can you see him? Because that is where he is.'

I wait and wait. No answer. Open my eyes. There are tears on her cheeks which tremble.

Stupid refugee.

And then I see Rebecca is staring up at us both. 'Hey, mucky,' I lift her on my hip. 'You OK?'

Her hands grip round my neck.

'All right. Now, you have to do this too, yes? You were singing Mama's song, weren't you?'

A little shrug. She turns her head away from mine.

'All right, all right. Well, it was beautiful. And I want to hear you sing it more, OK?' I shake her gently. 'OK?'

'OK,' she whispers.

'Good. Now you think of Mama singing and I'll think of Mama singing and Debs will think of her *ninka*. And then we will blow our flowers and we will remember them like that. Because they are free – just like your little seeds are, yes? Ready? One, two ... *blow*.'

A perfect feathered globe. Each spore is an umbrella turned inside out, or the wild rushing in a woman's hair as she runs smiling with her arms towards you. Over land and air and light and shade, they twist and flutter up. They scatter from the centre. Find their own drift, the current which will deliver them on.

I think I want to go home.

PART THREE

HOME

17. September

The Barras

Consistently voted 'top of the shops', Glasgow's stores are unrivalled for choice and quality. Wander through specialist enclaves, enjoy the city's stately department stores and find your high street favourites in trendy shopping malls. As befits Scotland's City of Style, there's a wealth of unique boutiques and artistic outlets too, and — for lovers of a quirky bargain — head east, where the eclectic wares and colourful characters of the Barras Market await.

Situated in the Calton, Glasgow's very own flea market was founded in the 1920s by a young woman with a smart idea. Having made a success selling fruit, Maggie McIver started hiring out barrows to other traders. Even in the Depression years, Maggie's Barras flourished, particularly when she had her site permanently covered. The unstoppable Maggie then established the famous Barrowland Ballroom, whose glorious neon starburst still lights up the east end today. The venue is now a hugely popular concert hall, attracting rock stars as well as the dealers, pedlars and punters for which the Barras was built.

Open every Saturday from 10am to 5pm, and with a farmers'
market once a month, admission to the Barras is free. But do watch
out for pickpockets — and the occasional police raid! Just do what the
locals do: shrug, and keep shopping!

★

'KYLE! NO! COME here this minute!'

The lady pulls her little boy away, is glowering at me. Change my mindset, change my mindset. She is frustrated, she is tired. Her look is not directed at me, a lanky black man who has the glazed stare of an addict. What was it Mrs Coutts said? *You're lookin right glaikit the day, son. When you stopping they daft pills?*

Soon, Mrs Coutts, soon.

There's no rush.

I hold a copper coin. My thumb conceals the queen-face, my index rests on a feathered plume. Work or college? I can do one but not the other, my doctor tells me. Too much will 'overload' me, and it's not fair on Rebecca. He's right, of course. I pretend I have a choice. I haven't officially lost my apprenticeship yet. In fact, Mr Maloney has telephoned me twice.

'We've no filled your place, Abdi. There's no rush, no rush.'

I can't believe that. People are watching my interactions with my child now; they're hardly going to let me loose with knives. Debs says she will speak with her brother-in-law, but I don't want that. I know he must have told Mr Maloney everything already — no person is that accommodating of their own volition.

Not where there's knives involved.

My doctor is right. Accept. Process. I forget the other one.

College will start this month. A warm, dry classroom and search-ing minds, a crèche for Rebecca – if I lie about her age. (Debs and I are still arguing about this, but I like the notion of Rebecca being in the same building as me.) What is this preoccupation with age? She will learn when she is ready. And Debs will mellow when I bring her my gift. I have an excellent idea, you see, to show her my appreciation. For all she does for us, I mean.

I let the coin drop. It is, as they say, a moot point. I enrolled at the college this morning. An Intermediate in Italian, Higher Mathematics and Higher English. Mrs Girdwood has presented me with the collected works of Shakespeare already. I wanted to do a science subject too, but I am not to overload. Yes, the world is oily and slow once more. Nice slow, like Deborah's bath oils. We have a rhythm, where I am threaded to my groupwork and my therapy, to Mrs Coutts's house and my new parade of shops and, once a week, to Deborah's house for tea. It's a pleasant web and its filaments give me structure. On a Saturday – which is today – Debs takes Rebecca to soft-play. They are in a club there, they meet others, have lunch. And I have a day of drifting. I have not felt strong enough for church, which is strange because I'm praying every day. It is the public nature of it, I think. The sympathetic hands I'll have to shake. My minister understands.

'There's no rush,' he tells me.

No rush at all.

I could go to the Somali Centre, I suppose, but it seems so far away. Anyway, do I want to talk about home, over and over again? What is comforting can end up suffocating. When I was very small, I remember huddling with my mother in our *aqal*. Poles stretched with skin and cloth, light to carry, but it stinks when the rains teem down. The air sags and drips until you are desperate for unlidded skies.

After the rainy season is over, the ground is malleable. I think of my days as warm soft mud. When I had signed my name at college, I walked here, to the supermarket. I've been here a while now, watching the shoppers come and go. Old ladies with wheeled message bags, single men who leave with cigarettes and drink. Smart people in big cars, who load up with their sunglasses tipped on to their heads. As they bend into their boots, the glasses sometimes slip, land awkwardly on nose or ground, and they will scowl to check who has seen. The joke is, it's not even sunny.

I fill my lungs with fresh air. Pick up my coin and my bag, and go inside the supermarket. Mr Maloney is at the fish counter.

'Can I help you – Abdi, son! How you doing?'

He grips my hand with two slimy palms, pumping and spilling fishscales. We laugh; I don't know what we're laughing at.

'Good to see you, Abdi. Good to *see* you. Here, Cammie, Sam,' he shouts. 'Away through the front a minute.'

The plastic curtain parts and Cammie takes the stage. 'Abdi! Nice one! Let you out, did they?'

'*Cammie!* So, what you been up to, Abdi? Cammie, where's Sam?'

'Eh . . . he's away for a slash.'

'You mean a fag?'

Cammie assumes a look of innocence. 'I wouldny know, Mr Maloney.'

'Um . . . I have come to say thank you, for your nice cards. Um . . . and to say thank you for . . . for all of this. And to bring you this back.' I take the freshly laundered white coat from my backpack. 'I have ironed it so the little tabs on the pockets don't stick up any more.'

'So you're no coming back to join us then? Sorry –' Mr Maloney snaps his gaze to the left of me. 'Yes, sir. What can I get you?'

I move aside to let a stout man in close to the counter.

'I won't be able to come back,' I say to Cammie. 'I can't . . . I am going to go to college.'

'Is that right, big man? Quality.'

Another customer arrives at the counter, a young woman with an exposed midriff. 'Yes, hen?' Cammie reaches for a plastic glove. 'Sorry, pal, I better get this.'

'No, is fine. Of course.'

'Gies a wee bell if you're still on for the football, mind. Sam was saying.'

'Yes, I would like that –'

He is gone towards the whiting. I wait until he dips back near the till.

'Will I give you my telephone number?'

'Ho, are yous gabbin or servin?'

Another woman is standing behind me.

'Eh . . . wee bit hectic the now, pal. Just gies a ring at the store, yeah, and we'll sort something out.'

'Sure . . . It is no bother.'

Cammie clicks his tongue, makes a reassuring phone-shape with his pinkie and his thumb. Mr Maloney, who is finished with his customer, comes back to lift my coat.

'Cheers for this, Abdi. You didny need to come all the way in, though.'

'I wanted to say thank you. And sorry. I am very sorry for all the confusion that I caused.'

'Ach, away. No harm done. I'm only sorry you're no coming back. I mean, don't get me wrong, we'll get another apprentice in – the scheme's still running – but they're all daft boys, you know? You had the makings of a great wee worker –'

'I'm off to college!'

There is too much brightness to my voice.

'Proper college, you mean, not catering?'

I knew it; I sounded like a child. 'For Highers. So I can be a teacher.'

'Well, son, I wish you all the luck in the world. Now don't you be a stranger, you hear?'

'Yes.'

He smooths the folded coat which I have scrubbed and bleached.

'Well. You take care then, son.'

'Yes, Mr Maloney. I will.'

We shake hands one final time.

'Here, wait –' He disappears for a second, returns with a polysty-rene tray. 'Smoked salmon. Disny even need cooked. You take that for your tea, all right?'

'Thank you. Mr Maloney – can I ask you something, please?'

'Fire away.'

'I want to buy my friend a present. Where is a good place to go? All she likes is old things.'

'Oh, it's a *she*, is it? Well, you canny go wrong with perfume – try aisle seven. See down at the bottom there?'

'No. Her house is full of old things. What you call antiques? But I don't have very much money.'

Mr Maloney scratches his head. 'Eh ... I don't know. Huvny a clue.'

Stupid refugee. Why would I think Mr Maloney should know? He is good enough to give me fish, and I embarrass the man.

'It is no matter –'

'Antiques, Cammie. Where would you get antiques roon here?'

'Up the Gala Bingo!' Cammie is serving the woman with no patience. She has a face on her that is narrow and foreshortened, a trace of liver-coloured veins around her nose.

'Cheeky bastard,' she says. 'What kind of stuff you after, pal? Furniture and that?'

'No. I think a vase ... or a jug maybe. For flowers? My friend only has a bucket. I have saved up ten pounds.'

'Och, you'll no get much for that.'

Mr Maloney is still trying to help. 'What about a second-hand shop –'

'Naw, wait. What day's the day? Saturday? Have you tried the Barras? You get all sorts there.'

'Away. He'll get ripped off something terrible.'

'No he'll no. There's a load of right decent stuff –'

'Aye, and dodgy DVDs and stalls wi jewellery that'll turn your skin black. Oh. Nae offence, Abdi, son.'

I smile at Mr Maloney. 'Where is this Barras, please?'

'See if you get a 9 into Argyle Street. Then head along to George's Square –'

'Naw, naw. When you're in the toon, get a 240. That'll take you right out Parkheid way –'

'Naw. See if you're . . .'

I glean enough from their argument to know one bus will take me near to the Central Station (I am better with buses now. They do not intimidate me so much).

'Please. From there I can walk.'

'You sure? It's quite a trauchle. Take you a good hour, I reckon.'

'Och, rubbish. The boy's got big gangly legs on him. Half an hour max.'

'No rush,' I say. 'There is no rush.'

What a place is the Barras! It reminds me a little of Dadaab in its confusion, but more gaudy. It is nothing like the markets at home; there are few foodstuffs I can see, except for a wagon selling burgers and hot do-nuts – which, I admit, smell delicious. If I have enough money left from my purchase, I will buy myself a hot do-nut. People mill without urgency; I feel no threat here, despite Mr Maloney's warnings. Yes, there are charlatans and snakes; all furtive glances and sleight-of-hand: a sensible person knows this in any language.

'Awright, big man?' A thin man drags on his cigarette, nods approvingly as I pass his stall. Which is selling prepacked processed cheese and pairs of shoes. I am wondering if, in certain situations, my height plus my blackness may become an asset in a city which is pinched and pale. The fact of this makes me uncomfortable. And still conspicuous.

'Err yir sportsocks! Threefurapun, threefurapun.'

A jaunty red-metal arch declares the perimeters of the enclosure.

I know there is one at either end for I have walked the length of the market twice. It is how you might read an excellent book – devouring first at a gallop, and then retracing your steps, slower, more reflectively, to appreciate the detailed colour, the precision of the piece. And I do. Pillars of sunglasses jostle by bales of towels and rolls of carpets, men at the corners sell CDs and cigarette lighters the way you would sell khat. There are stalls outside and stalls within the collection of long brick buildings and warehouses, spilling clothes and handbags and books and life. I very much like the Barras! It has a vibrancy that fills your veins. Turning left, I find another passageway. The smell here is of damp, the lane darker. Pitched on one brick wall I see a line of paintings. Old things. I hurry down. Up close, even I can tell the paintings are cheap imitations. One is of a green-faced lady, and there are several of horses: in fields, with carts, running through spumes of water. The surfaces of these paintings are flat, they are not possessed with the rough, real life of the pictures at Kelvingrove. In front of the paintings are trestles piled with artefacts: boxes, mirrors, lots of brass and glass. Some jugs are in amongst this mess, mostly small, mostly chipped. It doesn't have to be a jug, of course. A vase would be fine, if I can find one pretty enough.

I pick up a jug made with the face of a black man. Immediately, he is funny, with his fat, beturbanned head and ludicrous gold hoops in his ears. Is this perfect? Will Debs laugh as I give her irony? Could you put flowers in such a thing? I think it may be too wee.

'What is this please?'

'Toby jug,' says the stallholder, a man with sparse long hair. 'Totally unique, that one. Ba–Bru, so it is.'

'Baboon?'

Well, now I am quite angry at his effrontery. I slam the jug back on the table.

'Naw, ya eejit! Ba-Bru? Fae the Irn Bru adverts? Used to be a big neon one at the bottom of Renfield Street? Naw?'

'I don't know it.'

The jug is actually very ugly. I go to walk away.

'So, is it Toby jugs you're efter, pal?'

'No. Just a jug. I want a big jug to put flowers in. And no cracks. There must be no cracks.'

'Ho, Stumpy!' the stallholder shouts at another man across the way. 'Did we no get that stuff in fae Creggans Hoose yet?'

'Aye.'

'So, how's it no oot?'

'Fucking up tae ma oxters here, Jim.'

'I'm sure there were two of they big cream pitchers in wi it. Gonny have a swatch for us?'

'Whit's a pitcher?' says Stumpy.

'A fuckin big jug, ya plum.' He shakes his head. 'Just gies a minute and we'll see what we can do you fur.'

I am in no hurry. I leaf through some old books, gone rotten with mildew.

'Like your history, do you?' The man nods at where my hand rests. *Centuries of Glasgow.*

'Some.'

'So, where is it you're from then, ma man?'

'Somalia.'

'Aw, right. Dinny get many Somalians in here. Yous lot are all up the Red Road, aren't you? Sighthill, know?' He blows on his hands. Is wearing fingerless gloves.

'I live in Cardonald.'

'That right? Good for you, pal. There you go, then. That's it started already.'

'What is started?'

'Well . . . I mean, this is where it all started really. *This* is the heart of Glasgow – no all that Victorian crap roon George Square.'

'Where the city began?'

'Naw – well, aye, aye, it did, but I mean all the different folk. *This* is where they came to. You read that book you're hauding. You've got your Irish, your Tallies, your Jews. Aw roon here is where they were punted – the Gorbals, the Calton, Brigton Cross. After a while, they either head back home cause it's shite, or move onwards and upwards and the next lot arrive. So now you've got your Chinese in Garnethill, your Asians in Woodlands. And your Somalians in Sighthill. See – you've bucked the trend already.'

'That is good?'

'Oh aye. Stumpy, ma man. What you got for us?'

Stumpy carries a cardboard box, brimming with treasure.

'I didny know whit the fuck a pitcher looked like, so I just brought everything wi a haundle.'

'Good man. Using your *initiative*. OK, pal, have a wee rummage, see what you fancy.'

Already, I have seen it. Not the enamel pitchers the man is press-ing on me, nor the tubby milk jugs or the turquoise vase. What I have fixed on is nothing like I imagined. An elegant, lipped urn, made possibly of stone, but lustrous; there are layers of translucent colour which shimmer as the light turns. It is green then it is blue and pearl. It is pink and sunset and the sea. It flares symmetrically, out then in, with two tiny handles at the top, like ears. Gently, I ting the rim with my fingernail.

'Clear as a bell, that. Nae cracks, not a one.'

'No.'

'Totally unique. A lustrewear ginger jar. You don't get many of them tae the pound.'

I glance up, eager. 'It is only a pound?'

'Eh, naw. Figure of speech, pal. Much you got to spend?'

'I have . . .' I stop. 'How much is the bottle?'

'To you . . . twenty quid.'

'Ah.' I place the urn back in its box. 'I am sorry to have taken up your time.'

'Haw – hold up, pal. Hold up. Look, I could maybe dae it for you for fifteen pounds? As a favour, like.'

'I'm sorry,' I repeat. 'I have only eight pounds that I can spend.' I hold out the ten-pound note. 'This is all the money I possess. Eight pounds for the vase and two pounds for my bus fare home.'

'Sorry, pal. I canny let it go for under a tenner.'

The hot do-nuts are two for one pound. I wanted to get some for Debs and Rebecca as well.

'Nine pounds, and I must walk home.'

'Done!'

He takes my ten-pound note, wraps the urn in newspaper. There is a moment when I am waiting for my change and he has finished wrapping that I think he is not going to give me my one pound back. I hold out my hand and smile. 'My change, please.'

'Oh, right. What was it we said again?'

'You have to give me one pound.' I make my smile bigger. 'Or maybe it was two?'

'No, no. Fair dos. Right you are. One pound it is.'

As I am leaving the Barras, with my one and a half hot do-nuts (the other half is in my belly. Delicious does not describe it. I am thinking that they are better eaten hot. To keep just the one . . . yes, I chew down the remainder of the first one . . . yes, I fear it would become greasy if not eaten at once); anyway, I am passing under the red metal arch, when a voice calls out: '*Big Issue*, pal?' Immediately, I turn, in case it is my rescuer, Dexy, but this man is much older.

'I'm sorry,' I say. 'I have only got my bus fare.'

His focus has already glided; he is monitoring the herd. Seeking the stragglers and the slow.

I touch his sleeve. 'Are you hungry?'

'Eh?'

'I have this, look.' I unzip my backpack to reveal the salmon. The tray has become a little squashed. 'If you would like some.'

'Fucksake, man. That is totally honkin.'

'It is good. Is good fish.'

He folds his hand below his nose. 'Naw, you're all right. In fact, gonny move downwind of me? You're scaring off the custom – and I've a tona these to shift.'

There is a pile of *Big Issues* in his hand. More still in the poly-thene bag wedged at his feet. He has bare feet inside his trainers. Even engulfed in Mrs Coutts's hand-knitted socks, my own toes are cold. I wiggle them, making the blood come alive. Nipping and popping. And I think.

'Do you always work in the same place?'

'Aye. How? Gonny come back wi a fuckin big shark or that? Look, I don't want your fish, pal, all right?'

'No. I wondered – do all the people who sell your books have their own place? I mean, if someone was selling the books in one street one day, would they be in the same street the next? If you understand.'

'Aye? I'm no a fuckin numpty. How? You thinking of taking up the noble art of issuing the big?'

'Pardon? Oh – I see . . . No. I am wondering if you know a man called Dexy. He sells your books too.'

'Dodgy fucking Dexy?'

'Yes!'

'Naw. Never heard of him.'

'Ah.' I hoist my backpack on to my spine. The weight of the urn presses into me. 'I am sorry to have bothered you. Good luck with your books.'

It was a hasty notion anyway.

'Ho!' he shouts. 'I huv seen Dexy by the way.'

'Yes?'

'Aye. There wis something up wi the printers: they only started gieing out the magazines the day. There's a pure wad of folk doon the depot, picking up. I seen wee Dex doon there.'

'Is this depot near?'

'Saltmarket. Straight doon London Road, come tae a fucking great tower in the middle, hing a left and that's you at it.'

'Thank you. Would you like a –'

'NAW!'

'– do-nut?'

'Oh. Aye. Go on then.'

True enough, the Saltmarket is very near. The longer I have been in this day, the more I am alive. I could lope for very far: I will walk home. Maybe I will run. To feel the strength of my legs, and my heart pump, to surge with breath and be steady, steady, steady in my sway and pound and leap. To run for pleasure, not fear? Rushing. Yes, that is when you *want* the rush.

Before I reach the depot, when I am only at the *fucking great tower* – which is in reality skinny and truncated – some men saunter across the main road. They have bags and bundles; I quicken but do not yet run. (The heavy bounce of my backpack reminds me of my nine-pound cargo.) Today, walking quickly will suffice, for it is a good day and I *know* he will be in that group. Otherwise, why else would God have given me this fine idea?

'Dexy!' I shout. 'Hey, Dexy!'

The group stop. A small, tight man who is made of knuckle and wire scrutinises me. And it is. It is Dexy.

'How is it going? It is me!' I touch my head. 'Red hat?'

I don't actually know where my hat is; I haven't worn it since that day.

'Aw aye! That's right. On you go, lads. I'll catch yis later.'

His friends trundle on without him.

'How you doin, pal. Ali?'

'Abdi.'

'*Abdi!*' Said like he discovered the name himself.

'I am sorry, I cannot buy your magazine today. I have no more money.'

'Makes two of us, my friend.'

'Business is not good?'

'Fair tae shite, I'd say. Put it this way, if I don't get this lot puntit, there'll be nae dinner the night. Again.'

'Do you like fish?'

'What?'

I open my backpack. 'Here. Do you like fish? I have some smoked salmon.'

'Fucksake. You rob Marksies?'

'No, it was a present. Please. Would you like it?'

'Aye. Don't mind if I dae.'

The entirety of my bag smells of sewage. Big fish in an enclosed pocket. Not good.

'So, you like fish?'

'S'all right, aye.' Dexy peels a strip of pink salmon, drops it in his mouth. His teeth chop through it at a tremendous rate, and he delves for more. Begrimed fingers, filthy nails, and he couldn't care less. I wonder if he has ever scrabbled rice grains from a latrine. I wonder if he would like to work indoors.

'That is good that you like fish. And you are homeless still?'

He ceases chewing, tongue still wound with salmon. 'Fuck d'you think?'

'Tell me,' I say. 'How do you feel about blood?'

18.

BACK AT SCHOOL. First, the smell gets you. Rubbery, squeaky echoes that elide into sound as a bell rings. Overhead, a squeak of chairs dragged from desks becomes the thump of gym-shoed feet. My sister runs a tight ship – no outdoor shoes allowed. Not since they got the new lino in. Rebecca's hand is welded to mine. We're both a bit sweaty-palmed.

'Honestly, it's no problem.' Lara, our friendly neighbourhood educational psychologist, was visiting the school anyway. 'I'm not due at Southbank till eleven.' Gill has set aside a room for us – what in my day would have been deemed a 'medical room' but is in fact a lovely lounge. There's a blue couch, two green chairs, low tables, a basket of toddler toys and a set of scales, the old-fashioned kind you stand on and calibrate the weights. One of the tables has been set as if for dinner, but where the placemat would be is a pile of A4 paper, and the cutlery is coloured pencils, with more pencils and crayons waiting in a plastic cup.

'Wow! Doesn't that look nice?'

Rebecca glances at me, then nods at Lara.

'Do you like drawing, Rebecca?'

'Yes.'

'Me too. Why don't we do a wee bit drawing and Debs can get a nice cup of tea? She'll get you some juice too, won't you, Debs?'

We've already discussed how this will play out. I've to give Lara ten or fifteen minutes on her own. She'll have a chat, assess Rebecca's language skills, her confidence. See how receptive she is to talking to a stranger. Then we'll see how things go, take it from there. Lara's words, not mine.

'Sure,' I say. 'I'll only be a wee minute. Do you want apple or orange?'

' 'Rnge.'

I clamp my hands to my hips, put on a posh voice. 'I beg your pardon? What is the magic word?'

Rebecca grins. 'Orange *please*.'

'Hmm. That's better.'

So she toddles off happy and I toddle off feart. Get her juice from the vending machine, sit on a bench in the corridor. My stomach dips and rises. Feels like I've been very bad and am waiting to see the heidie. Except the heidie's my wee sister. Who is scared of pennies. Seriously. When we were kids, I superglued one to the handle of my bedroom door, to stop her coming in. It's only actual copper coins that freak her. Claims they are 'full of dirt'. I wonder what Lara would say . . . A door opens. Not her. I make a steeple of my fingers. Then I lock them. Then I do that wee cat's-cradle thing when you turn them inside out and wiggle. My mum used to say a rhyme about the steeple.

There's the church (hands together, fingers pointing up)

And there's the steeple (thread fingers of both hands together)

Open the door (turn hands to reveal wiggling digits)

And there's the people (ta dah!).

There was another, where she would take my hand, hold it palm upwards. Her fingers walking in teeny circles:

Roon aboot, roon aboot, runs the wee moosie.

Up one stair, up two stair and in a wee hoosie.

Shrieks and gales of laughter as she plunged her hand under my armpit, tickling and tickling and I'd be squealing: *Stop it! Don't stop!*

My baby would have learned these rhymes. My mum might have taught them to him. It comes again in a sharp searing rip, that blinding migraine in your belly, that dividing-your-spine pain until the marrow is rendered as fibrous and dry as split bamboo. No matter how resolute your denial, your insistence that it *will not* be true, it is. You were a mum; now you're not. You were a child; now you're not. You were a wife; and that's gone too, and, like the driven pounding of the tide, there's not a damn thing you can do.

'Debs. Can I speak to you a wee minute?'

Lara and her long mauve nails appear round the edge of the door. Steady eyebrows, mouth like a poker. My heart slides from side to side. What has she found? You hear horror stories about what happens in the camps – assaults, sexual abuse – even with babies. I try not to read these things but they're insidious, they slip in to your field of vision as you're reading the paper or watching

329

the news and before you know it there's some vile fat man proclaiming how sex with 'innocents' can cure Aids. I have no idea if we're doing the right thing. An anthropologist would accuse me of imposing my Western values, would insist that our love of self-indulgent psychobabble turns us inside out and stops us healing. Maybe Abdi's dandelions and Rebecca's planting would have been enough.

She's only little.

A fierce, muscular contraction. I love her. It's not a mother's love, I realise that, but it's strong and protective and supersedes this ridiculous need to know.

'Lara. You promised you'd go easy on her. You said this was just a chat.'

'It is, it was.' She comes out full into the corridor.

'Is she OK in there?'

'She's absolutely fine. Playing with a dolly. I just thought you might like to see her drawings. Look.'

There are three different pictures: one of Rebecca in her pink wellies (waving all three of her hands), then the standard one of a mummy, a daddy and a little girl, safe in a big circle. The big and small female figures both wear triangular skirts, and they have pleasingly neat round heads. Rebecca's a very precise drawer, I've noticed that before. She chooses her colours, takes her time. I've seen these types of drawings at in-service days, when the area educational psychologist would come and talk to us about their work.

'OK,' says Lara. 'So what I did was ask her about *her*, what she likes doing best.'

'Wearing her wellies?'

'Wellies certainly featured. But she also likes planting, and playing at nursery. And "blowing" flowers? I'm not sure what she means by blowing, but see: that's a flower she's holding in that first picture.'

So, not a third hand.

'Then I asked if she could tell me who was in her family and she did this next one. There's Mummy and Daddy and Rebecca. In the circle.'

'I got that.'

'She said all the names when she pointed. I'm guessing Aabo is Dad?'

'Yes.'

'Good. Then I asked her if there were any other people in her family, and she drew this.'

In bright-blue crayon, we have the circle once more. And in it is Daddy, Mummy and Rebecca. The big female is in the yellow skirt, the wee one in the blue. There's another circle above them, with a little stick figure hanging on its own. At first, I think she's drawn a person inside the sun, but the circle's green, not red or orange.

'I asked her who that was and she said "baby". I asked her why it was in the sky and she said he lives there. Then, on the same page, she drew this.' Lara points to a red circle, with two more stick people in it. They have triangles at their waist and shorter legs. One has a cloud of crazy hair, the other a strange fat hat.

'And these are?'

'Mama Coutts and . . .' she touches the mental curly one. 'Debba.'

Such a warm whole glow on me. It rounds off the angles of my shoulders, my elbows, my knees. It softens and makes malleable all the hard and sore and sad bits and it's how I would feel if Abdi's inflating pills *were* for real. Filled with warm light air. A wee bit giggly; wee bit weepy.

'I think she's captured your hair really well,' says Lara.

'Ha ha.' But I am glad, from the tips of my toes (of which, according to Rebecca's picture, I have seven) to the very last wire of my unpleasant hair.

'OK. Now, I know I may have overstepped the mark, but it seemed too good an opportunity to miss. So I asked why the baby was in the sky. And she said he was in Heaven?'

I nod. 'Abdi did have a son who died. But I've no idea if Rebecca knew. He died before she was born, I think.'

'OK, good. All right – and you have to believe me on this, Debs. I judged it very carefully, I only nudged her. I asked if she knew anyone else who lived in Heaven.'

'And?'

'She didn't answer.'

'So where does that leave us?'

'With my next question. Where does Mummy live?'

'And have you asked that?'

'Not yet. I wanted you to be there.'

We return to the bright painted room. Rebecca jumps up when she sees me. Flings her arms around my legs, forehead ramming into my stomach. Her tight-sprung hair is escaping from the neat braids Abdi put her in and I stroke a wayward coil, twisting it in my fingers, over and under with the soft fine silk. Her breath is shudders in my belly. I could snip off a strand and keep it. Who would know? I hear Lara cough.

We release each other.

'Here's your juice, mucky pup.'

'Qu'you.'

'I've just been looking at your lovely pictures. Is that me?'

'Yes.' Rebecca is shy, straw between her gappy teeth.

'Should I really make my hair green, d'you think?'

'Yes!' She is delighted at this, nodding so vigorously she spills her juice.

I tut. 'And that, Lara, is why we call her mucky pup.'

'I showed Debs all your drawings, Rebecca, and she really liked this one of Mummy and Daddy and Rebecca. Didn't you, Debs?' Lara smooths her lovely nails over Rebecca's drawings, laid out now on the primary red and yellow of the table top.

'Yes, I did.' A flutter of panic. She's not briefed me. Am I meant to join in, ask the questions myself? Thankfully, Lara carries on and I can wait in the margins, neither good cop nor bad. Just neutral. I don't feel neutral. I feel sick.

'Now, Rebecca. You told me that the baby lives in Heaven, yes?'

'Yes.'

'Where do you live?'

'In a flat.' Rebecca frowns directly at me, then lowers her eyes. She's looking tired. Or nervous maybe? Or is it betrayed? Shit, I want her to know this is fine, this is safe, but I don't even know that myself. My voice becomes more shrill than I intended. 'Good girl! It's up high, isn't it? You can see the park and lots of houses from up there, can't you?'

I – AM – TALKING – LIKE – THIS, each false bright syllable shone through the prism of my false bright smile.

'So, if you're up high,' says Lara, 'does that mean *you* live in the sky, Rebecca?'

'*No*. In the flat.' Her little head is pit-patting from Lara to me to Lara to me, unsure who is sanctioning these ridiculous questions. Not her, certainly.

'Who else lives in the flat?' Lara persists.

'Aabo.'

'You and Aabo. And where does Mummy live?'

Her bottom lip is trembling. 'That's enough,' I start to say, but Rebecca speaks over me. 'In the camp.'

'In the camp? Where's the camp? Is it in the sky too?'

'No!' she shouts, grabbing more sheets of paper. On one she scribbles a lone stick figure with her yellow skirt and a bright red sun, with laser-rays that shoot right off the page. Their angry redness covers everything, and this drawing is not remotely neat. It is all wild lines and jagged fractures.

'She will be too hot.'

'Is it very hot there?'

'Yes! Aabo leaved her!'

'Ssh, now, Rebecca.' I try to pull her on to my lap but she will not be held. She jerks away, continues inflicting furious scores and scratches on another page.

Lara holds up a professional hand which says *wait, this is fine*. It says *let Rebecca fill this space*. It says *I am a narcissist who spends too much time on my nails*. Her hand beneath her chin. Rebecca is being observed. I want to slap the psychologist.

'Bad men hurted her and Aabo leaved her.'

'Oh darling, I know, I know.'

Bugger Lara. I'm on my knees, reaching for Rebecca's scrawling arm. What do I say? What do I say; that he would have been killed too? That he couldn't go back because he'd to protect Rebecca? Yes. Let's fill her up with the guilt that Abdi ingests every day. That'll help.

'They hurted her head. You look, Debba. Look!'

She presents me with her picture. I don't want to look. There are five, no six shapes now. There is a crowd of three together: one is lying flat and there is gushing red everywhere and the other two stand over it with extra arms, or maybe sticks or guns. The remaining group of two figures and ... I don't know – a table? a box? are at the edge of the paper. The box shape has four legs, with a triangle at one end.

'What's this, darling?'

'Horse.'

This chimes with what Abdi told me. It was men on horseback who ambushed the trucks. I force myself into the detail of the scrawls. No red spurts on this side. Here it is mostly yellow. One figure is draped over the horse shape. There's a triangle for the legs, an arched line for the back, with two straight arms streaming outwards. The head is not round, but an elongated oval, lying parallel to the horse's back. The final figure has both arms raised, a thin wavy line rising out of them. I glance at Lara. She speaks quietly, over the top of her hand.

'I think we should contact Freedom from Torture. They have specialists working with children ...'

I wonder what it is I'm not seeing. Rebecca's upset, yes, but at our patent, slow stupidity. She is a crackling fuse, not roaring and greeting, nor catatonic. She continues to go over her picture, tracing and retracing the lines of the horse and the two figures by it. Carefully, she changes her yellow pencil to brown, begins to colour in the horse.

'Lara, look.' I indicate the initial group of three, the one where all the blood spurts. 'That isn't the woman with the yellow skirt. Rebecca. Becky, darling. Show me Mama in the picture.'

Emphatically, she points to the figure on the horse.

'Is this where you saw Mama? On the horse or on the ground?'

'Horse,' she says firmly, without a shade of doubt. 'And the man was whippin' at Mama's head and the horse was runnin' and runnin' away.'

You cannot shake this sense of urgency and dread.

You sit at your desk in the Refugee Council and you tap on your plastic keys. Mrs Casci passes by you on her way out for lunch. She is the only senior caseworker in today; you notice she hasn't locked her office door. Gamu, two empty desks away, is engaged in animated conversation with a tired and tearful man. She looks knackered as well.

You cannot shake this sense of urgency and dread.

Absurd, you know, but you are galvanised by trust. Rebecca's trust; her stout and placid stare as she pressed that drawing on you. Winding down into you. Her small hands folding gently over yours. You did that, you turned her inside out. And then she smiled at you. A smile against the shadows, and you go back to your plastic keys.

Once upon a time, they would have provided a tracing service here. Not any more. Another victim of the cutbacks, that pervasive snipping at the fabric holding this fragile mesh intact. Soon, it will fray too far and we will rip and plunge into oblivion. All of us. Don't they see that? This net holds every one of us. If a girl like Rula slips and I fail to catch her? Well, I slip too.

For now, I consign Rula back to the dark and scavenge in my brains. There was a conference paper circulating; I took a note in case people ever asked. Surprisingly few do, though. It seems that, once you scrabble ashore, you just keep struggling forwards. Unless you're a mother adrift from her kids, it's rare that refugees go searching for their past. All those loved ones, scattered. Perhaps it's better to imagine them still at home, waiting in the warmth.

Family Tracing Services.

I know I'm chasing ghosts. Rebecca was what, three or four when she saw her mother dragged away. At that age, you see fairies. You have whole imaginary worlds in which you live. But what if this is not imagination? It can't hurt to explore the possibility. All Abdi saw was blood, all he heard was Rebecca's cries. And Rebecca is adamant that she saw what she saw. Lara spent a long time talking to her afterwards. Filling the room with calm. It was like she'd unwrapped Rebecca, then was rebandaging her. Better, cleaner. There were no more allusions to Azira, no false promises. We talked a little about talking, about why sometimes we don't. Rebecca consented to it all. She let herself be swaddled. Even sat up on my knee. But that child is suffused with fierce intelligence. I know it. And she wants to be heard, about so many things. With Abdi's agreement, I think we should push for school. There used to be a second entry after Christmas, I can't see that it'd be impossible to let her start then. In the interim, we could ask for speech and language therapy – though I hardly think she needs it. We might even consider these Freedom people. Might. For now, I will say nothing to Abdi of the strange table-horse and its living cargo, and I don't think Rebecca will either.

To her, it's not a revelation. It's a long-borne fact.

Red Cross provides limited . . . That was who they mentioned in the conference paper. I click, search, scan . . . there's a form to be filled in, phone numbers to be called. As much detail as possible, it says. Where you last saw your missing person, when and how and why you lost them . . . I realise I don't even know Azira's full name. Mrs Casci is still at lunch. I'm pretty sure she's the line manager for Abdi's caseworker, who's away on leave. Volunteering in Namibia, God love him. There's no limit to the generosity of some of the people working here. If I were a full-time employee, I'd need a luxury spa break, where the world came wrapped in towelling robes. I ponder, muse, rationalise.

My fingers hover. I succumb.

We can access most of our client files on the database. It's quiet today. Lunchtime sun is shining, after the cold snap we've had. Folks' troubles ease on a ripe September day; they seem slow and grateful for a glimmer of extra sun. We'll sook it up, deal with the shit tomorrow. Even the phones are quieter. Into the uncanny stillness flies a rainbow peal of praise.

Blessed God!

It's Gamu's tired man, and he's literally jumping for joy. Gamu's clasping him to her bosom – against all protocols, but he doesn't

338

seem to mind. The letter they hold between them drifts palely to the floor. The man dips with grace, swoops it up, and I am witnessing his rebirth as the years and dust shake off him. His height and girth increase; he turns, bows, includes me in his ebullient glow.

'I am to stay!' he booms. 'You have invited me to stay!'

'That's wonderful,' I call, glad for him and for Gamu. Too often, we have to read out bad news to our clients. But the days when you get that letter, when a shaking hand passes you an unread sheet of paper and you say the words out loud:

You have been granted refugee status.

That's why you do this.

That is why I'm doing this. I return to my computer screen. The files we've got here are basic: a log of when and what help clients have received. I type in Abdi's name, just to *see*. Up it comes: age, address, children. Interactions with SRC. As I suspected, the self-sufficient bugger hasn't asked for much: help with that perennial, housing; wee bit of advice on learning opportunities; no complaints lodged about his mentor (yet). I scroll down, flicker when I see his wife's full name:

Azira Samatar Guleed (Hassan) (deceased).

Why is Hassan in brackets? Were they not really married? Or maybe Somali women don't take their husband's name. I should know these things, I'm supposed to be his mentor. I write all four names precisely; there's no date of birth, no last known address for either her or Abdi's families. All I have is the name of the camp, and a rough idea of dates. Under 'contacts', it lists the solicitor who must have dealt with Abdi's asylum application, me – which sends another silly ripple of pleasure through me – and not one, but two ministers – a Father and a Reverend. Abdi's as cosmopolitan as he is smart. He's clearly hedging his bets. All I know is that he goes to church, and Mrs Coutts goes there too. Fine. If church is a comfort to him, then good but it's not a crutch I want to discuss. So we don't. Such is my reductive reasoning, I've been limiting his horizons since we met. See Glasgow? See religion? The whole place seethes with its undercurrents. Our schools, our football teams, our whole civic life. In fact, it's the marker of where the city began. Glasgow Cathedral should have been the very first place I took him to.

'Goodbye, my wonderful friends!' The untired man is blowing us kisses. Gamu leans from her little booth, laughing. Laughing and waving until he is out of sight. Would there be any point in talking to Abdi's minister? I note down the phone number of the reverend, with the 0141 Glasgow code. The number for the priest is unrecognisable . . . ah, that's because it's some lengthy postcode that's spilled across the columns . . . for . . . I scroll back. Malawi. Africa. I reread the entry, see the priest has the first initial 'P'. Further down, it says Father Paolo Alessi. The friend called Paolo who Abdi lived with, it must be! I copy down the whole address, with its string of numbers and unfamiliar words. Surely Paolo could tell me where to start? I can put in a request to the Red Cross too. With Azira's full name, the rough date and location, the fact it was an ambush . . . Dadaab can't be entirely lawless. They must keep records in the camp.

A door swings in the lobby. No one comes in. Gamu is no longer laughing. In fact, she's crying. Slow, silent crying which she hides behind her hands. There's only me and her in the office. The whole world's gone to lunch. I ignore my ringing phone, go over. Funny how it's the good news that can finally knock you adrift. Grim vigour holding you together until a shaft of pure delight punctures your too-tight skin. Mrs Casci's office remains unlocked. The silvery handle is tactile, sleek. What extra files would be stashed in there? Whole swathes of Abdi's backstory, a phone number for the priest? It could be months before a letter gets there. Now that I'm doing this, I want to do it *now*. Jesus God, what if that poor woman really was left behind? If she limped and crawled to hide, or was carried away on a table-shaped horse? What if she's still waiting for someone to come and find her? The thought shivers in a flu-ache, it impels me to rush and demand, to scour out absolute facts. If it was a raid on the camp, there'd have been bodies, officials to count the bodies, to bury them, surely? Or maybe dead refugees become carrion. An image comes of still-live bodies, and the buzzards circling and my phone continues ringing and there's poor Gamu, crying. I scooch down to hug her.

'Och, come on, missus. It's all right. Just you let it out.'

She folds into me, hot hair tickling my mouth. We sway, me wobbling since I'm down on my hunkers and have terrible balance at the best of times, and — let's face it — Gamu's quite a big girl, so I grab the edge of her chair, which is on wheels and it shudders, which makes her laugh again, thank God.

'Hey, it's cool, Debs. I'm fine.' Heel of her hand, scrubbing at her eyes. 'Fine.'

'You sure?' I oof and uff myself upright: I probably have the joints of an eighty-year-old. *Weight-bearing exercise!* I know, I know. More calcium, too, but milk's such an unpleasant, chalky drink.

'Mmhm.' Her reply is unconvincing.

'Honestly?'

She's a nurse. She only does this job for light relief. Who am I to counsel her?

'Uh-huh.' Gamu gulps. Massively. Like she's gulping in the sea. Blinks through puffed-up eyes and gulps again. 'Huh ... no. Not really. No, I'm not so good today, my love.'

'What's up?'

She heaves up her giant handbag. Its patent leather gleams. Everything about Gamu is large and bright. Rummages until she finds a brown envelope, torn at the top. 'Will you read my letter?' she asks. Same simple phrase we hear a dozen times a day.

It's from the UK Border Agency.

... must advise you that we have been appraised of investigations currently underway in relation to your claims in respect of Working Tax Credits ...

I read the paragraph again. 'Is this a joke?' The letter flails as I gesticulate, prodding and pinching air. 'They're saying you're a benefits cheat? But that's ridiculous. I've seen you – you never even put in your travel claims for coming here. I'll write to them –'

Gamu licks the corner of her lips. 'I did it all right, you know? I phoned the helpline before I put in my form. Then, one year later, they phone me back – say I shouldn't be getting this. I even give them the name of the lady I spoke to. Date, time – I write it all down, but they don't care.'

'Bullshit. We'll fight this. No way are you getting labelled a fraudster. I mean, will they want you to pay them back? How much are we talking?'

She makes a weary half-shrug. 'Don' matter. Read the rest.'

... came here under the Fresh Talent Initiative, a scheme which has now expired. Consequently, you were informed that your visa would require to be renewed. I am writing now to inform you that your renewal application has been refused ...

The slick text crawls across the page. The page is shaking, the shaking is me.

'Refused? They're chucking you out because of a mix up over tax credits? No way. No bloody way. Have you appealed?'

'I only got the letter this morning.'

'Who's your lawyer?' Automatically, I reach over her, for her phone.

'I can't ... Not now, babes, OK? I ... I thought if I kept busy ... this doesn't feel so real, you know? I just need to go someplace, be a little calm. You be OK if I go ... ?'

'Sure, sure.' I help her to her feet. Pass her her gleaming bag, which matches her always-smart shoes. Gamu's hand clenches the strap, her expression clenches too. Desperation flames like a candle. Is bitten back. And there's me, mouth on hinges, standing like a chookie. Watching this splendid woman sail out into Glasgow's streets.

19. OCTOBER

SCOTTISH PARLIAMENT

'There shall be a Scottish Parliament.'

These words, inscribed on the Mace of the Scottish Parliament, form the opening of the Scotland Act, which led to the establishment of the first Scottish Parliament since 1707, and the creation of the stunning new Parliament building at the foot of Edinburgh's Royal Mile.

A sovereign nation in its own right, Scotland has never been conquered. In 1603, the Scottish and the English crowns united when James VI of Scotland succeeded Elizabeth to the English throne. Each country retained its own Parliament, Church, laws and coinage until 1707, when concerns about unified succession and a disastrous Scottish economic slump led to the dissolution of the Scottish Parliament and political union with Westminster. For the next 300 years, however, the desire for a return to Scottish self-government waxed and waned, culminating in 1997 in a national referendum — which produced a clear majority in favour of Scottish devolution.

The Scottish Parliament reconvened in July 1999, and, four years later, took its seat in the curvaceous building designed by Spanish architect Enric Miralles. Sitting in front of Salisbury Crags, the complex structure is formed from a mixture of steel, oak and granite, and has been hailed as one of the most innovative designs in Britain today.

Open to visitors six days a week, and home to the country's 129 MSPs, admission to the Scottish Parliament is free.

★

FROM THE OUTSIDE, it is fair to say the Scottish Parliament looks like a concrete block of flats. To which – in a misguided attempt to 'add interest' – some bright spark has appliquéd giant cow-hides, then glued on some garden canes.

Step through the low dull portal, however, and it is magical.

It is your country, your hope and your pride, all bound in sinuous pale oak and shafts of light, in echoing floors and ancient walls and modern vaults that are the fabric of cathedrals. Stairs and spirits rise as you ascend through metallic, marbled layerings. And the art – the spirited art that is the very pores of this place, breathing from walls and doorways in the carving, the paintings, the sculpted joys. Etched words on glass and stone speak of better nations and women's dreams, the Declaration of Arbroath is eloquently honest, and it hurts your chest. Glass-eyed girders blink above us in the Garden Lobby, which is where we're to be received, where the harled frontage of Queensberry House, forever walled within the parliament, is the old encompassed by the new.

There shall be a Scottish Parliament.

It all hurts your chest. This place, the fact of it, the procession of marching people – twenty of you, because that's all they would allow – bearing petitions to your king. Or to your MSP at least: a very nice chap who will make 'the most earnest protestations', but *immigration is not a devolved matter*, but what else can we do? Poor Geordie never got this chance. We're damned if Gamu will go quietly.

At the far end of our crocodile, Abdi gives me a cheerful wave. Our group has been crafted to be 'representative'. It's a mix of old and young, of refugees, asylum seekers, volunteers and – in our biggest coup yet – a well-known Scottish soap actress whose mum was nursed by Gamu. How lucky is that? (Not for the old lady, unfortunately, who has since passed.) Gamu stands centre stage, in her uniform. She'd wanted to wear a voluptuous red coat – *it is fire, my love, it will give me courage*. But Caro Winter and I overruled her. Entirely due to the presence of Ms Soap, the television news is here. You can't blame them – they only have sporadic interest and slots for these stories: if it is a clutch of wonderful angry Glasgow teen-agers, or a doe-eyed child whose mummy left her abusive husband and is no longer his dependant and so is no longer entitled to stay. *These* things get folk angry. Gamu is a healthy working woman, with no dependants and an uncompromising frown. Ergo:

There shall be a Scottish soapstar.

Gamu's MSP is a nationalist, which means he can be as direct and vital as he likes in his derision of the Home Office, of UK immigration policy, in his defence of Scotland's undeniable need and inalienable right to 'choose and welcome her own citizens'.

'Gamu is a woman who has done nothing but good since we

invited her to our shores nearly a decade ago. She contributes hugely to the fabric of her community – through her nursing, her volunteer work, her neighbourliness. It's a testament to this neighbourliness that the petition I'm receiving today has over 3,000 signatures –'

That petition is the fruit of four weekends in a row standing in various shopping centres. Abdi and I took St Enoch's, unPC Len and his girlfriend did Buchanan Galleries and a couple of Caro's mates drove out to The Fort and Silverburn respectively. Each weekend, we rotated location, figuring some people might sign twice if they thought it was a different petition. Gamu's next-door neighbour organised a local ceilidh to raise funds, and I encouraged Abdi to go.

'Och, you've not lived till you've done the Gay Gordons.'

'It sounds painful.'

'It is.'

I stayed home to babysit, but not before I'd taught him how to 'hee-uuch' (an essential sound-effect for any eightsome reel). As regards the actual dancing, Abdi was on his own. Ceilidhs are great fun, don't get me wrong. I love the way your feet know the airs and dances, some folk-memory revived and reinforced by all those hours in the school gym. But Mrs Coutts's hip was playing her up and Rebecca was going to stay at mine. Len and his girlfriend would drive Abdi over. We all had dinner here first.

'Just don't eat too much before you go. In case all the birling makes you puke.'

'Remind me again why is it that you're not coming to this cultural delight?'

'Oh, I've done a fair bit of Stripping the Willow in my time, don't you worry. And you've not, plus you need a babysitter and Gamu needs your support. So there.'

I picked up a tea towel and said they'd better head: Rebecca and I were going to make scones. I'm sorry I missed Abdi's face as he saw the kilts, that I never heard Gamu shriek as she was swung in a figure of eight. By all accounts, it was a brilliant night – they raised a wad of cash, and got three hundred signatures right there in the hall and the pub next door. But I'm not sorry for avoiding the drink and loudness, the arms linked to spinning bodies that would bump and hold me. I didn't want to be held. Abdi told me to imagine Callum at his finest, and it hurt so much; all that unseen weight demanding to be made visible. Each tiny seed flying into the air was all the years I've still to live without him. All the possibilities, and the decisions I must make. My unreadiness to make them.

Avoiding the ceilidh was a decision. Rebecca and I made luscious scones and did our reading practice – she's skipped two levels already. When she went to bed, I resumed my search. Every day since I'd written to Father Paolo, I'd anticipated the postman (I think he thought I was stalking him, this disturbing, dressing-gowned creature behind the door). All he brought was the usual round of bills and circulars. Nothing from Paolo – and I'd put my home address, home phone number, email, Refugee Council address and phone number on the letter, so he was spoilt for choice. I'd had a brief reply from the Red Cross, but it was just an acknowledgement of my enquiry. Most nights I'd be on the computer, visiting sites and chatrooms, posting requests for refugees who'd been in Dadaab to get in touch, seeking charities that might carry out searches. That night – with Abdi jigging at the ceilidh, with Rebecca sleeping and the smell of scones in my kitchen – I went as usual to the internet. Opened up my emails expecting the usual dross, and there it was! A message from Father Paolo. He apologised for the delay, apologised all the more for his not-knowing.

I cannot believe that Azira might be dead. We all believed the transition had gone smoothly. I am sickened to learn this is not so. I have written to our charity partners to find out what they know, and why I was not told. In the meantime, I suggest you try to contact a Ms Rose Gray. She no longer works for the charity in question, but was their Kenyan co-ordinator at the time. As she has moved on, I no longer have her contact details. I have asked for them to be provided to me, but perhaps you might also search yourself? I believe she is originally from Donegal in Ireland. The facilities I have in Malawi are somewhat basic & we often lose internet connection – hence my late reply. In the meantime, can you please tell Abdi that I pray for him and his beloved Rebecca, and that I commend both them and Azira to the mercy and grace of Our Lord. I will write as soon as I have news. With God's blessings on you all.

Fr Paolo Alessi

Rose Gray. Right there, I searched online for the Irish phone book. As if. Like we have a 'Scottish' phone book. Then I looked up Donegal. Did you know there was a Donegal in Pennsylvania? My only option was to work through a different city a night. If any similar names came up (and there were five in Dublin, three in Belfast and a Dympna-Rose Gray in Derry), I'd phone them. And I did. And, each time, I drew a blank. I even got my nieces trying Facebook and Twitter. It would help if I'd known what charity she'd worked for, but Father Paolo hadn't said.

And then he contacted me again. Last night, as I was checking emails with one hand and painting my Parliament banner with the other, I got another email. Still no details for Rose, but the soul had gone to the bother of finding someone who would scan and upload a photo of Azira. I read his email before I opened the attachment.

> I have sent this picture to Light of the World, who have still to reply, but I thought also that it may be of help to you. I suspect Abdi will not have such images. This was taken at my house, at Christmas when Rebecca would have been three, I believe – although Abdi is very vague with ages – it is a Somali trait! Please tell him how much he is in my prayers.

I couldn't, of course. *Why were you speaking with Father Paolo, Debs? Oh, no reason. Just because I think your wife could still be alive, and you left her there.*

I clicked on the attachment, and there she was.

Azira.

Black Rebecca-eyes, deep in their sockets. A heart-shaped face, skin sleek across her cheekbones, which were sickle-sharp; holding the light in perfect crescents. The flash had caught the starkness of her teeth, her long forehead, her coffee-cream neck. She was wrapped in some kind of checked plaid. I thought she'd wear a headscarf, but her straight hair hung in a middle parting, uncovered and made into tiny strands. One tendril flicked across her face as if she'd just that minute turned her head, was on the brink of . . .

From the flickering screen, Azira regarded me, her mouth a half-arch. I couldn't tell if her lips were painted; they seemed too stained to be real. It had to be make-up. To be that bare-faced stunning would be unfair. I touched my fingers to the screen. Whispered, 'Hi.'

You know when you're wee and bursting to tell a secret; when it's so imperative to relieve the pressure? And the other urge that accompanies your need for revelation: that, although you *know* you're doing the right thing, you need another to confirm it? Or not.

I met my sister for lunch today, before coming through to Edinburgh (clever Caro has arranged an afternoon appointment with our MSP, to catch the tea-time news). Brought Azira's picture with me, so that Gill would understand.

We ate, we talked, she blanched.

'Jesus.'

'I know. And it may be wishful thinking, but it *sounds* real. Rebecca wasn't play-acting. I thought if I could get her story checked out in some way . . . obviously I'm saying nothing to Abdi. Not yet.'

Gill picked up the photograph again.

'Yeah, but look at her. She's gorgeous.'

'So?'

'I said *look* at her, you idiot. You of all folk should know what happens in refugee camps. There was an article in the *Sunday Herald* last month – it's around one in three women, maybe higher –'

'Shut up. I know.'

'Well, have you ever thought maybe Abdi didn't look back on purpose?'

'Don't be so bloody stupid.'

'OK, you know him, I don't. But from what you and Richard have told me, he's a very proud man. Maybe he couldn't cope with the thought of what else might have happened to Azira. And maybe you going digging round where you're not wanted is a totally crap idea. The guy's already had one breakdown.'

'Piss off, Gill. You're telling me I should just leave her there?'

'You know, you swear much more than you used to.'

'Excuse me –' I ordered another beer. 'You wanting anything else?'

'Nope. *And* you're drinking more.'

'I'm not, actually. I'm just not hiding it.'

'Oh sister dear. You're such a thrawn besom.' Gill kissed me on the cheek. 'Gotta go. We have an HMI inspection tomorrow. Joy of joys. Look, you do what you've got to do.'

'I will.'

She got up. 'Just think about worms and cans, yes?'

'Mm. You'd better go and cook your books. I'm off to get the train.'

Gill's hand hung on the back of the chair. 'How's wee Rebecca doing, anyway?'

A quiet dazzle inside me. Glad that she asked, that my wee sister really cares and that we come from a family that cares, despite my dad's protestations. Callum would have cared too.

'Good. I've got her on some Primary Two readers already. I think

Abdi's coming round to the idea of school after Christmas. D'you still think you could swing it?'

'Leave it to your fairy-sister. If I still have a job after tomorrow, that is.'

'Ach, the inspectors will love you. *Everybody* loves you.' I reached up to hug her. 'Even me.'

Inside the Scottish Parliament, where we are standing, light pours in from the ceiling. It paints us brighter than we really are, enhances profiles and upturned faces with noble glows. The MSP is nearly finished, the cameras are swivelling to the soapstar. Virtually no one is looking at Gamu as she stands quietly to one side, observing her worth being measured. An appeal has been lodged with the Home Office, all we can do is wait. And keep on shouting. I go over and squeeze her hand.

'Will we go home now?'

'Yes. Please.'

I have the picture of Azira on the noticeboard, which hangs on the wall to the left of my PC. Beside the noticeboard, in front of my computer, is my window, from which I can see my street. Azira watches me from between a Scottish Economic Society calendar (they send me one every year, bless them) and a carry-out menu for the Golden Tandoor. I can see Mrs Gilfillan moving stiffly in her front room. She is watering her ferns. Next door to Mrs Gilfillan, Naomi's kids are playing with their new au pair, who is just as smiley and efficient as Rula was. Naomi, when I see her now, keeps her head down and is brisk, trailing out a 'Hi there' only when she's past. I rarely reply. Lovely bouncy Allison is walking with her children; no, now she waits patiently as the wee boy stops to examine his reflection in an oil-rimmed puddle, which is beautiful. Music lifts from the open window of the dance school and the trees are gradually giving up their leaves. All Azira can see is the top of my head – and the wall behind me, which badly needs a paint. I unhook my noticeboard, turn it so it rests diagonally across the corner of the broad windowsill, facing outward, with the edge nearest me balanced on my desk.

What does my little sister know?

In front of me are two letters. I slit open the first one. I can't make out the postmark, but it's been franked by the Red Cross. My hands are trembly; the paperknife slips, the bobbly brass head of it (an oversized thistle) dips forward and the knife presses up, catching a fragment of hangnail. Just a totey wee strip of skin, but, man, it stings.

I read. I read it again.

Dear Mrs Maxwell

Apologies for the delay in responding, but I am currently overseas and our mail is being forwarded by the Red Cross. I understand from my former employers Light of the World that you've been trying to get in touch with me, in regard to tracing a refugee by the name of Azira Hassan. As you may know, I no longer work for Light of the World, but it's my understanding that Mrs Hassan travelled with her husband and child from the Dadaab Camp in Kenya to the UK approximately two years ago now. I think it would have been the November possibly? Can I suggest therefore that you

contact the Home Office, or failing that, the Red Cross Tracing Service, for
information on where the Hassan family were then sent.

I'm sure you'll appreciate that we worked with many refugees, so it's not
possible for me to keep tabs on them all. Good luck with your search.

All the very best
Rose Gray

My excitement plummets as I read, then bounces, right at the end.
Rose has sent this message on heavy notepaper, the kind which
you order with your name and mobile telephone number inscribed
on the bottom of the page. It's dated two weeks ago. I pick up the
phone. Dial, my heart playing with my ribs.

'Hello. Rose Gray.' Her voice is cheery and hopeful. But definitely Glaswegian.

'Hello,' I say. 'Sorry. But is this Rose Gray from Donegal?'

'Eh – who is this, please?'

'You don't know me, but my name is Deborah Maxwell. I'm
hoping to speak to the Rose who used to work for Light of the
World?'

'Yes. That's me.'

'Oh, sorry. I was told you were from Ireland.'

'When I was a baby, yes. I'm sorry – what's this in connection
with?'

'You were good enough to send me a letter about Azira Hassan?
From Dadaab?'

'Azira … Hassan? Oh yes … yes. I was quite surprised when
Light of the World got in touch. But, like I said –'

'Sorry. Can I ... sorry to interrupt you. I don't think they told you why I was trying to find her. I'm sorry – this is so weird, you being Glaswegian. You see, Abdi and his daughter made it here, to Glasgow – that's how I know him. But he believes his wife was killed in the camp – on the very day they were leaving.'

'Oh my God. But that's not possible.'

'Were you there?' I don't mean this to sound accusatory.

'I ... well, no. We set up the transportation, then left it to the local agents. That happens quite often, you know. I mean, Light of the World is a small charity, and I was covering several camps – not just in Kenya, actually.'

'Of course. I'm not ... look, I only ask, because I'm not quite sure what happened the day they were due to leave. Abdi says there was an ambush – men on horseback.'

'Al-Shabaab?' It comes in a gunfire crackle.

'I don't know. He's never given them a name. But apparently they struck just as the trucks were loading up.'

'Do you know where they were loading? Was it the south gate? Bloody hell, I bet it was the south gate – they were expressly told not to leave from that location.' She halts, draws breath in. 'Sorry. Sorry, on you go.'

'I don't know much more, really. Abdi and his wee girl escaped, but Azira was attacked and dragged away, along with several others. Nobody knows what happened to them thereafter. There's a slim chance that she wasn't killed. Maybe. Her wee girl says she saw her being put on to a horse.'

'Oh Jesus.'

'Look. Abdi doesn't know any of this – he thinks his wife is dead.

All I want to do is find out if there are any records of an incident, if any bodies were recorded, names of people killed. Anything. And if there's even a glimmer of a hope that Azira wasn't killed, then I want to try and find her. What I need from you is the exact date they were scheduled to leave the camp. And any contacts you have, or advice you can give me on how I go about getting those records.'

I fling this last requirement in like it's a request for eggs or milk, all tumbling out in the rush. As if, slipped in with such subtlety, Rose is bound to go, *sure, no problem* and rattle off the home telephone number for the Head of the UN. She doesn't.

'Suffering God. Where to begin . . .'

'That's what I was hoping you'd know. Is it the UN we speak to? Or the Kenyan police –'

'Je-sus no! Ach,' there is a squelching sound, like she is rubbing her eyes or her nose, 'it's complicated. Really, truly complicated. I can't believe this. It's the very thing we were trying to avoid.'

'What is?' But I don't think she hears me.

'Problem is, soon as you start asking questions, any semblance of records or evidence – if there ever was any – will disappear. The only people you'll ever get the truth from are the refugees: people who were there, who actually saw it. And even then, the moment they hear a *mzungo* asking for help, they'll tell you anything you want to hear. For a price, of course.'

'So what do I do?'

'Deborah, isn't it?'

'Yes.'

'Deborah. Do you have any idea how big Dadaab is? I mean, it's not even the one camp. There's three of them, three great big filthy hellholes full of people disappearing every day. Charities: we go in like SWAT squads, wheech a handful of them to safety – and then you hear *this*.'

The fire in her's all sputtered out. Voice gone to ash.

'Have you got an email address, Rose?'

'I do.'

'Let me email you a photo I have of Azira. Please.'

'For why? D'you think if I send it on to the camp some beady-eyed policeman will track her down?'

'But you must still *know* people there. People you could trust.'

'Deborah, I thought I could trust my transportation agents. We'd been using the bastards for the last five or six years.'

She says this with such venom that I am knocked off course. 'Och God, I don't know then. Maybe Rebecca just made it all up, maybe your agents are fantastic. But whether Azira lived or whether she died – she bloody well didn't make it out the camp. And your agents never reported that, did they?'

I hear a massive sigh. My ragged finger's singing. Flayed flesh grating on air. I take it in my mouth, suck it.

'No,' Rose says softly. 'No, they did not.'

The line goes quiet. Has she hung up on me? As I say *hello?*, all miffed and querulous, she goes: 'Ach, right. Here's what we'll do then. You know how I'm with Oxfam now?'

I murmur *um*, don't want to interrupt her flow which I sense is building to a solid plan.

'Well, we've a new sanitation project launching in Dadaab. I'm not strictly involved, but part of my job is overseeing operational human resources. Now, I'm scheduled to be visiting Nairobi next month, but what I could do is work in a couple of days at Dadaab too. On the basis of visiting our water guys. Only two days at the most, mind. This lot work me like a Trojan – you're lucky you caught me at all.'

'You mean you'd go out there yourself?'

'Quickest way I can see. I know the girl, know the feckers who arranged the pick-up. And I daresay I'll still know the safest hand to slip a bribe in.'

'Right, of course. Bribes. How much are we talking?'

'Depends how high I need to go. US dollars usually hit the mark. Ach, don't worry – they have a bureau de change there. Right next to the camel-slaughter-and-sacrifice house, so it is.'

'I'll give you whatever you need. You have no idea how grateful I am, Rose.'

'I'm promising absolutely nothing, mind. There'll only be the one of me, and I'll have to do some proper work too, else they'll not pay my board and lodgings!'

She lets out a trill of crystally laughter, and if I merely thought she was wonderful before, now I've fallen in love with her.

'Can I come?' Three syllables release themselves from my unsuspecting mouth. *What?*

'Seriously?'

'Yeah, I'm serious.' Suddenly, I am. 'What would I need to do? Do I need a visa, jags, what?'

'Holy moly ... Um ... I'm not ... Look, Deborah. I don't know you from Adam. This is not a holiday we're talking about. It'll be roasting hot, it'll stink the enamel off your teeth, break your heart – and it's as dangerous as buggery.'

'Aye, but will there be karaoke?'

There's a beat before she laughs again. 'Tell me. Do you do duets?'

We exchange email addresses, Rose says she will send a checklist. I'll have to pay my own way – *and a sizeable donation to charity would be nice* – but she'll try to arrange for me to get a press pass to accompany her. *I'll say you're a freelance, doing a piece on the water project or something. Might give you that wee bit more leverage when we get there.*

I put the phone down, shocked. Sit for a full ten minutes until my pulse quietens and the saliva quits gushing in knots.

God oh God oh God. I am going to Dadaab! I want to run outside and scream it. How wonderful, how brave! How utterly bloody mad. But what if what if what if.

What if I go back to Africa, and find a life to save.

It's grown dark since I first sat down here. Hard edges of my street smudged by lamplight. We have special wrought-iron lanterns, installed by the conservation society. Very grand and curly-black, very solid. But they're an illusion. There's no Leary coming with his taper to flame the gas. We're all electric here, all mod cons. I remember the vast bareness of Africa, the circle of Callum's arms around me, the unseen presences that whine and howl. What will it feel like, to sit on the edge of the bush again? Is it even bush in Kenya? I have no idea, and it's too late to ask. What if I don't find out what happened to Azira? What if I do? What if Abdi is horrified?

I am shivering. Cup of tea, I think. Although whisky might be warmer. I reach to switch off the computer, and my sleeve brushes some paper off the desk. The other letter. I retrieve it from the carpet. Open it. It's actually a postcard inside an envelope. There's no return address, and the message is brief. In simple rounded hand it says:

Dear Madam

I write to thank you for being a friend to my daughter when she is living in Glasgow. I am told you found for her a good place to stay. I think Rula did not have so many friend. It is good that you were for her there. I am most kindly thanks to you and write to advise you that she is home now safe. We have buried her beside her mother. It is very beautiful there. You can see river. For you it makes I can imagine her with friends. This means very much.

With my grateful thanks
P. Kadyrov, Esq.

I lay my head on folded arms. Keep staring out the window.

'ANY CHANCE OF a refill, big man?' Dexy waves his empty glass. 'Just gies the can but.' His short legs drape over the arm of my couch. Politely, he took his boots off when we came indoors, so it's only his threadbare socks which swing against the newness. Rebecca watches, open-mouthed. She knows the penalty for jumping on the couch.

'Oh, here, here. Turn that up, man. You heard this song? It's fuc – it's brilliant, so it is. You like music, hen? Gonny do a wee dance for us?'

There's a knock, sorry no. A chap at my front door. I mean my front door is *being* chapped, not that there is a man. I put my glass down, go to let Debs in. Rebecca is staying at hers tonight, because I have an early start at college. Our English class meets at nine, and we've been getting in a guddle – Rebecca and I, not the class. Little heap of beer cans … kick them out of sight. Yes. Early rises no longer suit Rebecca; she is not sleeping so well; has once more been wetting the bed. Mornings see her fractious, huffy almost, like I am to blame. But I never shout at her. Except when she wrote 'couch' on the back of our couch. Debs says this is more reason she should go to school, and I am thinking she is right. About the Lara woman, I'm not so sure. It seems this wilful unease has grown since their meeting. Debs wants to take her again, but I have said no.

Have you spoken to Rebecca? Asked her how she feels about seeing Lara?

No. I said I do not want to know.

'Hiya!'

Deborah has cut her hair. It shimmers in neat flicks, elongates her neck. Her neck. I am aware I smell of alcohol.

'Here, there's that money I owe you for those comics.'

I demur, she insists, crumpling paper money into my pocket it is my jeans pocket, does she feel it as her knuckles graze me? I have imagined it but not her perfume, which angers me. Her perfume disturbs the atmosphere.

'No, please –'

'*No.* I said I'd pay. Hello, mucky pup! Whatya –' Debs halts midway into the lounge room, pressing her purse into her breast. 'What's he doing here?'

'Oh-ho,' smiles Dexy. A thin smile. 'It's yirsel, doll. Lookin good. *Not.* You put on weight?'

'Abdi?'

Her eyes are flint. It is my medicine, these pills dull thought and reflex, but they seem to heighten my sense of smell. That is all. It is the beer and it is my medicine. I am going to stop them. Soon.

Now. I want to drum my fingers. I swallow. 'Deborah. You remember Dexy? Well, we have some very good news.'

'He's just leaving?'

'Ha! No. We are not long arrived.'

'Really?' She has seen the beer cans.

'We have been to the supermarket. And, the very good news is – I have got Dexy a job!'

'You've what?'

'My apprenticeship is not yet filled, so I asked Mr Maloney, and he says he will ask –'

She darkens even more. 'Abdi, I got *you* that job. As a favour.'

'Indeed? It was not because I was a good fishman then?'

'No, what I mean is, you should have come to me. I could have spoken to my brother-in-law.'

'But *I* wanted to do this. I said *I* would help. And I have.'

Dexy expels a beery burp. 'Listen to the man, doll. We're doin fine without you. Chillax!' He grins at Rebecca. 'Will we give your auntie a wee beer?'

'Rebecca.' Debs throws her purse into her opened handbag. 'Do you want to come with me and we'll get your overnight bag packed? I'm assuming Aabo's been far too busy entertaining to sort it?'

Guilt and belligerence poise on the corners of my mouth. Turn one way, see her face, and *this* is what I will say. Turn the other, see him, and I will have to say –

So I say nothing.

Debs and Rebecca disappear. Is it my imagination or does Rebecca mimic the surly flounce of her mentor? *My* mentor, who has in fact dropped her purse as she flounces. And her mobile phone. I pick them up, lay them on the mantelpiece, right next to Jesus on the cross. Pour from the can into my glass. Glug, glug, glug. See it cloud and form and separate. The amber light, the friendly froth. Why would God not want us to enjoy this lovely stuff?

'*Man*. You shagging that?'

'I'm sorry?'

Dexy makes a lewd gesture, pushing the finger of one hand through a circle he makes with his other hand.

'No! Debs is my friend.'

'Aye *right*. Some friend. Keep your baws in her handbag, does she?'

'She is a very good friend.'

'Aye well. Takes allsorts. Anyway. Here's to you, ma man. Cheers.'

'Cheers.'

The beer is a little stale. But the fact of my good deed warms me hugely. Maybe I didn't explain it well enough to Deborah. I go to find them. Rebecca is in her room, carefully folding her pyjamas.

'Hey, mucky. Where's Debs?'

She shrugs at me, and it is *at* me, my extrasensory powers of perception have not confused this. As I go out, Debs is coming in, her hand stuffing something in her bag. The something crinkles, as paper would.

'What is that?'

'My handbag?'

'No, what you put inside.'

'Why? Do you think I'm robbing you or something?'

She is so brittle and bright. Snap-snap teeth. I have done nothing wrong.

'I only asked.'

'If you must know, it was a sanitary towel. For when women bleed?'

Aghastmortifiedhumiliatedmute a slug who drags its abject body away from harm's way. Back to my living room, my beer. My pal, who is picking his ear, then wiping it on the topmost cushion of the couch. I get a plastic bag from the kitchen, gather up the beer cans. Soon it will be tea-time and I have one lamb chop and one potato to bake. Maybe I could bulk it out with onions, and do plantains go with that? Dexy is turning up the telly and I am harvesting a can from the mantelpiece – ooh, a little is left, good – and as I do so, Debs's phone begins to ring. I lift it up, then I think. *No. Get it yourself.*

I finish the beer in the can. Has my new house ever been this full before? Close my eyes so I can hear the noise of mother and child as they laugh, as they are. As they are not. But it *is* laughter and a tenderness is there. My daughter uses a different voice to Deborah, one full of enquiry and need. Open my eyes. Who would have thought that Abdi Hassan would have a house of high bricks and women laughing again? On my couch, Dexy stretches, gently farts. Another expulsion a minute later, it's the quizzical noise of a text coming through.

Re our trip. Pal of mine on project spkn to man who says yes. R

I drop the phone as Debs returns to the living room.

' 'Scuse me.' Deliberately, I think, she nudges Dexy's feet as she passes. Her tone is ... tart. This is a new word I've learned, and I love its clever playfulness, how it mimics the sensation of sour rhubarb which is in a tart and sour expression which is in Deborah.

'Abdi, have you seen Rebecca's slippers? I can't –'

'Awright if I light up, big man?' An unlit cigarette already wobbles in Dexy's lips. I want to be a good host, but I don't want my couch to stink of smoke. Or my daughter.

'This is a no-smoking house,' says Debs. 'It's not good for Rebecca.'

'Fucksake. Who made you queen?'

'No swearing either.'

Dexy swivels himself to sitting. 'Ho. Abdi, man. Gonny control your wumman? Either that or gie her wan, because she's needing something –'

'She is not my woman.'

'She your fucking jailer then?'

'Right, that's enough, you. Out.'

'Deborah. Please do not speak to my guest like that.'

'Your guest? Abdi, he's a bloody junkie –'

'Ho! Ho, lady. You cool your jets, you. I'll have you know I've been clean for –'

'Shut up. I wasn't talking to you. Abdi – a word?' Debs motions for me to follow her. Dexy picks his teeth. My head is in my neck, I bristle then cower as I slink into the hall. Feel the muscles in my arms grow tight. Wait for her to rub my nose into my mess, for me to whine.

This is my home. There, that little head peeking from the haven of her doorway. That is my future and my past.

'Why the hell have you got in tow with *him*?'

'Because I want to help people.'

'Then why not volunteer at the Refugee Council, like I said? Or what about Gamu? D'you think going to a stupid ceilidh and getting some signatures is all it takes? Lobby your MP, do some leafleting – If you want to help folk, think about your own kind.'

'My own kind?'

I stare into the whiteness of her eyes, a thick gleam in them.

'I don't mean *that*,' she says. 'I mean refugees, folk who've struggled . . .'

'Maybe Dexy is my own kind, huh?'

'Oh really? A junkie arsehole who skives and scrounges his way through life?'

'You know nothing about him.'

'I know he's no good. And I don't want him anywhere near Rebecca. Have you forgotten you're still under Social Work supervision?'

'Have you forgotten this is my house? And that Rebecca is my daughter?'

Blotches on her throat and neck. 'Pardon?'

'Stop trying to control me. I am not your pet, Deborah. Nor your puppet. And I'm not some poor black boy you are trying to bring back to life.'

Slow

Motion

Strike.

We reel and dip. Her hand across my face. I let it come. Let it be firm and fleshly and explode. I feel the fallout burst across my cheekbone. Hold it.

'You utter bastard.'

'Debba!'

Extending the same hand to my baby. 'Come on, Rebecca. Let's go.'

'No. She is staying here with me.'

'Oh no she's not.'

'You want me to make her choose? Huh? Hey, Rebecca – who do you love more?'

'Jesus Christ, Abdi!'

Rebecca is terrified. An empty appeal hangs in her outstretched arms; Debs is there, scooping her up, gripping my wriggling fish until she flops. Rebecca rests her chin on Deborah's shoulder and regards me. It is the last look of Azira. She cradles my girl, and I can see how long her legs have become; they dangle down to almost Az to Debs's shins. Her own mother would not recognise her. Fucking beer and pills and talking and the window. My winking kitchen window that is wide and high if I run and run I could crash straight through. The sweet downdrift would wring the breath from inside me and I could scatter myself like seeds.

I could, you know. Plenty of 'my kind' do.

'OK, OK. Ssh. Aabo and I are just being silly.' Debs kisses Rebecca's forehead. 'Aren't we?'

'Please leave.'

'No!' wails Rebecca.

'Look, honey. I'm going to go now, but I'll see you very soon, all right?'

A sniff. 'For soft-play?'

'Yes – oh! No. God, no I can't this week. I'm sorry. Debba's going away for a few days.'

'Away where?'

'Just for a wee holiday. Abdi, I'm sorry. I meant to say ...'

'Can I not come?'

'No, pet. I'm sorry –'

'Deborah is going to meet men, I think. That is why you cannot go.'

'Have you gone mental?'

There is a pause.

I let my voice roll out until it hits her. 'Yes. Yes, in fact, I think that is exactly what my diagnosis was. But thank you for reminding me.'

Then Debs is crying and Rebecca is crying.

Stupid, ugly refugee.

'Ho! Gonny keep the noise doon, folks? I canny hear *Countdown*.'

'Please.' I open my arms. Debs relinquishes Rebecca without a fight. Oh, my girl is heavy. How did she get so heavy? I try to cradle her like Debs was doing, but her body is rigid and mine has no hips.

'I will see you *very* soon, I promise,' Debs says to the fierce hot head beside mine. Then she brings her face closer, until I can taste her breath. 'You better watch, Abdi. Cause see if Social Work know he's here –'

'He is not staying.'

'Good.'

A press of anticipation. Speak, speak do not speak swelling. I am trying to control this as I would steer the sea, abdicating to its strenuous insistence. I believe it is called *going with the flow*. Or is that too casual? Perhaps it is when you say *weathering the storm*, the hallway flooding with a silent *so?* But Debs seems to have decided I, we, Dexy are not deserving of further censure.

'Right. Well. I'll be off then.'

'Do not forget your phone. You dropped it.'

'Where?'

'Is on the mantelpiece. And your purse.'

'My purse? You left . . .' She does a little sigh, and her perfume flutters. Another kiss for Rebecca, then she goes to fetch her things. I hear Dexy mutter *fucksake*, hear a low murmur in response, and then she is gone.

Later, four beers later, I get rid of Dexy. It seems he had planned to sleep on the couch. Rebecca, thankfully, is in her bed. Took no dinner, and has refused to speak to me since Debs left. I wished Dexy had gone then. I need to wall myself in for the night. Stones in my skull, our fight clacking and colliding. I think I might phone Deborah. I was not fair to her. Dexy, though, is coiling himself around me. What do I fear most? Loneliness or . . . this.

'I can't accommodate you, my friend. Sorry. I have the Social Work lady coming later.'

Glib lies spilling. How civilised I am become.

'So? I'll be good. C'n rely on Dexy, pal,' he slurs. 'Brand new, so'n I am.'

'Ah, but I am not allowed to have guests to stay.'

'How no?'

I finger the little bread knife I had used to make us sandwiches.

'I can go a little crazy sometimes. With the knives.'

'Aye, very good.'

'And I threw a man downstairs. An old man.'

I harden. Make live wires of madness crackle. It is easy: merely involves the unpeeling of your soul, so that you are shiny and base. I smile, he smiles. Tapers and drips. Then musters himself.

'Ach, we're all a bit fucked in the heid department, pal. Fact, you're more fucked-up if you think you're no. Anyway,' Dexy slaps his knees, 'if it's all the same wi you, think I'll be headin. Big date wi a park bench, know?'

'Ah, but soon you will be in gainful employment.'

'Oh, aye. That.'

I bolt and lock the door behind him. Haze of beer and exhaustion. Will phone Debs tomorrow, after college. All I want is bed. Remember to check my hungry daughter, who is sleeping on her face. I turn her, gently, find my own room. Bed unmade. Climb in. Forget to pray. Just lie.

And lie and lie.

How are you feeling?

Better, thank you.

No, talking does not 'help'. Tapping my brow does not eradicate my visions. These pills, these pills and beer are symptoms of my weakness. Tomorrow, I will pour them in the toilet with the turds. I lie on my side, feel the blackness slide with me. My bedroom has blackout blinds; initially, I found them oppressive, but now I cannot sleep if they are not tight-sealed.

I am truly Scottish, see? I have perfected negative positivity. That and swearing.

What will become of me?

I just lie. Just stare at the smooth unyielding dark.

I am too big for my cloistered world. As a young, happy man, I had life. I knew my place, and knew I wanted more. Each day a spring to drink from, no *I* was the spring, bubbling forth and reaching for the sky. But now there is a rock perpetually laid upon me, crushing, blocking out the light.

To die would be to desert my daughter.

That is the only reason. Not your stupid fucking tapping on my skull.

Oh. I am. I'm drumming again. Fingers on belly, on my thighs. My counsellor told me I must write motivational notes. Put them in my sock drawer, so I commence each day with an endorsement to survive it. Debs threatened to phone his supervisor; I told her just to laugh. I cannot be without Debs and I am thrusting her away. Drumming again. Fingers on my groin.

Sleep is unkind, she will not come. Azira does, although I fight to keep her out, but she shivers in on drunken lust and tight-strung brainwaves that soothe when she is near. She curls into my back, is hot, burning hot in the black, black sun her hands on mine whispering *here I am, baby*.

I am so lonely, I whisper back. Willing her long slightness against me, bunching the covers up until they are a solid mass, each fold a leg, an arm, a breast. My hand her hand, the grip of her holding me, tentative, giggling, me firmer in the rhythm, the difference of her breath. Delight as I lessen and she quickens.

This is *not* my hand.

This is not.

I am a stupid refugee.

Azira, I whisper. I do not have her face. It is slipping, slipping. No possessions, no clothes, no books. *Wān ku jecelahay*. I no longer know what language I think in, but this is always the same. Distant, sharp, other – because it is her. I do not have a single image of my wife, not one thing that she is in or has touched. I wonder, was she ever real?

I wither. All the room is fading in the dark. What is real? Your taste, your words for ever? Things we know but have not seen? Only substances we can touch? Sounds that are the same, yet have no connection? Real and reel: to be the truth. To bring in fishes and to faint.

Have you swallowed a dictionary, son? Mrs Coutts has come to join us.

I lie. Just lie. Watching myriad rainbows burst. Breathe in oxygen and panic. Panic drumming panic winning my hand reaching for the light switch. GOLD. Eyes screw, then widen. Over there, between the wardrobe and the chest of drawers. My stolen red backpack. My *recycled* backpack, containing all my papers. Give a refugee some papers and he is rich. Azira is in there. Of course she is. When Father Paolo baptised Rebecca, he blessed our marriage too. We both signed our names on the certificate. Azira had prac-tised for days, embellishing her swirling instroke on the A, the loops uniting each letter into a word. Floorboards creaking with my bones. I get my backpack, will be calm when I can . . . no, it's not a backpack. Deborah says *rucksack*, I think backpack must be a child-ish word, *rucksack* is rougher, and I tug the straps to me . . . but it's lying open. I never leave it open. Look how easily Debs's phone slid away from her. Whatifwhat if? I shake the bag, upturn it. Count carefully through all my correspondence. Letters from Home

Office, Refugee Council, Housing. Department of no-Work and Pensions, my clinic, my counsellor, my doctor. And this and – no –. No. NO. The blessing parchment and Rebecca's baptismal certificate are missing.

I check, recheck. But they are gone.

21. NOVEMBER

DADAAB

Dadaab is a semi-arid town in north-east Kenya, but is also the collective name for the three refugee camps surrounding the town, known individually as Hagadera, Ifo and Dagahaley. Covering 50 square kilometres, the camps developed in this crisis-torn region in 1991, and have since become home to over 400,000 refugees. The vast majority are fleeing from civil war in neighbouring Somalia, although there are also refugees from Sudan, Uganda and the Congo.

Designed originally to accommodate around 90,000 people, the camps – which are served by a United Nations (UNHCR) base – suffer hugely from overcrowding and lack of resources. A further increase in violence in Somalia, coupled with ongoing famine, has seen an influx of up to 1,000 refugees a day. The area around Dadaab has suffered severe drought in recent years, killing livestock and severely impacting on the local economy and landscape, with food, fuel and building materials in constant demand. Growing tension between refugees and locals means that, as the camps are not officially demarcated, disputes over water, land and safety are common.

Several international humanitarian organisations deliver both emergency relief and long-term solutions, including food distribution, sanitation, counselling, training, health care, economic development and education. This vital work is only possible through the generous donations of supporters.

With many people living in the camps for up to ten years, much of Dadaab's economy now revolves around the provision of services for refugees.

★

Everything is gone! Stolen!

Calm down, Abdi. Slow down and tell me what's wrong.

Abdi's cries, my duplicity, drilling in my ears as the flat stone earth drills up from our tyres, sending tremors through the soles of my feet, my knee-joints, my bored-through back. We're on what's supposedly the main road: it is a crude track of rutted dust. Refusing to yield. *I am here. You chose to pass over me.*

Kenya. There is no give in this land, none at all. But it's true. *I am here.* On the edge of the weary desert. Pink-baked earth radiates vapours of heat and returns it to the sun: it is endless planes of thin and flat, surprised by spikes of green. Imagine sand dunes ironed smooth; it's that kind of scrubby hard grass, poking through sand. We're at the end of the short rainy season, which, one week ago, would have seen these pitted roads flood with mud and water. But the rains came early this year, and the thirsty soil has drunk it all down, flashing her thanks with these grasses, those bushes. That stunted bright tree. Flaming low and wide, clustered with scarlet on its highest spines, it's the flagrant red of rowan berries; the trees we Scots plant to keep away the witches.

'What is that?' I ask my driver, pointing.

'Acacia.'

Acacia Avenue. Epitome of Middle England. Wasn't that where Mr Benn lived?

'Christ!'

A crack of mortar fire, I cringe and duck. Realise our axle has just negotiated a large pothole. Resume my seat. No. Bananaman. It was definitely Bananaman.

Everything is gone.

I knew exactly what had gone, seeing as Rebecca's baptismal certificate and Abdi's marriage blessing are currently in a folder inside my travel case, which sits on my juddering knee. Rose said to bring anything I could that would substantiate a connection.

Even if we did find Azira, they won't just let us walk out. You'd be surprised what folk conjure up to try to get resettled.

No, I wouldn't actually. There's a man with one foot who hirples into the Refugee Council every other week. Rumour is he cut it off himself.

In the rush of his distress, Abdi had forgotten we'd fallen out. We were shriven by the urgency of the situation. I suppose I should be grateful, you could even say I'd engineered it, but it made me feel sick. All that fretting when he needs to be well. I hadn't thought he'd notice. Then you think, that rucksack is virtually an extra limb. Of course he'll bloody notice. I told him not to worry, that I would sort it when I got back.

Will I see you before you go?

When will you return?

Where and why and I trailed my answers, vague. Pointedly did not go to see him. Missed Rebecca like I am missing cool Glaswegian drizzle. Why am I consumed with such a weight of betrayal? This is a GOOD THING I am doing. It's for him, for them. And did I let him think Dexy might have stolen his papers? Did I make appropriate tutting noises and was I economical with the truth? What am I meant to do? Raise his hopes then rip what's left of him to shredded meat? Because this is never going to happen. In my graceless world, God doesn't answer prayer.

The scarlet tree burns hugely, tiredness weeping from my skin. Up at dawn to catch the shuttle, nine hours of no-sleep on a plane from London, two hundred and fifty miles from Nairobi to Dadaab. I was supposed to hitch a lift on the UNHCR flight, but it was full. Aid workers get priority, as they should.

If you read the press information we sent you, madam, you'll see there is no guarantee that journalists will get on these flights (oh yes, I'm a freelance writer, doing a piece for the Oxfam in-house journal. Rose says three thousand words should do it. And I don't think she was joking).

The flights leave twice a week from Nairobi to Dadaab, and if you draw a blank, the only other option is going by road. That too is dictated by timing: from Garissa, you need a security escort and they leave at 2pm on Sunday. Full stop. But we made it – just. Me and the Norwegian documentary team who've adopted me. (I think they know that I'm a fraud. They live perpetually with their mobiles at their ears; mine lies at the bottom of my bag, most likely switched off.) Listen to me – all casual about armed escorts and rough terrain. The rumbling tyres mark the truthful rhythm of my heart: scared-excited; scared-excited; scared-excited. Need a wee. And utterly, thinned-out knackered. No air-conditioning in the 4×4, so the humid air simply pours round us like languid soup. Sound carries for miles. Long-boned cows clack skinny haunches as a herdsman flicks his stick and it is all sharp, immediate. Incredible.

I lick the dust from my mouth. If I arrive today, I can stay till Wednesday, when the return convoy leaves. Only gives me two full days, but Rose has been at Dadaab since Thursday. One of her friends on the water project works with a refugee who says his father was a great elder. *Now he is the keeper of our truth.* He keeps records of atrocities. Hundreds and hundreds of incidents, stored in his head. Communication with Rose has been fragmented, but she was trying to meet with this man either yesterday or today. I turn my phone on, in case there's messages. Nothing. Settle down. Press my spine and squeeze my thighs. *Do not need a wee do not need a wee.* The cows meander, dull hooves dropping. I follow their progress, if you could call it that. Feel my head dropping and enjoy the dullness. Travelling is a hiatus; for now I'm in others' hands and I need not do or be anything other than tired.

I pass half an hour in monotonous dozing before I notice that the Norwegians are zipping and unzipping bags, that paperwork and visas are being produced because, from out of vast and vacant land, a city is rising.

A hellish one at that.

* * *

Humid blurring acre on acre of humped tents and wire; scarf over nose to expel the smells, the vilest smells how could you? How could people live –

Through here. Bundled, chickenwire and wooden latch, swing shut, inside. There's been rumours of unrest. *Bandits very bad* says the man who gives out towels. His downcast eyes are sorrowful, ashamed at the welcome he provides. No Rose when I reach the UNHCR guesthouse. The man tells me she and I are in adjoining rooms, so I figure she'll chap the door when she gets in. That a wee lie-down won't hurt. I think I kick off my boots, I *do* go to the plumbed-in loo, and am surprised at sitting, was all set to squat. Take my shaky legs back to the shaky bed and lower and lay and . . .

Wake to shouts and motors running. A beating heat. Someone coughing through the wall, my throat cracking. Eyelids held with lead-lined weights. Fumbling fingers, a rough, rough wall. I feel myself awake, come up slowly to avoid the bends. The mosquito net pats me like a friendly spectre. I shake my head. Press the heels of my hands into my sinuses – an old trick; it kind of 'pops' your eyes open. Shake again and smack my lips, the sticky skin adhering. Peeling apart. Remember I am here. Against every vow I ever made, I've come back to Africa. Thousands of miles away on this very continent, a wizened bitch who is still alive will be sipping G&T. No matter what the time is. The cough comes again. I respond in kind; a little expectorating code.

'Deborah?' A voice drifts through plaster. 'That you wake?'

I let out a pathetic: 'Rose?'

Within a second, she's knocking at my door. I'm expecting a khaki missionary, open up to a vision in pastel pinks and blues.

'Rose?'

'Deborah! Well, hello there! You made it!' A paper folder under her arm; she transfers it to one hand, enfolds me in a perfumed hug, the folder brushing the back of my head. I've not showered for . . .

'God. What time is it?'

'Nine am their time. And it's Thursday, in case you're wondering.'

'Oh shit! Oh, sorry.'

'Och, no sweat. Here, d'you want a wee coffee? I've a travel kettle in my room.'

'I would *die* for a coffee.'

'There's a cafeteria if you're hungry?'

My head thinks *hmm*, but my stomach says no. Gurgles it quite urgently, in fact. 'No, ta. Eh – I just need to nip to the loo . . .'

A knowing grin. Her teeth are perfect white; it's a lovely smile, framed by pale-yellow hair made paler by the dust which lies on everything. 'I'll sort you a coffee then. Black, no sugar, I'm afraid.'

'That's fine.'

'Back in a minute.' She lays her folder on my bed. 'Drink plenty water too – did you bring some bottles?'

I nod and scuttle off. Five minutes later, with my face and underarms washed too, I feel almost human. A shower would have been good, but my en suite doesn't run to that. Rose is waiting with my coffee.

'Oh, cheers.'

As she leans forward to pass me the mug, the neckline of her shirt gaps and I see spidery scar lines running up her breastbone.

'Sip it slowly.'

I do. Rose has an air of calm implacability about her: she smiles with a firm assurance, moves efficiently. Kind of woman you would cleave to in a crisis. But she has said nothing yet about her news.

'So. Azira? Where do we start?'

'Would you not like some breakfast first?'

'Not really. We don't have a lot of time. Did you manage to speak to that keeper guy?'

'Ah.' Rose reaches for her folder. Her very blue eyes flick to her feet. She's wearing gold pumps.

'Not so good, I'm afraid. I think his powers may have peaked some time ago. *Yes, yes, very bad bandits. All the time, there are many killings. Very bad bandits, all the time.* Which could indeed be your "men on horses". In Dadaab, though, they use the term "bandits" to describe pretty much any bunch of wandering heidbangers. They can thieve, rape, rustle with apparent impunity. You've got your fundamentalists too, of course, and there's also your clan warfare. You thought Rangers v Celtic was bad? Christ, it's got nothing on this lot. Problem is, the Kenyan authorities blame every single crime on the refugees, the refugees blame it on the Kenyans and we all do a merry dance of denial. And I'll tell you this – in the midst of it all, the fecking "bandits" have carte blanche to take – and do – whatever they want.'

'This isn't hugely helpful.'

'Agreed. But that was the sum total of what the old boy could tell me. That and that all the birds here are the "demons of the dead".'

'Shit.'

'I know. Guess it happens, though. If you cram every horror that takes place here into your head, you're bound to overload.

Eventually it all becomes one homogeneous mass. Just makes you go ga-ga.'

'How do *you* do it then?'

'I can't not.'

Rose pushes neat hair behind her ear, crosses her legs so one shiny foot rests of top of the other. 'Once you've . . .' Sighs. 'I'm not being noble or anything, trust me. I like a good time as much as the next person. Give me a party and a blast of Rod Stewart −'

'Rod Stewart? Sorry, don't think me rude, Rose. But what age are you?'

I mean this as a joke, but draw back immediately I say it. Who am I, quipping with the familiarity of a BFF, when I've known her for ten minutes, two phone calls and a handful of emails and texts? I can't help it, though, Rose oozes approachability.

'Put it this way: I've been married forty years.'

'Away!'

I had her down for being late forties. Early fifties at most.

'Och, I was a child bride, me. But, honestly − see when you've seen all of this fecking awful misery, you can't just walk away. I mean, you're never going to make a massive difference, but . . . one thing, you know? One family, one person even. If you can hold out your hand and −' Her foot jiggles, 'Well. You know, don't you? Otherwise you'd not be here. *Anyway*. I do have some news for you. Very positive news, in fact.'

'Yes?'

'Yes. I've been doing some checking with Médecins Sans Frontières.' Rose smiles, but it is a spasm of a smile. I balance on the thin rim of my metal bed; she takes a pair of reading glasses from her shirt pocket. Once more, I glimpse the silvered scars on her breast.

'OK. So. They have a record of a female with Azira's name presenting at the clinic here in Dadaab on the tenth of January 2009.'

No smile, so the quiet enormity of this fact takes a moment to impact; it hovers like a massive wave, then crashes, warm salt flowing. 'Oh my God!' All my dreams come true this easy, this easy. We'll return in triumph, charging through the sky, powered only by my mighty fist, my steadfast resolution.

'That's two days after Abdi arrived in the UK! Oh my God, Rebecca was right. She's alive!' I feel dizzy, delirious as it beats and bursts anew. I can see Rebecca's little face and –

'OK, OK. Don't get too excited. Bear in mind this was almost two years ago. Michel at the clinic was good enough to let me see the medical report.'

Kind and brilliant Rose offers me a sheet of paper but everything is blurred. 'You read it.' I listen through Rose-coloured glasses. Hugging myself. Will I phone Abdi, or just bring Azira directly to him?

'OK. It says the woman presented with multiple lacerations on head, back and thighs.' Rose coughs, adjusts her glasses. 'Severe trauma indicated to genital area . . .'

Little vicious bite I always knew was there, like when you touch your breast and feel a lump and pretend there is no shooting pain. Then you return to it in the night-time on your own, and prod and wince and remove yourself from its malevolent possibility. But you know it all the same.

'She was raped?'

Say it aloud. Let delicate folds of language bleed.

'I reckon so. I'm so sorry, Deborah.'

'But she's *alive*.'

'Possibly. Problem is, they never treated her.'

'Why?'

'She disappeared. In the cubicle one minute, gone the next. It's not that unusual, Michel says. Often, women will be brought in by well-meaning friends or neighbours. But the shame's too much for them. That or the thought of another person touching them.'

'What are you saying?'

'I'm not saying anything other than that we know, in January last year, a woman by the name of Azira Samatar Guleed Hassan was injured, but alive. Thereafter, the hospital has no more information.'

'What about other clinics?'

'I've checked them all.'

'Do we know who brought her in?'

'Nope.'

'What about the police?'

Rose slips her glasses back into her pocket. 'Look. Security here is shite. Even for us. We're confined to our compounds from dusk to dawn – no exceptions, by the way. They have approximately three hundred police to cover all three camps. In reality, that translates to ten or fifteen on duty at any one time. And, since coming here's seen as a punishment duty, they're usually young, inexperienced – and seriously pissed off.' She's flicking through her sheaf of papers. 'Notwithstanding the numerous allegations of police taking bribes and being involved in rapes and violence themselves. Here. Take a wee look at this report on security. That'll give you a flavour of life in sunny Dadaab.'

The brief shine of my optimism is rubbed away. I glance at the top paragraph. Can't bear to read the rest.

> *The security situation in and around Dadaab has been deteriorating . . . Despite additional live fencing being installed, banditry attacks within the camps (including looting, shooting and sexual assault) have become almost daily occurrences. One or two bullets being fired is now considered a minor incident and violence is often not reported to police. In any case, the investigative skills of local security are very limited. Investigations rarely lead to arrests and convictions, while those suspects who are handed over to police are often released shortly afterwards.*

'OK? So, I definitely think we should leave off going to the police until the very last resort. They do have a station here, and they keep "records" of a sort. But their records rarely correspond with what we hear on the ground. Plus, once we start going all official, we're casting aspersions on their professionalism. Which will very much limit our other options. You with me?'

I nod. From a distance, bells peel. Tiny tinkly bells. I feel the press of Rose's hand on my arm.

'To me, the best thing would be to gather as many facts as possible. We need eye witnesses to tell us exactly what happened, who survived, who helped who. So, I'd say our first avenue would be to speak to the transfer agents. They've an outpost in the camp. Oxfam don't use them – and, if I have my way, no bugger will ever use them again. Our main problem is we're meant to have a security escort whenever we travel outwith the compound. Which is also ... limiting. So you'll have to bear with me – act daft and say very little, yeah?'

'OK.'

'And you might want to turn your rings inwards.'

My engagement ring – a modest twist of diamonds, and the eternity ring of sapphire and diamonds Callum got me when ... he called it my maternity ring.

'Nice. I'm an emerald girl myself,' says Rose. 'Emeralds and diamonds – the more bling the better. But not here.'

'Of course. Will I – should I just take them off?'

'No! No, God. I know we're in the compound, but ... no. Just keep them with you, but hidden. You could put them inside your bra, I suppose ...'

I consider my meagre cleavage with its shaved-off edge. 'Nah. You're all right. Think they might slip out.'

'Nice shirt, by the way,' says Rose.

It was, two days ago when I set out. I'll need to ask about showers sometime, but to wash seems a very dirty thing when there are standpipes and tankers and huddles queueing for water. On the way in, we had passed one of the water stations: hundreds of bowed heads waiting; their canisters laid in the dust. Great snakes of yellow, orange, cream containers segmented and twisting in patient coils. I brush the worst of the red stour from my chest.

'Thanks. And I love your shoes.'

'Yeah?' Rose twinkles her upturned foot. Pinpoint bursts of golden light flit from wall to wall. 'They weren't cheap, you know.'

★ ★ ★

389

The transfer agents are worse than useless. We crowd on to a stepped verandah, people jostling in and out as Rose makes herself heard. A plump and sweaty man with a plastic visor to hide his eyes chews his pen. Shakes his head. Scratches his arse.

'We're talking tenth of January 2009. You had a convoy then, leaving for resettlement to the UK.'

'No remember, no.'

'Well, can I see your records, please? You're required to keep a log of all journeys – it says so in your contract.'

'All gone. Records gone in fire. Big fire.'

'Bullshit. Right, let me see your boss. *Boss* man.'

'Me the boss man, lady.'

'Indeed you are not. I've done business with your company many times. Now you get me Mr Obama. Right now.'

'He not boss. I am boss.'

'Don't contradict me!'

Our armed escort – I'm not clear if he's a policeman or a soldier – comes closer at this sound of raised voices. He adds his own to the mix, which has slipped into Swahili. Luckily, the irrepressible Rose can handle this challenge too; her quick-fire questioning is menacing. Or maybe it's just the unfamiliar tongue and the threat implicit in our escort's rifle, and the raging sun which is utterly cruel: all are menacing. I stand dumb. A sheep.

'C'mon, Debs.' Rose takes me by the arm. 'We're wasting our time here.'

'Did you try him with a bribe?' I say in a stage-whisper.

'Shut up,' she hisses, dragging me on. Outside, she whispers: 'Never acknowledge that money's changed hands, OK?'

'OK. Sorry.'

'But yes –' She stops as our escort emerges from the shack. 'All right, Mo?'

He clicks his tongue. 'Man is right. Obama gone now.'

'Did you not hear – he got elected president?'

Neither of them crack a light. I think I'm hilarious, manic with the skitters and lack of sleep. Gibbering, I'm gibbering. The volume of humanity pressing on me is terrifying. To find one person in *this*? Worse, to find the memory of one person? We're in a kind of marketplace, people on cycles, or dragging carts by hand. Archetypes of Africans with swan-necked élan carrying unfeasible loads on their heads. What strikes me most is how bright and clean everyone's clothes are. That and the men with their bright-red beards, the children with aqualine noses and bleached-gold hair. If you saw this on television, you'd think it looked . . . pretty. There are even stalls with some fruit and veg. But then you notice the slowness of the people's gait. The harsh and sickly stench that pervades, the brutal thorns and chainwire. The sitting. Interminable sitting in non-existent shade. The huge black-winged storks that flurry and stand on bony legs, and peck and preen and peck. The fact that no one's actually buying anything. Our escort mimes smoking a cigarette. 'Two minutes, OK? I need get more.'

'Sure, Mo, take your time.'

I tug Rose's shirt sleeve. 'Will we be all right?'

'We'll be fine. Just stay with me, and walk slowly. Fancy a –' she picks up a gnarled purple plum. Smiles at the stallholder. '*Je ni?*'

'*Passion matunda.*'

'Ah. Passion fruit. Hey. *Kubwa!* They're big!'

391

The girl giggles, hides her face. Rose gives her money without asking the price.

'*Asante.*'

'No, thank *you.*'

As we're leaving the stall, a young man emerges from behind a rusting bus.

'Missus, missus. Excuse, missus.'

Rose links arms with me. 'OK, just keep walking, Debs. Don't make eye contact. Let's go to that other stall, the one with the fabric.'

'Missus, please. You shouting 'bout bus get hit?'

Rose touches my wrist. 'Let me do the talking.'

The boy wears cut-off shorts, is barefoot. Bare-chested. Puts his arms behind his head as if he's showing off his pecs. Rose sighs and produces a single dollar. 'Here. That's all till I hear you speak.'

'When you say this was?'

'No, you tell me first what you know.'

'I work there sometime. Two time this year, bus hit by bandits.'

'Well, that happens.'

'No, lady. Boss; he tell. He take-a money, tell whena Christian going.'

I lower my voice. 'Rose. Did you mention about Christians?'

'Nope.' Her chin pushing air. 'OK, sunshine. Tell me more. Who are these bandits? Where do they come from?'

He shrugs. 'Bandit.'

'Why do they pick on Christians?'

'Lot money. And *mzungo* no get good guards.'

'That's fecking true,' she says. 'Do they kidnap them?'

'Huh?'

'Do they take them away?'

'Uh-uh. Take-a money. Passe-port. Take-a shag.' He grins. Thrusts his hips.

'What about the year before? Did the buses get hit then?'

'No know no more, lady.' He holds out his hand.

'And would you be willing to tell what you've told me to the police?'

'P'shaw. Money go two-way, yeah?'

I can see Mo walking back towards us.

'Here.' I give the boy five dollars. '*Asante*.'

'*Asante*, lady.' With an elegant swagger, he's absorbed in the rolling crowd.

Rose returns to her browsing, fingering a cloth of satin sunflowers.

'You like?' asks the stallholder.

'*Ndiyo*.'

'OK.' My throat is hoarse. 'What do we do now?'

'All right, Mo? Get your fags?'

'Fag?'

Rose puffs her empty fingers. 'Fags. Cigarettes.'

'Yeah. Want one?' He slips a cigarette between his lips. Sparks his lighter.

'No, ta. Debs and I are good girls. *Nzuri wasichana*.'

Our escort chuckles. Breathes out smoke. 'Where you going now?'

'Um, UNHCR.' Rose speaks directly to me. 'There's a researcher from Human Rights Watch over. And they're looking at setting up a security partnership. They might have pulled together stats, or interviews that . . .'

But I'm not really listening. If this was my forsaken life, where would I go? What does your mum tell you when you're wee? *If you get lost, you go to a policeman.* Aye well, clearly not in this shithole. But she'd also say: *Just stay where you are. Stay where we last saw each other, and I will come back and get you.*

'It's a braw bricht moonlicht nicht the nicht!' I declaim. Stop short of doing a Highland fling.

'Whit?' Rose is scowling at me.

'If the lassie was bidin' awhile, might be in her ain hoose, eh?'

'Debs, what the hell are you wittering about?'

If only they'd taught us Gaelic at school. I try to think of other ways to circumnavigate this lumpen armed guard whose ears are twitching. 'Her ain hoose?' I repeat. 'D'ye mind her ain hoose?'

'Oh God, aye. Now I get you . . . Actually, that's not such a daft idea. They put most of thepeopleofanotherfaith in the same area. Mo!'

Mo pretends he's not been listening to us, that he's only been straining to relight his fag. 'Mo, I think I'd like to go and see some of my old pals near the church. You know, Father Paolo's old church?'

'Is gone.'

'I know *he* is, but I'd like to show Debs the church.'

'Is gone too.'

'Oh. Och well, I still fancy a wee look round.'

He gives up on his unobliging cigarette, flicks it away.

'Back in jeep, please. I only got one hour, then finish.'

'Sure, no problems.'

The jeep's parked beside the transport depot. We scramble up. Mo is a gentleman of sorts – he stands outside to pee, turning slightly from our view.

'Lovely,' says Rose. 'Right, listen. When I met them they were in an absolute hovel, right on the bare edge of the camp. It's not very safe, but it's out of the way, you know? Far away from hospitals, and police and officialdom and that. So she might have tried to make her way back there. Plus, if it's true only Christian convoys are being attacked, most of the Christian families are dumped in the one place anyway –'

'So there might be others there who've had the same thing happen to them?'

'Exactly. Or know someone else who has.'

Mo wrenches the driver's door open, climbs inside. It's the fastest I've seen him move all day.

'We go now.'

'Yes, that's great. It's up by the –'

'No. We go back to the compound. Big shootings near hospital. Not safe. You stay inside till safe.'

'Och, c'mon, Mo –'

'No argument, lady.'

We hang on the sides as the vehicle clatters and bangs away at speed. I don't like Mo, don't trust him, but I'm suddenly aware of what a burden we must be. Ten cops, four hundred thousand people, unilateral poverty and violence – and here's Mo, babysitting two middle-aged women on a sightseeing tour.

'Ach weel,' says Rose, pragmatic. 'Such is life. At least we can talk to the researcher girl. She's in our compound. We'll head out to where the church was tomorrow.'

I whisper, although Mo is driving with one hand and shouting into the radio clamped in the other.

'Surely the authorities must be aware of these attacks? I don't mean the police, I mean, like the UN? If they're happening on a regular basis?'

'We knew there were attacks, yes. But not that they were orchestrated by the bloody people we were paying to get folk out.' Rose shakes her head. 'And it depends how "regular" you mean by regular. It takes a lot to give violence a pattern here. Fuck. I'll tell you one thing. No matter what, before we leave, I'll be filing an official complaint about the transport agents – with the UN and the police. Make sure their licence is revoked, with immediate effect.'

'But we don't have any evidence.'

She reverts to grimmest Glaswegian. 'No yet we huvny.'

All that evening, we are cooped inside. The researcher isn't there after all, has gone home for two weeks' leave. We eat a little, drink a little. Talk a lot. I learn that Rose, like me, grew up in Glasgow. That she has two daughters and a husband called Bernard. That her scars are not from breast surgery, but a quadruple bypass, aged thirty-nine. *After that, I just thought – seize the day. Life's precious, you know? So do something fecking precious with it.* She asks me why I'm doing this and I say *to help my friend.* One raised brow, her finger singing on the rim of her glass. *I take it he's a very good friend?* Then I tell her about Callum, how deep in my bones I miss him. How Abdi and Rebecca make me less empty. We clink our glasses, shout *Carpe diem!* The next day, Rose has to go to the water project.

'I'll only be a couple of hours.' She hands me a key. 'That'll get you in the office. We share it with a load of other charities. Why don't you photocopy the picture of Azira? We can hand them out in the Christian area. Put your mobile number on the back too. Code for the copier's 2991, all right?'

What can I say except, *fine*? I'm conscious that today's my last full day. The UNHCR flight back to Nairobi leaves tomorrow at 10am, and Rose and I both have seats confirmed. The alternative is to make the return trip by road, which would mean I'd miss my flight to London. Do that, and my government authorisation will expire before I can get the next one. It's only paper, I'm sure it could be sorted, but the thought of being trapped here is appalling. I feel I'm looking through a kaleidoscope, with time fragmenting into a smaller and smaller hole. You could lose your mind here, I think; if only to escape. That Abdi – that my wee Rebecca – survived this; no, not survived, that they are whole and human still.

That they are wonderful.

The photocopier hums; I've been warned it overheats. I make fifty copies of the photograph, fiddling until I work out how to get two images on one page. I keep Azira face-down as I work. Mobile number . . . I can never remember my own number, but it's in my contacts list, under ME. If I can find my phone . . . Check my pockets, check my fetching bumbag. Ah. I have two missed calls, and three texts. Abdi, my sister and Gamu.

Hope u r njoing self. A

Don't bother to tell me you got there ok or anything. Your loving sister.

Home Office reconsidered my case. Visa application turned down. Lawyer to appeal, but not hopeful. Thank you for all your help though. Your friend, Gamu.

Shit. I wave the phone about, trying to get a signal. Gamu was one of my calls too: she phoned me yesterday, waited a polite half-a-day before dropping me the text. I wave more frantically, bend my knees, stand on tiptoe. The signal is resolutely absent. Try the office phone, but there is no cheerful buzz to it; it sits mute, even when I press nine, then zero, then all the stupid buttons one by one. Mute. Rose returns around two, by which time I'm utterly scunnered.

'All right?' she says.

'Nope,' I say. I tell her about my friend Gamu, and how I've made a hundred postcards of Azira. And how it's all a waste of bloody time.

'That's the spirit,' says Rose.

And we go out anyway, because that is what we're here to do. If we have no joy in the Christian area, Rose says we'll go next to Group Four.

'Security?' I say dumbly.

'It's the block that houses *dhilo*.'

'What are *dhilos*?'

'Prostitutes.'

A raptor floats above us, broad wings motionless as it hangs and drifts. I think of the elder Rose spoke of, and of his crawing feathered demons. Rula sits on my shoulder as we drive. She is skinny, and doesn't preen. There are no pickings on her. Like this land: there is no bush here as I envisaged; it is arid outback, it is the bare dry bones of the earth. We are driving on a giant corpse. But on my other shoulder rests Callum, and he is fine and glossy. I crane my neck to look up. Almost too high to be seen, the raptor wheels and turns. He is majestic. Part of this landscape, and above it all. It's much nicer to be looking at blue-blank sky than the viscera we're navigating. Yet Callum would be very proud of me, I think, and I don't mean this to be glib or self-satisfied. I know it as a fact, just as my husband is a shining fact. Each fragment of him, from the clear young man I met to the broken mosaic that left me. I have a vibrant memory of Christmas, our first Christmas when we couldn't afford a tree. In a fit of festive extravagance, I'd already bought the fairy lights. I was going to string them above the radiator, but Callum had a better idea.

'Nah. You want them to be voluptuous.'

'Everything I'm not?' I'd pretended to go in a huff, knowing he would reassure me. And my breasts. Very nice it was too – so much so that we forgot about fairy lights. Next morning, I came down to fresh coffee, a yellow-white dark room and a softly glittering orb of light. His solution had been to pile up the fairy lights in a goldfish bowl. Outside, new snow was falling in steady deliberate drifts, casting yellow and pewter in the sky, swallowing the lampposts, layering itself on our windows. It quietened us in its yellow light. Contained within our square of house; our ball of light with all its flickering episodes of lights, made voluptuous by my clever husband, instead of stretched out and thin.

The raptor leaves us, or we leave it, and carry on past interminable rows of cylindrical tents. It could be an endless market garden. Eventually, even these peter out, and there is no regularity at all – excepting the sun of course, with its precise and searing beats.

'Here we are.'

The Christian area is even bleaker than the rest of Dadaab. It lacks colour, lacks form, clinging to the outer reaches of the camp. Unfettered access from the scrub beyond.

'That's new,' says Rose. 'There used to be a fence here.'

Grey-cloaked figures, streets of crude mud-and-tin huts, some tattered tents. It's as if the whole place is hunkering down, hoping for the storm to pass it by. *If we don't draw attention to ourselves, we'll be fine.* Rose hops out of the 4×4. Today, she's wearing pale-lemon pedal-pushers and a mint-green blouse. An exotic flower in the dust. People begin to stare.

'Mo, we'll be fine. You chill out in the jeep. Debs here is a journalist. She just wants to talk to some of the people about life in the camp. I know my way around, it's cool.'

'I have to stay with you. Lot of troubles with bandits.'

We can't shake him. For three hours we trudge the area, no longer bothered what Mo thinks or does. But he never once looks at the photographs we distribute. I don't think he cares; we are a duty he has to discharge. The ugly sun sucks the moisture from our skins, my swollen feet ache, my head aches. All I hear is clanging; the doleful clang that it's all too late. What could Mo do now to stymie us? We hand out pictures, people nod and smile. See Mo, and remove themselves from our sphere. Eventually, all the photos are gone. The shelters are dwindling too. We've come to a clearing with a wide spreading tree in the centre; a single piece of almost-green.

'Over there. That's where the church was.' Rose points to some white rubble. Rebecca would have been baptised in there, in the heat of the day with a white shawl tying her to her mum. My wee Glasgow girl.

'And look, Debs. This is the old schoolroom.'

It's just a mass of broken mud, the odd strip of corrugated iron. Several of the huts nearby have metal roofs, built with the spoils of war; you can see the dust-trails from school to homestead marking the spot. A part of one school wall does remain, and on it – incongruously – hangs a tatty blackboard. I stand where Abdi once stood. Smooth the surface of the blackboard he would have written on. Chalk traces of my hand make a pattern; I think of Rebecca's finger people and Rebecca's men on horses. I face outwards: teacher's stance. Survey the class with my teacher's face. The air is full of spirits.

'Excuse!'

Mo is shouting us over. Beside him is a woman, wrapped in a plaid shawl. Her head is covered, she holds part of the scarf across her face.

'Missus Gray. She want speak to you.'

'Hi there.' We pick our way across the rubble. 'Hi,' repeats Rose. 'How can we help?'

The woman drops her scarf. 'Missus Gray. I am Mariam. You help me to get passage?'

'Mariam?' Rose is frowning, eyes back and forth like she's scanning, scanning. Connecting. Clicking. 'Oh, yes. Mariam! And ... Sarah?'

Briefly, the woman shuts her eyes.

'Yes. Sarah.'

Mo nudges her. 'Hurry. You want talk to Missus Gray? *Dhakhso.*'

'Mo. Please. There's no rush.' Rose leads Mariam to a stump of wall. 'Please. Sit.' We squat beside her. 'Yes, of course I remember you, Mariam. But I thought you'd be ... but you didn't get away?'

'No'm. There was bandits come. We wait to gate to go on wagon. Then bandits came. On *farado*?' Mariam raises her hand high.

'Horses,' says Rose.

'They come, and they hit us. Bam, bam – big knives and spears. They take her, yes.'

'Her?' I hold up one of my photos. 'Do you know the woman in this picture?'

'Yes'm. I know her. Zira, yes?'

'Yes!'

'Zira, yes. They take her. And my firstborn.'

'Your first – Oh my God. I'm so sorry. Is she –'

'*Wey dhimatay.*'

It is the saddest, most graceful smile I have ever seen. 'She virgin, she very very good girl. So they rip her with their spears. She so much pain. I pray to God she die. Is OK. She die in my arms. Like when I birthed her.'

A tight jag of tears. Beaks pecking. My throat in bits and surges. Mariam holds my hand. I feel her, can see nothing in this bright sun.

'Is OK. Zira, she live. We take her doctor. Proper doctor, no witchdoctor. But she run away.'

My heart is tearing, this good noble woman comforting me, but I am crying for her and I want her to know this, how selfish I am that I want her to be grateful for my grief, I want to give her something, anything to take away this pain. To die like you are birthed.

'You know where she ran to?' asks Rose.

'*Tana.*'

'Is river,' says Mo.

'Zira no want live no more. But is a sin. I pray, pray. Always pray.'

I remove my hand from hers.

'She killed herself? *Wey dhimatay?*'

'Yes'm. *Wey dhimatay.*'

It is definite. It is definite and defined and a dam comes down, you hold it in place, all the tension and tides, roaring in your ears. Sharp points of your knees in your chin. Your arms bind your legs to your breasts. You wonder how small you could make yourself. People talk above you, but you have your roaring. No tears any more, just the roaring.

'Debs. *Debs.* Mariam's asking if you've got kids.'

I hold my index finger up. 'One.' Rock my arms in a cradle. 'One son. But he died. *Dhimatay.*'

Mariam holds my face. 'They safe now.'

Everything silent, because there is nothing to say. I let Mariam nurse my face, sit in fawn dust. Fawn and yellow, pink and gold, it covers my arms. Rests on my eyelashes.

'Debs. C'mon, Debs. Time to go.' The back of Rose's trousers bloom with dust. Wings of dust are spreading across our cheekbones.

Mariam nods. Urging me. 'They safe'm.'

We rise to go. Except I am left behind. I want to be, want to give her something. I want to *say*, not with words. Smooth blue of the sky, clear tears, my ring. My sapphire ring is in my hand, in Mariam's hand. She is wide-eyed horrified.

'No'm! *Maya, maya*.' Appealing to Rose, to surly sweating Mo.

'Please,' I say. 'Please take it.'

And then I rise to go.

All sorts of problems I've caused. Mo had to take Mariam to a man called Khadra. *He's like a pawnbroker*, Rose tells me. Then to the bank. *You realise she'll be a target for thieves? If Mo says anything to anybody* —

I'm sorry. I didn't think . . .

After half an hour, Mo returns to where we're waiting in the jeep. He has locked us in, and left us his radio. Some months ago, two female aid workers were abducted by Al-Shabaab. They've still not been found. He adjusts his trousers. Replaces his gun in its holster.

'Christ, Mo. What happened?'

A grunt, but no answer.

'Mo. Is Mariam OK?'

'Yes. See?'

From the doorway of the bank, Mariam waves at us. Her smile splitting the sky with its brightness.

'Did she get a good price?'

'Yes.'

'Mo,' says Rose. 'You won't say anything about this, will you?'

Meaty hands grip the steering wheel. The engine screams, and we are off, bumping over the grit and ruts. He takes us straight back here, to the compound. Furious with us, I think.

'Tomorrow you go home, yes?'

'Yes.'

'Good.'

'Mo, thank you for . . .' I give him thirty dollars. Wordlessly, he pockets it. Drives off.

'Honestly,' says Rose. 'Huffy bugger. *I take no leave of you, nor send any* – what is it again?'

'Don't,' I say. I go to my room, get into my nightshirt. Everything's packed for the morning. I have a passport; I can leave this place.

Later on, Rose taps my door.

'Debs? You want some dinner?'

'No.'

'How about a drink? We've a couple of *very* crappy bars. The Grease Pit's my personal favourite.'

'No. Ta.'

There is a long slow pause in which I hope she's gone away.

'Debs?'

'What?'

'I'm really sorry. But we always knew this was a long shot. That she'd still be alive, I mean.'

'I know.'

Morning comes. Not soon enough. I think I slept a wee bit, but it's hard to tell. I get up, brush my teeth, wash my face. I long for a bath, a big deep bubble bath where I can sink right under, feel the bubbles burst on my eyes. In water, no one can hear you scream. Enough. I just want my bubbles. Want to go home. Before we get the plane, Rose says we've to go to the police station. She reported the transport agents to the UN last night.

But I'm going for the two-pronged approach.

I don't want Mariam getting involved.

Don't worry. Once they check the manifests, see the discrepancies between who left and who arrived, they won't need to speak to Mariam.

Our driver – who is not Mo – takes us to the police compound. What an ugly place. Surrounded by a high wall, surmounted by barbed wire, the only break in the dirty bulk of it is a blue door, which opens after an age of Rose thumping. The door's actually a gate, we drive through the thick brick wall, into a dusty courtyard. Various outbuildings align themselves round a central office. There are bars on all the windows. By the far wall, a stooped figure holds a long stick. It's a hoe, they are hoeing at the straggle of plants that have been carefully embedded in two straight lines.

'You wait here, Debs, right?'

I concur. All the fight in me is spent. Our driver gets out to have a cigarette.

'You want?'

'No. Thanks.'

The heat of this place slides in like a drug. Thick, cloying. The vehicle we're in's a posh one, has air-conditioning, but the engine's off and I'm sweltering. I get out too, just to stretch my legs. The hoeing figure straightens up. Wipes her – I think it's a her – hand across her brow.

'Missus Deb. You OK?'

'Mo.'

From the verandah of an outhouse, our erstwhile guide is frowning at me.

'You OK?'

'I'm fine. Just a bit hot.'

'Huh.' He lights up a cigarette. I notice our driver begins to walk away. Poor Mo. He smokes in silence, blowing blue puffs, breathing heavily. Our driver's moving closer to the police station. Looking at his watch, rubbing his head. He's got a point: Rose is taking ages, and we need to be at the airstrip now. Eventually, when there is only a stub of cigarette left, Mo clears his throat. 'You no worry 'bout that Mariam, no? I tell Khadra if she be robbed, I will come for him, OK? Take his business, take his wives –'

'Oh, Mo. Thank you.'

I can hear our driver shouting. 'Missus, we need to go. You miss-a plane.'

'I'm coming, Omar, I'm coming.' Rose appears at the doorway of the police station, screeching a final riposte at whatever poor soul is quivering inside. 'But I mean it. I will be on your back like a fucking black widow spider, every day, every week, no matter where in the world I am, until you can tell me that you have investigated, prosecuted, and flung those bastards in your shittiest jail. You understand me?'

Mo grins at me. 'We got new-made corporal. Stupid boy. He will hate your Missus Rose.'

'Missus, please!' begs our driver. 'We got go.'

Mo opens the door of the jeep for me. 'Goodbye, Missus Deb.'

'Goodbye, Mo.'

The others bundle themselves in. Rose has barely shut the door before Omar slams the glass partition that separates us from him, and shunts the vehicle forward.

'Ooh!' says Rose. 'Temper, temper.'

I see Mo signal that he'll get the gate. He lumbers towards it, Omar revving his impatience. As our engine roars, the hoeing woman turns to look. She wears a black shroud around her hair and body. A tiny strand of hair flicks free and there is a terrible wistfulness in this, the soft wild hair that is not hidden.

The gate shuts. Just a window and a wall.

We move off. Tyres on unyielding earth. My loose head lolling, thump then shiver on seatback then glass, over and over. Judders in my chin, through my teeth. From the rear window I watch Dadaab retreat, shrinking its people and its lumps and rags and coils until it is a shimmering mirage. We trundle at all the speed this rattling heap can garner. My eyes unfocus. Absently survey the pink-yellow dust as the wistfulness in me grows. It sharpens as Dadaab recedes. Has piercing teeth.

Omar crashes open the partition.

'You going miss-a plane, missus.'

I notice there's a young girl swishing twigs, a flock of ruminating goats who claim the road as their own.

'No we're not.' Rose lowers her gold-rimmed sunglasses. 'Because you are such an excellent driver, Omar. You don't think we use you for your sunny disposition, do you?'

'I tell you. You miss. There no no more this week.'

'Well, we don't miss then, because I have to be in Mumbai in three days. *Unaelewa?*'

Omar slams the glass shut. Shrieks the horn; the girl jumps but does not falter. He opens the window to shout. She swishes her stick more brusquely. At us, her animals? We rev and screech, bullying our way through. The girl turns her head to frown. And it bites. A heart-shaped face, skin sleek across her cheekbones. She wears a bright gold shift not a black shroud that hangs around her hair and body but a tiny strand of hair flicks free because she has just that minute turned her head, is on the brink of . . .

My heart stops.

'Rose! That woman. I think that was her. I think that was Azira!'

'Who? Her? For the love of God, Debs, that lassie's about twelve.'

'No! The one doing the garden. When we were leaving the compound! The police compound. Oh, stop the truck. Hey!' Banging on the sliding glass. 'Hey, you, stop the truck! Go back.'

'Debs! For Christ's sake, get a grip! Omar, it's all right, on you go.'

'No, Rose, no.' Shaking my frantic head. My hair is suffocating me. 'I'm sure it was her . . . She looked right at me.'

'Did she?'

'Yes! No . . .'

'And you've only just realised this now?' Rose's scar gleams as she leans to wipe the hair off my mouth. 'C'mon, Debs. You're tired, you're upset. But you've got to let this go. You did your very best for her, but she's gone. Azira is dead. You know that, don't you?'

Just a window and a wall.

'Debs? We really tried. But she was fished out a bloody river. *Deid*. It's tragic, it's awful. But you have to lay this to rest.'

As we speed by, the goat-girl scowls fiercely. She doesn't even have hair, is shorn to baldness. No flicks. In fact, she is possibly a boy. I know that Rose is right. I know it, I know it, and it crushes me. Squashing my face against the hardness of the glass, I watch the world unfurl, blank and pink and spiked with green. As nondescript as concrete. Just longitude and latitude. On and on and on. My breath mists the window.

Far off to our left, another mirage begins to form. Shimmering, shifting. It's the haze of burning kerosene. The false flatness of the airstrip.

'But what will I tell Rebecca?'

'Oh Christ, Debs, I don't know.'

DEBS IS SICK. Ever since she got back from her holiday. All day, she's in her house; she did not tell me she was back for a week. She is upset for Gamu, we all are, but I would have thought the injustice would galvanise her. *Wait till Debs gets back*, I tell Gamu. *She will sort it.* It was very difficult, this lady crying, and me awkwardly patting her back. The moisture from my hand staining like guilt. I hardly know Gamu, but I had been at Refugee Council for a seminar on voluntary work (this news I will share with Debs when she is better) when Gamu flooded into the office and deposited her news. One should not presume because we have a similar shade of skin and have both fled our homelands that we are kindred. To be truthful, I find Gamu a little coarse at times, all that chucking you under the chin and spooning endearments on you scares me. It is her cloak, I suppose, her crutch. It is that element of her personality she has worked to hone and project in her bid to be acceptable. That is one commonality all us refugees possess. Cast off without family or culture, we must decide what new person we are going to be.

Well. I am a father. I am a man who grieves his family, his wife. I am a man who has been given a new life, and opportunities to make it great. And I'm done with all these treatments. I rattle when I walk; the medicines are a gauze through which I blink at my world. Talking therapies are hollow. Being exposed to your greatest fear does not conquer it, it simply solidifies. You can weigh it now and carry it, pretend to lay it down. But you can never have the freedom of 'imagining' how you would react, the luxury of closing your mind to it because it is not real. A strange liberation in that.

Our Father. Reveal your glimpses for my world.

Oh, I wish Debs would talk to me. I thought we had built a friendship where you could fight and still be friends. I suspect the man she was meeting on holiday was unkind to her too. She doesn't want to see people much – except Rebecca. Gaunt face lightening with my daughter in her arms. So I'm letting Rebecca stay there for a couple of days. She hates the nursery at college anyway. Complains they 'baby' her, that the crayons are rationed. When I told Debs I'd let Rebecca go to school after Christmas, she started crying. It was my best news. I had saved it up to make her happy.

I tell some of this to Sandrine – not about Deborah's love life, of course, for that is none of my business. Sandrine and I sit next to one another in our English class, but are early. This has happened the last three times. So we go for coffee first, it is not a fixed arrangement.

'Aren't you worried about infection?' she says. 'If your friend is ill.'

'I had not thought,' I reply. Now, I am worried about infection. If Rebecca if she was there are jags she must get, many jags before school. If anything were to happen to my daughter, all the manu-factured posturing of *ABDI REBORN!!* would be revealed as smoke and ash.

Sandrine fingers her scarf, watching me. Scarves are her crutch, I think. Every day a different colour. Today her neck is wound with bright yellow and green leaves.

'I'm sure it will be fine. It is more of a malaise Debs has, yes?'

Sandrine is from the Ivory Coast, I worry I have used this French word incorrectly, but she nods. Sagely. 'And your little girl – she loves this woman too?'

'Too?'

'I'm sorry. What I mean is, she is happy to be with her?'

'Yes. Very happy. Rebecca loves her, very much.'

I think of the force with which Rebecca propelled herself at Debs, the expectant charge that wired her little body as we neared the house. Quivering like a tethered foal waiting to bolt. My cheeks feel hot at the confusion of before. I must resolve it; this is part of my reinvention.

'When you said "too", did you mean that I also must love Debs?'

'Oh, no. I'm sorry.' Sandrine dips her head. 'It is my mistake. You talk of her with such pride and affection.'

'Sandrine, she is my friend. Only my friend.' The side of my hand glides upwards, connects briefly to her chin so I might hold her gaze directly. Hot coffee flavouring my tongue. I am amazed at my bravery, and at the little – no, the wee – blaze of light glowing off her skin.

'Come,' she says. 'We will be late for class. And today it is Shakespeare. Again.'

'My joy is unconfined!'

'Is that not Twain?'

'Yes.' A little sigh escapes. I must try harder to give big smiles.

Our lecturer is a horrible woman. This is not a random malice I feel, I have come to the conclusion after several observations. She is big-jawed and square. Sniffs, continually. Rolls her phlegm with a rasping sound and deposits it in her gullet. Not nice. She drones in a monotone, enlivened by the occasional spike of sarcasm or vitriol. We are a class of mixed abilities, and it's clear she has her favourites. *Quite right, Malcolm. Farida – do you have any idea what book we're reading?* This, I believe, is a cardinal sin for a teacher. Am I jealous of her? Yes. When she stands before our class and talks her incoherent nonsense, yes. It pains me that this woman has the job of shaping minds, and clearly despises it.

'OK, class. Turn to page forty-three. Now we're not gonny have time to finish this before Christmas, so what I'm gonny do is bring in a DVD. It'll give you the gist of –'

My hand is up.

'Yes?'

'Could we not simply read more quickly in the classroom? It seems we have been on this scene for several lectures.'

Her hands fold themselves into hooves, and she leans on her

knuckles, on her desk. Rarely does this woman come out from behind her desk.

'Is that right?'

'Yes. Also, I wondered if we might study some other literature after Christmas. It says on the prospectus that we will cover a range of writers and styles.'

'I'm sorry if we're boring you, Mr Hussein.'

'Hassan.'

'Potato, po-tah-to.'

'I beg your pardon?'

'So tell me. What other writers would you recommend for our curriculum? Bearing in mind that we're studying Eng-lish lit-er-ature, and that Shakespeare is the finest exemplar of English literature in the known world. Or would you disagree?'

Her tone is less slovenly when she is engaged. I have noticed this before. It is a warning sign, like when a snake retracts the bluntness of his snout. He appears to retreat, when in reality he is building his momentum.

'I wondered if we might read some Scottish writers, bearing in mind that these are the Scottish Highers we are studying for?'

'But we're doing Eng-lish literature.' A dramatic tossing of her head. Clearly, for the benefit of this tableau, I am cast as the imbecile. Ah, but maybe I am a mongoose to your snake, Ms Irvine. (That is Kipling, but I paraphrase.) There is an animation to me that is not unpleasant. In fact, it is sparkling. Tension pulls at the strings of my neck and wrists. Muffled in her scarf, Sandrine conceals – a cough? Mirth?

'Yes,' I continue. Shoulders broadening, expanding wider than the air around me. 'But surely this denotes texts that are written in the English language, not those which are confined exclusively to being written by persons originating from the country of England?'

Her small, dead eyes shutter. I await the sly transmission of her forked tongue, which I will tie in copious knots.

'Maybe we can discuss this later, Mr Hussein, otherwise we'll never get past the scene you find so objectionable. Right, class. Page forty-three, please.'

Denied. (This is not from Shakespeare, but a film which Dexy insisted I would enjoy.) The class embarks, once more, into *The Merchant of Venice*. I try to pay attention as Ms Irvine speaks of *misbelievers and cut-throat dogs*, but find I am thinking of this film. It was very funny, about a man who loves music and has a friend called Garth with whom he produces a most amateur television show. They play hockey, lust after beautiful girls, see a rock band, stab do-nuts. It zooms with puerile humour and catchphrases, many of which have lodged in my brain through Dexy's copious repetitions. When I bring him some *anjara* with his tea, he bows and winks at Rebecca. 'Cakes and aw? Man! We're not worthy!'

I cannot think it was Dexy who would take my certificates. If he was truly in need, surely he would have helped himself to my books or my little television? What use would my memories be to him? More than that, it's not his way. He is not duplicitous. *There's nae side tae him*, said Mrs Coutts after she met Dexy on the stair. *Cheeky wee runt, mind.* (I believe he called her 'doll'.) He is settling well, into his job. Mr Maloney gave him my white coat and a set of knives – which he makes him keep in the store. Once or twice a week, Dexy comes after work to say hello. Occasionally he brings some sell-by food, or sweeties for Rebecca. And he never asks to smoke. Soon, he will be moving from his hostel, to share a flat with two other apprentices. I want to tell Debs all of this good news. I don't care that she promised to help get new certificates. It's my fault for not keeping them safe. I convince myself I dropped them – at the Barras possibly when I was buying Deborah's vase. Maybe, as I sit and contemplate Shylock, they are being sold as curios on that very stall, packaged up with musty books.

'Ah. Now. There's a phrase.'

There is a change in Ms Irvine's inflection that causes me to pause. Look up. As if her pronouncement is directed at me and only me.

'*Temptation is the fire that brings up the scum of the heart.* "Scum of the heart" – isn't that wonderful? Now, what Shakespeare's saying here is that wanting stuff we can't have makes us jealous. It makes us do bad things, even when people have been good to us. Especially, actually, when folk have been good to us. Because we end up wanting to have everything they have. All the nasty stuff inside us is drawn up to the surface, and we get angry. Violent. Greedy.'

And it is now that her tongue appears. Pink and pale, it meets her lips. Traverses them and slides back inside.

'Just think about it nowadays. All they asylum seekers, for instance. Our taxes paying for everything they need, all their travel, putting them up in nice flats, then before you know it they're on the phone back home, going *Come on over. It's free money here, free hospitals, free schools.* Then more of them come, and they start to get sneaky . . .'

All of the class is listening; they are more transfixed by this piece

417

of social commentary than by any meditation she has delivered to date. But it is an uneasy rapture. Even the dimmest eyes flit from her to me. A collective breath is held. By my side, Sandrine shifts uncomfortably. Her hand is on her scarf, twisting it as she twists and turns her knees, her feet. In the movement of the yellow flowers, I see another twist, livid like barbed wire. Recognise it as a scar, one made by a chain.

'Ms Irvine.' I am on my feet. 'Perhaps we should return to Shakespeare? I understand your knowledge of the world is limited, but perhaps your knowledge of the Bard is limited also? Let me enlighten you with some of his other quotes: *In time we hate that which we often fear. Antony and Cleopatra.*'

She makes a snorting noise. 'Am I supposed to be impressed? It may have escaped your notice but we're no studying *Antony and Cleopatra*, Mr Hussein.' Folds her arms. 'As I was saying –'

'*The empty vessel makes the loudest sound: King Lear* – and Plato, of course.'

'Ho. Excuse *me* –'

'*The man that hath no music in himself* –'

'*Mr* Hussein. That is enough.'

'I quite agree, Ms Irvine. And my name, as I said, is Hassan. Would you like me to spell it for you?'

'Sit down.'

'Or you will what?' I pick up my back-rucksack, my *Collected Shakespeare* Volume II and my apple for later. 'I have no wish to continue with this lesson. When you begin to teach literature, I will return. And, in the interim, I think you should apologise to the class.'

Oh the sound of the door whumping shut. The thickness of my

breathing, reminding me I am alive, that my simple act of ingesting air will power all this wonderful machinery of pumps and pistons and exploding, thrashing, multiplying cells. The corridor is unusually quiet. It is stripped of ornament so you will not linger, but hurry forward into education. Windows line one side, giving on to a concrete courtyard. I see a reflection of my sneering face, and my pride mutates to humility. What will I do now? My actions seem so flagrant as they deflate. Will I be expelled? I only want to learn.

Behind me comes Sandrine, then Farida. In the corridor we stare at one another. A little startled, a little crazed. A residue of shame hangs about us. The door opens again and out come three or four other students, no five. No seven. Around half of the class is standing in the corridor.

'Aye well, up yours.' A girl called Tanya is last to decamp. She slams the door behind her. She has deep-black hair which she must straighten with a flatiron. She has never spoken to me before.

'Ho! Nice one, Abdi. She's a cheeky bitch, so she is. You should complain about her.'

'I should?'

'Fuck, aye. She canny talk to folk like that.'

'Perhaps I will.'

'Good on you.'

Another student, a lad in his late teens, says, 'You thought about the student council, Abdi? I think you'd be good on it.'

'I don't know . . .'

'There's a few positions coming up.'

'It's not really —'

'Look, we're having a meeting on Tuesday. Why don't you come along, see what you think, eh? No pressure. Right.' He claps his hands at the assembled renegades. 'Seen as we're all oot early, who's for a drink?'

Several of the younger ones troop after him. I want to leave before Ms Irvine's wrath boils over. Farida smiles her goodbyes and follows them. Tanya shoves her folder in her bag. 'So, what you up to the night then, guys?'

I shrug. 'Not sure.'

Sandrine shakes her head.

'Och, well I'm away up to see my mum. She's no keeping so well. I'm gonny take her up a big bar of Galaxy and a bottle of wine.'

'Sounds nice. I hope she is better soon.'

'See you, Abdi. Bye, Sandrine.' She bounds out. Sandrine and I continue to wait. For what? My limbs are clumsy, my elbow clunks the window frame as I adjust the strap on my rucksack. Sandrine is rounded and petite, she is compact while I spill over. A slow tension unfurls. Should I make some lively remark, or let the conversation wither?

'You came out also.'

Stupid refugee.

'Mmm.' It is an unformed, urgent sound. Flicks up at the end.

'Sandrine, what is it? What's wrong?'

Her brow is creased with the effort of restraint. It's our blank mask. The one we learn early, behind which we feel terror or despair.

'It's nothing. What that teacher said – to phone home? *Phone?* And then she said . . . *she* is going to see her mum. And I can't do that.' The smooth composure of her face dissolves. She cries very quietly.

'Sssh. Please. Do not be sad.' I let my eyes close momentarily.

'Sandrine. Would you like to go for a drink?'

23. December

Glasgow Cathedral

Religion could be said to be at the root of Glasgow's development. The city was founded by a saint; the university established by a bishop. 'Lord, let Glasgow flourish through the preaching of Thy word' is the city's motto. For centuries, people of all faiths — and none — have settled in Glasgow, and this has sometimes led to tensions. Even today, the rivalry of Glasgow's footballing 'Old Firm' and the colourful processions of Orange and Hibernian walks inject a reminder of times past. However, the city is now a cosmopolitan multi-faith community, boasting mosques, synagogues and temples — as well as four cathedrals.

Of these, Glasgow Cathedral is the best example of a large medieval church to have survived the Reformation. The first stone-built cathedral was dedicated in 1136, with the present building consecrated in 1197. It's believed St Mungo's original church was on the site of what is now the Blacader Aisle. Mungo died in 603 AD, and his own tomb can be found in the Lower Church. Thousands of pilgrims came to this shrine in medieval times, with the pope declaring a pilgrimage to Glasgow was as meritorious as travelling to Rome itself.

Today, the cathedral is part of the Church of Scotland, with serv-ices held every Sunday. Located at the top of High Street, it forms the centrepiece to an enclave of historical sights, including the city's oldest house, the Museum of Religion and the poignant statuary of the Necropolis, Glasgow's City of the Dead.

Entry to all is free.

★

'I SHOULD HAVE brought you here before.'

The three of us, in the front pew of the cathedral. Rebecca sits on me like I'm the chair. Her legs over mine, hands resting on my wrists, fine line of her spine between my breasts. *Ba-hoom* goes my heartbeat through my flesh. Since Dadaab, I've been struggling. I'd let myself be excited by the world again, with all its limitless complexities. Rose thinks *carpe diem* means to reach and strive. I think it means to be content.

Three weeks till Christmas, and the cathedral is resplendent in green. The nave is hung with ivy, fir boughs strung in virile garlands over windowsills, under arches. There is a crisp blaze of tree-bark and peppery pine which hits your nostrils as you move. They must have got a job lot of Christmas trees because they're sprouting like . . . well, trees. There's a huge one in the nave, glistening with silver strands. Other trees are potted in front of the stained-glass windows, their packed-green needles unable to compete with garnet, emerald, sapphire. I kiss Rebecca's plaited hair. She shuffles.

Settles in again. Two more trees stand either side of the communion table: pagan evergreen on the altar. Abdi gazes at the ceiling. It
is a soar of vast pointed arches sustained by clustered pillars.

'It is so old. A thousand years, Debs. Nothing in my country is
this old.'

Rebecca yawns. We've been to see Santa and bought new shoes.
School shoes. The polo-shirts and sweatshirts are on order and Mrs
Coutts – God help us – is making a grey skirt (I bought a wee
pleated one at Debenham's just in case).

'Does this not touch you, Deborah?'

'It's beautiful, yes.'

'I mean your soul.'

White Christmas roses shine like lard. Beady baubles glint and
wink. Below the purple fall of the pulpit, there's a nativity scene.
Apologetic in its smallness but illuminated by a hidden light. The
Calvinists would be birling in their neat plain graves. During the
Reformation, icons were smashed here, and burned, stone noses
severed from stone faces. You'd probably have been crucified for
depicting God in a manger.

'Why do they have all these trees inside?'

'Bringing in nature. It's an orgy of nature, Abdi. To remind us
that winter will end. And how small we are. See, if you look at the
pillars – they're meant to represent tree trunks too. And the arching
vaults are the branches.'

'That real tree with all the silver. It makes me think of fishes.'

'Fish.'

'Fishes.'

'Whasan orgy?' asks Rebecca.

Abdi starts to giggle.

'Um – a big party.'

Rebecca wriggles off my knee. 'Can I see the dollies?'

'There are no dollies, mucky pup.'

'She means the nativity,' I say. 'OK, but don't run. And DON'T TOUCH!'

'It's fine. We can see her from here.'

As she is bidden, Rebecca tiptoes neatly towards the pulpit. So careful is her progress, you could almost imagine she's mocking us.

'Abdi. Can I ask you something?'

'Of course.'

'When you became a Christian, it was a priest you had, right? In Kenya?'

'Yes.'

'But now you're here, you have a minister? A Protestant minister, who has a wife?'

'Mm.'

'Why the conversion?'

'No conversion.' Abdi glances sideways. Rubs his nose. 'It was the closest church to our house.'

He is laughing. First just him, a grin that bubbles over; now me. Louder and deeper until people start to stare and Rebecca, too, looks up. I blow her a kiss then cross my eyes, and her throaty laugh rings loudest of all.

'You're something else, Abdi.'

'Truthfully, it is all God. He is with us in the dust and the sewers, and in these trees: the real ones and the stone ones.'

I shake my head. 'I can't believe you still have faith. I think the best thing's to believe in nothing, expect nothing. Do nothing. That's how you stay sane.'

'Maybe your faith does not have to be in God?'

He is so forlornly beautiful. I wonder if he knows this? My Christmas gift for him's wrapped and in my handbag. It was a simple choice: Azira's photo in a nice gilt frame. Now I'm scared that it's a terrible idea. I'll buy him some socks. And a jumper. Rebecca's present is a little charm bracelet. My sister and I both had them; one charm a year: your birthstone; your first day at school; ballet pumps; your dog. I brought their presents with me because our time is officially up. In January the mentoring scheme is over. Technically, this is our last meeting.

'Debba!'

Rebecca tumbles towards us, her face on fire with joy and light.

First day at school.

Arrows of coloured light pierce her heart-shaped face.

Your sixteenth birthday.

A tiny strand of hair flicks wide and wide.

Graduation.

And what if you never came back?

Your wedding day.

Ah, but what if? What if you did?

Call it a revelation – it's not, of course. Call it what you like, but it's the play of light, it's a trick of the light, how it seeps and curls, is coloured smoke inside you. How it forms a shape, which becomes a substance. How that substance becomes you.

You.

What if that woman really was you? What if there's one singular stone left unturned? I know your face, I *know* it.

'Abdi.' I stand. Abruptly. 'I have to go away again.'

'Why?'

I gather up my bag and gloves. 'I dunno . . . not for long. A week? Few weeks, maybe.'

'Will we see you before Christmas?'

'If I can, yes. *Yes*,' I insist.

'You are coming back to us?'

'We goin' now, Debba?' Rebecca jumps to a halt. 'Ah'm *bouncin'*.'

I pull her into me. 'Um–um–um. I could *eat* you.'

'No!' she shrieks, pushing me off. In her shoving hand I see a pair of feet. A tiny pair of feet are protruding from her fist.

'Rebecca?'

'What?' she says, with wary defiance.

'Let me see what you've got.'

'Nuffin'.'

'Open your hand.'

Slowly, very slowly, she unfolds her hand. A fat baby Jesus looks surprised at all the fuss.

Before I left, I went to see Naomi. It was the invite to the cocktail party that did it. Came in a thick cream envelope, gold ink on thick cream card.

Dear Friend

You are invited to join Naomi and Duncan for drinks and canapés, to celebrate our exciting news! Following recommendation from the Lord Justice General to the First Minister of Scotland, Her Majesty the Queen has appointed Duncan as Queen's Counsel, and we would love to share this happy time with you all. RSVP. Dress: smart / casual. PS – no gifts, please. Your company is all we desire.

I waited until her house was hoaching, countless cars spilling chic little dresses and elegant overcoats – you know, the type with black velvet collars. Slung on my anorak and stomped over.

'Hey, Naomi!'

She was a confection of cream and gold. Hair stiff with spray and a weight of gold trinkets on her wrist. Big gold boulder round her neck. Yes, Naomi was quite beside herself with jangling.

'Oh, Debs! You made it! Come in, come in. Let me get you a drink. Fizz all right?'

'I was wondering if we could have a quiet word?'

'Oh. Gosh.' She surveyed her teeming household, all the braying laughs and teetering heels. A woman bumped into me, wine slooshing over her crystal flute. 'Oops!'

'Watch the carpet, Lindi!' Naomi's trill was kind of desperate. 'Well, look. Why don't we do coffee tomorrow?'

'I'd rather it was now. It's about Rula.'

'Oh Christ, Debs. Really? You're going to do this here?'

A fat bloke in a pink shirt came out of the downstairs loo. 'Lovely party, Noo-noo.' He had sweat rings under his arms. They fake-kissed, *mwaa*, then Naomi hustled me, and her, inside the loo. 'Oh, for God's sake.' She put the seat back down. 'OK. What about Rula?'

'Nothing really. Except I think it's payback time.'

'For what? Christ, shit happens, Deborah. Who died and made you a saint?'

My mouth got all loose and ready, but what would have been a fitting response? Really? I just swallowed, counted the little sticks in her fancy air freshener. Seven, there were seven sticks sooking up the woody goodness of *Forest Nights Ambient Oil*. At least she had the grace to examine her nails.

'Naomi,' I said eventually. 'I'm going to need Duncan's help. How is he with immigration law?'

So. Now I have the direct telephone numbers of two legal experts. One I've instructed to look into Gamu's case again – and then again, until he has fully exercised his incisive and expensive brain – and the other . . . Well, the other I have in reserve.

Dadaab. The very name of it flops in a dollop of misery. If you're looking for venal despair, here it is. They've built a city on it! Dadaab exists, and it should not. To return there would be a madness.

Yet. How do these things stop? At what point do you define a story, craft the frame and glass it in? State with a triumphant flourish: *it is done*? Where do the ends fall when you snip them off? I don't think Dadaab will ever be done, I think it is a mouth of infinite need. And even if it were possible to sate it, another mouth will open, demanding to be shovelled full. You can keep on staring at the blue-blank sky, or out your window, or at your navel if you prefer. Dadaab will grind on regardless.

I still have my press pass, and my previous letter of permission. It's the Republic of Kenya that grants you passage. Their online form is relatively simple; I must state my name, my nationality, my organisation and my purpose. This is key; I must prove how my presence will benefit refugees. The website informs me, sternly: *Using the camps as tourist sanctuaries is highly discouraged*. I tell the same untruths as last time: I am a freelance journalist, I am continuing my story about the water project. I compound this lie by scanning my previous permissions, and Rose's official letter of endorsement. I've not told Rose I want to go back – I think she'd have me sectioned. She's in Sudan at the moment, sending me cheery postcards from the edge.

Duplicitously, I attach both documents to the form. I wait ten days, ten days in which I have no contact with Abdi. I am in purdah. I am simmering but inert. Only a dull compulsion driving me on. Most of the time, I stay indoors. It's Yuletide: there are cards to be written, parcels to be wrapped. I keep busy with distractions. Random interactions and occurrences: I know that's all there is. But we persist in weaving narratives. It might be God, or Fate or Karma. Astrology, or aphorisms. For the realistic amongst us, the tugging thread might be nothing more than a blind imperative to get up each day and keep breathing.

On the eleventh day, a letter arrives. I read, reread. *Request is a continuation of an earlier project. Permission granted*. My heart ignites. I book my flights to Nairobi. Christmas, last minute; the tickets are extortionate. I could have given that money to Abdi. Or donated it to Oxfam. Guilt-ridden – and very possibly insane – I write a cheque for nearly a grand but do not post it. I prop it on my mantelpiece. If I get her . . . if I get her. I make a deal with Abdi's God. If I get her, I'll post the cheque. How's that?

The flight from London to Nairobi lasts nine hours. I read a nice fat airport book where the words dance and I must keep respooling to get the gist of it. I never do. I'm exhausted, too tired to battle through the teeming airport, hunt for my bag, find a way out. I knew when I left, the aid flights to Dadaab were full: I have the option of paying around three hundred dollars for a dodgy cab, or taking the local bus, which works out at twelve dollars, and – I reckon – has the advantage of safety in numbers. It's cramped, hot, noisy, but I do sleep, a little, once we've negotiated Nairobi's bubble of bodies and beasts and traffic chaos; my money in a pouch beneath my bum, my bag embraced tightly on my lap. We jolt and rumble onwards. My stomach shrinks as the landscape expands. Bleak yawns and dry earth dirt. Two white men behind me speak in French for almost the entire eight hours, but I find the softness comforting.

Forever onwards on our flat, sandy track. No journey of discovery this time. Under limitless skies, I feel claustrophobic. Sweat slicks in little tongues; on my brow, my neck, my joints, my groin. Goes crisp in my armpits. I'm so stiff. Press my forehead on the seat in front. Retract at the ripe smell lifting from it. Doze and read and stare and listen and do not think beyond the forward, forward, forward until.

Again, it rises.

Dadaab.

On our approach, the vast stretches of tents and makeshift shelters seem even wider than before. In only one month, this virus has spread. It is definitely bigger, even messier than I remember. At the periphery reams and reams of bright barbed wire form higher fencing, newer pens. And in these pens, as we get closer, I see people. Quiet and undemanding, their natural elegance grotesqued to skeleton and skin. They wear brightly coloured wristbands; I have a horror they're somehow condemned. That happened in Ethiopia, I remember it on the news. How nurses had to choose who were still worth saving. Snip-snip-snip. I turn round in my seat, to face the Frenchmen.

'*Qu'est-ce que c'est?*' I ask, touching my wrist.

'*Comment?*'

I brandish my wrist again. '*Les* . . . band thingies? *Pour quoi?*'

'*Ah. Ils sont en raison de la famine. Pour des rations de secours?* Um . . . to permit emergency ration?'

'*Ah. Oui. Merci.*'

We arrive on a cloud of dust. My press credentials allow me to book an escort in the camp.

Tomorrow?

No. Today. Can you ask for Mo, please? I get an expansive shrug. I get my stamp, go in, get my towels and sheets. Jangly nerves and vicious coffee. I sip, drum my fingers. Refuse to be overwhelmed. My escort duly arrives, and is a surly, skinny man with a red neckerchief and a missing tooth.

'Where's Mo?' I ask.

'Huh?'

'Mo? Mohammed? The policeman. You know him? Big . . .' I blow my cheeks out. 'Big heavy guy.'

He picks at his ear.

'I would really like to see him. Is it possible for Mohammed to escort me, please?'

'He busy.'

I offer the man ten dollars. 'Please?'

The money evaporates. My escort beholds me blankly. I try another ten, then another.

'I go see.'

Two hours later, when I've given up hope of having any escort at all, Mo appears. He's wearing his khaki uniform trousers and his gun, but with a flapping grey T-shirt on top.

'Huh. Is you.'

'Mo! Yes, it's me. Oh, I'm so glad to see you.'

He rolls his eyes. 'What is you want, Missus Deb?'

I ask him to take me back to where Mariam lives, pretend it is a follow-up. 'Is she well? Have you seen her?'

'No.'

We travel in almost-silence, past the hooped white tents and matchwood shacks, the sofas made of mud. Past the tyres and scrap, the miles and miles of chickenwire, the shuffling dense mass going nowhere but round in circles. It's more starkly awful than before. Greasy, infernal heat shimmers over man and beast, me on tour with my big white face. I feel as if I have flu.

Finally, the jeep stops.

'You know which house?'

Mo nods. 'Not house. She at the school.'

'What school? I thought you hadn't seen her again?'

'You come.'

Hat on, sunglasses on, scarf on the back of my neck, I follow him towards the clearing, that same one from before with the stunted tree. But something's different. I can hear children's voices, the familiar chant of rote learning. I can see a structure where there used to be a wall. Quicken my pace towards the sound. There are three white walls, an open awning. I remove my glasses. Discs of flattened oil drums painted red and green pock the lower part of the walls. They look like happy shields. Under the awning, a teacher addresses her class. *Mariam.*

'Oh my God.' I grab Mo's elbow. 'She fixed the school!'

'Yeah, but they no have money to keep it going. One year, two year, then – *phu*.' He snaps his fingers. 'You kind OK, Missus Deb. But stupid.'

'Mizz Deb!' Mariam cries, hurrying out. 'You come back!'

We hug, the children giggling. None of them leave their school-room, just extend their necks to see, and chatter in their place.

'Oh, I am so very happy to see you. You like?'

'It's amazing.'

'Is you gold, Mizz Deb.'

'But I wanted you . . . I thought you'd use it for a better house. Or maybe buy your way out of here.'

'Go where?'

'Home?'

'Who I go with?' She pats my hand. 'Whena fighting stops, I go home. For now, I gota children.'

Heat wiping me, sky live with flies. I hug her again, feel the

435

bones of her. She is thin and strong. Then we stop, are holding hands. I beam, forgetting why I'm here.

'I better go back'm . . .'

'Oh, yes. Of course. They are very well-behaved.'

'Thank you.'

'Mariam. Before you go. Please. I wanted to ask one thing. When we talked about Azira, you said she went in the river. What happened after? Did someone find her? Was she buried?'

'Uh . . . no. *Tana* take her.'

'You mean her body was never recovered? But someone saw her jump in?'

'Yes'm. Two peoples saw her. You want talk to them?'

'No, no. It's OK. Thank you, Mariam. Thank you so much.'

'OK.' She nods, clasps my hand for a final time. 'Hey . . . you want say hello?'

'Och no, I don't think so.'

But Mariam is off. Mo and I follow. She speaks rapidly to her pupils, who all clap like crazy.

'What did you just say?'

She grins. 'I tell'm this you school. Because you.' Mariam takes her place before the blackboard, scratches on it with flinty chalk.

DEB SCHOOL

'No. Oh, no, no it isn't. Please.' I shake my head. On white plaster, the painted oil drums gleam. Each child's white shirt, blue top, green dress is a bright thirsty fire. The colours pooling, the children clapping. Even Mo is smiling. I wave, blow kisses. Try not to feel like the Queen. No body was found. I clasp my positive negative, hard. Feel the solid press of it.

We return to the truck, Mo waddling, me waving, not looking where I'm going until I realise I've bypassed him altogether. Mo has stopped by a circle of low bush-huts. Their threadbare straw is clumsy, the struts which hold them gaping. He lifts one fat hand. 'You wait. Bad smell.'

'Bad smell? Mo, this place is absolutely stinking.' I wind my scarf higher, so my nose is buried. 'See? Don't worry, I'm used to it.'

'No. Not stink. Is dead-smell.'

'What?'

We're out of sight of the school, and in five seconds I will be hugely grateful for that, but for now I watch, stupidly, as Mo sniffs, shuffles, sniffs, then dips. It is all over very quickly; I barely see a thing. Just a roof of straw, and him, yanking at the straw, sheaves of it torn out and a tiny arm and a part-furled fist. Tiny. Mo bundles it up and a woman emerges, launches herself, wrestling with Mo and the tiny corpse. Everywhere is shouting, Mo bawling, the young woman bawling, a tired old man crawling from an adjoining hut. He is whickering. The woman weeping. Mo shouting some more; he speaks into his radio, the bulk of his shoulder blocking the woman from reaching the dead child. I can't look. I can't inhale, the smell is too thick. I take myself away to a pile of plastic containers. Sit on them and pull my scarf all over my nose and mouth. Another van arrives, two more police. They remove the woman and the baby. Mo addresses the old man, I think Mo's going to shove him in his feeble chest, but he doesn't. Eventually, he lumbers over to me.

'You go back now.' It's not a question.

'What happened? What happened to that wee baby?'

'Is not baby. Two, maybe three. It die, what happened.'

'Did she kill it?'

He snorts. 'No.'

'Then why . . . ?'

'She hide him. So she keep getting his rations.'

Deep blue dusk is settling when we finally leave, falling in a cloak which Dadaab gratefully receives. Mo and I drive in silence, faint smells clinging and drifting between us. The gap between day and night comes like snow here. Sharp barbs become undulations. The plastic fluttering is blossom on trees. It will pitch rapidly, though, to absolute dark, the thick lightless panic of nature versus man, of bad versus good. You would be mad to be in Dadaab in the dark. The tip of Mo's cigarette glows in the windscreen. All the edges of my nails are stinging. I take my hand from my mouth.

'Hey. No cry, Missus Deb. Is not your fault.'

'Mo. What if I set up a fund? So money could come here regularly for the school. Would that work?'

'Why you ask me?'

'Because you, my friend, are a fat wise man.'

'And youa very rude.'

My rudeness is his Achilles' heel, because he starts to chat a wee bit as we trundle through the dusk. He has two sons and two daughters and his father was a policeman too. At every gap in the conversation I hesitate. *Will I say it now, will I say it now?* Does it matter any more? Is it safe? We are alone in a growing blackness which chases us in

438

waves. He could shoot me, dump me … anything. One wrong move … and I am now in a cowboy film. I hear Rose, feck-saking me. *Carpe diem, you silly cow.* Mo scratches his abundant thigh. In another police truck, a little body rolls in a blanket.

'Mo,' I say when we're in sight of the UN compound. 'Can you stop the car? I'd like you to look at something.'

'No got time. Am day off, you know.'

'Please.'

He tuts loudly and slows the vehicle, pulling in by the side of a feeding station. Keeps the engine running.

'What?'

I bring out the picture of Azira. I won't show it to him yet.

'You know how we were asking Mariam about Azira?'

'I no listen when women yi-yi-yi.' He snaps his hand like a jaw.

'Aye you do. You listen to everything. I am trying to find this woman, Mo. And I think I saw her, last time I was here. D'you know where I think I saw her?'

He lights another cigarette.

'In the police station. In your compound, Mo.'

'S'no my compound. I don' live there. *Work* there, yes.'

'But people do live there, don't they? I mean, I saw a garden, other buildings.'

He removes a shred of tobacco from his tongue. 'Some does. The men. The corporal stay sometime, and inspector when he come.'

'And women?'

A dry laugh. 'They keep some animal there.'

'The women do?'

'They not women. They *dhilo*.'

439

He means the women *are* the animals, I think. My nails press sickle-shapes into my knees. Azira's face shines from the glossy paper on which she is printed; the swing of her hair, how her mouth folds and opens. How she demands attention. When Mo looks at her, he'll . . . And then I remember he already has looked at her, and if not her, then hundreds and thousands of other Aziras, reduced to livestock and kept satisfactorily remote. What if it was his wife? I lift her up, flat on my palm.

'Could you look at this photo, Mo? Tell me if you know her.'

Eyes barely skim the paper. *Look at her.* She is my last gasp and I am hers.

'Don' know.'

'Mo, please. I'm begging you.' I put it on his lap. 'This is someone's wife. Someone's mother. *Hooyo?* Please, she has a little girl. Please let her go home.'

He looks for a long time, until his cigarette has burned to nothing. Ash crumbles, falls and the tiny breathing light extinguishes. Night has finally caught us fully, so I can only see his outline. Smell the desert, our breaths twining with residual curls of smoke. A bird screeches, there is a tumbling clang of metal buckets. People shout inside the compound. I want to be inside the inhabited warmth. Close myself in and tuck it all around me.

Mo's disembodied voice comes slowly. 'I no know her, Missus Deb. I sorry.'

Wife, mum, victim. *Dhilo.*

Wife, mum, killer, widow. Victim.

Victim.

You could rearrange labels all night when you can't sleep, you've nae pals, there's no electricity and all your lovely magic medications are at home or in the bin.

Economist, husband, disabled, dead.

Fisherman, husband, father. Refugee.

Now, isn't that interesting? When I write them down: it's only the men who get their professions first. You can extend the game by cutting up the paper to make actual labels. Rearrange them, shuffling them in a deck, deal them out in random allocations. Luckily for me, I get bored with this quite quickly, go wandering to find a drink of water (the stuff in the washroom tap is a funny brown). Meet a lovely girl in the desolate canteen.

When I was first diagnosed with breast cancer, I wanted to die. Not one shred of brave fighting spirit. Just a terror of decay, the imperfection, the corrosion of my body. *My* body. How could it do that to me? The hormones that had struggled to make a baby could whip up a tumour with ease. Better to die intact than have bits lopped off. Then, when I finally succumbed and had a bit lopped off, I came home to a husband who unbound me, kissed me. Told me he'd always been a cup-half-full man.

Which is true. And was very funny at the time.

Even if I had found Azira, what part of her would have come back to Abdi? Would he want it; would she want him? Jesusgod, how am I meant to know?

The pale blonde girl in the canteen, scribbling in an A4 notepad, is Inge. She is the researcher Rose had wanted me to meet last time. We get talking, as you do in your vest and jammy bottoms when you find another insomniac with haunted eyes, and I tell her why I'm here. The true version. Inge listens as I describe Abdi to her, tell her anecdotes of Rebecca, try to sketch Azira's short life. Inge rarely interrupts. She has very bright-blue eyes.

'I keep thinking, I keep thinking, I mean, that river's a totey wee creek . . . ach, Christ, Inge. This is so stupid.' And there it is, I physically feel the last vestiges of resolve shudder from me.

Inge nods. Passes me a hankie. 'Yes, but last two years we have had terrible floods. For women . . . the shame can be very great, you know? And sometimes, if others know; women can be burned alive, you see. Or scalded with boiling water.'

'For being raped?'

'For having sex.'

'How can you go digging for all that stuff? Listen to their stories, write it all down?'

'So others can hear them.' She smiles, briefly. 'You say you have been giving pictures of her?'

'Yes. I've still got . . .' I'm in my jammies. 'Can you wait a sec? I've got one in my room.'

'Sure,' she says in her lovely curdled accent.

On the way back from the accommodation block, I'm halted in the yard. Dawn has painted the town red. A low, rose-tinted glaze is creeping over first the water tower, then all the rooftops. Light thickens, begins to assume its hazy forms. There are little staff huts dotted here and there: round stone buildings with thatched roofs, then the low verandahed buildings where we sleep, then bigger blocks for meetings and administration — and recreation. Rose's Grease Pit was jumping last night when I got in; a leaving do for

some CARE staff. Kenyan music pumping, the rich roasty goodness of barbecued goat. Stray beer bottles still litter the ground
around a group of empty chairs. I crunch on dust and stones
towards the man who waves urgently at me.

'Ma'am. There's police here to see you.'

Mo waits at the entrance to the compound. He looks exhausted,
wears the grey T-shirt of yesterday. Not an attractive look.

'Hey. Have you not been to bed, you?'

'No.' With him is another man, a plump, glossy man in an elabo-
rate robe. His thin beard is hennaed red. Mo dunts him in the back,
so he is stuttered forward. The shiny man is appalled, his heavy
jowls sway. He composes himself and extends his hand. 'Khadra,
madame. At your service.'

'You have plenty money, Missus Deb?'

'Mo. What's this about?'

Again, he pushes Khadra. 'You tell.'

Khadra gazes nonchalantly at the sun above us.

'Yes, I have money. I have money!' I grapple with my watch strap;
it's all I have on me but I can get more, *I can get more*, I'm gibbering
as I force the watch into Khadra's fist. He turns the silvery strap
over, over, as if he might reject it.

Mo cannot contain himself. 'He know her. He know your Azira.'

'You know her? Her?' Thrusting the photograph I'm clutching
in his face. 'You know Azira? She's alive? Is she alive?'

Khadra continues to examine my watch. A glancing blow to the
side of his head. 'You tell her. She is live!'

Khadra shakes out the folds of his rich blue-green robe. Into
them, my wristwatch disappears, silver running silver, threaded

time pouring and repouring. The heavy sun crawls higher, gapes on us. The air, unhurried. 'I find things.' With his little finger, Khadra wipes sweat from the side of his mouth. 'I find things, I sell. Pretty things.'

It is late afternoon and I am panting. Steady puffs: a runner before my race. My heart is uncontrollable, it's bound to give me away, me and Inge and Huq in our car with the windows open, Huq's car, who is Inge's boyfriend/escort/not sure but there is much glancing and careless touching between them. He's lovely, Huq and I'm havering utter nonsense, both at them and in my head. This morning, Inge said this was a crazy idea.

You have a police who will help you?

I think so.

Be careful this is not a trap. He's already taken hundreds of dollars.

One hundred, Inge. He said he needed them.

In Inge's experience, the police can never be trusted. She has spoken to too many women who've gone to them for help. The lucky ones are ignored, the others robbed or beaten. Or worse. She urged me not to trust Mo.

But why would he tell me this?

To extort more money. To have you abducted? Whatever you do, you must not go inside.

They've still not found those two female aid workers.

This man is a very powerful chief. You understand this? These people have links with militia, police, some of the staff here — and with politicians too. Drugs, guns, money laundering: they all buy big bribes.

As do human beings. Azira is not fresh enough to have been trafficked. But, in a world where people eat bare unidentifiable bones, she is not so stale as to be worthless either. Khadra tells Mo she cleaned up well. *Very fine, very pretty.* He has a team of scavengers who search the dumps, riverbanks, the refuse. Azira is now the property of a tribal chief, a man of great stature, great power. He and his extended 'family' live in a small compound of their own inside the camp. I hadn't realised, until Inge told me, that people cling to their tribe structure here. Even the design of their bird-nest shelters can denote which tribe they come from. How it was negotiated that this chief gets an entire compound, no one is quite clear. Apparently, he is so important, it is necessary for his own safety. Where Khadra is a useful man, this chief is mighty. His compound has been used as a storage facility for smuggled arms: Inge knows this for a fact. The guns were removed, yet he was not.

I think you must report this officially.

Look, Inge. Interrupting her plain, Nordic flow. *You're just after telling me this tribe's a fucking cartel.*

You must also consider this, Deborah. It may be that she is happy there.
Happy?

Yes. If she is safe, and well-protected. Victims of sex crimes are often rejected by their communities. They are left with very few options.

Christ, Inge. Do you hear what you're saying?

I had listened to her sigh, and the hum of the kitchen generator cranking up, the dryness of a sleepless night flattening my tongue. We sipped stale water. Watched the sun rise fully for its daily onslaught.

Mo will sort it. He's risking a lot for me as it is.

Then Inge asked if she could help as well.

Mo cannot get involved beyond getting Azira out of the chieftain's compound. I'm not sure how he'll do this, but we are to wait, just far enough away that we can see the gate and the freshly painted corner of the wall. We sit, shaded in the lee of the transport yard, washed by this constant stream of disinterested people who are walking for rations, for firewood, for water, who are walking because it's better than standing still. We've to wait here until I see them come out. I asked Mo to make absolutely sure it's her.

Ask if her daughter's called Rebecca.

And have her go crazy inside his house? No way. I see her face; I know. OK?

After he gets her out, what then? I've not to approach until Mo has gone and Azira is far enough away from the compound that she can't be seen. Inge says normal procedure is for refugees to be referred to UNHCR. They undergo case creation, then pre-screening and verification, so any gaps in their story can be filled. Defining and refining as they are shuffled in and on. Then a resettlement interview, a medical examination . . .

It can take for ever.

But she's already done all this. She was going to be resettled.

After five. Mo said it would be late, once the men are 'on deliveries'. I need to pace, to grind my heels and press my soles in lulling ambulation and make my mind still as my body moves whatifit's not her? Whatif we get shot or she doesn't come and it *was* her or Mo is shot I am sick, jesusgod I'm swimming in nausea on a belly of rotten water and some orange juice Huq has offered amid joking apologies for the fact it's not fresh.

The yellow gate cranks open. We tense, suspend our animation.

A people-carrier rolls out, turns right when we are left. Disappears behind a pile of old tyres, and we breathe in again. Ten minutes later, and Mo chugs up. He clambers from his jeep, hammers on the gate. Hammers again. Shouts theatrically.

'What did he say?' I whisper to Huq.

'He says: "I have important information".'

Mo is eventually admitted access, but his jeep remains outside. Another twenty minutes pass. We're melting, melting. 'Your window, please?' Huq starts up the engine and the air-conditioning. I teach him and Inge the delights of I Spy. *Yup. D for dust.* Again. We are packed and trembling in our dinky jeep, no back seat to speak of; knees up round my ears. I look away, through the window as Huq leans in to whisper-flirt with Inge. Their heads meet briefly. Flaxen and jet. Finding each other in Dadaab. They are a beautiful couple. Please, please let them be happy. Outside, more beautiful people wrapped in cloths of cream and blue and green. A camel is led to the slaughterhouse: its graceful plod heartbreaking. My calves are in spasm; I need to move, muscles bubbling, there is a tourniquet on my legs. And then the yellow gate reopens. Huq kills the engine, winds the window down. Straining to hear over the tumult of the day, can only see an arm, then a humphy back, bowed down with a bundle.

All your worldly goods.

Thrust out into the open glare, the cloaked figure stumbles. Is weeping, I can hear her crying, then Mo appears. He shoves at her again, too rough. Too rough! Steps forward to yell into the gathering crowd. 'What's he saying?' I hiss.

Huq translates. 'Um . . . She is dirty bitch thief. He says: "You steal from your master? You are lucky he does not kill you." '

'Oh my God!'

Mo has struck her on the face, she reels and clutches for her bundle.

'Oh God, stop him, Huq,' cries Inge.

'Ssh. Now he says: "You take your . . . um crap, effluent? . . . you get out now. You get out, whore, and you never come back." '

The woman falls down, sobbing and clutching at Mo's legs. He kicks out, but doesn't make contact. I'm sure he didn't make contact. For an instant, his stare wavers, like he is searching, then the yellow gate slams. Mo stops kicking. Moves back to his dirty jeep. The cowering woman lies in the dust. A man walks over to help her. Spits on her face, then walks away.

'*Herre Gud.*' Inge is unlocking the passenger door. 'We have to help her.'

'No!' shouts Huq. 'You go now, that police gets killed. The man inside is nasty, nasty bastard.'

Mo screeches at her one last time, his sturdy finger poking at the air. Then he hauls himself into his jeep. Is gone. I've still not seen her face. Remain dispassionate, this scene is sterilised by the frame of open window, the metal casing of the jeep. I am observing a distant far place, these are actors and puppets and the puppet pulls herself up, walks in imprecise steps, her strings newly cut. Arms behind to heft the load of her burden. She shakes her head and her headscarf shifts.

And I can see that it's Azira.

I get out, quietly. Mouth 'no' at Huq who wants to follow. We are less than a hundred yards from where she teeters. A length of plastic sheeting hangs from the wall of the depot. Inert in the still, searing heat, it offers me a little cover as I move from the side of the wall to the depot entrance. I can see better from here. *Come this way.* I'm willing her, I'm saying the word *Rebecca* in every ripple of my brain. Spine long and high, Azira examines her surroundings. Growing confidence in her steps, in her ability to bear her body. The churning mass of people had never really stopped; it meanders on without her and she turns, is turning away from me. An older woman shouts something, Azira flinches. Turns back. *This way.*

This way. Please. And she does; I watch her come towards me. Taller than I imagined, thinner than she should be. Skull and cheekbones and broken teeth. Rebecca's mummy. Abdi's wife.

There she is.

Sunlight invading me, it churns behind my eyes in needle-fine whorls, obscuring then revealing a flash of face, her hair, her wrist. The flicker of her moving. Closer, closer: I could touch her. I do, and as I do, I say her name. Say it soft as you would coax a child. She shrinks, the distance of her all held in. Glances, then stares ahead. Waiting.

'Azira. You are Azira?'

Unblinking. Hands manacled to her bundle of rags.

'Mother of Rebecca? Ree-be-ca? *Hooyo?*'

Full gaze on me. She begins to scream. A torrent of urgent words which I can't understand.

'Ssh! For Christ's sake! Huq!' I shout. 'Huq!' as Azira is grabbing me, the rags of her nails tearing flesh. 'What's she saying?' Huq and Inge are running over. I'm wrestling with Azira. 'Stay quiet! Stay

449

quiet!' Huq reaches us first. He seizes her by the shoulders and is pulling, dragging her in the direction of our vehicle. As he tugs, he's talking, gesticulating, pleading. Immediately, Azira stops. Folds her hands beneath her chin and drops towards the earth. Inge takes her by the wrists. 'No. *Maya. Maya.*' Between them, she and Huq pull Azira upright.

'She says: "You have my baby?" '

'Yes!' I nod. 'Yes. She is safe. Tell her safe. Tell her her husband's safe. *Abdi.*'

'Abdi?' Azira repeats.

'Yes! Tell her we've come to take her to them. Tell her she's coming to Yookie!'

Huq translates this. Oh, the thrills coursing through me, I could almost burst in flames. I'm anticipating the same delirium that's overwhelming me, grinning like a heidcase to receive her delight. Azira looks plainly out at me, then bends her knees so we are equal height. The bundle on her back is distorting. Liquid. The rags part, the bundle shifts and yawns.

'She says: "What about my son?" '

24.

TODAY IS A good day. Rebecca is making paper chains in the living room; I am round and full from the ham Mrs Coutts delivered. Ham is pork, of course, but I am no longer a Muslim. My Christmas tree is testament to that. Even so, I hesitated. It was the salt smell of it, the ragged pinkness and the blackened edge.

'That's marmalade, so it is,' Mrs Coutts told me, poking the sticky rind. 'The Scots invented marmalade, you know.'

Yes, but only the Scots would eat it, Mrs Coutts. Marmalade is not a subtle confection: it is loud and orange, laced with bitter lumps, yet the resonance is robust and sweet. Surprisingly delicious turned to caramel on ham. Two slices were not enough. So I had four. Yes, I still feel guilt when my belly is full; but I feel hunger in greater measure.

Tomorrow is Christmas Eve. On Christmas Day, Mrs Coutts is coming to dinner with us, and the day after, Rebecca and I have been asked to Sandrine's home. There we will have fish, Sandrine says: Scottish salmon and dill. I didn't mention it, but we are also having salmon for our starter here (smoked offcuts which Dexy has acquired). For the main course, Mrs Coutts has told me how to stuff a turkey, but there is no need. My minister has gifted us a turkey crown, and a cake with nuts and currants. He said he won them in a raffle, but I think it is charity. No. It is kindness. Our Christmas tree is courtesy – again – of Dexy. Small, but perfectly formed (this is true of both Dexy and the tree), it sits in a pot under our window. My only concern is the chewed nature of its base – it appears to have been snapped rather than sawed.

'You are very kind, Dexy,' I said. 'But did this belong to someone else before it came to us?'

'No *exactly*. Well, put it this way: no a person, any road.'

I thought it best to smile and thank him again. Then he gave me a present for Rebecca.

'I know the wean's into reading an that, so I brung her a book. It's fae a wee second-hand place – disny mean it's shite by the way.' He thrust a tattered hardback at me. 'Oh, and I huvny wrapped it. Mostly because I huvny any paper.'

The book is a compendium of sorts. It's called *The Girls' Book of Heroines* and shows a young girl with dreamy eyes staring at a vision of a maiden in a chariot. The colours are bright and delicate, blurred at the edges as if painted by hand.

'Dexy. I know she will love it. Thank you. I am very touched.'

'Fucksake, we know, pal. *Leverndale?* You don't need to boast about it.'

I invited Dexy for Christmas too, but his response was apologetic.

'Nae offence, but you're no the best of cooks. Apart fae they wee cake hings. And they do a cracking Christmas dinner down the Lodging Hoose Mission. So, if it's a the same to you . . .'

In a way, this is good because if he came, I don't think Debs would. She is arriving shortly to drop off gifts for Rebecca, and I plan to ask her then. Doubtless she'll be spending time at her sister's, but I know Rebecca would be so happy to see her, even for a little while. Deep, hidden down, I had wondered if we might be invited to hers, but Debs has grown distant. Today will be the first time we've seen her since the cathedral and her mysterious dash abroad. It can't be work, it must be love that drives her to long quietnesses and sudden absence. I have to think this, for I cannot bear to believe she's growing tired of us; am extremely aware that the mentoring period is done. My pleasant fullness abates. 'Dropping off gifts,' she said. Does that denote a duty discharged? Anyway, I will give her the antique vase and it can be a parting gift or a seal of friendship, or simply a place for flowers.

I am in my bedroom, sorting through my rucksack. I feel a little foolish. Carrying it everywhere has not protected my papers, it has endangered them. My Christmas gift to myself is a grey box with a key. The box has a handle, it is almost a suitcase, but metal, with folding files inside. I can keep my papers in this, then I need only carry the key. I survey my bedroom. They should be safe enough here. If I place the box in the wardrobe, behind my extra blanket.

'Debba!'

My mucky pup is thumping down the hall, streaking loops of coloured paper from her arms. 'Aabo! It's Debba!'

Ach, I'd meant to tidy away the plates, the glistening pork-meat.

Can you have ham with a cup of tea? I think Debs would like it, but it's the middle of the afternoon and I have no clue about pork-eating etiquette at Christmas. It seems, though, that you can gorge all day without delineation; for a two-week splurge you may drink alcohol with fruit juice at breakfast time, then eat chocolate for lunch. All this plenty.

All this plenty. Does it not make people sick?

'Come in, come in.' I am bright and cheerful, then stutter when I go to shut the door. There is more to come. Debs has company, a lady of a similar age oh oh it is Social Work. They have found out I hit my neighbour, Rebecca will be seized –

'Becky-boo! Oh, I missed you!'

Debs bundles Rebecca up, they are two clutching monkeys who jig and pet.

'Abdi!' Still holding Rebecca, Debs reaches to cup my face, draws me in for a kiss. 'Oh, it's so good to see you.'

The other woman leans between us. 'Hi. I'm –'

'Sorry, sorry. Abdi, this is my sister Gill. My *wee* sister.'

I shake Gill's red-gloved hand. 'I am so pleased to meet you. Please tell your husband I say hello. You are the lady who is helping us with school?'

'Absolutely. You looking forward to school, Rebecca?'

'Yes,' she lisps, feigning coyness.

'Don't go all shy and silly, you.' Debs tickles her. 'You *know* Gill already. Remember when we saw Lara, then we went for lunch?'

'Remember chocolate ice cream?' says Gill.

'Yes!'

'Well, I know a really good ice-cream shop not far from here.

Abdi, I wondered if Rebecca would like to go and get ooh . . . I dunno. A ninety-nine? A double nougat?'

'Nougat! Nougat!' my greedy daughter shouts. So much love and fun in my hallway; it is confusing.

'Would you not like some tea first?'

'Och, you and Debs can have a nice cup of tea and I'll take this wee monster for a TREAT! How's that?' Debs's sister addresses this to a near-bursting-with-glee Rebecca, so my only option is to say *yes*.

'Great!' Gill pauses, as though expecting further conversation. Neither Deborah nor I speak. I don't understand, because there is a weight of anticipation compressing us all. What's happening? This woman is Deborah's sister; I can trust her, but why does she want my daughter for herself? Are Social Work outside?

'Right. Well. Grab your coat, missy, and we'll go stuff our faces, yeah? And you can ask me all about school and I'll tell you how brilliant it's going to be.'

Radiating smiles, an animated Rebecca is swung to the ground, takes Gill's hand, and I am led inside my own living room.

'Hey, Abdi.'

'Debs.'

'Will we sit down?'

'How was your trip?'

'Yeah. It was good. Good.' She nods. Her brow buckles, her mouth opens. Closes. A troubled preface to whatever she must say – she is leaving us, that is it, she is moving abroad, ach I *knew* it. Why can nothing stay the same? Human beings are born to strive, that is a fact. But we need the peace of stepping stones; some occasional gap in which to rest and consider. Surely we might be granted that?

'Deborah. Would you like some ham?'

'Oh God, Abdi. I'm just going to say this and you must listen, please, and be prepared for a shock, a massive, wonderful shock, OK?'

'OK.'

Slow, suspicious, the panic of another man.

'Jesusgod, OK.' She puffs and puffs, ties her scarf. Unites it. 'Right, I'm just going to say this and I'm not going to stop. Right, so. When I went away, I went to Dadaab. To your camp because Rebecca told me she'd seen her mummy alive and I didn't believe her, but I kind of did?'

All the while she is stroking my hand. The movements are big, too clumsy; my skin is beginning to chafe. My abdomen pulls itself in.

'So I went and I checked and she'd only been injured, Abdi! Azira had only been injured, and I found her. I found her, Abdi. Azira's alive!'

I am in a vertical shaft falling from dark to light to dark to light. In the humming dark come threads of distorted colour, they sing to me and the dark is growing bigger it is a black hole which mutates and spreads, I hear Deborah calling I hear Azira calling I hear my mother calling I hear Deborah sobbing, calling butbutbut a chittering yicker to bring me back.

My life.

My life.

There is a but.

'You have to understand, Abdi, it wasn't her fault. None of this was her fault.'

Warm flowers open, surge to liquid. All the times I have heard her calling! Beloved God who never fails me; I remake the world in the hollow of my skull, it is a million threads of delicate gold, a million distinct impulses. I can neither sit nor stand, am consumed by agitation butbutbut

There is a but.

'Say again?'

She makes a noise; I hear her make a noise. It is *gape* and *shape* and *ape* I am hearing with the beat in my head. With the but.

'She survived, but she was hurt pretty badly. She . . .' Deborah sucks in her mouth. My hands are very slow, my brain detached; it floats outside, is watching me watching her. Sucking. 'Afterwards . . . she tried to kill herself. Threw herself in the river. But someone found her. They took her to a man for help, or the man found her; I'm not sure. But he took her to another man. A . . . He hurt her too. They cleaned her up, gave her shelter, but this man . . . used her. You understand this, yes?'

He hurt her? He fucked her HE EE EE

'He had her in his compound all the time you were here. She had nowhere else to go. She tried to kill herself. Abdi, Abdi.' Debs is kissing my head, the murmur of her heart in her breast. 'I am so, so sorry. It was nearly two years. You understand that? She has a little boy.'

Tear my head from my hands tear tongue from mouth and my guts my guts are spilling let me die Lord let me die I left her to be this ah. From outside of this world dull clunking words, hands pulling me and pushing me

STOP FUCKING PUSHING ME!

'Abdi, please! Abdi, stop it! You're bleeding, stop it!' Debs pulling my fist sour with metal dripping blood and my knuckles, my teeth biting blood.

Let me die.

'No. You will not die. You will face this and you will deal with this. Abdi. Look at me!'

She may have slapped me or my head strikes off an angle. Pain blooms in perfect circles perfect clarity. Perfect sense.

'Was he scarred? Tattoos on his forehead? Or pale-eyes? Young?'

'Jesus, I don't know. Some rich man, who sells guns. She didn't want it, but he made her. Christ, the main thing is she's *alive*. Azira is alive. She's arriving today, on a plane from Heathrow, and then they'll come up by train. I'm going to meet her at the station. I'm so sorry I couldn't tell you before. But you need to be there. And Rebecca. Maybe. Oh God, I don't know. I know this is a terrible shock; you need time. But I didn't find out until yesterday if we were going to get her out. Abdi, please. Can you be there for her?'

Deborah is pressing on my drumming fingers with the beat and the blood and the muscle rising and my breast rising. I am only flow and breath.

'If you're not there . . . She's . . . Azira's not in a good way, Abdi.'

I have grieved and mourned. I am grief, the thing relentless. Unable to set it down, until my flesh has grown around it. I have mourned death. Yet death itself is quick and clean. You are, then you are not. There is a resolution in that, an acceptance I have come to. But this? This is death then life. Then death.

We have many legends about the spirit, and there is one, of course, of a man who descends into the earth, to beg the darkness to return his wife. There is this story in every culture, I think, one that is fantastical, absurd. And so, so basic. How wonderful, you imagine. How beyond all words our lips can form would it be to hold that which you had lost, to regrow your limb, remake the dust into the substance it once was.

My wife lives! I want only to cradle bones and flesh that are mine, to make her never hurt again. To kill the people who harmed her. I will use my hands and teeth so I might taste their final pain. She is not her past. But a part of it is. There is her and there is it. Deborah said she would not leave it. That is my Azira. If it had been I who was felled, she'd have found a way to protect me. It. She is so full of love, she could not leave it behind. But it is a waste product; she will want to be rid of it. I know my Azira. There is adoption, homes, good grateful parents without issue who will remove it and we will never mention it again. Ever. Will she ever let me touch her?

Can I touch her? Oh God yes I want to run and scream.

My dead wife is alive.

I want to rush her by the hand and show her my world, every tiny detail she has missed. Remake her with our daughter, we will go to Kelvingrove and to the Science Tower, to the pub – and to Loch Lomond! I can show her my loch. Once she has gazed into its tranquillity, she will forget . . . she will forget.

It is not possible that the world is so made.

A frosted puff of breath distracts me, comes past my nose. It's mine. There is my glove, and the sleeve of my coat. *Second-hand but good as new.* There are my feet. Transfigured. They are the feet of a husband. These limbs, this brain is connected to the earth and flesh and heaven. I look up from the glittering pavement, see slate-grey clouds, their bellies full of cold. See an angular street of broad sand-stone blocks with the occasional darkened window, but mostly joyously lit. Pinpoint silver lights, beats of colour, garish livid Santas and snowmen with flashing hats. Uprooted trees propped on carpet, hung with baubles, topped with stars and angels and how do you choose? What is it that they celebrate? Intercession versus blank celestial observation? I don't recognise this road. I think I'm lost. I *want* to be lost.

Beneath distant marching skies I plough the streets. Rebecca has gone to Debs's house. I didn't see her again – I am ashamed to admit Debs put me to bed like a baby. Sat and stroked my brow and wept with me until I asked her to leave. Promised her I would *do nothing stupid.*

Stupid refugee. Other men fuck your wife.

Blessed Lord. You have given me back my wife.

But to ask me this, God? To ask me this? And how can she love me? I let go of her hand.

Sweat rises, then cools on my skin as I circle and stomp ever nearer to my destination. Or perhaps I am spinning away.

You'll walk *to Central Station? But it's miles, Abdi.*

When I was a boy I would walk for ever. My mother would make me patties and I would wander with the camel herders, then slip off when they reached the pass. An occasional stream – no, a burn – trickled the length of where the mountains dipped and met. The sparse water was delicious; I would pretend it had magical powers which gave me further impetus, and I would walk and walk until nightfall, and always find my way back home. Once, in the rainy season, I saw a rainbow there that was circular. Tiny water droplets splitting sunlight in a coloured ring. Revealing its embrace. It struck me that all rainbows must be circular, but we only concern ourselves with the half we can see. And, if they are circular, they have no end.

'*Assalamu alaikum*.'

A low greeting creeps from shadow. Makes me jump. I search for the source of it. There is a boy, squatting in a boarded doorway. He cups his hands, catching the beginnings of the sleet.

'And also with you,' I reply. '*Wa'alaikum Salam*.'

He has offered me a politeness: it is customary to shake hands.

'Hey you are cold, cold, cold.'

'Cole?'

I shiver. Make a *brrr* noise.

'*Bêë ni*. Cold.'

'Here.' I give him my gloves. 'Put these on.' Wiggle my fingers to show him.

'*E se*.'

'These are gloves. You must have gloves here. Don't lose them!'

I wrap my arms round my body, trying to mime keeping safe. 'You keep them. They are good.'

'*Gud*.'

I think he must be Nigerian. What words of Yoruba do I know? '*Odaa*. Good. OK ...'

From far away, a clanging commences. It is *one* bell, *two* bells. The boy and I suspend our pidgin exchange, waiting until the ringing stops. *Seven*. I have to decide where I will go. What would it be like to keep walking on and on and never be still? Or sit in this doorway with this boy, my pale bones knitting? Inertia or momentum – whichever I choose there is a train grinding its way from London and it bears.

It bears scars.

My rucksack lingers on my back. I free my arms from the straps. There is a five pound note in the inside pocket: I still must buy Christmas crackers for the table. Celebrate with loud bangs.

'Here. Take. Buy coffee.' I pretend to sip.

'Co-fee?'

'*Kaffa? Kahwa?*'

He nods.

'It tastes different here. They make it different. Is all different here.' I point at the pitiful hang of moonlight. 'Even the moon is smaller. But you have the streetlights.'

We consider the bundled clouds and the uneven light. I take out a pen, and one of Rebecca's drawings of her hand. 'Tomorrow . . .' on the reverse of the picture I scribble the address of the Refugee Council, 'tomorrow, you go there.' Tapping urgently on *Cadogan Square*. 'They *odaa*. They good. Um . . . Good? Help?'

'*Bëë ni.*' The boy folds up Rebecca's drawing until it is a neat square in his hand.

'In fact, you take this. Put your things inside.'

On the damp-sparkling pavement, I empty out my rucksack. Apart from my mobile and my keys, there is little to retrieve.

'Please. Take.'

The boy seems unsure. I come a little nearer. He retracts.

'OK, OK.' I move, make more space around him. 'You keep your things safe in that, yes? And tomorrow –' I lay my head on pointed hands, 'after sleep, you go to Refugee Council, OK?'

'O – K. *Insha' Allah*.'

'Good luck, my friend.' I check my mobile phone. It is 7.05pm. The train from London arrives in ten minutes. I have no idea where I am.

'You know train?' I ask the boy. 'Train?'

A half-shrug.

'OK. Is good.' I raise my hand. '*Odaa. Ma' asalama*.'

'*Ma' asalama*.'

In the gutters, the sleet is turning brown. The brittle crunch underfoot becoming slippery, drainpipes muttering, running with icy flow.

'Excuse me –'

A woman turns up her collar and hurries on.

'Excuse me,' I ask the next person. A man lugging a box of full bottles.

'Canny really stop, mate.'

'Please. Which way is Central Station?'

'Eh. That way.' He juts his chin to the right. 'See when you get to the river, go straight across the bridge, then swing a left, OK?'

'Thank you. Um – how far?'

'It's a straight road. Twenty minutes maybe?' he calls behind him.

Find the river. Many times I have thought of death, but Rebecca has held me. I have asked Debs to say nothing to her about Azira, yet. Would preparation help? It is not helping me. Children are resilient.

Oh.

Shards of conversation form into sense. Debs said Rebecca knew. She knew, yet she did not confide in me. What manner of clumsy father have I been? Of course Debs will take her; my baby will be waiting there, now.

Unexpected brightness of headlights, the road unravels; I lurch, return to the pavement. There is a long dark glow of gleaming hardness; I find the centre of it, align myself. Strings of streetlamps, furrowing. I inhale, gathering all the thick night air. March straight through the heart of this city.

In the blackness I am eyes and teeth, but my speed makes me visible; people move, respectfully, as I pass, always keeping to the centre. Windows blurring, traffic flashing. I smell the river before I see it. Find my elegant, swinging bridge, which pings with the thud of my shoes. Breathe cooked fat and sick and alcohol, push past revellers who are celebrating the birth of Our Lord with shrieks and pink bare legs. It is a quarter past. I begin to jog, but my feet slither from me. Azira will arrive and I will not be there. Rebecca will be confronted by a ghost. The city writhes with people and noise, a discordant carnival of trumpet bands and elbows barging, the shiny bounce and bump of full-stuffed plastic bags. I jog faster, tense my fists. So many buses shunting, slowing. I squeeze between two of them, sprint across the stop-start street.

Central Station lurks in a tunnel, over tawdry shops and a chip restaurant, its Victorian elegance obscured. I slip under a square, modern arch, find the escalator to take me up into the concourse; it is not fast enough; I leap and slide through bodies. Reach the top. Scan the shiny hall made livid with Christmas lights. It is twenty past, nearly twenty-five past. We are to meet beside a bullet? Debs says there is a giant bullet, near the door to Gordon Street, I am running and looking for a lump of metal when I see –

I see Azira.

I see the curve of my daughter and the stoop of my wife. Bound in a ball of joy. Unmoving.

It is real now. To my God, I give a prayer. I am Thomas. I witness it is real. Huge flares of drumming seize my heart. I melt, re-form. Am balanced and am light. I see Azira's long hand, her graceful folds. Whirls of people navigate me, each with their definite lives. I see the vulnerability of her neck exposed. My feet will not work and then they are running running while the space expands; I will never reach them.

I am there. This is where I am. With my arms out wide and my wife inside them. Our daughter at our feet.

I have no words.

We touch each other's lips, relearn each other's skin. To feel her skin . . . I am aware of Rebecca, of my Deborah shushing her and shushing some dark package which is passed from her to Azira. Brushing me. Azira accepts it calmly as I flinch, I put out my hand to repel this thing, to push it from me, but I cannot touch it. Azira moves the bundle closer: it is her offering, I understand, without meaning to. Without meaning to, my hand nudges the shawl. Falling from brittle curls, a cautious swell of cheek. A damp black

465

eye which blinks above the cheek. It has lashes. Thick lashes. I see the down on his skin catch the radiance that beats through bright glass. His wide black eyes. He is afraid.

I see my daughter's face.

And I see my wife's face.

Wān ku jecelahay.

And I see my wife's face. Echoed in my son's.

ACKNOWLEDGEMENTS

MANY PEOPLE AND sources helped to shape this book. I'd like to thank: my niece Dr Deborah Wilson and her colleague Dr Mary Cawley for advice on clinical psychology and mental health-procedures in Glasgow; my friends Dr Michael Rennick for a GP's insight, and Dr Maureen Myant for advice on educational psychology; all the many blogs, internet footage and reports I was able to source on Dadaab; the lovely Omar Kettlewell for advice on Muslim greetings; Mohamed Ibrahim for all his help with Somali words; everyone at the Scottish Refugee Council; my husband Dougie for being my rock and my inspiration; my girls Eidann and Ciorstan for their reading and encouragement; my excellent agent Jo Unwin, Carrie Plitt and all at Conville & Walsh; Bernadette Baxter; Lisa Moylett for all her support; Sarah-Jane Forder for the careful copyedit; my editor Helen Garnons-Williams, Erica Jarnes and all at Bloomsbury for being so welcoming and enthusiastic; Rose Gray, who so kindly bid to name a character at the Lord Provost's charity auction; and, finally, huge thanks to Abdul and Farida Nasri. This is not their story, but without them, it would not have been written.